Annie Edwards

Susan Fielding

Annie Edwards

Susan Fielding

ISBN/EAN: 9783337047337

Printed in Europe, USA, Canada, Australia, Japan

Cover: Foto ©Andreas Hilbeck / pixelio.de

More available books at **www.hansebooks.com**

SUSAN FIELDING.

A NOVEL.

BY

MRS. ANNIE EDWARDS,

AUTHOR OF "ARCHIE LOVELL," AND "STEVEN LAWRENCE YEOMAN."

ILLUSTRATED BY

SOL. EYTINGE AND WINSLOW HOMER.

NEW YORK:

SHELDON AND COMPANY,

498 & 500 BROADWAY.

SUSAN FIELDING.

CHAPTER I.

IT was a drowsy, silent afternoon early in summer. The outlines of the scarce-clad trees showed lifeless against a neutral-tinted sky. The dull white London road, brisk thoroughfare in the old coaching days to all western England, looked duller and whiter than usual, as it stretched away, without a spot of color to break its monotony, across Hounslow Heath. Even the canal seemed to drone in a sleepier voice than was its wont, as it stagnated by, its brief life spent, under the wilderness of poplar, alder, and sycamore that grew around the powder-mills.

"Is my life to be like this?" thought Susan, as she leaned across the parapet of the little wayside bridge, and watched, as much as excessively short-sighted eyes can be said to watch, the dreary heath and drearier overshadowed stream. "Have warm suns and cheerfu. sounds, like love and home, and all other pleasant things, gone clean away from me forever? Oh, papa, if I could see you once—if my watching here meant anything! If I could hear your voice, scolding me, even—there's no one to scold me any more—but hear it. Ah, I'm sick of silence! I want papa's face to kiss; I want his arms to hold me as they used."

And now great tears rose slowly in the short-sighted eyes; every tinge of color ebbed from the childish, round cheeks, and, with a passion of pain, the girl realized the irrevocableness of her loss, the emptiness of a world from which her own narrow world of love had been newly blotted. "If he had loved me less I might bear it! Oh, why was I left? What good was it to leave me in this big world, where no one will want me—no one be fond of me again till I die?"

Susan Fielding was seventeen years old on this day when I first bring her before you, watching at the spot where, ever since she was a child of six, she had been accustomed to watch for the return of her father across the heath; and knowing that she watched in vain. Mr. Fielding had now been dead three months. April rain and May sunshine had already brought up a thin green covering over his grave in Halfont churchyard. The servants had got new places—the house a new tenant. At midsummer, scarce a fortnight hence, the furniture would be sold and Susan have to seek a home among relations of whose very existence she had not known until her father's death left her desolate.

Throughout a lifetime of fifty-four years, Mr. Joseph Fielding had been a man neither possessing nor wanting friends—one of a class rather more numerous, I suspect, than some genial-minded people would have us think. Unsociable by temperament a: d through long habit; holding crotchety, unpopular opinions on every subject under the sun; engrossed with his bookselling at Brentford during the day; engrossed of an evening with his cockney road-side home; his violin in winter, his garden in summer; where was such a man—he often observed this of himself—to make friends, and what good would they have been to him when made? He was on terms, odd to say, with the parson of the parish, but with no other soul the parish contained (I must remark, for the pleasure of writing the words, that the dear old vicar of Halfont was a village priest of a type seldom to be met with now—a village priest with the untroubled belief, himself, of a little child, but tolerant, from fine breeding and wide culture alike, to every variety of opinion among his parishioners); once a year, even, dined, with little Susan, at the vicarage. "Fielding is a queer fellow," the vicar would say; "never comes to church, holds terribly wrong opinions about rates and tithes; but he and his little girl dine with me every Christmas, and I can't help forgiving him all his wrong-headedness when I hear them sing together. If our orthodox people only had the divine voices of these latitudinarians, what a choir we might have!"

And this yearly dining-out was the solitary dissipation, the one act of social intercourse that broke Mr. Fielding's lonely existence. During the lifetime of his wife, whom he tenderly loved, he had been brought, perforce, if not into friendliness, into some degree of contact with his neighbors.

Mrs. Fielding, a quiet-tempered little woman, unrivalled in her pastry and damson-cheese, and regarding books much as the wife of an ironmonger would regard stoves or saucepans, made it a point of faith to air her best cap and hear the village gossip whenever opportunity offered; and on rare occasions would prevail upon her husband, very miserable in his dress-clothes, and with his song-books and violin under his arm, to accompany her to some of the village tea-parties. After her death, which happened when Susan was six years of age, he fell back at once and forever upon his own society. "The morose nature of the man showing itself," said the village people among whom he lived, and yet from whose companionship he held himself so utterly, so suspiciously aloof.

He fell back upon his own society; and from the day of his wife's burial until that of his own death, led (in a roadside villa, ten miles from London) the life of a hermit. And yet it must not for a moment be supposed that Mr. Fielding was a philosopher, raised by superior reason above the common weaknesses of humanity. He was, on the contrary, the least philosophical, most sensitive of men—as open to offence, as famous for "taking the law" of everybody, with or without provocation, as Tom Touchey himself. He would no more dine or drink tea with a neighbor than he would go to church or abstain from openly pruning his pears on a Sunday; but let any man, from the lord of the manor downward, attempt to fire a gun across the bookseller's orchard, or fish in the hundred feet of canal that ran along the bottom of the bookseller's garden, and he would speedily discover with what manner of hermit he had to deal!

"Human nature is the same in us all," the old vicar would say, his kindly optimist spirit ever thinking the best that could be thought of every man. "If our social instincts don't show themselves in one shape they will in another. Poor Fielding's actions and lawsuits and ejectments are just his fashion of holding communion with his fellows. If it had not been for that willow-fence case between him and Dicky Ffrench, I believe he would never have held up his head again after his wife's death."

And possibly the vicar was right. Still a social instinct that takes the form of perpetually dragging other people into the hands of lawyers is scarcely one for ordinary minds to appreciate. Mr. Fielding died; and his little daughter reaped the fruits of all his long dissent from the common opinions of the world. A London solicitor whom she had never seen, an uncle in France, whose name she had never heard, were appointed by her father's will, as Susan's legal guardians; friends, with the exception of her morning governess and the vicar, she had none. Even Miss Jemima Ffrench, the kindest-hearted old woman in the whole country round, declared openly that she could take no interest in the concerns of a man who, for more than a dozen years, had embroiled her brother in a lawsuit about the willow fence! For Mr. Fielding's radical opinions Miss Jemima had never cared a straw. Church and state were not going to be upset by the half-crazed notions of a poor little Brentford bookseller. His atheism lay between himself and his Maker. But to go to law about the willow fence, the fence that the oldest people in Halfont would swear had always belonged to the lord of the manor! No, Miss Jemima could not forgive him that. And so now that Joseph Fielding lay dead, the querulous sharp face, querulous no longer; the brain, with its oddities and disbeliefs, quiet; the heart, with its superficial hatreds, its deep affections, cold—not a servant from the great house was sent to inquire for his child. We pay these penalties for eccentricity. Men and women will forgive us every vice, nay, every virtue that they can understand. Some out-of-the-way whim, some crank about a willow fence will freeze Christian charity at its fount, even charity as genuine and as broad as Miss Jemima's.

"To inquire." It would have mattered nothing to Susan if every inhabitant of the parish, of the county, had come to inquire for her, to sympathize with her. She mourned for her father, as she had loved him with her whole strength; mourned as these natures that love through sheer physical necessity do mourn; and when, a month after his burial, one of the servants led her, passive, to morning service, her childish face had so altered that scarcely a woman in the church could look at her without remorseful tears. Whatever Joseph Fielding had been, the child, they began to recollect, was alone and friendless; dwindling, too, in another six months would rest, likelier than not, beside her parents. And coming out of church, old Miss Ffrench, a world of contrition at her warm heart, walked straight up to the forlorn little creature's side, took her hands, and kissed her in the sight of all the congregation. "I'll come to see you this evening, my dear, and I'll bring Portia—we ought to have come sooner. Portia will cheer you. Poor child, you must not be left to mourn by yourself any longer."

Portia came, and Susan was cheered—not consoled; two months later you see her standing in her old place on the bridge, weeping the old tears for the voice, the step she should know no more—but cheered by the magnetic irresistible influence that youthful laughter, a sunny youthful presence must ever prove to a mourner of seventeen! The good old vicar had visited her, and left her spirit dull and crushed as he found it. Her governess had read her admonishing lectures about the paganism of this sorrow without hope, the duty of resignation and self-control, in vain. Before she had been five minutes in the room with Portia, before she had listened five minutes to Portia's airy chatter, Susan's cheeks actually began to dimple again as they used. I don't know whether, as we grow older, we feel our losses lightened by being brought in contact with the possession of others. Children—and Susan, though she was seventeen, was a child—can be lured out of their sorrows by the sight of pretty toys, of other children at play, without an envious pang. The beautiful face in its tiny bonnet, the soft peach-colored silk, the little trinkets, the dainty collar and cuffs of this girlish visitor (immensely bored by the work of charity she was performing) were better medicine for her sad heart than either physician or parson could have administered.

" I shall see you again to-morrow ? " she asked, very shyly, as her visitors were leaving. And when Portia gave a careless promise to visit her every day —oh well, twice a day "if it could possibly do anybody any good"—Susan Fielding once more felt that life was not wholly and absolutely without flavor.

The poor little girl *must* love ; there is the truth ; she could no more live without loving than without breathing, and in default of stronger support, her arms stretched themselves out instinctively to Portia Ffrench. Portia, who at times found the love even of an affianced lover a weight too heavy for her ease-loving shoulders to sustain !

CHAPTER II.

SUSAN raised her face at last, and saw a man's figure standing about three yards distant from her on the bridge ; a figure which her short-sighted eyes, additionally blind at this moment with tears, failed to recognize.

She drew back with a little frightened cry, and found her hand taken and held in a firm warm grasp.

" I'm not going to let you pass me like that, Miss Susan, indeed I'm not. I've been watching here for the last five minutes without your knowing it, and I say it's a sin for you fret as you do. As if—ahem ! these things didn't happen to all of us. As if young people musn't *expect* to survive their parents ! And to say (yes, you've been talking aloud)—to say that no one will ever be fond of you again. Why shouldn't lots of people be fond of you always, I should like to know ? "

The grasp was hearty, the voice pleasant, the face of the speaker emphatically what would be called a good face, ruddy of hue, well-favored of feature, open of expression. But Susan shrank away as if she had been hurt.

" I can't help fretting, thank you, Mr. Collinson, and I don't want to make any new friends. It's very good of you and Eliza to trouble yourselves about me as you do, but—but I like to be alone." Saying this she tried, in vain, to take her hand from her captor's, then stood silent ; evidently biding her time, like a frightened child, to break away from him anew and run home.

The young man looked down with a mixed expression—part contemptuous pity, part ardent tenderness—into her face. In common with most of the people about Halfont, Tom Collinson did not consider Susan as over-bright in her intellect ; but he fancied her—to use his own language—as he had never fancied any woman during his whole three-and-twenty years of life. A vagrant freak of the imagination it must be confessed ; Tom Collinson's tastes generally being of the earth, earthy, and Susan's face one for all, save the most refined beholders, to pass over with careless notice. A delicately modelled forehead, on which the dark hair rests in thick natural curling rings, a sensitive full-cut mouth, a pair of grey eyes, to which extreme short-sightedness lends almost the pathetic unanswering look of blindness—what is there in this pallid child's face to rouse the admiration of a man to whom ruddy lips, and pink and white complexion, yes, and plenty of animal life and audacity, have hitherto been the highest idea of feminine charms ? Collinson put the question to himself as he looked down on Susan's white, tear-stained cheeks ; and the only answer he could get was—that he did passionately admire it ; more, perhaps, at this very moment when the girl stood, shy and unwilling, and drawing her little cold hand away from his, than he had done since he first began to lose his head about her at all. The fact was a fact, but inexplicable ; save, indeed, on a favorite hypothesis of the vicar's, namely, that in the commonest, coarsest natures there must exist some one fine instinct, some latent affinity with superior sweetness and beauty which needs but the right influence at the right moment to call it forth.   But this is quite the last explanation of his folly that would have offered itself to Tom Collinson's mind.

"If you were to go a little more into company, I'm sure it would do you good ; Eliza says so, too. Now, why couldn't you walk across the heath and take tea with us sometimes, and I'd meet you and bring you back—only too glad of the chance. Oh, I forgot," a distinct change was discernible in Collinson's voice, "I quite forgot ! You are too much taken up with your grand lord of the manor set to care for Eliza any more ! "

"You are very good," was Susan's hesitating answer, "and so is Eliza. Now that the evenings are so long I shouldn't mind coming sometimes, if you're sure it would be no trouble to you to walk back with me ? You see the servants have both gone to their new places and I've only old Nancy Wicks, from the Ffrenches' lodge, to stay with me till the sale."

"Trouble ! very likely I should call it trouble to walk with you," answered Collinson, coming a step nearer.   "As if I wouldn't like to walk with you every day of my life, if you would let me ! Now, this evening—its only just five o'clock, why couldn't you come back with me this evening ? We could walk after tea to the Firs, I have heard you say you like seeing the sunset from the Firs, and—oh, well, there's no sun to set, as it happens, but we should have the walk just the same ; and I—I mean Eliza and I—would bring you back." He made this amendment in answer to the denial that he saw was coming from the girl's lips.

"But I am going to spend this evening with the Ffrenches," said Susan, "Its the first time I have ever been asked to their house. Mr. Josselin, the gentleman Portia is going to marry, will be there and—and any other evening, you know, I could walk with you and your sister."

The blood rose on Tom Collinson's face. "Eliza and I, of course, must wait until you have no better engagement !" he remarked, bitterly.   "We couldn't, for a moment, hope to keep you from such fine company as Mr. Josselin's ! But you surprise me when you say this is the first time you have been asked to the Ffrenches' house. I thought you and Portia Ffrench were sworn friends ? called each other by your Christian names, and the rest of it ? "

"Portia has been extremely kind to me," answered Susan, warmly, "I had never spoken to any of the Ffrenches' in my life—I suppose because papa and Colonel Ffrench both wanted those willows on the river bank—but when I was in my trouble old Miss Jemima brought Portia to see me, and I got fond of her at once, and she told me I might call her Portia, and sent me a photograph of herself next day. I haven't seen so very much of her since." Susan's countenance fell as she recalled the numberless days when she had stayed indoors, expecting her new friend in vain. "But then Portia has been paying a visit in London, and she is so much sought after, and engaged to be married so soon— how could she have time to remember me ?"

"Portia Ffrench, if what folks say of her is true, remembers precious little but her own pleasure," remarked Collinson, savagely. His passion for Susan was sincere enough to render him vaguely jealous, already, of every one she liked. " I hear this last lover of hers is little better than a fool ; but, whatever he is, I don't envy him his bargain. If Portia Ffrench wanted to treat you as a friend and an equal, she would never have gone all these weeks without asking you inside their doors."

" Any one in mourning like mine doesn't look to be asked out," said Susan. " The Ffrenches' house is always full of company when Portia is at home ; and Miss Jemima has too much consideration to invite me among strangers. My being asked there this evening is all a kind thought of Portia's. To-day is my birth-day, and she was resolved, she said, to give me a great treat on it, and let me make Mr. Josselin's acquaintance. I hope you will never say anything against Portia again. It hurts me."

She got her hand resolutely from Collinson's as she spoke, turned, and began to walk fast along the two hundred yards of path which lay between the bridge and her home. Tom Collinson turned, too. After a minute—"And so it's your birthday to-day ? " he began. " Don't be cross with me for speaking against Portia Ffrench ! I can't bear the thought of any one slighting you. What a fool Eliza must have been not to tell me so. Now, if I bring you something to-morrow, instead, will you take the will for the deed, and accept it as a birthday present ? "

" I think you had much better not waste your money," said Susan, half-displeased, half relentant. " Papa never liked me to take presents when he was alive."

" And you mean to go on in everything just according to his old-fashioned ideas ! " cried Collinson—not, as you see, a man of super-delicacy in thought or speech.

" If I can I will," said Susan ; " though, to be sure, that will be almost impossible ; for he was clever, and saw—oh, in an instant—what was right to do and what was wrong, and never made a mistake ; while I—"

She stopped, her lip quivering.

" And you'll want some one to be at your elbow, and advise you, and look after you, always," said Collinson, promptly. " That's about what you'll want. You know you never could go on living alone as you do now, Miss Susan."

" I know it very well," said Susan, shrinking, as every word of Collinson's seemed to have the power to make her shrink. " Don't talk about it, please. I've a fortnight left to me of home. Time enough to talk about leaving when the dreadful day comes. You don't know what home is to me—how awful the thought is of going away and living among strangers in a strange place for the rest of my life ! "

" Well, home is home, be it ever so humble," said Collinson, glancing up, contemptuously. They were now close to Addison Lodge, at the stucco road-side villa, with its prim lawn and fish-pond, and dusty summer-house surmounted by a huge weathercock that would have been in proportion on a church-steeple —the cockney villa which, to Joseph Fielding's daughter, was the one abode worth living in on the earth. " But I don't think you need look far to find a place just as good as Addison Lodge. Now, Eliza's cottage—"

" Mr. Collinson ! "

" Oh, well, small, I'll allow, but big enough for you two little women to get on in. Why couldn't you come to us, and you and Eliza set up housekeeping together, as you don't particularly relish the thought of this French uncle you are to go to? I was talking to Eliza about it this morning, and—"

"And I am sorry you wasted your time so much," interrupted Susan, not without temper. "Uncle Adam, my French uncle, as you call him, is the guardian papa appointed for me, and he has offered me a home, and I shall live there—'till I'm an old woman, I dare say—because it's my duty. I want to keep house with no one. Eliza must know that she and I would never get on together—never! I wish you good-day, sir."

And before Tom Collinson could find time to collect his ideas into a conciliatory speech, the garden gate had opened and shut, and Susan's small figure shot away behind the hollies, which, tortured into different varieties of pyramids and monsters, stood on either side the entrance to Addison Lodge.

The young man waited until he had caught one more glimpse of her as she ran quickly up the steps before the front door; then he took out a cigar, lit it, and, with his hands thrust into his pockets and a complacent smile on his ruddy, good-looking face, set forth upon his homeward walk across the heath. Susan breathed freer when, from the window of her own little room up-stairs (helped by the spectacles which, with no one by to see her, she was not too shy to put on), she watched him depart. That Tom Collinson could be in love with her— in love, as people are in books; that his intrusive questions about her "lord of the manor friends," his interest in her future prospects, could be prompted by any deeper feeling than curiosity, the child was far from guessing. He was Miss Collinson's brother, and, at his sister's bidding, doubtless, took the daily trouble of these long walks across the heath to see how she was getting on. Still—still there was enough of her sex's nascent instinct in Susan's heart for *something* in Tom Collinson's attentions to frighten her. Every time they met she was forced, against her will, to feel that, while she liked him less, his kindness brought her more and more into this man's power! In her love-sheltered child's world she had never, during her father's life, experienced the feeling of positive dislike toward man or woman. As coldly, perhaps, as it was possible for her to regard any human creature with whom she was constantly thrown, she had regarded her governess, Miss Collinson; partly because her governess was inseparable from French verbs, English grammar, and sums (and in every branch of education Susan was alike obtuse), but also from another unconfessed and still more cogent reason. Miss Collinson, a faded, half-pretty little spinster, under forty, had for a great many years cherished a subdued, not altogether hopeless fondness for Mr. Fielding; and this fondness—wholly unrecognized by its object— Susan, almost since she could remember anything, had divined. She was too sing.e-hearted, too thorough a child, for any secret fear of her father's making a second marriage to disturb her happiness. The bare notion of Miss Collinson at his side—of Miss Collinson filling the place of the dead mother in their little household, would have been profanity to her. What she knew; what, with all a child's passionate jealousy, she resented, was that Miss Collinson forever, and in a hundred small, underhand ways, strove to please Mr. Fielding; would not gainsay him when he advanced opinions at directest opposition to her own; gave way, without even the form of contradiction, to every eccentric crotchet about his daughter's education; worst crime of all, on days when she was certain of his coming home early, would attempt such poor blandishments in the way of personal adornment as her frugal wardrobe could furnish forth. "As if papa so much as looks at her!" Susan would think, watching some oft-darned

bit of lace, some faded neck-ribbon of Miss Collinson's with silent, jealous aver-
sion. "As if he cares for any one looking nice but me!"

The child's nature was too really generous, and Miss Collinson—mildest of
sentimental women! too really inoffensive for the feeling ever to strengthen
into one of more than potential bitterness—indeed, now that her father was gone,
now that she had seen Miss Collinson mourn for him dead as sincerely as she
had striven to win his affection living, Susan's sensitive conscience reproached
her for many a small wickedness that jealousy had prompted her to commit in
by-gone days. But, as regarded Miss Collinson's brother, her feelings were
widely different. Susan Fielding had no acquaintance whatever, theoretically,
with the words "vulgarity," or "good breeding." Her father, a Brentford bookseller, clad in his tradesman's black suit, abrupt of speech, unconventional of
manner, had to her been as much a gentleman as the old vicar in his fine silk
stockings and cambric neckkerchief, and with his polished well-rounded sentences, and courtly past-century air. But in her heart was the instinct, the
essence of true gentle breeding—immaterial essence which finishing-schools,
dancing-masters, and diligent study of books of etiquette fail sometimes to instil
into the daughters of higher commercial persons than Mr. Joseph Fielding!
And everything Tom Collinson said, or did, or looked, came with a sort of jar-
ring shock to her nerves. He wore grand chains and rings, but his hands were
coarse; and Susan's blind eyes saw the coarse hands clearer than the good-
looking face. He loaded his handkerchief with bergamot. His clothes, smart
though their cut might be, were not accompanied by the snow-white linen that
it had been the pride of the little girl's life to attend to "as mamma used" for her
father. And then he stood so near her when he talked; and it was always so
horribly palpable, despite the bergamot, that he had been smoking cheap cigars;
and he would hold her unwilling hand, so infinitely longer than was necessary,
in his own hot clasp whenever he got the chance!

"I don't like him, I shall never like him," thought Susan, as she stood and
watched his short square figure disappear across the bridge. "I suppose I
should have more chance of making friends if I could care for men and women
like the Collinsons, but I can't. I want a world full of people like Portia, only"—
with a sigh, this—"they mustn't all have found a Mr. Josselin. Ah, if I could
meet some one handsome, and graceful, and good as he is, yet who would not
be above loving me! Some one—quite unlike poor Tom Collinson, of course—
yet who would watch, and wait, and take the trouble about me that he does."

And then she fell into a day-dream; a marvellously innocent one—the
old vicar and Tom Collinson were the only men she knew, to speak to, in the
world—but the day-dream of a girl of seventeen for all that.

CHAPTER III.

THE Ffrenches' dinner-hour was six; and by seven o'clock Susan stood before her glass, "dressed" for this first grand dissipation of her life! Her shock
head of hair had been duly wetted in the hope of making it smooth and neat,
thereby causing it to twine in more profuse little waving rings than ever round
her forehead; her every-day stuff frock was replaced by her Sunday one of silk
and crape; an old-fashioned jet necklace, one of her mother's scanty stock of
trinkets, was clasped round her babyish white throat.

"I hope Portia won't be ashamed of me before Mr. Josselin," she thought, looking close and with extremely distrustful eyes at the charming little picture her glass gave back. " Papa thought me pretty, but I don't! I'm like no other girl living, with my great eyes and odd hair, and by Portia—oh, by Portia's side —what shall I look like? However, Mr. Josselin won't trouble his head much about me—that's one comfort, and Portia herself is too good and generous to mind my being plain."

And then Susan ran down stairs, put on her scarlet garden-cloak, and with its hood drawn close round her brown curls—a dearer little picture than before —ran along the hundred yards of high road that divided Addison Lodge from the gate of Colonel Ffrench's avenue. A minute or two later she found herself within the house; hitherto an inaccessible holy of holies in her childish imagination; with a beating heart followed the majestic old butler, Jekyll, up a noiseless velvet-carpeted staircase; was sensible that a door opened, that she was shown into a room full of light and color, and the perfume of flowers, and then—then shyness and short sight mingled got the better of her and she stopped abruptly, a confused singing in her ears, and a sense that twenty people at least must be looking at her frightened face and rough hair with pitying wonder!

A note or two of subdued treble laughter broke on her ear with welcome relief; and, guided by the sound, she ran across the room to an open balconied window where Portia Ffrench, a gentleman by her side, was standing.

"We watched you up the road, my dear—such a funny little Red-riding-hood as you looked!" And Portia Ffrench stooped and touched Susan's cheek with her lips. "Why didn't you come sooner? We have been expecting you this age. Mr. George Blake, Miss Fielding. You must call her Susan, all the evening, mind. Young ladies, until they come out, retain the privilege of being called by their Christian names."

Mr. George Blake! Susan looked up, startled, into the face of this man with whom Portia was on such evident terms of easy familiarity, yet who was not Mr. Josselin, not Portia's lover.

"Yes, we expected you long ago," he said, good-humoredly, for Portia had told him Susan's story, and he believed her to be, as she looked, a little girl of fifteen. "We are going out for a walk by the river by-and-by, and shall sadly need a fourth, Susan. You are to be the fourth. You are to be my companion, and I hope you mean to take care of me, and amuse me the entire evening?"

The tone of this speech was so kind, the shake of the hand that accompanied it so hearty that Susan's dimples began to show themselves, a faint blush to overspread her cheeks.

"Ah, but you mustn't frighten the poor child with fine speeches," cried Portia, quickly. "Susan will not understand you unless you call black, black, and white, white. She is not worldly and artificial, and—what was the other word—like the rest of us, you must remember?"

This, with a little imperious toss of the head, and carelessly moving so that her own pure-cut profile was the contrast to which George Blake's eyes turned from the irregular childish beauty, if beauty it could be said to possess, of Susan's face.

Portia Ffrench was a wonderfully handsome woman; she was only one-and-twenty, yet it never occurred to you to think of her, or speak of her as a girl; finely-built, long of throat, graceful; the forehead somewhat too high, perhaps, for fashion, but well carved, and smooth as marble; the nose and upper lip, and chin, all without a fault. What a noble, what a high-bred looking woman, you thought, the first day you were introduced to her! Then, when you had watched the play of feature, the delicate nostril, the small curved mouth, so prodigal of smiles—what charm, what endless mobility of expression ! Then, later (unless you happened to have fallen over head and ears in love with her, meanwhile), your first opinion of Portia Ffrench changed a little, and you thought—if only the smiles were *less* prodigal ! if the mouth, even at the expense of its perfect symmetry, could grow passionate or tender ! if the coal-black eyes, the least handsome feature of the face, could tell any story, good or bad, concerning their possessor's soul ! Well, it was some time before you got to this ; and the chances were, as I hinted, that your reason was subjugated long before your first admiration had had time to cool. At this instant, the soft evening light resting on her jetty hair and deep-tinted Titian-like face, it struck George Blake with sudden force that he had never yet seen Teddy Josselin's betrothed look so handsome. But then this was a thought which on an average struck him about four times an hour whenever he was in Portia's society ! For George Blake was in love. As well tell a truth in three words that three elaborate pages could tell no better ! a truth which Susan, unsophisticated though she was, could not be five minutes in the company of these two persons without discovering.

"Grandpapa and Aunt Jemima will be here directly, Susan. They are still over their port—I mean their toast-and-water. I shall introduce you to grand-papa as ' Susan ' only, remember. Grandpapa is so queer—I mean he will like you a great deal better if he don't know how near a neighbor you have been all these years. Now, please put away your terrified look." Susan had frozen within herself anew at the awful thought of being introduced to old Colonel Ffrench. "Take out your spectacles—yes, this child wears spectacles, Mr. Blake—and assure yourself that there is no one here but us, and that we are not very awe-inspiring when you come to view us closely."

Perfectly obedient, Susan took out her glasses and held them, but without putting them on, before her eyes. Already she had a dim dread of being made to look ridiculous in George Blake's sight. A long country-house drawing-room, all easy-chairs and natural flowers and open windows, Portia in her dainty dinner-dress, a tall man's figure standing by Portia's side ; this was what she saw.

"I'm not frightened in the least, thank you," returning her glasses to her pocket; "and I'm very glad no one else is here. Only, you know, Portia, you *said* I was to see Mr. Josselin ?"

Portia laughed ; one of the pleasantest laughs you ever heard ; trilling, na-tural, yet full of sustained quality ; a laugh to have made the fortune of an actress of manners, in the days when actresses of manners existed.

"Mr. Josselin ? Of course you shall see Mr. Josselin, little Susan. Teddy, where are you ? Come—not and be killed, but be looked at, immediately—why, I verily believe he is asleep again."

She moved across to the easiest chair the room contained, rested her hand on its back, and looked down, as one might look at a pet cat, at something lazi-ly curled up inside. "Teddy ! do, if you can, arouse yourself, and come and speak to Susan. I told you about Susan, you know—well, she is here, and wanting to see you."

"Dear little Susan, how good, how natural of her !" said a sleepy voice. "I like Susan already, now, for that very—what is it ? trait, that is the word—trait in her character. But couldn't she be brought up here ? Are Susans, like syllabubs and cowslips, and everything beginning with an ' S '—no, cowslips don't begin with an ' S,' but it is all the same ! Are Susans—you've put me out, child. I don't know what I was going to say. The thread's broke."

"Are Susans always to be looked at in the open air? (When I am by you need never mind losing the thread of a discourse, however important. Teddy! *I* know what is coming). As a rule, yes; but in the present instance, no. Miss Susan Fielding is standing about four yards distant from you at this moment, and I am waiting, if you please, to introduce you to her."

Upon this the curled-up figure rose languidly, and advanced: and Susan, for the first time in her life, saw the picture of a real London dandy in evening dress. It was a very finished picture of its kind; and she looked at it curiously, and with admiration ludicrously visible upon her simple face. Portia watched her, well-pleased. These unhackneyed critics are often the ones most to be dreaded, and Mr. Josselin was sufficiently one of Portia's personal possessions by this time, for her to be jealous of the effect he produced, even on the village perceptions of Susan Fielding.

"You two are to be great friends, remember. Shake hands, Susan, Mr. Josselin is not quite an ogre when you know him better, although the first impression he gives is, I must confess, of an ogreish and forbidding kind."

"Oh, I don't think so, I'm sure," cried Susan, eagerly. "Quite the reverse."

At which remark, or at the sincerity of voice with which it was uttered, George Blake laughed aloud. His was a delightfully hearty laugh, notwithstanding the hopeless malady from which he suffered; and it broke forth abruptly the moment anything tickled his fancy, like a school-boy's.

"I never had a thing like that said to me since I was born," he cried. "If I had—from lips like Susan's! it would flatter me so that I should look in the glass a dozen times a day for a week to come, and you, who are satiated with pretty speeches, get as many of them as you choose, Josselin. The injustice of the world!"

"Did I make a pretty speech?" said Susan, opening her great eyes. "Oh, I didn't mean it. I only meant—Portia knows what I meant."

"That Mr. Josselin is not absolutely like an ogre," finished Portia, with a glance at her lover's boyish face.

"Well, I am very glad you think so, Susan, and now let us all try to be sociable, and to get to like each other, if we can."

She moved back to her place beside the open window, her head brought negligently in contact with a drooping spray of guelder-roses (an admirable foil, that sultry yellow, to her clear dark skin), and before a minute had passed, was engrossed in the one occupation in existence that cost her neither trouble nor weariness; running on, that is to say, with all manner of airy nonsense to the man of whom she was sure, yet holding captive some other poor wretch, George Blake for the time being, by furtive looks, by plaintive little undertones, at her side.

Susan stood, unnoticed of all three, and watched and listened. What wit was Portia's, she thought, as subject after subject—it might be justice to say person after person—was brought forward just sufficiently to receive a few of Portia's off-handed, half-jesting, half-bitter strictures, then dismissed! What grace, what beauty! How natural that these two men—that all men—should be Portia's slaves! And then she fell to comparing the merits of the slaves themselves—trying to think, if she were in Portia's place, which of the two she would smile on most; or whether, like Portia, she would smile, doling out short-lived hope and despair, by turns, on both.

"I dare say I should smile equally on both," she decided, after serious

thought. "It must be so delightful to see people waiting for one's words like
that. Perhaps, in reality, I should care for Mr. Josselin least; and yet he is so
good-looking, and has such a pretty manner, that I couldn't keep from liking
him in my heart. Oh, how pleasant Portia's life is! How different they both
are to Tom Collinson!"

And in her journal that night—a journal in which the number of fish her
father had caught in the canal, or the way she had shirked an exercise, or her
sensations on first wearing a trained skirt had hitherto been the kind of matter
recorded by Susan—the two portraits were thus sketched:

"Portia's lover—her *real* lover, I mean—is the prettiest man I ever saw. I
got to feel at my ease with him afterward; but when he first spoke to me my
breath seemed almost taken away, he looked so beautiful. He wore a coat with
white silk trimmings, and a lily of the valley and rosebud, and beautiful embroidery over pink insertion, and shoes such as I never saw before, and silk stockings. Altogether, he made me think of those court gallants in Charing Cross,
who separated Alice and Fenilla from Julian. His pocket-handkerchief was fine
cambric, worked in the corners; his hair was parted like a girl's. He made me
laugh a great deal, and yet, when I come to think of it, I can't particularly remember anything he said. I thought he smiled more to show his white teeth
than because he was much amused himself. When he winked his blue eyes he
winked so slowly that I always thought he must be going to sleep. Portia
seems fond of him, and yet to like to laugh at him, which I don't understand.
Mr. George Blake has a dark, serious face, something like the frontispiece of
Oliver Goldsmith. He has no pretty ways, like Mr. Josselin, and was dressed
as other men dress. Although, of course, he thought of nothing but Portia (for
I am afraid he is in love with her, too), Mr. Blake was so kind to me, and walked
home with me, and"—here three or four words were diligently obliterated—
"and spoke of papa as if he had known him."

And then, in a line by itself, carefully written and understroked, this confession: "I like Mr. Blake."

CHAPTER IV.

AT the end of another quarter of an hour old Colonel Ffrench and his
sister came up to the drawing-room. Susan started round at the sound of the
opening door, all her shyness returning at the thought of being in the awful
presence of Colonel Ffrench; and Portia, a world of graceful protection in her
manner, led the little girl across the room to her grandfather. "Here is Susan,
grandpapa—my friend Susan. To-day is her birthday, and this is her first visit
to Halfont Manor."

It was a plan devised by Portia and Miss Jemima, that Susan's surname
should be withheld from Colonel Ffrench, the greatest misery of whose self-
centred life had, during a long course of years, arisen from the litigations and
lawyers' letters of Joseph Fielding. "Susan—I beg your pardon, my dear, but
I did not catch your other name; poor Portia speaks so indistinctly. I am very
glad to see you at Halfont—very glad. Jemima, will you see that some of the
windows, indeed, that all the windows are closed. Our little friend looks delicate. We must not allow her to stand in this thorough draft."

Miss Jemima ran dutifully and shut all the windows, except Portia's, with
which she dared not interfere. Colonel Ffrench seated himself with difficulty,

for he was a martyr to rheumatic gout, by the fire. Susan stood close at his side, too frightened to get away, trying to reconcile to her senses the fact that this bland old gentleman, with his soft, slow voice and good-natured manner to herself, could indeed be Dicky French, her father's enemy, the wicked lord of the manor, of whom even the cottagers spoke in a certain tone and with a certain shake of the head implying that more was known of Dicky Ffrench than was good to repeat. Could this be the man who had married two rich wives and gambled away the fortune of each ? Glancing at his delicate, well-shaped old hands, Susan could not but remember, with a shudder, the popular misgiving regarding the suddenness of those wives' deaths. The man who, in his youth, had been a duellist, in his middle age a gambler, and who now—his sons, it was whispered, working as common laborers in the colonies, old Miss Jemima and Portia dependent upon him—had sunk the last remnant of his riches in an annuity, for the sake of an extra two or three per cent. of income.

"Our tumble-down old place is tolerably pleasant in the spring, my dear," he remarked, looking up with kindly courtesy at the shy embarrassed little girl. What a handsome old face it was ! Portia's features and jet-black eyes, set off, as if by powder, by his well-preserved silver-grey hair. "There are too many of these high elms about us for health, and we hear the working of the powder-mills a great deal more distinctly than is pleasant, but a poor man—and I am a very poor man, Susan—cannot always choose his residence. This little Halfont box is the only place belonging to me now."

"I—I should call yours a very large place, sir," said Susan, struggling between her terror at speaking at all and the bewilderment she felt at hearing the manor and its grand old elms, yes, and the powder-mills themselves, disparaged. If these things were of small account, what was Addison Lodge ? "I suppose it's larger than anything in Halfont, even the vicarage ?" she added, with an appealing look in the direction of Miss Jemima.

"That is right, my dear little—Sarah ?"

"Susan, sir."

"Susan, to be sure—poor Portia speaks so indistinctly—quite right, Susan. Always make people contented with what they possess. I try to be contented myself—we grow, perforce, to be philosophers, as we get old, my dear. Mine is the largest house in the parish, and has some pretty grounds around it, as Portia would show you if the evening were not so damp. Now, from these windows, the side windows especially, we have a charming peep of the river, so we call our little canal, and in a week or two shall have a better one. There are a couple of willows I have been trying to get down for the last dozen years, but a cantankerous fellow next door—"

"Susan, Susan, dear, come and talk to me, and I'll tell you all about it," interrupted old Miss Jemima, quickly. "Don't you see your paper, brother ?" —and she drew a little table, his glasses, and the "Times" to Colonel Ffrench's side. "Now I know you want to read last night's debate, and not be troubled by us. Susan, come and help me pour out the tea. We shall have it cold, as usual, if we wait until Portia remembers her duties."

Saying which, Miss Jemima led Susan away to the farthest and pleasantest window in the room, a window overlooking the lawn and flower-garden, not the canal ; then, by a kind squeeze of the hand, a whispered "You must not heed my brother, child, we old people are crusty and need forbearance !" managed to charm away the child's indignation ; indignation which even the dreadful presence of Colonel Ffrench himself would not have restrained, had the subject of the willow fence been allowed to progress.

Dear Miss Jemima—kindliest of all kindly hearts! if custom did not forbid our interest in a heroine of sixty-five—did not imperatively exact that lovers, marriage, and again lovers should fill nine-tenths of every three volumes—what a pleasant task it would be to write the story of your life! "I have brought up fourteen children," Miss Jemima would say, not without a flush of maternal vanity "five of one generation, nine of the next; and I have lived in all climates, and have nursed people in yellow fever and cholera, and been under fire twice. And now I have the charge of Portia!" This with a shake of the head implying that the most onerous post of her life had, as indeed she felt to be the case, been reserved for the last.

At twenty years old Jemima Ffrench, as ready, it may be assumed, for her own share of life's sweets as other young women of that age, had been suddenly called upon to take the place of mother to a nursery full of motherless little boys and girls, her brother Richard's children. Colonel Ffrench was in the Guards, a man of fashion and pleasure, at the time of his first wife's death—no violent death, poor lady, as Halfont gossip would whisper, but a gentle, not wholly unwilling one, with a little face a fortnight old beside her on her pillow! and the management of the whole household, as of the nursery, fell at once upon his sister's shoulders.

To ward off ultimate ruin from a man leading the life Richard Ffrench then lived, was as much beyond Jemima's power as it had been beyond the power of the neglected wife who now, happily for herself, lay in her grave. All she could do was to check the tradesmen's bills, dismiss such servants as she caught in flagrant and open robbery, and—love the children. The small economies in domestic management, the dismissal occasionally of dishonest servants, could do little for the fortunes of a house, the master of which would lose a thousand pounds of a night at Crockford's. But love for the children—love for five small human beings to whom "Aunt Jem" was to be the one tender recollection of after life, the father and mother of an else unloved childhood!—who shall over-estimate the value of this?

Struggling in vain against ever-increasing debt; fighting at heroic odds against cooks and butlers; nursing babies through teething, hooping-cough, and scarlatina; sending small boys, with tears, to school; taking them to pantomimes and Astley's during the holidays—in these employments Jemima's youth passed by. When Colonel Ffrench had been a widower some dozen years he married again; through his second wife's fortune saving himself, as by miracle, from the crash of absolute ruin; and Jemima was wanted no more. Her children —with true maternal jealousy she thanked heaven for this—her children were no longer of an age to be dependent on a step-mother's care. The eldest one, a daughter, was already married; the four lads were public-school boys; all could get on without her now. And quite cheerfully, without a spoken regret for the youth that had blossomed, faded, and brought no fruit to herself, Jemima prepared to settle down into the grey monotonous twilight of an old maid's life. Her parents were both dead, her means small; smaller from the numberless little loans, a hundred at a time, that Richard had incurred and forgotten; but she would be able, she thought, to take a modest house, not so far from London but that the boys could run down and visit her in the holidays, yet sufficiently far for it to be a nice change whenever anybody, the boys, or her niece, or her niece's babies might happen to need country air. Loneliness, however, fortunately for others, was not Jemima Ffrench's destined portion. Colonel Ffrench's daughter, Mrs. Elliot, had, three years before, made what her friends generally, her father most of all, deplored as a wretched marriage ; her husband being a young man of spirit and character whom the girl loved devotedly, but who possessed barely more than his soldier's pay for her support. And six weeks after Colonel Ffrench's second marriage ; just when Jemima's mind was torn by the conflicting merits of a farm-house near Tunbridge, a nutshell at Bayswater, and a ten-roomed house (said to be haunted, and therefore let cheap) at Teddington ; Captain Elliot wrote and proposed that instead of attempting separate housekeeping she should throw in her lot with theirs, for a twelve-month at least. His Lucy was ailing, he wrote, and the children, and constant moving were too much for her. If Aunt Jemima had not been over-dosed with nursery already, and could stand a roughish soldier life, all wandering and no home, how grateful they would both be for her presence !

It was not without regret that Jemima gave up her project of setting up her own household gods. She really did feel that she would like a little respite from nursery cares ; still more to possess a place which "the boys" could look upon as home, if they choose. Still, this call to go to poor helpless Lucy and her babies seemed too definite a duty for her to hesitate long about accepting it. Her house-hunting was given up ; her luggage reduced to regulation-compass ; and, at the end of a fortnight, Jemima found herself in barracks at Corfu —at the age of thirty-three beginning the charge of another family, only with the additional one of a delicate grown-up baby added thereto, and with perpetually shifting foreign quarters—instead of Colonel Ffrench's comfortable London house, for her home !

The visit began for a twelve-month and lasted more than sixteen years. Children were born, had to be tended (once or twice died) in such quick succession as to efface—no, I will not say that, but gently to wear away the remembrance of those first-forsaken little ones in whose Grosvenor Square nursery Jemima's youth had been past. She got letters at intervals from them all ; not one of those four nephews from whom she was parted but felt that at every turn of fortune, good or bad—and with Colonel Ffrench's sons it was mostly bad— Aunt Jem's was the sympathy to turn to, sympathy that no number of years could estrange or chill. And over these letters Jemima shed tenderest mother's tears ; returning, if it were possible, a bank-note or money order, or, if the Elliots' exigences had drained her purse too dry for that, an answer worth more than money to the scapegrace boys—they always remained "boys" to Jemima —for whose worst misdeeds her only feelings were those of pity. Still her heart, perforce, clung warmest to the children of the younger generation ; children born in every quarter of the world, and to whom "Aunt"—not the delicate little white lady on the sofa—was indeed mother.

As years went by, and as Elliot rose in rank, the hand-to-hand struggle with poverty of Lucy's early married life of course lessened ; but never Jemima's duties. It was necessary twice during a term of foreign service, lasting nearly twenty years (for Elliot's scanty means compelled him to exchange whenever the battery to which he belonged was ordered home), that Mrs. Elliot, with detachments of children, should visit England for health's sake ; once from Mauritius, once from India. And each time Jemima—no climate hurt Jemima— remained behind. In Mauritius she gained her experience of yellow fever ; in India of cholera, also of the sensation of being under fire. But never did this fine old soldier's courage flag, or her spirit droop. Stories that would fill a volume are told still of Miss Jemima Ffrench, by grey-headed veterans whom a quarter of a century ago she nursed in fever, or cheered through weary convalescence—only, as I said before, what writer dare take a lady of sixty-five for his heroine ? At last, to use her own words, she got "promoted to general's rank, and was laid upon the shelf." Lucy's husband left the service, the death of his father, together with his pension, giving him at length sufficient means to live in England, and Jemima Ffrench, at fifty years of age, was a free agent once more.

Her ideal of happiness for the remainder of her days had certainly now been to live with the Elliots in their pleasant Devonshire cottage, and with her children of the second generation growing into tall men and women round her. But no ; there was some one still to be nursed, this time a baby of threescore, with rheumatism, gout, and selfishness, instead of the pains of teething, to make him fractious ! In a charmingly-worded fraternal letter—and no man living wrote prettier letters—Colonel Ffrench pointed out to Jemima how her plainest duty was to spend the remainder of her days with him. "The young want us no longer," he wrote. "We are the last leaves left on the old branch. Let us flutter together while our little day lasts, and fall side by side !" And then followed such a picture of his maladies and his loneliness and poverty—his second wife had long ago died childless—as dissipated whatever doubts about duty still lingered in Jemima's mind. The Devonshire cottage, with its bright young faces and cheerful atmosphere of home and love, was given up, and replaced by Halfont Manor, a damp-stained, sunless house, with no young voice, no young step to break its silence, and with her brother, a querulous, sick, disappointed old man of the world, for sole companion.

But wherever the good sun shines he fructifies ; wherever Miss Jemima went, love sprang up beneath her feet. Colonel Ffrench, "Dicky Ffrench of the Manor," was disliked by every man, woman, and child in the parish of Halfont. He was known to have been a gambler, a spendthrift, a duellist, a faithless husband, a cold father ; and, that this little catalogue of ill-doing might be neatly rounded off, the Halfont gossips liked to inquire in a whisper whether it was known of what disease the lord of the manor's two wives had suddenly died ? He was weakly ease-loving ; like all weak men would break out occasionally into fierce raids against the persons who grew fat upon his weakness ; so even the Halfont school-children were taught to regard him askance, as the old tyrant who on any fine morning would wake and turn half the servants he possessed adrift upon the world ! Unlike his neighbor, Joseph Fielding, Colonel Ffrench went regularly to church when his bodily infirmities allowed him ; and a much better sign the Halfont people would have held it, had he stayed away ! The atheist bookseller at least was honest ; acted up to what he professed ! To see Dicky Ffrench's face, the imperturbable old face, with its high-bred air of reverential attention, in the house of God ; to have to kneel with Dicky Ffrench before the altar, at Easter, a season at which the old gentleman made it a point of duty to receive the sacrament, was, to the moral sense of Halfont, something very little short of positive sacrilege ! But wherever the sun of a warm heart shines, human hearts respond to it. Miss Jemima came, every soul in the village prejudiced against her as Dicky Ffrench's sister, and before three months were over had made to herself friends of them all. She had not means to give much in substantial charity among the poor ; and no argument could change Colonel Ffrench's opinions as to the vanity of alms-giving ; but she had enough to buy calico and flannel, and time to make them into baby clothes ; time to sit up with the sick, to stand by women in their hour of anguish, to mourn with those who mourned ! And soon her fine old figure became as well known and as welcome among the Halfont cottage wives as it had been abroad among the bearded occupants of barrack-rooms and hospitals in days gone by.

" If I had only something to care for at home ! " Miss Jemima would think during the first year of her changed life, " I could be happy. If everything young wasn't outside the house, and only Richard and me, with our complaints and our age, within ! " She contrived occasionally to get some of the Elliot's children to visit her ; but could rarely prevail upon them to stay out the time for which they were invited. Children shrank away instinctively from Colonel Ffrench's presence. Grandpapa did not like whistling or singing, or disturbance of any sort ; and the old manor, with its stately butler, its dull gardens and silence, seemed, in spite of Aunt Jem, a poor place after the homely Devonshire cottage, where mother minded no noise, and father had his boat and workshop, and where nobody scolded or dressed for dinner, or reminded one, by any chance whatever, about one's manners ! So the Elliots' visits waxed fewer, and Colonel Ffrench grew more and more averse to children, and Miss Jemima was begin- ning to realize that one old life was indeed all she would have to care for more in this world ; when suddenly Portia came into her hands, her great-niece. Por- tia, who in her own small person possessed more mischief-power than all the fourteen children Miss Jemima had brought up ; Portia, whom she would not only have to look after as a child, but chaperon and rule—Heaven save the mark —as a grown-up young lady on her entrance into the world.

" I can scarcely believe that I really am to lose her at last," Miss Jemima whispered, as Susan's eyes forever wandered, in their blindness, toward the window where Portia was standing. " There has been a talk so often before of Portia's marrying, and now—"

" Now, ma'am ? " Susan ventured to say, as old Miss Ffrench hesitated.

" Well, now, it is impossible not to feel that she has chosen the wrong man. I don't mind saying so to you, Susan, for I know how fond you are of Portia. Teddy is a nice little fellow, poor lad ! upright and honorable, I do believe, un- der all that foolish exterior ; but not the husband for Portia. I've often won- dered," went on Miss Jemima ; " and I'm sure I have never yet made up my mind, who *would* be the husband for Portia ! "

" The man she loved, I should think," said Susan, without a moment's hesitation.

" Ah, perhaps so," answered Miss Jemima, with rather a doubtful shake of the head. " But then, the next question is, could Portia love anybody ? Portia is a Dysart. poor child. That is a circumstance, Susan, that one never must forget. Portia is a Dysart."

Susan was silent. The incompatibility of loving with being a Dysart was a mystery beyond her grasp.

" Portia is a Dysart, heart and soul," went on Miss Ffrench, "and Teddy, in his feeble way, is a Dysart. They are first cousins, Susan. The late Earl of Erroll had two daughters, one of whom married a Josselin, the other my poor nephew Harry, and how two Dysarts are to get on and stand upright—"

" Aunt ! " cried out Portia's animated voice, " I know from the way you shake your head that you are talking about me or Teddy, or both of us ! Now confess "—she moved across the room to the tea-table. George Blake following, as if magnetically drawn, and Teddy slowly sauntering behind—" confess you have been poisoning Susan's mind against us ! Now, the truth, Miss Ffrench ? "

She came close to Miss Jemima's side ; stooped, smoothed the old lady's gray hair on her forehead ; then, with the prettiest little mock-abigail air, set her

cap straight on her head. "Aunt Jemima insists upon a certain Watteau-like
fashion of wearing her cap on one side, Susan, and I disapprove of it. Now
Mr. Blake—you have an artist's eye—I appeal to you. Does not Miss Ffrench
look better with her cap straight as I have put it, than in her usual flowing and
dishevelled style?"

"I think Miss Ffrench looks well always," said George Blake. "When I
look at Miss Ffrench, the fashion of her cap is the last thing that I should re
member."

A faint color rose on Miss Jemima's cheek. At sixty-five she still loved a
compliment as well as a girl of seventeen, "Ah, Portia, you see you are not
the only person who has pretty things said to them! Portia won't believe me,
Mr. Blake, when I tell her that I am handsomer than she is."

"But I swear that you are, a hundred times handsomer," said Teddy, who
by this time had mastered the difficulty of crossing the room. "You have better eyes—oh yes, Portia, you must hear the truth sometimes—and a fairer skin,
and are a handsomer woman altogether. Now, Susan," he sank down into a
low chair, not by Portia, but between Susan and old Miss Ffrench; "Susan at
her age is sure to speak the truth. Which of the Miss Ffrenches do you think
the handsomest? Don't be afraid."

Susan glanced across at Portia, then looked up straight in Miss Jemima's
face. Not in its fairest day could that face have been handsome, still less
pretty. It possessed none of the hereditary good looks of the Ffrenches. The
graceful turn of head, the pure cut profile, both were wanting; and the mouth
was large, and the eyes were commonplace grey not black. But it was a sweet,
fine old face to look at, notwithstanding. In spite of Indian suns, and the wear
and tear of her soldier's life, some inalienable bloom of youth seemed to have
clung to the cheek that so many little lips had forever kissed; some inalienable
gayety of heart gave the eyes and brow a lightness that Portia, with all the
beauty of her one-and-twenty years, did not possess.

"Susan can't make up her mind," cried the girl, "or is too much afraid of
you, aunt Jem., to say. So we will look upon the question as settled. You are
far handsomer, and have a great many more people in love with you than I can
ever hope for. What an awful trouble it would be, by the way, to have people
really, heavily in love with one! I know nothing about it practically, but I
should think affairs of that kind, taken seriously, would make life insupportable."

She gave a careless glance at Teddy, who, from the force of habit rather than
malice aforethought, was beginning to look with soft eyes at his little neighbor,
and to whisper pretty speeches in her ear as he helped her pour out the cream.

"Don't interrupt us, Portia. Susan and I are so happy; and after tea we
are going to listen to the nightingale. For people in the spring of life, like us,
nothing is worse than to be forced to listen to these cynical opinions of the
world. A serious passion a trouble! You should have seen the Dormouse at
Sheldon's house last night."

"What, with Laura Wynne?"

"Of course."

"Ah, that is an exceptional case. A dozen years difference in age, and all
on the lady's side, may give a pleasant sub-acid flavor to love-making that we,
in our *blasé* youth, know nothing about."

Miss Jemima sat down the teapot with a start. "Portia," she exclaimed,
"that is one of the most shocking speeches I ever heard you make! You, in
your *blasé* youth, indeed! You are obliged to use a foreign word for what you

dare not say in English. And comparing yourself for a moment to Laura Wynne! You seem to forget, child, that Mrs. Wynne is a married woman.

"Don't heat yourself, aunt (please throw open the window, Ted; if you do it softly grandpapa will never be the wiser; thanks), and don't be unreasonable. Can I help it that poor Laura is married, and that the Dormouse is a dozen years younger than herself?"

"You can help speaking of such people, Portia. When I was a girl, no decorous young woman ever appeared aware of—of conduct like Mrs. Wynne's," said Miss Jemima, blushing.

"Decorous young women must walk about the world in blinkers, if they would not appear aware of conduct like Mrs. Wynne's now," cried Portia. "Depend upon it, Aunt Jem, as I often tell you, the only difference between successive generations is, that hypocrisy is rather more in fashion at one time than at another."

"Heaven help the age when hypocrisy was more in fashion than at present," remarked Mr. Blake, under his voice.

"Oh, of course *you* say that," said Portia, turning upon him quickly. "It is part of your profession. Mr. Blake is an author—author and artist, Susan! I didn't like to frighten you by saying so sooner."

"The celebrated author of a novel called 'Ixion,'" added Teddy Josselin, twisting the ends of his fair little moustache into finer needle points. At which remark George Blake gave a kind of groan.

"And naturally, as a writer," went on Portia, "supports the popular fiction about the rapid pace of to-day surpassing the pace of all the yesterdays there have been in the world. What would become of smart young essayists if they had no frisky matrons, no girls of the period to write about?"

"Writers, at all events, could not write about such things unless they existed," said good Miss Jemima, in her innocence. "If, instead of reading satires upon yourselves which make you worse than before, you young people would improve your minds with the solid standard literature of the past, how much better it would be for you!"

"You dear, good, believing old aunt," cried Portia, with the frank impertinence that sat so well upon her. "How often am I to tell you that that faith of yours in standard literature is a mistake? I read half through the 'Spectator,' a little time ago, to please Aunt Jemima, Mr. Blake, and what did I find? Proposals of a fair for marriage, complaints against hoops and mantuas, accounts of the Romping Club, of the dissection of a beau's head and of a coquette's heart! After this I went through a course of Miss Austen. Has any one here read 'Northanger Abbey,' and can any depiction of modern young ladies outdo that of Catherine and Isabella pursuing the gentlemen in Milsom street, then driving out with them, unchaperoned, in gigs? The fact is, the world has always been divided into two classes—people who amuse themselves, people who don't; and those who don't—very naturally, poor wretches—abuse those who do!"

Portia tossed off this generalization with the easy assurance that characterized her; and seemed to consider the subject exhausted.

"I know nothing about the 'Spectator' or the other fellow. Something Abbé, wasn't it, Portia?" remarked Teddy. "For, I am thankful to say, I never read"—Teddy Josselin said this, with some natural pride—"unless when any very dear friend writes a book. If the statements of a novel called 'Ixion' are to be relied upon—and a sense of duty has made me read the work carefully—old Rome, at its worst, was a garden of Eden compared to London now."

"But then," said Portia, trifling with her tea-spoon, "has the author of 'Ixion' ever penetrated beyond the servants' hall, nay, the scraper of the aristocratic mansions where his scenes are laid?" The measured way she spoke evidently marked the sentence as a quotation.

"Has this miserable witling," added Teddy, in the same tone, "this grovelling impostor, this libeller of every thing good and noble in human nature, ever calculated upon the evil which even the spurious malignity of a pen like his may have the power to effect?"

"Miss Ffrench," interrupted George Blake, turning to old Miss Jemima, "I throw myself upon your compassion! I have, as you know, written a novel —the very worst novel, I should say, ever written in any language—and this fellow Josselin, and I am sorry to add, your niece, have learnt the different criticisms upon it by heart, so as to torture me at any time when their spirits want that kind of stimulant. Is this fair?"

"No, indeed," said Miss Jemima, seriously. "Portia, it is not at all pretty of you to behave so. I remember a dear sister of my own wrote a novel —her name was Rosamunda, Mr. Blake, and the novel was called after her, 'Rosamunda, or the Sufferings of Virtue.' It was published by subscription, and in the family we always attributed Rosa's early death to the heartless attack made upon her book in the 'Hampshire Gazette.' My father, it was afterward remembered, had not employed the editor's son, a worthy young man in his way, to new-glaze the greenhouse. You should never wound an author's feelings, Portia. I read 'Ixion' through, without missing a word, Mr. Blake, and thought the last volume extremely pathetic. When they are all weeping round —round—I can't remember names—but the bad young gentleman's death-bed, I was fool enough, I assure you, to shed genuine tears."

"Thank you, Miss Ffrench, thank you," said the author. "Yours, I am quite sure, were the only tears shed over 'Ixion'; unless, indeed, I wept with shame over it myself."

"And would be still more valuable, if aunt did not weep so copiously over everything!" said Portia, as she rose from the tea-table. "Unfortunately, not only bad young gentlemen's death-beds, but all death-beds, and all railway accidents—yes, and bishops' letters, and royal speeches—anything about death, or that contains fine, long, puffed-out sentences, makes Aunt Jem cry! Now, who is for the garden? You and Susan are going to listen to the nightingale, Teddy. Mr. Blake, do you feel in the least inclined to take care of me?"

She put her hand as she spoke under Susan's arm—such a contrast as they made, as Portia knew they made! Her own tall figure in its graceful London dress; the little village girl in her black frock, fashioned by a Halfont milliner —then, followed by the two young men, left the drawing-room.

"Portia, Portia," cried old Colonel Ffrench, waking up from his newspaper, "it is much too chilly for you to venture out. All this opening and shutting of doors fills the house with damp air. I must really put my veto upon your going farther than the billiard room."

"Oh, very well, grandpapa, no farther than the billiard room," Portia answered, then tripped down stairs and straightway through the hall, without hat or cloak, into the garden. "Obedience is not one of the cardinal virtues in my code," she remarked, turning round, with a repentant look, to George Blake.

"Nor truth-telling, either," added Teddy Josselin. "Come away with me, Susan. Portia is going to confess her sins, and you and I will listen to the nightingale."

CHAPTER V.

THERE were no nightingales to listen to; nevertheless it was a right pleasant evening for loitering through old-fashioned garden shades like those of Halfont Manor; the idle wash of the canal to lull one's senses, a congenial companion at one's side. The leaden clouds of the afternoon had parted above an amber sunset; the early roses smelt sweet; the rooks were cawing jovially in the high elms; and Susan, as she walked along by Teddy Josselin, could not but feel that the world was a much more endurable world than it had seemed when Tom Collinson joined her on the bridge that afternoon! For the first time for months she found herself laughing aloud—at such infinitely small jokes, too, as those of Teddy Josselin! Her fingers no longer twitched with shyness as they rested on his arm. The color deepened in her cheeks until Teddy began to decide that Portia's village friend was really a very pretty girl indeed, also that he might as well begin a flirtation with her in earnest, and without delay.

"Let us make ourselves happy under the cedars, Susan—oh, Portia and Blake are miles away by this time, you needn't look after them. My maxim is, never exert yourself after the unknown when the present moment is pleasant. And our present moment is very pleasant—don't you think so?"

He stopped; took both her hands; made her sit down on a little rustic bench upon the lawn; then sank into an American rocking-chair, Portia's special property, close beside her. The evening light slanted rosy upon his refined fair face, upon the white jewelled hands lazily clasped up over his head, upon the elaborate evening-dress, which in his boyish dandyism he did not, it must be confessed, carry off ungracefully. And, for the second time, it crossed Susan's mind to think how much Portia was to be envied. Beauty, wit—or what possesses more than the effect of wit from lips like hers—for her own portion, and a companion like Mr. Josselin, handsome, light-hearted, rich in this world's goods, to saunter, well-contented, by her side through life!

Until now, Susan, unlike most girls of her age, had been positively without an ideal as regards love or lovers. Tom Collinson, the only young man she knew, was repulsive to her; and Teddy Josselin was attractive. This was the extent of her experience up to the present moment. And if it had so happened that Teddy had been free, and the fates had willed it, she might, just like the majority of women, have never come within a hundred miles of passion while she lived; only have married, slipped—half awake, but contentedly—through existence; then gone to her grave, ignorant of the meaning of stronger love than the love which a Teddy Josselin can inspire! But George Blake was coming; was within twenty yards, his face turned toward her already; and the girl's soul was about to awaken. This childish half-envy of Portia—this momentary heart-whole admiration of Portia's lover—was just the brief rose-flush, the ten minutes before dawn, in Susan's life.

"Yes, I say we are very happy," murmured Teddy, caressingly. "If your head was turned a very little more my way—thanks. How jolly it is to look at a dear little outline of round cheek against a background of sylvan green; how jolly a long life in the country would be, all spent like this. Portia is a very nice girl, Susan?"

"Very nice, sir."

"Oh, not 'sir!' You must never call any fellow 'sir' till he's sixty years old, and—and I forget what I was going to say."

"Something about Portia, sir—Mr. Josselin, I mean."

"Don't trouble yourself about my name; or, if you call me anything, say 'Teddy.' I should like to hear you say 'Teddy,' Susan."

"Oh, indeed I couldn't!" and the child flushed rosy-red, then laughed.

"Yes, please do—for Portia's sake! You know you said you thought Portia was a nice girl."

"So I do, but I can't see any connection—I mean I couldn't call you what you asked me, if I tried for an hour."

"Ah, then, don't try," said Teddy, placidly. "I never like to see pretty people trouble themselves to think about anything; it spoils the expression of the face. Do you like lilies of the valley, Susan?"

This, after a full stop, during which he had amused himself by lazily leaning down and plucking minute portions of grass, then throwing them, blade by blade, upon the girl's black dress.

"I'm very fond of them," answered Susan, in her shy voice. "But those are not lilies of the valley that you are throwing at me, you know, sir!"

"Ah—'sir' again! and did I say they were, you wise child? Will you have mine, then?"

He unpinned the liliputian bouquet from his button-hole, and arrested the rocking-chair at such an angle as brought his hand within two inches of Susan's, his handsome boyish face not very much farther. "Don't say 'no.' It's the only favor I've ever asked of you yet."

"I don't want to say no," said Susan. And then this child of nature takes the first (mock) love-gift that has been ever offered to her, and smells the flowers—hanging her head so as to hide that she is flattered—and finally pins them in her waistbelt; all these baby coquetries acted with no more self-consciousness than a little kitten feels when, dancing round its first worsted ball, it curvets and purrs and growls with the undeveloped instincts of torture of its kind!

Teddy found her a charming study—the study of pretty faces was the only one he ever permitted himself. With the aid of a friendly cigarette the remainder of the evening might pass, he thought, as not all evenings at Halfont Manor passed, without his once feeling bored.

"You don't know how to roll a cigarette, I conclude, Susan? Well, then, I'll teach you."

And Master Teddy had taken out his book of cigarette paper and his embroidered tobacco-case, and was just—the rocking-chair finally brought to a stand-still—training Susan's awkward fingers in the way they should go (a piece of education, it seemed, requiring much close assistance) when Portia and Mr Blake emerged from a shrub-shaded walk not six paces away from where they sat.

"Never mind," said Teddy, "it's only the other people," for Susan had given a start at discovering they were not alone. "You have got too much tobacco—now too little—dear, dear, why is not everybody clever! Now let me show you once more."

He took the girl's small fingers within his, and Susan, a tremendous accession of shyness overtaking her at knowing she was watched, blushed violently as Portia came up to them.

The blush, the down-drooped face, the transferred lilies of the valley—Portia noted all in an instant, and an expression George Blake had never seen them wear before, came round her lips. Violent jealousy, the love-born unreasoning jealousy that can rise to passion, was probably beyond her compass. But there are many degrees of the same feeling and—little though she would have acknowledged the weakness—Portia could never brook the sight of Teddy Josselin getting to the end of his chain with complete equanimity. Absolute freedom, conquest at every step she took, with every breath she drew, were *her* prescriptive rights ; rights at which let neither present lover nor future husband demur. For him, lover or husband, slavery. A man's pride is, or ought to be flattered by witnessing the world's approbation of his choice. A woman's self-respect is lowered by seeing herself put aside, even jestingly, for another. This was Portia's creed ; not an uncommon creed among women of her type ; perhaps—so long as they have round them a bevy of slaves all more or less in the state of George Blake—a pardonable one. Only, curious to say, the person most nearly concerned, the actual lover, the actual husband, does not always subscribe to it unmurmuringly.

"Admirable, by Jove ! No machine could have turned one out better rolled. By the time I am ready for my next, in about ten minutes that's to say, you will be perfect."

"You will smoke no other cigarette than the one you are smoking now," remarked Portia, coolly. "Indeed, I doubt whether you will have time to finish that. I am going to take you over the powder mills."

"Portia ?"

"Didn't you say the other evening you wished to see them ? "

"Yes, but we had no other amusement then. We were so out of spirits that we thought even the remote chance of being blown up better than going on living."

"I should always think that," said Portia ; "the other evening or now, or any time ! Should not you, Mr. Blake ? "

George Blake, when out of love, was no fool ; but on the present occasion he made the speech of one—the substance of it being that to explode in Portia's company were better than to continue to live alone, *et cetera*.

"Then do, my dear fellow, give yourself a chance at once," cried Teddy, with thorough good humor. "Here are two romantic persons wishing to be blown up and have done with the bore of living, and two commonplace persons perfectly ready to live till they are ninety, and to be allowed to make cigarettes. Why can't we all be happy in our own way?"

Without deigning to reply, Portia turned and walked off, with stately dignity toward the house. For a minute Teddy Josselin watched her, a careless half smile on his face, then rose, slowly, and moved a step or two across the lawn. "Portia, Cousin Portia!" he called. "Won't you wait for me? I am quite willing to be blown up, but I don't see why I should be put out of breath beforehand."

Upon which Portia's pace at once quickened; and then—then Teddy actually ran and caught her up, and George Blake had the pleasure first of seeing the beautiful face turn round with a frown, then melt into a smile; finally of watching the lovers turn into a narrow side-path and saunter off, most lover-like in mien and proximity, toward the canal.

He stood still, his eyes fixed gloomily on the point at which Portia's figure had vanished, for some minutes; at last, abruptly seemed to remember Susan's existence. "What! you and I left to amuse each other, after all, Susan? Come here, my dear?"

George Blake's life was spent among theatrical people, painting people, writing people, unconventional people of all sorts; and he had contracted a trick—wholly innocent—of speaking more affectionately than is the custom of the world to his associates; I may add that older and wiser persons than Susan were not always offended by it. She jumped up, and came, as he bade her, to his side.

"What are you looking so solemn about? What are you thinking of? Are you cross that Portia has taken Teddy Josselin away? He is her property, remember."

"I wasn't thinking of Portia or Mr. Josselin, either; and I'm not cross at all, thank you."

"Thank you," repeated George Blake, mimicking her prim little shy voice. "Then if you were not cross, and not thinking of Portia, or of Portia's lover—may I ask what you *were* thinking of?"

"I was thinking of you!" said Susan, with a jerk. She had not forgotten Teddy Josselin's lesson in good-breeding, but only pulled up just in time to keep in the obnoxious "sir."

"I was thinking you were annoyed, and—and I wished Portia had offered to take you to be blown up!"

"Complimentary! That you and Josselin might make cigarettes undisturbed, I suppose?"

"No—that you might be with Portia."

For a moment George Blake turned his head aside; then he looked down closely on Susan's face. "And what do you know—what have you heard of me, child, that should make you think I wished to be with Portia?"

"Nothing, Mr. Blake. I never heard your name till an hour ago; but—but I think you said you would rather be blown up with Portia than live alone; and you did look *so* disappointed as they walked away."

"The fact is, my dear, you are a witch. I am not deluded by that childish appearance, that shy little mock-innocent manner! Nothing but witchcraft could make you divine such an unlikely thing as this. Susan"—after a minute, and still closely reading the transparent, girlish face—"you and I would be great friends."

"Would be?" said Susan, lifting her eyes to his.

"Yes, would be—will be, if we see enough of each other. Now, suppose you talk to me just as you were talking to Teddy Josselin when we disturbed you. It will do me good." He made her sit down again, and took his place, one arm on the back of the rustic seat, beside her. "Go on, my dear—talk."

"But I've nothing to say," said Susan, horribly frightened at this prospect of having to sustain the burden of a conversation.

"Rubbish! say what you were saying to Josselin."

"I couldn't—indeed I couldn't! That was all nonsense, and it was he who said it," cried Susan, logically.

"And you couldn't talk nonsense, or roll cigarettes, or laugh aloud—such a good little laugh, too—with me? You like Josselin much the best, don't you, Susan?"

She turned away, setting her lips like a child who has been asked for a kiss, but means to contest it, and colored.

"You like Josselin better than me," repeated George Blake. "Now, tell the truth."

Susan caught down a bough of acacia close beneath which they sat, and buried her face in one of its clusters of cool white bloom. George Blake began to forget the powder-mills a little.

"Susan," said he, severely, "you incipient, small coquette, tell the truth. You like Josselin best?"

"I like Mr. Josselin."

"Best?"

"I did not say anything about 'best,' sir."

George Blake had sufficient experience of Susan's sex to be contented. After a minute or two spent in watching her (he looked upon her as a child, remember, and watched her with purely artist eyes, thinking how fair a rustic model she would be; not for a Greuze or Watteau—she had not piquancy, not conscious innocence enough for these French pencils—but rather for one of Sir Joshua's serious, sweet, child faces)—after a minute, "And so I looked disappointed when Portia went away?" he said. "Are you sure of that, now? I attach a great deal of importance to everything you tell me."

"I am quite sure of it," said Susan. "And no wonder," she added, quickly (nature had conferred on her, as on all gentle natures, that best gift for a woman —tact); "I feel a kind of blank, too—though I've only known her these few weeks—whenever Portia goes away. How beautiful she looks to-night, Mr. Blake."

The subject of Portia's beauty was one on which Mr. Blake, in his present state of madness, would mercilessly descant to any man, woman, or child whom he could force into listening. Once set going, indeed, and he forgot time and place, the slight monotony of the subject of short upper-lips and graceful throats, when pursued unremittingly; the sufferings of his victims, their slackening attention, their attempts to escape from him—everything. But the hearer he had got now was too sympathetic, too thoroughly fresh to be bored, even by a man in love. At every "and what grace, and what variety!" and "have you noticed this, or that?" Susan, in perfect good faith, gave the required affirmative interjections. She was really interested—the first listener of that kind he had ever found—not only in Portia, but in Mr. Blake's hopeless admiration of her; the more interested, probably, because it was hopeless; and when at last he paused, rather from want of breath than because he felt the subject exhausted, volunteered this little chorus of her own: "And, in addition to all her good looks, what an unselfish, what a generous heart Portia has!"

George Blake looked up at the throngs of gnats that were dancing quadrilles between him and the sky. That Portia had a Titian-like complexion, an exquisite throat and profile, he knew to his cost! Also, that he loved her (as men love) violently; had been led astray by her for weeks past; had given up the easy, cheaply-bought pleasures of his old life for the expensive necessities of cabs, bouquets, and white gloves, in order to haunt her through parties and balls. This he knew to his cost, likewise. But heart! Portia Ffrench's an unselfish, a generous heart! Blake had lived twenty-five years in the world—eight of them by himself in London—and could not now fall in love quite as boys do. He would have been ready to swear a mole on Portia's cheek a loadstar of beauty; for all the admiration his senses could give was hers. In the matter of forming judgment upon her moral qualities, reason, to a certain limited extent, was his own, still.

"I speak," said Susan, as she watched the expression of his face, "from what I know. When I was in my great grief, Portia came to see me"—not a word of good Miss Jemima!—and she has thought of me in twenty kind ways since—Miss Jemima had sent the child presents of sweetmeats and early strawberries—"and asked me to-night because it's my birthday. And 've enjoyed myself *so* much!" added Susan, irrelevantly.

George Blake felt a sudden strong impulse to snatch the little creature in his arms and kiss her. It was a common kind of impulse with him when he was in the company of children; but Susan's advanced age, and a certain wistful gravity that never quite forsook her face, withheld him from carrying it into effect.

"My poor little friend, how sorry I am to hear that word 'grief' from your lips."

Up welled the tears into Susan's eyes. She tried to say something and couldn't. The tears brimmed, then fell, wetting her hands as they lay clasped on her black frock. "I didn't mean to trouble you like this!" she faltered out, at last.

"Trouble me!" said Blake, and all his light manner fled, his face softened a vast deal more than it had done when he rhapsodized about Portia's upper lip. "Why, my dear, what do you take me for? We might have talked to each other the whole evening on idle subjects, and have remained strangers still. At that one word grief, Susan—at that word I feel in a moment that I have known you since you were so high!"

On paper this speech does not read eloquent. Spoken in a kindly voice, and coming straight from the speaker's heart, it sounded so, or comforted the little girl it addressed, which is better. Susan realized, as she had not done since her father's death, that she was being felt with—not consoled, not advised, not pitied; but felt with.

"If you had only known him," she said, presently. "You would have liked each other—have got on so well. I'm sure you would."

(In the interval before dinner, Portia, mentioning the guest who was to drink tea with them, had said: "And the miracle is, where the child gets her pretty little lady-like ways and looks! Her father was a Brentford shopkeeper—a gentleman who smoked a long clay pipe on Sundays, and christened his

roadside villar after *Haddison.*" "And who kept my brother in hot water for
ten years about a willow fence," Miss Jemima had chimed in. "Joseph Fielding's 'h's' and 'r's' wouldn't have mattered—by the way, Portia, you never
heard him speak—or his clay pipe, either, if his nature had been a better one."
This was the man whom George Blake would have got on with and liked !)

"No one in Halfont knew papa," went on Susan, "except the vicar, a little ;
and I'm beginning to feel now that no one liked him. He never wanted to be
liked, I think—except, of course, by mamma, and, after her, by me. Directly
he came home, he used to work in the garden, or take his fishing-rod ; and then
of an evening he sang—he and I. There was no room for strangers in our life.
If we had had just one friend, like you, sir, to come and talk to us, it would
have been different ; but we had no one, and so we lived alone. We were contented."

"And you have never, till you knew Portia, had a companion in your life ?"
said Blake ; "have never been to a dance or read a story-book, I'll be
bound ?"

"I've never been to a dance," said Susan, "but as to stories—" she wiped
the tears from her cheeks and began to reflect—"well, I should say I've read
nearly all the novels that were ever written."

"Tell me the names of them."

"The whole of 'Waverley,' Fielding's collected works, 'Sir Charles Grandi-
son,' 'Evelina,' 'Rasselas,' and the 'Vicar of Wakefield.'" She ran through
the list with conscious pride, speaking volubly to show her thorough acquaintance with English literature. "And then, of course, 'Pilgrim's Progress' and
'Robinson Crusoe,' and all those *childish* books," she added ; as George remained silent, just the least startled it must be owned, at the strong food on
which his little "Sir Joshua" had been nourished. "And as to poetry and plays
—oh, I could never remember the names of the plays I have read, if I was to try."

"And were these the books your father and mother picked out for you ?"
asked Blake. "Richardson and Fielding, and more plays than you can remember the names of !"

"Mamma died when I was six years old," said Susan, "and she never read
anything. I remember she used to say it took off your taste for reading to be in
the trade, like confectioners with sweet things."

"And a very true remark, too," said Blake, thinking, no doubt, of his own
branch of the trade and "Ixion."

"And papa said he would never force me one way or another about reading
—this was when Miss Collinson was angry once about my reading some book—
'Rasselas'—no, 'Amelia,' I think it must have been. He took care, he said,
never to have any trash in his own house—nothing but the standard editions—
and I might please myself as to which of them I read. So long as a book was
well bound and one of the standard editions, papa didn't trouble himself much
about the inside."

"A wise man !" said Blake. "Susan, you teach me something new every
minute. I feel as I never did before ; how much better a thing it is to sell
books than to write them !"

"Now, are you telling the truth ?"

"Susan !"

"Oh, I beg your pardon, but I never am quite sure. You speak like earnest,
and yet—its the same with Portia—I'm never sure you are not laughing at me !
Now would you really not be above selling books ?"

"Its the very occupation I've been long trying," answered Blake, with a laugh, "and in vain. The public won't come to my shop! I have put verses, story-books—just the wares you are fondest of, Susan—upon my counter; all without effect. No one will buy. Don't let us talk of books, child; 'tis a sore subject to us who are in the trade. Suppose we go for a twilight walk instead." As he said this, he rose and turned down an over-arched pathway toward the canal, Susan following. "You have told me about your studies; now talk to me about yourself—a pleasanter theme, my dear, than all the novels and poems that were ever written."

CHAPTER VI.

YES, books were a sore subject just then to George Blake, the books called novels sorest of all. And here probably, was fatalest sign that nature had not destined him to be a master—he was cast down by failure; he believed in his critics! Worse books than "Ixion" have proved the basis of a great fame before now. Why? Their writers have had faith in themselves—no sign of genius, perhaps, this faith; who shall define for us what genius is? but an excellent prognostic of the faculty of success. But George Blake felt in his inmost soul that, as far as novel-writing went, he could never rally after "Ixion." He had written verses, a thin volume of boyish fancies, crude, not wholly contemptible, already. "Poems," by "G. B.," no critic had stooped even to annihilate; and all the young author's poetic fire had gone out under the cold shade of this neglect. Poetry was not what he was born for, he acknowledged; still, most great men try their 'prentice hand on verse; defeat in verse-making, however complete, is not shameful. He was born to write prose—and he wrote it —wrote "Ixion." And "Ixion" was cut to shreds by such critics as noticed it at all, and left alone by the public; it was also a dead loss to the publishers. "You may succeed in some other line, very possibly, but you will never write a story," said these gentlemen. "You have not the knack. There are authors and authoresses, Mr. Blake, with no genius or pretence to genius, who sell their so many hundred copies, certain. But you, my dear sir, *would* you step round to the warehouse and see the numbers of "Ixion" we have still got upon our hands?"

And then Blake began to see he was not born to write prose—prose fiction, at all events. What was he born for? To go diligently through the plain duties of his calling. the daily red-tape routine of work as clerk in a public office, and leave art and literature to other men? If Blake could have felt this, the failure of "Ixion" had not chafed him so sorely. But he could not feel it. He belonged to the class of men who, without any marked creative power themselves, have ineradicably strong art proclivities; and it frequently takes a lifetime of dilettante trial to teach such men what they cannot do. "Ixion" was a failure. He was not a poet; he was not a novelist! Grimly reading his book over in cold blood, and with his eyes opened by the wisdom of reviewers, he perceived that the sentiment of his story was sham, the cynicism sham (Blake was the most kindly, happy-natured of creatures, and only wrote bitterly because A, B and C had written bitterly before him), that his plot was impossible; that every one of his puppet characters uttered the same falsetto opinions, in the same falsetto voice. All this he acknowledged; and still he could not but feel that some other road *must* yet conduct him to success. What if he should try a play? He was intimate with half the theatrical people in London, and when you know actors, personally, few things seem easier, on the surface, than to supply them with fitting parts. Or turn musical composer? he had a pretty taste for weaving other men's thoughts into reveries and nocturnes of his own; had some acquaintance, too, with thorough bass. Or give up his clerkship in the treasury and study as a painter in earnest? His talent as a draughtsman was the most positive talent Blake possessed. As many drawings on wood as he chose to execute he could sell, and sell well; proof that they were at least up to the market standard of sentiment and perspective. A young lady, ten feet high, jumping into the arms of a young gentleman, half a mile distant, from a rock; a dislocated young gentleman stooping, with his card, over a young lady (dislocated also) in a ball-room; a young lady and gentleman, impossible as to anatomy, but with beautiful eyes and small mouths, looking at the moon from a balcony. In the exercise of art like this he might really have made an income; if he had possessed worldly sense enough for income ever to be a point of importance in George Blake's schemes! Well, he was just in this undecided frame of mind when he met Portia Ffrench; and the difficulty, for the time-being, was solved by his falling in love.

The property of love, we hear, is to act as a stimulant upon artistic faculty; to quicken the poet or the painter into nobler effort. Love did this for Blake; took up his time, wasted his money, incapacitated him more than ever from serious work, nay, as his infatuation progressed, put the thought of work altogether out of his head. Who would write a play when he might act the first part in one? paint a picture when he might gaze at one? rack his brain over form or simile when, without exertion, he might hear the praise of beautiful lips, feel the sympathizing pressure of a beautiful hand upon his arm? A man must have herculean strength who can bring the life of ball-rooms and the great world to alternate with the strenuous work that all honest art demands. Play, under the laborious guise of white gloves and the London season, is not the kind of play for ordinary workers; and so George Blake discovered. He had been Portia's slave now for a good many weeks; had gone where she bade him go, held her fan in ball-rooms, watched her as she danced with other men, watched the back of her head as she talked (to other men) in theatre-boxes, spent his days, after office hours, in waiting to catch a glimpse of her in the park—and what was his reward? Portia had engaged herself to Teddy Josselin! Well, he had anticipated some kind of tragic ending to his love from the first; how could a poor wretch, with a treasury clerkship and a hundred a year of private means, offer this divinity the affront of proposing that he should support her? The hope of winning Portia was irrevocably gone—his happiness with it. But, as regarded art, what inspiration, what single influence for good had she proved to him?

Once or twice, after a ball or opera, he had essayed verses to her, and had invariably lit his pipe with them next morning. Her face, with its faultless line of profile, its sweet, cold smile, its dark, unchanging eyes, he had drawn in every conceivable change of attitude, yet had never made of it aught save a catalogue, from right to left, or from left to right, of lips and brow and chin—a catalogue informed with no more soul than he could have found in the first plaster cast he had chosen to copy. He had composed a nocturne and an addio, both inscribed to Portia; and these had certainly more merit in them than the verses—perhaps than the drawings—yet were not a whit more original than the countless nocturnes and addios that he had dedicated, in old days, to the Violets and Claribels of his imagination. His senses, in a word, were enthralled—nothing mo.^. He himself, George Blake, was George Blake still—a good deal the poorer, in spirit and purse, for the little dance he had been led, and as far from "inspiration" as on the first day when Portia met him and decided that the holding captive a man who was neither marriageable, dandy, nor fool, would be a new stimulus, a new emotion to herself.

Their acquaintance began thus: Portia, who really liked pictures, or really liked to be able to talk about her liking for them, had gone up to town for a day's exhibition-seeing. The exhibitions were very convenient institutions, during the whole season of spring, to Portia Ffrench. To tell Miss Jemima she must go up to town for shopping, or to see any of her London friends, was, as a rule, to enlist Miss Jemima, in her village dress and sensible bonnet, as an escort. Portia, with her extravagant ideas, could no more be trusted alone in shops than a child; and as to her acquaintance—"Of the two I would sooner you should go and half ruin us all at the milliner's," Miss Jemima would say, "than spend a couple of hours in the society of any of these women of fashion whom you call your friends. When you stay with your grandmother, the responsibility is hers. You are a Dysart then, and must have Dysart associates. As long as you live at Halfont you are a Ffrench." But at the word "exhibition" Miss Jemima was silenced. Once, long ago, she had consented, at Portia's instigation, to have a bout of picture-seeing; had been ruthlessly dragged through Royal Academy, Water-colors, young and old, Suffolk street, National portraits—all in the course of one very sultry summer's day. And on that day Miss Jemima had inwardly sworn that no temptation should ever lead her into the regions of art again. She hid her sufferings like a Spartan; enlarged, to Colonel Ffrench, at home, upon the delightful treat they had had; and ascribed the pain in the nape of the neck, that lasted her for a week afterward, to the chill evening breeze that met them as they were driving back across Hounslow Heath. But she never broke her resolution—she never set her foot within the doors of another picture-gallery. It was good, doubtless, for young people to see everything that was going on; good for them to enlarge their minds, to take an interest in any subject unconnected with expensive dresses and frivolity; and, as the girl always chose the name of her very soberest acquaintance as her art chaperon, it grew in time to be a settled thing that Miss Jemima should not say nay whenever these opportunities of intellectual improvement offered themselves. Thus, as I remarked, the ordinance of picture-seeing was an ordinance of whose manifold resources Portia, during the whole London season, availed herself pretty freely.

Upon the day on which George Blake met his fate, she really had gone to an exhibition—the one in Suffolk street—her cousin Teddy with her; perhaps some more lawful chaperon (Blake saw none). But in these days who can say of two ladies which is married and protecting, which spinster and protected? Both of the cousins were a great deal bored—Teddy the least so, perhaps, for Portia did really conscientiously look at every picture which the fashionable art critic of that season had pointed out as noteworthy. Indeed, when Blake first came upon them, the poor little fellow was sitting down, placidly asleep, while Portia, some yards distant, stood in a proper attitude of admiration before one of the pictures of the year.

The young men had been at school together—were friends still, as far as their different means, their different habits of life allowed—so Blake went up, and, after waking Teddy Josselin from his nap, asked him what he thought of the pictures. Teddy possessed no more knowledge of art than of Arabic (it

would be hard to say on what subject Teddy did possess knowledge); still, he
was just one of those sketchy, inconsequential, shallow rather than empty human
creatures, to whom you will so often find that people with brains in their own
heads delight to listen. Wittier men, wiser men, better men than Teddy jostle
one at every turn. But Teddy had the rare gift of being absolutely natural—
unconsciously suggestive as a child in every word he said. Lazily rousing himself, he cast his blue eyes round—Blake having further explained that his own
business was to make picture-notes for a newspaper—and for five minutes or so
gave utterance to whatever opinions came uppermost in his nutshell of a head
respecting the score or so of pictures that he could see without moving. "And
though, thank God! I know nothing about high art or high criticism," he finished, "I believe I have eyes, and a grain or two of common sense, and, my dear
fellow, you are welcome to make professional use of all I have said." Then he
he rose and sauntered away after Portia, whose graceful figure Blake, meanwhile, had been furtively watching.

She asked, before Teddy could open his lips, who that person was to whom
he had been talking—the person with the sallow face and black moustache, like
a singer. No one?—that was nonsense. Was he one of the men who sold the
pictures, or the catalogues, or what? "Now, I insist upon knowing. Teddy.
He is writing a book, and must be something dreadful of the kind. Who is
he?"

"In the language you talk, no one at all," answered Teddy. "He is a clerk
in the Treasury. He has about ninety pounds a year of private means. He
won't even dance. He is non-existent."

"Go on, Teddy, dear."

"He writes novels and verses, and things for the newspapers. He doesn't
care for ladies."

"Bring him and introduce him to me this moment."

"Haven't I said he does not care for ladies? There is Liddell just coming
in, I see; and there's Brett, somewhere about, and me. Why should you want
to plague this poor fellow? He has never hurt you."

"Have Colonel Liddell and Johnnie Brett?"

"No; and you can't hurt them," said Teddy, with his small laugh. "Now,
Blake—well, you see, Cousin Portia, you could hurt a poor fellow like Blake immensely."

"Will you bring him here at once, little Teddy?"

"With the thermometer at ninety, I will do anything rather than argue,"
said Teddy Josselin; then went away after his friend, who was busy again with
his note-book at the other side of the room. Blake looked round horrified on
being told he was to be introduced to a young lady—Was in a morning coat, had
come for work, must beg to be excused, and—and which was the lady? He
would like to see her first.

"She stands over there, in a black silk dress and a white muslin scarf," said
Teddy. "No, not the sphynx of sixteen stone, heaped over with pink roses—
the slender, dark young woman, who carries her head on one side, and at this
moment shows us her profile. She is my cousin, and thought rather good-looking, and—oh, you are coming, then, after all?"

Blake came, was introduced, and wrote no more notes that day. Portia was
afraid, although she had the celebrated Mr. Blanque's guide in her hand, that
she had been admiring everything she oughtn't. Could it be possible there were
only eight pictures worthy to be called pictures in the rooms? Would Mr.

Blake mind the trouble of taking her once round with him? She was utterly
ignorant, but loved pictures from her heart. Oh, how different looking an
exhibition was with some one who really cared for art to direct one's admiration! "I have heard enough of faults," she said, making a shrewd guess at
George Blake's turn of mind. "What I wanted was to enjoy, and you have
taught me how to do so."

She gave him a beautiful hand at parting—or a hand clothed in so perfect a
glove as to look beautiful; Portia's gloves were always miracles of good taste,
indefinite of hue, symmetrical of cut, firm of texture—gave him a hearty pressure, too! and no woman living had a pleasanter way of shaking hands than
Portia Ffrench, when she liked. Next week she came up to pay her yearly visit
to her grandmother, and through Teddy's agency, at once had George Blake
brought to Lady Erroll's house in Eaton square. She had no need long to keep up
the intellectual strain in which the acquaintance began. The trouble of reading
Mr. Blake's poems had to be gone through; the exertion of forming an opinion
differing from that of the reviewers, on " Ixion ;" after this Mr. Blake himself
took all further difficulty off her hands by falling in love. Now there was no
very novel amusement to Portia Ffrench in having a man so circumstanced at
her side; but there was wonderful novelty in the type of man she had at length
had the good fortune to conquer! As a companion to spend her life with, Teddy
Josselin was, and continued to be the girl's ideal. Teddy held the same beliefs,
on all momentous questions, as herself, namely, that pleasure is pleasant, and
trouble troublesome; that after them would come the deluge; and that excitement, bought no matter at what cost, is the end-all and be-all of an otherwise
worthless existence. And then he had a handsome person, and the air of a
man of the world, and did whatever he was bidden, and altogether—altogether
as much as it was in Portia Ffrench's nature to love, she loved him. She never
asked herself whether it would be possible to fall in love with George Blake.
She cut him short whenever he began to talk sentiment—sentiment, no audience by to listen, wearied her to death. All she cared for was that the world,
from cynical old Lady Erroll down to Aunt Jemima at home, should see that a
man of genius (throughout his aberration so she loved to call poor Blake) did
not find her so frivolous but that he could take delight in her society. She was
like a child who, angling for minnows, unexpectedly brings a magnificent perch
—three or four inches long—to land. Such a prey would probably never come
to her little hook again; and she wanted every one to look at him as he lay
gasping on the bank. As to the perch's sufferings—ah, that was his concern.
There he stood in the same plight as the minnows. Her own small momentary
triumph was all with which Portia troubled herself; and of this she certainly
made the most.

Mr. Blake must come to dinner; "a quiet dinner, with one or two ap-
preciative people to meet him, and with sensible conversation, grandmamma, and
a little music afterward." Next he must follow her to balls. " You don't dance,
I know, Mr. Blake, but it will be profitable to you to stand out and moralize
on us foolish people who do!" After this, to operas and to the drive of an afternoon, and the Zoological on Sunday. Finally, when her own London visit
was over, nothing would content her but the poor fellow must be invited to
come down and dine with Colonel Ffrench at Halfont.

The pleasure of showing off her conquest at home proved limited. Miss
Jemima looked carefully through her spectacles at Blake—the only author, besides Rosamunda, she had ever known—during dinner, and, when he was gone,

remarked that, for her part, she couldn't see that writers talked cleverer than other people. Colonel Ffrench said he must really request Portia not to encourage the young man too far. Mr. Blake might be a gentleman by birth—very possibly; still he was connected with the press—with painters, too. Art and literature—ah, ah, all very well in their proper place, but Colonel Ffrench must confess he had never seen persons of that description at his table before. What a change after London, after liberal, art-patronizing London! Portia saw plainly that, with no audience save these two prejudiced old people, very little pleasure was to be got out of George Blake's Halfout visits; so the next time he was asked, bade Teddy Josselin come, too; and, as we have seen, invited Susan Fielding in the evening.

Teddy, whom nothing could make jealous, and poor little, shy, ignorant Susan were not much; still they formed a gallery, and without a gallery Portia could seldom bring herself to feel real interest in any game. The subjugation, alone and unseen, of the cleverest, bravest man in Europe would, I verily believe, have yielded her pleasure less acute than the subjugation of some well-looking fop, chosen at random from her London partners, the world or any small section of the world looking on.

An inborn coquette would as soon make a conquest in the midst of Salisbury Plain as elsewhere; her zest being in the conquest, not the mere glory of it. To Portia the glory was all in all. She had not the effervescence of spirit, the quick pulse, the enjoyment-power, which characterize the real coquette—as I understand the term. Constitutional melancholy, constitutional inertia lay at the bottom of all her brightness, of all her restless activity in the pursuit of excitement.

Unless life could be forever dramatized to her, she sank oppressed under its burden. And George Blake, no mean reader of character, although he could not write novels, already divined that it was so. He was not a whit cured of his passion by the discovery of this or any other weakness in Portia's character; nay, it seemed to him that he was but attracted toward her more, now that he knew what weary lip-laughter half her lightness was! But he did often speculate—had speculated half an hour ago, as he wandered with her through the silent garden—what sort of lot that man's would be, who, without money and all that money brings, should become Portia's husband? So very little of the married life of poor people is spent before the foot-lights; the hours of excitement are so few; the hours of dual solitude so many! Why this little village girl, this little shy Susan Fielding would be a better every-day companion, in very fact, than Portia Ffrench, with all her cultivation, with all her brilliancy!

Before three or four people, Portia's powers of conversation never flagged. Alone—positive love-making interdicted—and it was wonderful how little you found to say to her, or she to you. You got a reply never void of intelligence; often a caustic—even a witty little aphorism in answer to whatever you advanced; and then—then you must think of what you would say next. No remark seemed in Portia's presence to open out to graver interests. You never got an inch nearer to Portia's soul! The beautiful face, the graceful attitudes filled up all absolute blanks delightfully, still the blanks existed; while with Susan—

CHAPTER VII.

"Susan," said Blake, taking out his watch and trying, as well as the fading light would permit, to make out the time; "you are certainly a witch. I was quite right in my estimate of your character. Here we have been out an hour and a half together, and you have made it pass like five minutes."

Susan's heart gave a flutter of pleasure at the speech.

"An hour and a half? I never thought it was so late—time goes so quick out of doors—and—and if you are tired we had better go in at once," she added, demurely.

"Go in?" said Blake; "no. It is much pleasanter here than in the house, and Josselin and Miss Ffrench haven't finished seeing the powder-mills yet—rather dark, by the way, for seeing anything. This is the best hour of the twenty-four."

"It is the best for me," said Susan. "What other people call dusk is my day. At this minute I can actually make out the bank the other side the river."

They had walked as far as the long-disputed willow fence—the extreme boundary line of Colonel Ffrench's property. The light had died into one dull crimson streak above the flat horizon, but sufficient after-glow yet lingered to show the forms of near-at-hand objects; of the water-flags with their pale broad blossoms; of the narrow canal path, of the canal itself, as, brimming and level with its banks, it floated past, with its low, scarce audible murmur, toward the powder-mills.

"Poor little Susan!" said Blake, kindly—to him with his keen-strung, artist's delight in every object of the external world, this fact of Susan's near sight seemed an affliction very little short of actual blindness—"you must take comfort in one thing, remember; as you grow older, as you approach the age when the rest of us get mole-like, you will begin to see better. When you are ninety, what sight will you have, my dear!"

"I am not quite sure that I want to see better," said Susan, diffidently, for she had a consciousness that there might be an implied slight to the rest of the world in her contentment. "At least when I look through my glasses and see everything so plain, I don't feel half as much at my ease as before. The world seems all at once too big for me, you know; and whenever I have a bad dream, a nightmare, this is what I dream: I can see as every one else sees, and there are trees and houses ready to fall and crush me, and crowds of people, with their faces distinct, as I never see faces really, looking at me. No. I am sure I don't want to be different."

"But then your short sight makes you helpless?" said Blake. "You always need some one close at hand, as I am now, to keep you out of mischief?"

"Not a bit," Susan answered. "When once I know a place I can find my way everywhere—not with my hands, but by feeling, you understand. Papa might send me for any book he liked, in the dark, and I never brought the wrong one, and Miss Collinson says she never saw such eyes as mine for fine needle-work; and then they never get tired, however many hours I sew, even by lamp-light."

"And you are fond of needle-work, I'll answer for it," said Blake. "I think I see you with a needle and thread in those prim small hands! like the heroine of one of your favorite novels. You are great at pies and plain sewing, are you not, Susan?"

"I don't know about pies, sir, but I can do every kind of needle-work well, and I like it. Portia never sews; she says it is a slave's employment to sit and drag a needle to and fro, to and fro, through a bit of cambric or muslin all day long. If that is true, I suppose I was born to be a slave! I like to work—work even at plain sewing—and think. I don't know how it is, but I never have such nice thoughts as when I am sewing."

"And what are the 'nice' thoughts about, Susan?"

She made him no answer.

"What are your thoughts about, child? Come, you have told me so much about yourself already, you may as well tell me this."

"If I tell you my thoughts, will you tell me yours?"

"Ahem—on due consideration, I think not. I have a great many bitter hard thoughts to trouble me, Susan—thoughts that you would never understand."

"Then we will each keep our own secrets, Mr. Blake. If your thoughts would be too hard for me to understand, mine would be too silly for you to care for; and besides, I'm not quite sure I haven't told you them all, as it is!"

"Poor little Susan! If we meet again some day when you are older and wiser, I wonder whether you will remember all that you have said to me to-night?"

"I wonder," said Susan, becoming suddenly grave at the suggestion. And after this both were silent; and side by side—Blake looking out for the first flutter of Portia's dress through the gloom, Susan with I know not what dawnings of new emotion in her child's heart—began slowly to retrace their steps toward the house.

They found Portia and Teddy Josselin waiting for them under the portico. "What, not drowned?" said Portia, carelessly. "We were just beginning to think it was time to send out the men with drags."

"What, not blown up?" remarked George Blake, in the same tone. "We were terribly afraid something had happened to you, but knew we had been so much engrossed in our own conversation, that the explosion might have taken place without our hearing it!" For the feelings of Portia Ffrench and Mr. Blake were just at that kind of ebb when small mock warfare, semi-bitter speeches before other people, are the food of love—if vanity on one side and (conscious) infatuation on the other may be dignified by that name!

Susan ran away from Blake's side and got close to Portia. "I hope you have not been really frightened about us?" she said, in a whisper. "I am very sorry if I have stayed away too long."

"Dear, innocent, penitent little Susan!" cried Portia, but in a perfectly good-humored voice. Into whatever jealousies her craving for dominion might betray her, Portia Ffrench was too self-collected a woman ever to show animosity toward another woman; retribution she kept for the offender himself, not the rival. "Of course I forgive you, but you will have a fine scolding from Aunt Jemima and grandpapa, depend upon it. Come here, and let me make you look respectable," for they were now within the lighted entrance hall, "and unless we are very hard pressed we can let everybody believe we have been no further than the billiard room. Why, child, what a color you have got."

Susan had a brilliant color; the more brilliant because standing full under the lamp she felt that all of them must be looking at her. Her eyes were animated, and, as is the nature of short-sighted eyes, had lost their vacant look now that daylight was gone; the damp night air had made her brown hair twist into a multitude of little soft curls round her forehead. For the first time in her life Susan Fielding looked more than pretty.

Portia tried to smooth down the child's hair with her hands, in vain. The curls curled tighter and tighter. "You will never look respectable, my dear, never. I give you up."

"Then I'll go home at once," cried Susan, aghast; "indeed I will. I can run home in two minutes. I could never appear before Colonel Ffrench—"

"In this wild disreputable state," interrupted Teddy Josselin. "Hair dishevelled, face on fire, and worst of all, my lilies of the valley gone. I should think not, indeed! you reprobate Susan."

Susan felt that she must cry. Like most sensitive, lonely-nurtured children, she was intensely matter-of-fact in small things; had no conception that any one could mean to jest with her as long as his face was serious, his voice steady. And then the obstinately rebellious nature of her curls had long been Susan's weak point—her thorn in the flesh. "Everybody else's hair gets smooth in damp weather," she said, appealingly, "and mine gets rougher! I can't help it—it's not my fault!" A distinct foreboding of tears was in her voice.

"And when it is rough you look prettier than ever, little Susan," said Blake. "Don't you see that they are chaffing you? Mr. Josselin is jealous because you have lost his flowers—"

"And Miss Ffrench because your curling locks and bright eyes make you look so much prettier than herself!" interrupted Portia. "Come up stairs, Susan, dear, before these foolish people persuade us to quarrel in earnest." And casting one half-scornful, half-softening look at Blake, she swept up the broad staircase; Susan—all in a flutter of terror at the prospect of Colonel Ffrench scolding her, all in a flutter of happiness at spending another hour in Mr. Blake's society—following.

Colonel Ffrench had had his basin of water-gruel, and betaken himself to the hands of his valet half an hour before, for it was nearly ten o'clock; Miss Jemima sat alone at her work-table, a half-finished baby's sock on knitting pins in her lap, the "Illustrated Gazette" in her hand. Belief in church, queen, and state; nay, belief in the British army itself was scarcely stronger in Miss Jemima's mind than belief in the "Illustrated." When the resources of this paper enabled its artists to depict the interior of the last exploded coal mine two days before the reopening of the shaft, Miss Jemima would shudder, unquestioning, over the truthful details of the picture. When an errant railway train had leaped into mid-air from a viaduct, and the "Illustrated" gave a sketch of it, "drawn by our own artist, on the spot," Miss Jemima would grow perfectly breathless over the sensational terrors of the situation. "I take a deep interest in the accident because I have actually seen it," she would say, "seen it, I mean, in the 'Illustrated.'"

She looked up with mildly reproachful eyes as the young people entered, and laid down her spectacles. "You have not been near open windows, this damp evening, I hope, Portia? You look white. I shall be having you hoarse again."

"We have not been near an open window," said Portia, sinking down into the first easy-chair that presented itself, an example followed at once by her lover; "and all we are in want of is support. Billiard-playing *is* so wearying."

She really did look pale and weary. An hour's exercise, without excitement, would, at any time, tire Portia Ffrench to death, body and mind—and she had not been at all excited this evening! Miss Jemima jumped up, obediently, to the bell, and in a few minutes a servant entered with a salver on which stood wine, brandy, and seltzer water. Teddy Josselin, more actively than was his custom, rose and asked Miss Jemima what he should give her?

"A glass of water, Ted," cried Portia. "Don't you know what Aunt Jem always takes?—half a tumbler of beer at lunch, one glass of port at dinner, ditto of water at night. It is only we washed-out younger generation who cannot live without the wicked help of stimulants. What, you take nothing. either, Susan?" Susan had tasted wine about six times in her life, and then a third of a glass at a time. " What sober people you all are ! "

Teddy poured out some madeira into a tumbler and handed it to Portia; then helped himself generously to brandy and seltzer water—very little seltzer water. And, after a time, nature recruited by these kindly aids, the powers of both seemed gradually to revive.

" Did we see the powder-mills, I wonder ?" remarked Teddy, after a silence. " There was a great deal of canal, and bull-rushes, and all that ; but did we see the powder-mills ? I can't, for the life of me, recollect."

Portia looked up at the ceiling, her eyebrows elevated ; Miss Jemima, who held imbecile questions of all kinds as Teddy Josselin's special prerogative, resumed her knitting. " There *are* powder-mills, the worse for us, within a stone's throw of the house," she observed ; " Portia, I suppose that is what your cousin means ! "

" I suppose so, Aunt Jemima," said Portia, sententiously ! "

Teddy Josselin rose and again helped himself to seltzer and brandy—the seltzer still perceptibly decreasing ; after this his brain seemed to grow clearer. " How could we have seen powder-mills, or any mills, when we have been playing billiards !" he said, smiling a little smile to himself over his own perspicuity. " I know as well as possible what I meant, now. We were all of us to have seen the powder-mills, you know, Portia, only Blake and Miss Fielding roamed away and prevented us." Teddy Josselin called it " woamed away and pwevented us."

" Susan, my dear," said Miss Jemima, seriously, " I hope, if you went out, that you put something worsted over your head ?" The good old soldier never troubled herself about other dangers than physical ones. " I knew a young lady just about your age, oddly enough, her name was Felton—it was in 'forty-six, we were at Gibraltar—poor thing, she married into the Sixtieth rifles, and led a most unhappy life, and she had entirely lost her hearing in the left ear through going out bare-headed in the damp. Since then I always say to young people, 'walk about at midnight, if it gives you any pleasure, but put something worsted over the head.' Now, I knit very nice little *capooshaws*"—Miss Jemima's French pronunciation had not been acquired on French soil—"they come down well all round, and protect not only the ears but the throat. I always wear one myself when I go out at night. I'll make you a capooshaw, Susan."

" Thank you, ma'am."

" You may well say 'thank you, ma'am' in that devout tone, Susan !" As she spoke, Portia rose and loitered across to the piano. " Considering that if you don't wear a capooshaw you'll lose your hearing in your left ear, marry into the Sixtieth rifles, and lead a most unhappy life forever after ! Aunt, you logical old philosopher, what shall I play ?"

" Anything you choose, my dear," said Miss Jemima, turning round her placid old face so that she could better watch the girl's graceful figure at the instrument. " All the music I hear now-a-days sounds much the same to me."

George Blake, who ever since they returned to the drawing-room, had been silently watching his opportunity for making peace with Portia, now came across to her side, and, in a low voice, duly humble and penitent, petitioned her for something out of " Faust." They had listened to " Faust " together, one even-

12

ing when the poor fellow had talked especially great nonsense, and Portia had not taken the trouble to check him, an evening or two before he knew of her engagement to Teddy.

"'Faust?' I'm not sure I know anything out of 'Faust,'" answered Portia, indifferently. "Ah, yes, I do though—just *one* thing." And then, of course, played the very chorus which Blake, which both of them, remembered so well!

She had been excellently taught; played, as she did everything, with real good taste ; and, on an imperfect instrument, like the piano, natural faculty for music is a gift, the want of which good teaching can almost hide. After the Faust chorus she glided into a nocturne, then an addio ; both extremely like thousands of addios and nocturnes written by greater composers than Mr. George Blake; then stopped tired, the momentary amusement of putting back the truant mouse over, and proposed that they should play *écarté*.

Cards, played for money and good high stakes, be it understood, were a genuine amusement, very nearly a passion, with Portia Ffrench ; another point of sympathy between her and Teddy. Winning or losing, Portia's interest over a card-table never flagged ; and the time of all others when Blake came nearest to disenchantment, was when he stood and watched her face growing keen and flushed—wonderfully like her grandfather she looked at such times—over the triumph of turning kings, and scoring tricks. "Let us have more music," he pleaded, quickly, "Let us have a song or two. Cards are for short days and Christmas, not for summer."

"That is my opinion, Mr. Blake," said Miss Jemima. "But nothing will cure Portia of being a gambler. The other day I found her and Mr. Josselin gravely playing piquet, for I don't know what a game, at four o'clock in the afternoon."

"And the daylight constitutes the sin!" said Portia. "Every game but chess is sinful, so long as you play it by daylight. How can I alter myself, Aunt Jem? I'm a Dysart. Its part of my maternal inheritance—none of the Ffrenches having ever touched a card to gamble!"

"But not to-night," said George Blake. "Let us have music, not cards, to-night?"

"Oh, as you like. The thing is to find performers. Teddy, will you sing ? No, you shall not. I *abhor* comic songs, and it makes me abhor you when you sing them. Susan, will you?"

Susan jumped up instantly and ran over to the piano. She had not the faintest idea that a young lady who is asked for music should look modest. Music had been the one keen enjoyment, the daily sweetest solace of Mr. Fielding's life, and Susan was as simply ready to sing as she would have been to carry a foot-stool or pick up Miss Jemima's knitting-needles had she been so bidden. "The songs I know best are duets," she said, looking up at Portia, who had given her her place before the piano, "but I will sing whatever is wished."

"Tell me the name of your duets," said Blake, "and I will see if I know any of them." Susan's fingers had already touched the keys, and something in the touch, something in the way her large eyes lighted up, made him augur well for what was coming. "I have just enough voice to sing a tolerably inoffensive second, no more."

Susan went through the names of five or six English songs, time-flavored and sterling as her novels.

"Sing that," cried Miss Jemima, looking up suddenly from her knitting. " 1 have not heard 'Drink to me only' for five-and-forty years." And, a minute later, George Blake professing sufficient knowledge of the air to take a modest second, the duet began.

Never, perhaps, by two non-professional people, were rare old Ben's love-words married to truer melody. Susan Fielding's voice was exquisite. You wanted nothing finer or more cultivated when you listened to her, the piercing sweetness of that fresh soprano contented your sense so utterly. Very likely in Italian opera she would have failed, for the order of her voice was sustained rather than flexible ; but it was a voice that suited such music as this to perfection. And then Susan sang out bravely—sang, as so few drawing-room singers do, with her whole heart, with frankest delight in her own singing. " The thirst that from the soul doth flow doth need a draught divine." What a volume of feeling the little girl threw into those words ! What subdued, lingering emphasis into the next couplet—" But might I of Jove's nectar sip, I would not ask for wine." George Blake's "inoffensive second" proved an admirable one. He possessed a tenor voice, moderate of compass, but full, every note of it, of honest music—and then, was not Portia's beautiful face before him ? Were not Portia's dark eyes—more expression in them than their wont—drinking to his ? Of his fellow-singer, all whose ignorant, passionate soul was shaken by new feeling as their voices flowed forth together, he thought no more than of the piano. Luckily for the execution of the duet, however, there was no glass window to inform Susan of this.

When it was over, Portia and Teddy Josselin applauded loudly. Miss Jemima was silent. Her knitting had fallen in her lap, her spectacles were pushed up on her forehead ; she sat listening, listening, with a sad, far-away look on her old face.

"You are very ungrateful, Aunt Jemima," cried Portia. " The song was sung for your pleasure, and now you don't offer the performers a single compliment."

" I hadn't heard it for five-and-forty years," said Miss Jemima, absently. " How you startled me, child ! "

And then she bent down her face again, and, with a flurried little gesture, took up her knitting. No one had ever heard any whisper of romance connected with Jemima Ffrench. She said, herself, that she had never been pretty —had never had a lover. Yet in this old heart, that had so long beat for others only, *some* remembrance of youth—the one supreme romance of every human life—must still have flickered, and the song, unheard for five-and-forty years, had power to rekindle it.

" That was real music," she said, after a minute or two ; " not like what you hear now-a-days."

" Yes, if I could sing—if I could move people like that ! " exclaimed Portia, looking across at Susan. " I think to have no voice is really to be dumb. When others sing I always feel what I, too, could have said, if the same power of expression had only been given me ! "

Few accidents of human speech sound more graceful than the praises accorded by one young and pretty woman to another ; and Portia paid this little homage to Susan's superior gift in the prettiest tone conceivable. and with a genuine look of self-deprecation on her handsome face. The tone, the expression went straight, as they were meant to go, to George Blake's heart. All the fire of his quickly-wrought nature had been stirred by poor little Susan's voice, and now an adroit word, an adroit expression, had already turned aside the current of his feelings toward Portia. To appropriate, in this cool kind of fashion, emotions caused by the gifts of others, is a faculty, I think, that exceptionally-handsome people nearly all of them possess. Your senses are carried away by a piece of admirable acting, by a strain of touching music; and if a beautiful face chance to be near, ten to one but you will transfer to its owner a good half of what you feel. The poor little man or woman, with sallow complexion and snub features, beside you, may have a brain to understand, a heart to sympathize with yours—in vain. At such times, all you need, if you are the kind of foolishly-susceptible creature George Blake was, is a faultless lay figure to clothe in the purple and fine linen of your own imagination. And Portia was this, and more than this. He forgot to ask Susan to sing again—forgot Susan's existence. All he saw, all he wanted to see, was Portia's face glowing with this flush of new and softened expression; and when, presently, she moved away into a window, still declaring herself "under the delicious influences of that duet," drew aside a curtain and began to whisper about the beauty of the night (as it chanced, it was pitch dark, and beginning to rain a little), the young man, his pulse beating almost as it used to beat in the first days of his infatuation, kept at her side.

The sociability of the little party was hopelessly broken up. Teddy Josselin sat quietly asleep in his easy chair; Miss Jemima held silent counsel with her own thoughts over her knitting; Portia and George Blake continued to murmur in indistinguishable tones at the window. When some minutes had gone by like this, a timepiece struck eleven, and Susan rose from the piano, and, crossing over to Portia, wished her good-night—did not, however, hold up her lips as usual to be kissed. The whole world had deepened, grown into new significance to Susan during the last two hours. Even her sentimental worship of her friend was modified.

"What! going so soon?" cried Portia, with innocent surprise. "Aunt Jem, Susan says she is going. Has any one come for you, my dear?"

"Oh no, I can run home quite well by myself; I told old Nancy I would not be late. Good-night, Portia. I shall not forget my birthday treat. I have enjoyed myself very much!"

"And Jekyll shall see you home," said Miss Jemima, stretching out her hand toward the bell. "Yes, indeed, child, I hear rain on the windows, and Jekyll shall carry an umbrella and see you home. Very likely indeed that I would allow you to run along the highway alone at this time of night!"

Susan began to beg and entreat. The idea of Mr. Jekyll condescending to hold an umbrella over her unimportant head was too overwhelming.

"Better wait till our carriage comes," suggested Teddy, whom all this talking had aroused. "We ordered it somewhere about midnight—didn't we, Blake?"

"Better let me take you home, Susan," said Blake, who would at all times have foregone pleasure of his own to humor a child, and who read aright the terror of the little girl's face at the proposal of Mr. Jekyll's escort.

"It rains in torrents!" remarked Portia, laconically.

"Then Susan must put her cloak over her head, and wear my galoshes, if she can keep them on," said Miss Jemima. "Now mind, Mr. Blake, I trust to your getting her home dry and safe."

And then the old lady came across to Susan, and, as she kissed her cheek, thanked her in a whisper for the song, and bade the girl come and sing to her, alone, another day.

Susan could never help loving old Miss Ffrench a little better than she loved Portia, after that night.

The rain, as it turned out, did not pour in torrents yet, only an occasional big drop splashed down through the thick cover of the avenue ; the trees and grass smelt dewy sweet ; the frogs were croaking a vociferous chorus of joy over the approaching shower—not a romantic sound, but I try to be truthful, not romantic, and about Halfont, wherever you did not walk by a canal, you walked by a ditch, and the ditches were deep and green scummed, and full in the summer season of frogs. Rain or no rain, Susan would have liked that walk to last forever.

When they were half-way or so down the avenue, George Blake turned and looked back at the house. He could see the lighted bay-window within which he had stood five minutes ago with Portia ; she stood there still—alas, with her rightful lover at her side now ! and Blake heaved a despairing sigh. He was apt, in perfect sincerity, to be just a little bit melodramatic at times ; saw, as most imaginative people do, the picturesque capabilities of a situation at a glance, that is to say, and could not refrain from throwing himself with spirit into the fitting attitude as hero.

" 'The thirst that from the soul doth flow,' " under his voice he hummed the line. " Oh, Susan, little Susan, how I envy you ! You who have never felt a thirst that a cup of cold water wouldn't slake. How can you sing so well about feelings of which you know nothing, child ?"

" I sing *what* I feel, Mr. Blake," answered Susan, simply, then walked on by his side again in silence. She was not jealous, consciously, of Portia ; not vexed at Mr. Blake's treatment of herself ; the grass smelt sweet, the rain-charged air blew soft ; there was a walk of a hundred yards by Mr. Blake's side before her still. Susan was satisfied.

The old village woman who was at present the solitary guardian of Addison Lodge, came to the door in answer to Blake's knock, the loud London knock which echoed and re-echoed through the silent garden. At sight of a gentleman, tall, moustached, not of the Halfont world, standing beside "little Miss," the good old soul set down her candle and fled.

" And now indeed, good-night !" said Blake, holding out his hand. " Susan, what are you going to give me for all the care I have taken of you ?"

" I should like you to come in just for a minute, Mr. Blake," said Susan, hesitating as she made the request. " I have nothing to give you, but I should like you to see something I hold very dear—something that I may never have a chance to show you again after to-night."

She took up the candle, and threw open a door on the right, about a yard and a half distant from the entrance—there was no space lost within the small area of Addison Lodge. " This was our sitting-room. The auctioneer says the furniture will all have to be arranged differently before the sale, but you see it now exactly as it was when we—when papa and I lived in it. There is his violin." She walked across the room, and tenderly rested her hand on a very old, very shabby violin case ; " he played it, Miss Collinson said, as if he had been a master—and there are the books, all he was fondest of, in the Russia backs ; and there—Mr. Blake, I asked you to come in and see this—there, above the mantel-shelf, is papa himself. Of course the portrait will not be sold, but I like you to see it to-night among the old furniture and in the old room, just as it all was when he was alive."

The portrait was in oil, and a fair one, had at least the merit of being strik-

ingly like the face from which it was painted ; a thin, pale face, insignificant of
feature, broad of brow, and with prominent grey eyes, like Susan's, which
seemed at this moment to look down half with kindliness, half mistrust on the
man who stood by Susan's side.   George Blake never forgot either the picture
or the room—the room with its smell of Russian leather, its silent instruments
—a meerschaum pipe left piously as Fielding's hand had laid it on the mantel-
piece ; in the branched sockets of the music-stand two ends of wax-candle, never
lit since the night when Fielding and his girl played their last duet together.

"I'm glad you asked me to come in, my dear ; I feel now as if I had known
your father, as if I had smoked my pipe with him scores of times, and heard
him play, and heard you sing together, in the winter evenings."

The color faded in Susan's face ; her eyes filled.   "We shall never sing
again," said she ; then turned away abruptly and lighted George Blake without
a word to the front door.

He took her hand, held it a little space in his, then, with loyalty as absolute
as if the girl had been seven, not seventeen, raised it for a moment to his lips,
and left her.

In that moment was shut the last white page of Susan's childhood.

CHAPTER VIII.

PORTIA FFRENCH was charming throughout the remainder of the evening. Either that passionate old love-music had really subdued her, or she felt, for the first time since their acquaintance began, the possibility of George Blake wavering in his fealty. She did not want cards, did not want to chatter town scandal with her cousin. Real animation lit up the finer beauty of her rich, deep-tinted face; real feeling, gay and pensive by turns, was in her voice. Even Teddy Josselin—the least impressionable of men—went away with a vague idea in his mind that he must be much more in love than he had hitherto suspected; while George Blake—no, of George Blake's state of feeling I need not speak!

"Thank Heaven, we are alone at last!" cried Portia, the moment the two young men had taken their leave. "How mortally tired I am—don't go to bed, dear Aunt Jem, sit down here and talk to me a little—what a fearfully tiring creature a clever man in love is!"

Sleep had been weighing heavily on Miss Jemima's eyelids for a good hour or more past, but she seated herself obediently, at Portia's bidding, just as in by-gone years she had been wont to seat herself by inconsistent babies who chose to keep vigil at midnight, or as she would do now at her brother's bedside, whenever old Colonel Ffrench, additionally fractious under an attack of gout, would take it into his head that he needed "watching."

"You ought to say, how tiring two men in love are, Portia. It seems to me, Mr. Blake is quite as lover-like as your cousin.

"I am speaking of Mr. Blake. Did I not say how wearying a clever man was in a certain state? Teddy never tires me, now I am accustomed to him, but George Blake! (I confess I am weak enough to be pleased by his attention, just because it shows I am not so frivolous as you have all called me) but for any pleasure his conversation gives me—oh dear, how I shall pity the woman that young man marries!" Portia yawned prophetically.

"Mr. Blake seems to me a young man of great ability, and what is more, of very excellent feeling," said Miss Jemima. "I don't judge him by his novel—indeed, except the death-bed scene, I thought it all rather foolish—but by his manner. How prettily he behaved to Susan Fielding. Few young men now-a-days, if Teddy Josselin is a sample of them, would have turned out in the rain as he did, to take that poor child home. The man who is kind to a plain little girl like Susan, or to an old woman like me, is the man with the real stuff in him, Portia, depend upon it."

"Well, then the real stuff bores me," said Portia. "I'm not a plain little girl, I'm not an old lady like you—I often wish I were you, Aunt Jem! I like people who never require me to think, like Teddy. I could talk to Ted for a year with less exertion than that last hour of Mr. George Blake's society has cost me.'

"Then why ask him here at all, Portia? You insist upon having him invited; when he is here you encourage him—yes, child, I've not had much experience in such matters myself, but I have watched you since you were seventeen—"

"Four years," interrupted Portia. "How old I am—how old I feel!"

"And I know very well it is your pleasure that George Blake should not go. Now, Portia, as you have chosen the subject," Miss Jemima drew herself very upright, indeed, as she said this, "let me put one question to you. Do you think, engaged as you are to your cousin, that your conduct to his friend is honorable?"

"I am a Dysart, Aunt Jem," said Portia, coolly. "Has a Dysart a conscience? Teddy is not jealous, Mr. Blake seems to like coming here to dinner —he has an excellent appetite, still, by the way! Who is hurt?"

"Yourself, child. If you cared for Blake's society I could find an excuse for you, but you do not. You have just confessed as much, and yet you like to have him forever dangling after you—you, who in a few weeks will be another man's wife! In my young days we called such conduct by harsh names, I can tell you."

The girl stole her hand into Miss Jemima's; not a usual action with her, for Portia's was the least caressing, the least demonstrative of natures. "In your young days, depend upon it, human nature was just as bad and just as good as it is now," she remarked. "There were people like you, generous, unselfish souls who always acted right, because they couldn't help it, and people like me who thought of nothing but themselves and their own vanity—and they couldn't help it! and young men, like George Blake, who ran about falling hopelessly in love with every one they oughtn't, for the same admirable reason! Aunt Jemima," after a pause, "I've often thought of late that I should like to know why I, Portia Ffrench, am what I am. As we are not going to bed, and as we have nothing better than Mr. George Blake to talk about, suppose you help me a little in my speculation. What sort of woman was my mother?"

"Your mother?—Portia, the past is past," cried Miss Jemima, hastily. "What has put this into your head to-night? Your mother is in her grave. Let her faults rest with her." Old Miss Jemima rested the palms of her hands down on her knees, looked up austerely at the ceiling, and pronounced the word "faults" with emphasis.

"And I am living," said Portia, quietly; "living, and wearying myself, and running after excitement that I can never reach, because I have her nature in me, I suppose. I'm a Dysart, as you so often say. I could no more be like you, Aunt Jem, than I could be like that small child next door, with her odd face and passionate voice and jog-trot commonplace nature. It all came upon me as I watched Susan singing here an hour ago. I've often thought before when I have listened to her and you talk—the interminable talk about that horrid old bookseller, the interminable grief at leaving Addison Lodge and selling the dear old cups and saucers—I say, I have often thought before, that Susan Fielding and I could not, in reality, belong to the same species, and to-night I felt sure of it. I've much greater capacity for enjoyment, one would say, than she. I want change, excitement. I want money. I want a thousand things just as I want air; and Susan could live contentedly in the damp shades of Addison Lodge (pity George Blake does not marry her!) and make shirts and puddings and mend children's socks forever. And yet—Aunt Jem," the beautiful face saddened, "there's something in that girl I haven't got, shall never have! Her jog-trot little nature, such as it is, is complete. I am incomplete."

"Most people would not say so," answered Miss Jemima, who, severity itself in her own judgments, could never listen to any censure of Portia, even from Portia's lips. "What additional gift do you want to possess? A voice like Susan's? It would be the worst thing you could have, with your disposition. I knew a very beautiful young woman, once, with just that kind of sweet piercing voice, a niece of Colonel Harding of the Engineers, and she turned out shockingly—after her marriage, too—and every one attributed it to her voice. I think I heard she went on the stage eventually, but I'm not certain. No talent for leading people astray like music!" Miss Jemima's generalizations were somewhat broad, as you perceive; her deductions from actual personal observation unhesitating.

"I don't envy Susan her voice," said Portia. "Yes, I do; I envy every gift under the sun; but it is not of my want of voice that I am thinking when I say I am incomplete. I want what she, like all commonplace people, has in perfection—the gift of taking an interest in her own life! I looked at her face as she sang; her color coming and going, her great eyes afire; and I saw that she enjoyed her singing as she enjoyed seventeen years of father-worship in Addison Lodge, and one day will enjoy darning socks and baby-worship elsewhere. Why is life a weight to me, Aunt Jem—a weight I am always trying to put away from me and cannot? What kind of human beings were Harry Ffrench and Lady Portia Ffrench, his wife? I am one-and-twenty, I am better-looking than ninety-nine women out of a hundred, I am going to be married, if grandmamma will give us anything to live upon, (did Ted give you her message, by the bye? You are to lunch in Eaton square the day after to-morrow, and talk about settlements.) Yet every morning when I wake I feel how bitter the taste of a new day is in my mouth! What were the people like who bequeathed this charming inheritance, this incapacity for life, to me?"

Miss Jemima looked, as she felt, thoroughly taken aback. Portia—indolent, self-contained, self-satisfied Portia—breaking out with a confession like this!

"You have had an excellent education—the best masters, I am sure, in everything. You know French and German—"

"Music, the use of the globes, and perspective; the whole art of polite insincerity, and every game that can be played on the cards! Aunt Jem, dear, do you think education, as begun by the Miss Davenports, and finished by Grandmamma Erroll, is what is wanted to make one enjoy life?"

"I'm sure I don't know what else it is for," said good Miss Jemima. "We paid forty pounds a quarter, without masters, the last five years you were at the Miss Davenports', at Fulham—"

"And you think that any of that fiddle-faddle, that outside layer of accomplishments, changed me, Portia Ffrench, any more than it changed the shape of my nose or the color of my hair? I was restless and dissatisfied when I was little. That's what made me so wicked."

"Ah, wicked, indeed!" groaned Miss Jemima, as she thought of Portia's childhood.

"I am the same now. I can help it no more than the black kitten can help not being tortoiseshell. From papa, I know, I must inherit my looks." She turned and glanced at herself in the different mirrors around the room. "From the Ffrench side of the house, probably, I get my little taste for extravagance and card-playing, also my fashion of carrying my pauper head so well aloft. But the unseen part—the weight, the weariness—is that a Ffrench inheritance, too, or am I merely the kind of woman my mother was?"

"God forbid!" cried Miss Jemima, hastily. "Portia, it cuts me to the heart to hear you talk like this. The past is dead. All that concerns you is the future."

"Which is part and parcel of the past," said Portia. "Does yesterday belong less to this week than to-morrow will? I ask you to sit up for half an hour and talk to me about papa and mamma—do you refuse? Harry Ffrench, handsome, spendthrift, ruined Harry Ffrench, died by his own hand, and his wife, Lady Portia, married again, and lived till I was twelve years old; and I was never allowed to see her from the day I came to Halfont. There is the outline of the story. Now fill in the details. I ask Lady Portia's mother, and she yawns and answers, 'another day;' I ask Harry Ffrench's father, and he says his feelings are too much for him—grandpapa's feelings too much for him!—that even yet he cannot bear to speak of his Harry's loss. Did grandpapa ever really love any human creature as much as all that, I wonder?"

Miss Jemima's hands clasped each other tighter; her lips twitched a little. "Your grandfather never understood poor Harry, or, indeed, any of his children, Portia. He was fond of them, of course; but he never understood them. When they were young and he used to come near them so seldom—they had the scarlatina once and Lucy and Dick were in danger; but 'twas Goodwood races, and he never saw them for a week—when they were in the nursery, and their father's affection for them seemed so cold, I always thought it was because they were in the nursery. A man like Richard could not be expected to feel anxious about babies and babies' ailments. When they grew older, grew to be companions to him—he would love them better. And then, when they began to grow up, when the boys left school and, one by one, went into the world, and—and settled to nothing, things became worse. They were fine-natured boys, every one of them; not a fault in their characters, but that they were slow at learning the value of money or the necessity for work; but Richard never understood them. My poor lads! Richard never understood them."

"Except Harry. Grandpapa's emotions overpower him still at the mention of my father's death. Surely, he must have understood him while he lived?"

Miss Jemima was silent. "Portia," she said, at last, "it seems you mean to insist upon my speaking of old days, of old sorrows, to-night. Very well; I will speak. Perhaps you are right. Perhaps you are old enough to hear what manner of marriage your father's was, the more now that you will so soon be a wife yourself. But remember, child, I have not the art that Richard has, of making unpleasant things sound pleasant. What I feel I say, and Harry was my favorite boy. I loved all Richard's children well, but Harry best; and I never loved his wife. I saw her twice, and it was enough. I could not love her. Even now I don't think I can speak of Lady Portia Ffrench with fair words. And she was your mother."

"Oh, don't mind that in the least," said Portia, cheerfully. "I recollect one thing with extreme clearness of Lady Portia Ffrench—a whipping she gave me with her own hands, for upsetting a jug of cream on the coat of one of her friends. She used to lie forever on a sofa and play cards. There were some horrible old women, I remember, and some foreign officers in uniform, and one man in black who always came to play with her. I upset the cream on the man in black because I hated him. I did it on purpose, and Lady Portia beat me when I was in bed. I hated them all worse after that."

"And you can remember all this?" exclaimed Miss Jemima. "Why, you were not six years old when you left your mother for good. What made you never speak of it to me before?"

"Where was the use?" said Portia; "I did not feel certain, perhaps, when I was a child, whose side you took, and latterly I suppose I forgot all about it. Besides, I was not brought up to tell tales. Sophie used to bribe me not to tell my lady when I caught her in my lady's clothes, and Lady Portia used to bribe me, and so did the man in black—Mr. Molyneux, my future step-papa, that must have been. I don't know why, but it seems to me that I was bribed all round to tell stories, and I told them—very well, too ! I loved nobody, except poor Lurly a little. After that beating, I loved Lady Portia least of all. You needn't be afraid of hurting my feelings in speaking of her."

"And you never knew your father. You were a babe, asleep in your cot, the morning he kissed you for the last time. Ah, Portia, you would have loved him ! Yours would have been a different life if Harry had been the one to survive."

"I should have loved him for his handsome face, at least," said Portia. "My mother was not handsome. She dyed her hair ; her voice was gruff ; she wore rouge. Whenever I kiss grandmamma I remember her. They are of the same texture."

"And Harry," said old Miss Jemima, warming into sudden animation, "was the handsomest of all Richard's handsome sons. You have his miniature, Portia, taken when he was five-and-twenty, and you think that handsome. No picture can give you more than a map, a shadow of Harry's face, for it was not the features only—the fine-cut nose and mouth, the fair complexion, the dark, full eyes—it was the goodness, the brightness of my boy's face that made him what he was. From the time he was a baby he was the same. People would all turn round in the park to look at him in his nurse's arms. 'What a lovely face !' every one said who saw him ; and there was no exaggeration in the word. As I remember Harry Ffrench in his youth, he *was* lovely, in face and soul. When I saw him years later, as a man, he had altered so that I should scarce have known him in the street—but that was when he was your father, when he was Lady Portia's husband !

"I came to England for a month, in 'forty-seven, just before our battalion was ordered up to Scinde (the only time in nineteen years that Lucy and Elliott were able to spare me) ; and on my way back to Marseilles managed to run round and visit Harry and his wife in Brussels. They had never had a settled home since their marriage, and were now living about in different continental towns economizing. I have always remarked, Portia, that when any member of our family is going faster to ruin than ordinary he calls it economizing ! I found it so with Harry. His father, he told me, had grown unpunctual with his allowance, the price of his own commission had gone long ago, and, as far as I could make out, they had very little to depend upon but the scanty sum Lady Portia got yearly from her mother, and what poor Harry could himself contrive to pick up at cards and billiards. So what do you suppose was their way of economizing ? Lady Portia had her opera-box, and her evenings of reception, and her own set of friends—a very fast set, too. And Harry had his friends, rather faster ones, I believe, than his wife's, and played higher, and lived altogether more recklessly, 'twas said (and that was saying a good deal), than any other Englishman in Brussels. Oh, child, how altered he was ! A man little over thirty, but looking any number of years more than his age—the handsome features of the face the same, but all the goodness, all the bright expression blotted out."

"Portia, I think I was unjust. I have often thought since I was unjust to your mother," said old Miss Jemima, humbly, "and I have tried to make some amends to you, her child. But when I saw Harry sunk to what he was, I did lay half the blame upon his wife. We women are like that; anything, anybody must be guilty rather than our son. And Harry had been more than a son to me! I was a girl of one-and-twenty, your age, Portia, when I first went to Richard's children; I had no hopes, no interests in life but theirs; and from the first and through every trouble, Harry, poor little soul, made himself my companion and comfort. Well, and Harry had sunk to this. The rest of the lads were adrift, God knew where, on the world, and Harry had sunk to this! Harry was an outlaw, a gambler, and hopeless—oh, so hopeless, at thirty years of age! with a wife who thought of nothing save her own pleasure, her opera-box, her dinner-dresses, her receptions; and you—poor neglected, little year-old baby—in your cradle. I wander, Portia. You must let me think for awhile before I try to tell my story, such as it is, in order."

CHAPTER IX.

"MY nephew Harry was already an officer in her majesty's service when I went abroad, in 'thirty-three, to join the Elliotts," said Miss Jemima, at length; Portia, with an expression of eagerness very unusual to see her dark face wear, waiting to listen. "He was gazetted about six weeks after he left Eton, and—I remember it as if it was yesterday—put on his uniform for the first time the day I sailed. I had to get on tip-toe to reach his face, he was so tall, and as I kissed him I bade him to be brave and truthful now that he wore a sword, just the same as he had been when he was a boy. He promised me, sobbing the while like a child (for he and I were alone together) at my going. Often I remembered him afterward, his eyes swollen with tears, his dear arms round my neck —this fine dignified young officer with his simple heart, crying as he said good-by to me just as in the days when he was a little lad going back to school after the holidays! I remembered him thus, I say, and used to think—and half reproach poor Lucy and her babies at the thought—that life might have gone differently with him, perhaps with the other lads, if I had stayed behind in England. It seems foolish to say that one unimportant old maid, old Aunt Jemima, living in her little cottage in loneliness and poverty, could have been any help to young men of pleasure and the world. But you see I should have loved them; and I believe in love!"

Miss Jemima looked rather ashamed of herself as she made this assertion before Portia.

"Its old-fashioned to talk so, I know, but I do believe in the power of love to ward away evil. I have seen it among all ranks. As long as a man has some woman who loves him unstintingly—wife, or sister, or mother—he does not despair of himself; and a man who does not despair of himself can be saved. No chance of love came to Harry. I am wrong; the chance came, and he lost it. Then began the ruin of his life. Portia, if you loved Teddy Josselin—mind, I suppose it only—and if to marry him against Lady Erroll's will would insure to you absolute poverty—"

"It would simply insure starvation," remarked Portia.

"I would still say, marry him. I know the real meaning of that word poverty. I have stood face to face with it during half my life. Elliott and Lucy were steeped in poverty, had children born to inherit nothing else, but they both led happy and dutiful lives, and now have sons doing well in the world and a ring of bright faces around their table at Christmas."

"Poor, dear faded Aunt Lucy!" cried Portia. "I'm quite sure I would rather die at once than live and be happy after that fashion."

"Yes," said Miss Jemima, drily, "you must remember I said, if you loved Teddy Josselin. Harry, your father, had a heart full to overflowing of tenderness, when he was young. When Harry's love was betrayed his best chance of life was over! You are of a different nature, Portia—I think, at times, you are more like your grandfather than any of his children were—and Richard's is a temperament that wears well. No disappointment in affection would have altered your grandfather's character or ruined his happiness."

"Any more than it would mine," said Portia, smiling. "I like Teddy really very much indeed, poor little mortal, but I am entirely dependent on grandmamma's opinion as to the wisdom of our marrying. I could much better bear to lose Teddy Josselin than to live with him in poverty. Go on with the essential facts of the story, Aunt Jem, and repress sentiment. Remember, I have had a whole evening of Mr. Blake."

"There spoke Lady Portia Ffrench!" cried Miss Jemima. "Portia, when I hear those withered remarks from your lips I feel myself back in the Brussels lodging, and could be hard on you, child—only that I look in your face and see Harry there. Repress sentiment! There is the true maxim of the world; the maxim which, put into practice, ruined your father's life. You shall hear, quite short and plain—I won't tire you with my old-fashioned opinions—the story of a life in which sentiment had been repressed effectually. Take what moral from it you like.

"I went away, as I told you, leaving Harry, at seventeen years of age, an officer in the army. Well, he wrote to me, as punctually as boys do write, for the next three or four years. I could show you the letters now, only you would laugh over the spelling—Harry never could learn to spell, bright though he was in most things. They lie in my dressing-case "—Jemima Ffrench's dressing-case was a black regulation dispatch-box that, in the old campaigning days, had travelled with her over half the civilized world, and was now a receptacle, not for trinkets, ivory-handled brushes, or filigree bottles, but for packet upon packet of faded letters; "love letters," most of them from her boys—"they lie in my dressing-case, together with the one he wrote me in large text from his first school—with the last paper he ever put his hand to on earth! I read them through on his birthday—yes, now you may know why I shut myself in my room every fifteenth of March, Portia—I read Harry's letters."

Old Miss Jemima broke down; and Portia's dark eyes sank, with a sensation of abasement, to the ground. Here was something beyond her, like Susan's emotion in singing: something, which ludicrous or not ludicrous, awoke her anew to the sense of her own incompleteness.

"They were not well-spelled, as I told you, or well-composed, or witty. None of that generation wrote such a letter as Richard—you write more like him, my dear. But they were letters brimful of such unflagging spirits, such perfect contentment with life, as did one's heart good to read. He liked the army, liked his brother officers—never had any man such capital fellows to live with as had Harry! To whatever station he was ordered it was invariably a 'jollier' station than the last. If he rode a race he won it. If he went to a ball he was sure to dance half the night with the prettiest girl in the room. During long leave his only difficulty was to choose the pleasantest out of the dozen pleasant country houses that were open to him. Even Richard, never sanguine about the prospects of his children, used to write me hopeful accounts of Harry during those first years. He was the handsomest, the most popular man in his regiment; the best shot, best dancer, best rider; extravagant, rather, yet not more so than might be expected of a young fellow in his position. 'Above all, he was well-principled.' This Richard said in one of his letters when Harry had been some years in the army. 'A lad, unlike the younger ones, to whose future establishment in life it was possible to look forward with a degree of satisfaction.' The remark pointed, I imagined, toward some prospect Harry had of making a wealthy marriage, and I confess I felt in spirits over it. We wanted money more than ever just then. The twins were babies and ailing, both of them, with their teeth."

Portia gave a shudder at the picture!

"And the doctors were beginning to hint that our poor delicate Lucy must either return to England or die. It really did seem to me as well that some one out of Richard's children should try the experiment of competency, and I wrote and told Harry what I thought. The following mail brought a letter from him in reply, a much longer, much graver letter than it was Harry's custom to write. By what odd coincidence I had guessed that he was thinking of marriage he could not divine ; such, however, was the case, my only mistake being that I imagined the young lady he loved had money. Money! did I think him capable of marrying for money, for any other reason than affection ? And then came such long description of chestnut hair and brown eyes and angel smiles as made me almost think the whole letter must be a hoax. It was so hard to imagine Harry seriously in love, so hard to believe in Harry writing about anything but races and balls, and his own amusement in them, or finding more to say of a woman than the 'capital dancer—beautiful figure,' which had always been his style hitherto in describing his flirtations to me.

"My poor boy was stationed at that time at Chester, and had fallen desperately in love at first sight—I tell you the story as I heard it, long afterward, not as I made it out from his letter at the time—with a Miss Morgan, the daughter of a small country solicitor in the neighborhood."

"And what was Miss Morgan like ?" interrupted Portia. "What kind of woman was this, who, if the course of true love had run smoother, would, you think, have influenced all Harry Ffrench's life for good ?"

"I never saw Miss Morgan ; I never saw any picture of her," answered Miss Jemima. "I do not even remember the name of the man whom, a few months later, she married. I know only that when I saw Harry in after days a hopeless and a ruined man, he could not speak of this girl without his color changing, and that when he died a curl of brown hair—not his wife's, not his child's—was in his breast. I have that curl now, Portia. I keep it, with one or two little notes written to him by Amelia Morgan in the first bright weeks of their engagement. They were put into my hands, long after your father's death, by Lady Portia, as you shall hear.

"I say he fell in love at first sight with the girl, proposed at the end of a week, and was accepted. The engagement went on for some months unknown to all Harry's friends, except me away in Mauritius, then his regiment was ordered to Ireland, and unable, so Harry wrote, to exist without the woman he loved, he took sudden courage, went up to London, and broke the news of his engagement to his father.

"Richard listened to the whole little romance with perfect patience, without a sign of anger. You know with what marked courtesy your grandfather always does listen to anything for which he feels the most profound contempt. First love—plighted word—a girl that a prince, that any man might be proud to marry! Well, he congratulated Harry heartily on so much good fortune, hoped he would find every blessing he expected in the married state, and—as a matter purely of curiosity—would like to hear how he proposed to support his establishment?

"'Your intended has only her face for her fortune,' he remarked; I know the exact words, for when I saw Harry in Brussels he described to me the whole scene, 'it would be unjust, perhaps, to look for money as well as beauty—then, my dear boy, *how* do you mean to live as a married man? I ask from curiosity, having myself married twice—both times, as you know, with heiresses—yet have never been able to do much more than keep the wolf from the door. How do you propose to live?'

"Harry, who, poor lad, was a good deal in debt, and had not a farthing but his lieutenant's pay and what his father chose to allow him, stammered out that he supposed—he hoped—they would get on pretty well, if they were economical, and through his father's generosity.

"'But I am not generous,' said Richard, raising himself up, and looking quietly in his son's face. 'I have made you a tolerably good allowance hitherto. If you marry in your own rank of life, and with my consent, I will increase it, and pay off your debts as well. But I am, constitutionally, the very reverse of generous. Your brothers have chosen their own paths in life; I do not interfere with them; but I do not and will not give them one farthing of money. Marry this young lady of whom you speak, and on your marriage day I write to Cox's and stop your account there. Now, let us change the subject.'

"Poor Harry entreated, stormed; finally swore with a great oath that he would brave poverty, go to Australia, as his brothers had done, would tend sheep, drive bullocks—would do anything but forfeit his word, abandon his love.

"'You will do exactly as you like,' said his father, calmly. 'The life of a gentleman is really not such a pleasant one that I should urge upon you the disadvantages of becoming a blackguard. Marry your fair Amelia Morgan; go abroad; found a new colony, you and your brothers between you, and call it Ffrench's Land. Do anything, my dear boy, rather than discuss a subject upon which it is impossible for our mutual prejudices to allow us to agree.'

"Harry flung away from his father's presence, as he thought, forever, and on the afternoon of the next day went down to Chester, resolute to stand by his engagement. He called at the lawyer's house, and was shown, not as usual into Miss Morgan's sitting-room, but into her father's office, there to receive his dismissal. Colonel Ffrench had come down to Chester by the early morning train; had explained the precise state of his son's affairs to Mr. Morgan, and, 'in consideration of the very handsome way the Colonel had behaved,' Mr. Morgan was willing not to publish Harry Ffrench's dishonorable conduct further. In other words, your grandfather had bought Mr. Morgan off!

"'And Amelia?' exclaimed poor Harry, 'does she call such a sacrifice as I was prepared to make for her, dishonor?'

"'Amelia thinks as her parents think,' said the lawyer. 'Amelia engaged herself to marry a gentleman, and has not the slightest inclination toward colonial life.'

"And a few cold lines written by Miss Morgan herself reached Harry in the course of the day, at his quarters. When, years later, he was telling me the whole story, he tried to make me believe, as he believed himself, that the girl's love for him never really changed. She was sensitive and timid of nature, and this letter must have been written under compulsion, under threats of personal violence from her father. For my part," said Miss Jemima, " I don't believe over-much in compulsion in such matters. A woman who loved a man, although she might obey her parents up to the point of refusing to marry him, must find some means, must write some letter to soften his pain. And no such letter came to Harry. He wrote to Miss Morgan. His letter, unopened, addressed in her own hand, was returned to him. She turned her face aside when she met him in the street. It was over.

" ' My calf-love over,' he wrote to me, lightly, and yet with something in his strain that made my heart ache. ' My belief in a cottage, all bliss and roses and earwigs, shattered. Congratulate me! Write to me soon, Aunt Jem, and con-gratulate me, laugh at me, do anything but pity me, for, indeed, I don't need it. I'm not hurt, not very badly hurt, at least. In six months I shall be cured!'

" After this fashion, Portia, the sentiment in your father's life was ' repressed.' He never fell in love again. Richard had plenty of extravagance of every other kind to complain of in his eldest son ; of an extravagance of sentiment, never. Time went on ; and, at last, five or six years it must have been after that first ill-fated love affair, I received a letter from your grandfather, telling me that Harry was on the eve of making a capital marriage. The lady was not very young, not actually pretty, wrote Richard, still was a decidedly charming person, the possessor of thirty thousand pounds, and—"

" Thirty thousand pounds!" exclaimed Portia, with animation. " I didn't know that a Dysart ever owned thirty thousand shillings ! If my mother had all this money, why am I a pauper ?"

" Your mother had just three hundred a year, allowed her very irregularly, for her life," said Miss Jemima. " The lady whom Richard destined to be Harry's wife was the widow of a Liverpool merchant, 'a lady innocent alike of good looks and good grammar,' poor Harry wrote, 'unearthed, the Lord knew how or from whence, by the governor himself ; but the undoubted owner, it seemed, of thirty thousand pounds ; also, of a slumbering interest—whatever that might mean—in the business of her late husband.' Well, the whole thing was arranged ; guests bidden, wedding breakfast ordered ; then, at the last, the marriage fell through ; Harry declared, through his father's parsimony as to settlements ; Rich-ard, through his son's gross negligence of the lady. This was in the summer of '44, just at the time we were under orders for India. At the beginning of next year, seven or eight months later, I got a few lines from Harry, telling me he was a married man. His wife was the daughter of the late Earl of Erroll, ' ætat. thirty-nine,' said Harry. ' When young ladies' names are written in the book, impossible to be delicate as to age. There was no money to speak of, at present,' he added, ' but a prospect of a moiety of a sum of twenty-five thousand pounds, should the dowager Lady Erroll inherit it ' (the twenty-five thousand pounds, Portia, which it is now in your grandmother's power to leave, or not to leave, to Teddy Josselin). ' His father,' Harry continued, ' seemed to like the marriage, and it was planned, he believed, that he should have his debts paid, leave the army, and, through the Dysart interest, be appointed to some consulship abroad. Lady Portia preferred the Continent to England ; and Lady Portia's husband, so he said, was in that beautiful frame of mind in which every place and every em-ployment would be the same to him.'

" I augured well from this letter, I must confess," went on Miss Jemima. " I knew too little what kind of man Harry Ffrench had grown to discern the hidden bitterness of tone in which he spoke of his own prospects and feelings. I augured well from the letter, I say, and, in my simplicity, wrote off what you, Portia, would call one of my gushing epistles to Harry and his bride. I also sent her an embroidered India muslin dress and an ivory work-box, not very valuable gifts, but the best it lay in my power just then to afford. In return, a good many mails later, I got a few scrawled lines from Lady Portia—if Harry had married Amelia Morgan, what a sign of her plebeian birth we should have considered such a hand! She was extremely obliged by my good wishes and gifts, hoped I would excuse a longer letter, but really she detested letter-writing, and was overwhelmed just now with engagements. Mr. Ffrench was away, in Ireland, she thought—oh, no, somewhere in the Highlands—or he would join her, she felt sure, in kind remembrances, and she remained mine sincerely—Harry's wife, mine sincerely !—Portia Ffrench.

"This letter was dated from Paris, and gave me no clue whatever to their future prospects. Harry, it seemed, could find nothing of interest to write to me about now that he was a married man ; from Richard's letters I could never gather more than that 'Harry was living out of England,' or 'Harry continued idle still,' or 'Harry, as usual, wanted money ;' and it was not until I came home, in '47, that I learned, definitely, how my boy and his wife were getting on. They were now living in Brussels. Either the Dysart interest had not been exercised, or had failed in procuring a consulship for Harry Ffrench. Richard, I found, would scarcely hear his name spoken before him. The second Mrs. Ffrench had lately died, without children, and, by the conditions of her marriage settlement, your grandfather's means, as I have often told you, were reduced—"

"To Halfont Manor, a brougham, pair of horses, butler, valet, and old Madeira—grandpapa's idea of excessive poverty !"

Miss Jemima shifted her position. She would condemn Richard as flatly as she would condemn Portia, with her own lips, yet could never listen unwounded to a word in his dispraise from others. "All our ideas of riches and poverty are relative, child. The diminution in your grandfather's income, at all events, was such as disabled him from keeping up the allowance he had promised Harry when he married. And, Portia, I have remarked—I say it with no unkind feeling toward poor Richard—have remarked all my life that we, none of us, care to talk much of people toward whom we know we have been ever so little unjust. Harry was incurably a spendthrift, your grandfather said ; he had paid his debts until he was tired of paying them, and, at the present moment, Harry was an outlaw. The more money he got the faster he would go to ruin, and the wisest course his relations could pursue was to leave him alone. If his wife and child actually came to want bread (for you were in the world now, Portia), he might perhaps make an effort to save himself, and then would be the time to help him. Meantime, let the absent prodigal's name be unspoken. It was wisdom, nay, it was positive duty to banish a man leading the life that Harry had led since his marriage, from our hearts.

"Well, I could not argue on such a matter," said Miss Jemima. "I could not argue, and I could not deny that Richard's sense of duty, however harsh, was just. Still—still a dozen years of absence had not moved my boy by one inch from his old place in my affection ; and so, when the time came for my return, I just took my carpet-bag in my hand one winter evening, and sending my other luggage on through Paris, started off, without writing to warn Harry of my visit, to Brussels. I travelled all night ; and it was about eleven o'clock in the morning when I reached the house in which I had ascertained that my nephew and his wife lodged. An English man-servant, not over-polished in his address, not over neat in his person, answered my ring. He inquired my business; his head upright in the air, his arms straight down by his side. I saw at a glance that the honest fellow, at some time of his life, had been a soldier, and felt friends with him at once.

"I want your master," I said. "I am Mr. Ffrench's aunt, now on my road back to India. Can I see him?"

"'His Aunt Jemima?' exclaimed the man, his face in an instant losing all its surly expression.

"His Aunt Jemima," said I, and in another minute I was shown into a room, half bedroom, half smoking room—an untidy room, full of the smell of stale smoke, with glasses and decanters on the table, and a pale dissipated-looking man outstretched in an arm-chair beside the fire.

"He stared at me a moment, sprang up and caught me in his arms. It was Harry. He had altered so that, for the first few minutes, I felt shy at calling him by his name. Other faces I have left young, and at the end of a dozen years found grey and care-worn; but I never saw any face so absolutely changed as his. By degrees, as we talked, and especially when anything chanced to make him smile, I might catch a gleam, an expression, bringing back to me, for an instant, the Harry of old; then it would fade, and in its place come back the horrible unlikeness to my boy; the hard, set mouth, the vacant eyes, the hopelessness—there was the essential change—the hopelessness of the face that I had left so sunny with the fairest hopes, the fairest promises of life.

"I asked him about his prospects. Oh, well, he had none in particular—yes, he thought he meant to go to Baden in the summer, unless something turned up meanwhile. About his wife? Thanks; she was as well as usual—poor Portia! They did not see very much of each other. Portia ran about to balls and parties, which he hated, and was never up before noon. I should see her by-and-by. At last, I asked for the child—for you.

"Harry's face grew brighter than I had seen it yet. 'Charles, go for the baby,' he said, calling out to his servant, who all this time had been standing, in an attitude of attention, just outside the door. And then, when we were alone, he explained to me who and what Charles was. 'An old soldier'—that I must have seen at once; 'his soldier-servant, who had kept with him all the time he was in the army, had left it when he left, and remained with him ever since; and is now valet, cook, housemaid, and, as often as not, nurse, too,' said poor Harry. 'Portia can never keep her women-servants. I'm sure I don't know where the fault lies; but she can't keep them—and if it was not for Charles, the baby would, often enough, be badly off. When the nurse-maid of the moment has struck, and Portia is away of an evening, Charles sits by the child and gives her her bottle. I came in at two o'clock one morning, and found him at it, by Jove! And the baby screams to go to him from her mother—by Jove, she does!' This was the sort of way he rambled on. 'He's the last friend I have left—is Charles; and if I apologize to him about his wages, is affronted and puts his hands behind him. What man of one's own class, what gentleman would do as much?'

"Upon this, he laughed; and I thought there was less of the Harry I remembered, in his laugh than in his face.

"The servant came back presently, with you in his arms. A muslin and lace pinafore, tied on evidently by male fingers, gave you a smart outside look;

HARRY FFRENCH'S HOME.—PAGE 59.

but your frock was torn and dirty, your socks did not match, your toes were through your shoes. Charles bore you aloft on his shoulder; you drummed with your hands on his close-shorn head, and showed your little white teeth as soon as you caught sight of your father. I went up, holding out my arms, and you came to me.

"'She won't do as much for her ladyship!' cried out poor Harry."

CHAPTER X.

AT this point of her story, Miss Jemima paused.

"Why do you hesitate?" said Portia. "We have come, at last, to the part that really interests me, the description of my mother. How did she talk to you when you met; how was she dressed; what was your first impression of Lady Portia Ffrench? Let me hear the truth, and the whole truth."

"She told me, during the first quarter of an hour of our acquaintance, the whole story of her married misery, and how little she and her husband suited each other. She was dressed in a loose morning gown, hair unbrushed, slippers down at heel," said old Miss Jemima, with grim veracity. "And my first impression of her was that she was the last woman on earth my nephew Harry Ffrench should have married. I knew nothing of the Dysart family, of the Dysart history, then. I did not understand that, being a Dysart, Harry's wife *must*, by some unhappy law of transmission, be—what she was! My life had been passed with wives who loved their husbands and their children; old-fashioned wives to whom the words home and duty had a meaning. I found in Lady Portia a woman, as far as I could discover, without a rational resource, or human affection; a woman to whom forty years of life had taught no wisdom; a doll who, well-painted and seen by candle-light, carried off satin and diamonds with an air—in short a fashionable fine lady, a Dysart!

"And why, in God's name, did you marry him? I asked her, point-blank, after listening, with my heart a-fire, to the list of Harry's failings.

"'Because he—I mean because Colonel Ffrench asked me. Because all mamma's grand matrimonial schemes had fallen through. Because I was thirty-nine years old,' Lady Portia answered, looking straight in my face with her great blue eyes (outwardly you show not a trace of Dysart blood, as I have often told you, Portia. Your mother was a fair, faded woman, with a high arched nose, a receding chin and forehead, a mouth that could not close over glistening prominent teeth.) 'Colonel Ffrench liked a certain poor handle I have to my name, and mamma liked that I should be married, any how! And so they made it up between them. Harry really was a victim.'

"And, whatever other question I put to her, she answered in the same unhesitating style. There are different varieties of truthful people in the world, I've remarked," said Jemima. "To speak absolute unblushing truth at all times, is not quite such a test of human character as the copy-books tell us. Harry's wife, it seemed to me, was the truthful, partly because Nature had constituted her without the quality of moral shyness, partly because she was too indifferent to everything to care whether she shocked you or not, partly because she had not energy for the trouble of thinking, which falsehood would have involved! 'The Dysarts are an awfully bad race,' she remarked to me, within an hour after I first saw her. 'So are the Ffrenches'—to my face, Portia, this to my face! 'How could a marriage between members of two such families be expected to turn out decently ? Mamma made Colonel Ffrench believe I should some day come into the half of twenty-five thousand pounds. And that is all in the air, for mamma is not certain to inherit the money herself, and if she does, will leave it, I've no doubt, to my sister Josselin's boy. And Colonel Ffrench made mamma believe Halfont would be at his own disposal at his death, also that his income was derived from capital, not an insurance company. We all know better now, and love each other accordingly. How long shall you stay ? We have not a room to offer you. We have plenty of smart paint and gilding, as you perceive, but no bedrooms. Charles—you have seen Harry's detestable man, Charles ?—folds himself up at night and sleeps in a cupboard. That was a sweet dress you sent me from India,' she ran on ; ' I suppose you haven't got any more of the kind with you ? '

" I had brought her, not a dress, but a scarf., a Cashmere scarf, embroidered in green and silver, that had been given me by a native woman I was able to help once in India, and was much too magnificent for me to wear. I had packed this up in my travelling bag. for it was as fine and soft as a cobweb, and I drew it forth and gave it to Harry's wife.

" ' Pale green and silver !' she exclaimed. ' The blonde colors ! The very colors that suited her !' They did not. In truth, Portia, your mother was a woman who took no exercise, and her skin, by daylight, was not the kind of skin that green becomes. Harry coming in for a minute, burst out laughing at the sight of her before the glass, slippered. in a dressing-gown, with hair unbrushed, and wreathed round in my gorgeous Indian present ! However, I was pleased to see her pleased, and during the remainder of the afternoon, until it was time for Lady Portia to dress for the dissipation of the evening, we managed to talk to each other.

" I think, Portia, those were the longest hours of my whole life. For Harry's sake I wanted, if not to like, to understand the woman who was his wife, the mother of his child. I tried her on every subject under the sun. Did she work ? No—a little. Embroidery got so dirty, and one could buy it from the convents nearly as cheap. Read ! Yes. of course. But there was no remembering the different people's names a minute afterward ; French books. of the two, were better, she thought, than English ones. The baby, I suggested. must be a resource to her ? Well, unfortunately she did not understand babies. and Miss Portia seemed to know it, and preferred Charles's society to hers. Could she be expected to enter into rivalry with Charles ? Brussels was a tolerable place ; just tolerable ; cheaper than Paris, and a place where doubtful people or beggars might get some sort of society. She and Harry were in—let her consider—well, she in the second, and Harry in the third or lowest Brussels set. Impossible to say how long it would all last. If Colonel Ffrench continued in his present loftily-virtuous frame of mind ; and if, as was extremely probable, her mother should die, leaving her nothing, they might come, as likely as not, to actual want. All this with the same open eyes. the same blank truthfulness ; Lady Portia lying on the sofa, yawning after every dozen words she spoke, and I in what you call my most bolt-upright frame of mind, child. and starving— starving ! for no one had offered me bit or sup since my arrival by her side.

" At five o'clock Charles brought in tea. ' Why in the world are you so late ?' said Lady Portia, sharply, ' I've rung twice. Don't you know I have to dress and go out to dinner ?

" ' I have taken Miss Baby for her walk, your ladyship.' said the man, laconically, but with perfect respect of tone. ' And I have give the baby her

tea, your ladyship. Miss Baby, she couldn't wait.' Then he set down the
tray beside his mistress's sofa, wheeled round short, and marched bolt-uprigh'
as if he had been on parade, from the room.

"'A fearful creature,' said Lady Portia, yawning anew. 'If I could bring
myself up to the exertion of hating anyone, it would be that man. Still, he serves
us for nothing. Skim-milk, instead of cream, again! Would you believe it, the
monster gives me skim-milk that the child may get cream! Such are the indig-
nities poverty brings one to! My dear soul, that man has been with us ever
since our marriage, and has had just seven pounds ten shillings of wages during
the time, so I feel I am in his power. Oh, if some good kind creature—yourself, say—had a spare fifty pound note to lend me. What a deal of small honesty I should be able to do, what independence I could buy, on only fifty
pounds!'

"I gave her, not fifty pounds, but the promise of a very much smaller sum,
and Lady Portia kissed me, remarking, with tears in her eyes, that I was the
only one of Harry's relations she could endure. Then she went off to get ready
for her dinner-party. I saw her for a minute, an hour later, in her satin dress
and diamonds—diamonds, she frankly confessed that had been paste ages ago.
'Don't forget your promise,' she whispered. 'If I'm pretty well I'll see you in
the morning. If not, good-by, as you must go so soon. Don't forget your
promise, and by the way, mind you address the letter *poste restante*—Lady Portia
Ffrench, *Poste Restante*, Brussels. Harry hates my having any thing to do with
money.'

"After this she went away; and Charles, when he had conducted his mistress
to her carriage, came softly into the room and asked me if I would please to see
the baby asleep? Her ladyship was without a maid at present, he explained, as
I followed him out, so he must make free to apologize for the untidy state of
the nursery.

"The nursery was next to poor Harry's own room, a dark, airless closet,
neither tidy nor over-clean, and there, in your cot, the cot that ought to have
been at your mother's bed-side, you lay asleep. You were a wonderfully handsome child, I must confess, Portia, however you may have altered since; dark
and dimpled, with cheeks like wild roses, and the loveliest pair of naughty lips
in the world. 'Miss Baby's a picture,' said Charles, creeping up on tiptoe, and
bending his stiff figure over your cot. 'She's the Captain's image and the
pride of his heart. When he wakes in the morning, madam, the first thing he
calls for is the child—even before his soda-and-brandy, poor gentleman. "Bring
me the baby, Charles," he says, or, "Where's the child?" or, "How is it I don't
hear the child's voice?" She's the Captain's one delight,' the faithful creature
added, with a tremble in his voice. 'But for Miss Baby, I don't see what there
would be to keep the Captain to life.'

"Saying this, he set down the light and left me, and throughout the long
hours of that winter night I waited and watched alone, Portia, by you. I counted the hours by the different city clocks till past midnight; then—it must have
been getting on for two o'clock, I should say—there came a loud ring at the
house bell. Charles, one of whose many duties was evidently to sit up and
have refreshment ready for Lady Portia, entered from Harry's room in a few
minutes' time, with a cup of hot soup and some bread, for which, as you may
imagine, I felt grateful. An hour or so later poor Harry himself made his appearance."

"Don't tell me in what condition," interrupted Portia; "I don't want my

ideal of my father spoiled. I would rather hear no further of him, poor fellow !"

"Your father came in not a bit less cool, less sober than I had seen him in
the forenoon," said Miss Jemima. "He walked up wearily to the table in the
centre of the room, mixed himself a glass of brandy and water, drank it off at a
draught, then pushed open the half-closed nursery door, and looked across at
your cot.

"'Aunt Jem ! Good Heaven, I had forgotten you were here !' he exclaimed
coming up and kissing me. 'But my memory—my memory's all gone. To think
you should have been left here alone, and on this cold night, too !' And upon
this he took me back into his room, with his own hands lit the fire (Charles,
by this time, I suppose, had folded himself into his cupboard) and, after making
me comfortable in the easiest chair his room possessed, came and sat down
close, just as he used to do when he was a little lad talking with me over the
day's troubles, by my side.

"'I really did not mean to leave you,' he said, 'but you know you were
with Portia.' When people are with Portia I never seem to have a word
to say to them, and so I went out, and some of the fellows at the club persuaded
me to stay, the worse luck to themselves !'

"And then he went on to tell me he had been winning twenty or thirty
pounds. 'A paltry sum,' he added, turning out a small heap of gold upon the
table—a paltry sum considering what his losses had been of late, but enough to
give the baby a cloak, and Portia a couple of new dresses. She wanted them
badly enough, poor Portia !

"'And Charles's wages?' I exclaimed, on the impulse of the moment.

"Harry looked at me sharply. 'Portia has been asking you for money,' he
cried. 'Don't deny it. She asks every one who comes near us for money—to
pay Charles's wages ! If you send her a single shilling I'll make her send it
back—mind you that. Poor old Aunt Jem !' He caught my hand and held it
between his own thin feverish ones. 'I did'nt think we had quite sunk to fleec-
ing you !'

"We sat there together till day-light," went on Miss Jemima, after a minute
or two, "but even to you, Portia, not even to his child, could I repeat half that
my poor boy told me. Harry was generous of spirit, still. This wreck of his
old fine nature still remained to him. He would allow no one to be blamed but
himself for his misfortunes ; not his father, not his wife. If he had married the
woman he loved—as I told you, he could not speak of her even now, without a
change of color—if he had married Amelia Morgan he believed his life would
have turned out differently—still, who should say ? everything was a chance !
He had never been oversteady, and for certain his father only acted as any other
man of the world would have done, in hindering such a marriage.

"'If I had had the real stuff of a man in me.' he said, 'I supposed I should
have stuck to her, have made her marry me. and gone away like Dick and the
others to Australia. For my part, I'm a fatalist. I turned fatalist when I heard,
a few months after she had done with me, that she was married. Nothing a fellow can do really alters his life by an inch.' While he talked he helped himself
freely from the brandy bottle at his side. 'I married Lady Portia because it
was "written," and we have been going the pace downhill ever since, and nothing seems to hinder us. My father is right, I dare say, in stopping my allowance. Money does not help me. I'm sorry for Portia, poor girl ! She don't

love me, never did, but I'm sorry for her all the same. She will be better off when I'm gone, and so will the child—so will the child!'

"He stopped when he had said this and buried his face down between his hands. I can see him, I can see the whole room as clear as if it had been yesterday when we sat there, my boy and I together, in that chill daybreak! At last, after a long silence, he lifted his face. Oh, the worn, worn face that it was! In the cold morning light I could mark, as I had not marked the day before, how the delicate lines had grown coarse, how the dark hair was streaked with white, the forehead furrowed with lines of premature care. I saw what a wreck Harry Ffrench had become, and—and loved him better so!

"'Aunt Jem,' he said, 'I never kept any secret from you when I was a small boy. I won't let you go away without telling you of a certain burthen I have on my mind now. It haunts me day and night. I tear myself from it by going into the company of other men, and it follows me. I come back to this solitary room of mine—'tis with me still. Shall I tell you what this burthen is? Well, then, I am a coward. I haven't got the courage to live my life out! Now you understand.'

"Portia, I burst into tears; I threw my arms round his neck; I could do nothing else.

"'You love me too well to argue, to preach me a sermon,' said Harry, very gently. 'And I don't suppose any argument but coming into twenty thousand pounds would have much effect upon me. 'Tis fatal. Poverty to a man with a hope in life may be endurable. I have no hope. There's something altogether wrong with me.' He put his hand to his head again. 'I drink brandy enough to kill a better man over and over again, and I keep sober. I play, and, whether I lose or win, I am not excited. I've tried every pleasure under the sun and—and after the turning-point you know of, found them all pleasureless. The play's over!'

"And the baby? I cried. The child whose whole future life depends on you?

"'The baby's life, like mine, is written,' said poor Harry, but a softer look came over his face as he said this. 'Miss Baby prefers Charles to me as it is, will be much better without a father like me than with me. You'll care for her, Aunt Jem? Promise me, when I die—well, then, if I die, that you'll care for the young one; let my father see her? Bring her up, if you can get hold of her, not quite upon the Dysart model.'

"I promised him, Portia. We went together in the room where you lay asleep, and as we bent, side by side, over your pillow, I promised Harry that if ever you were left alone in the world I would try to restore you to the place that he had forfeited in his father's heart."

"And having promised this, you left me with my mother!" cried Portia, "left me for the first six years of my life, knowing what blood ran in my ill-fated veins, to become a Dysart!"

"Until you were six years old I never dared mention your name in Richard's presence," answered Miss Jemima. "We were quartered at a remote station in India at the time of—of the bitterest sorrow of my life. Richard never wrote to me or Lucy—we first learned through the newspapers what had befallen us— and it was only through indirect sources that I afterward heard of the fearful horror his son's death had wrought in him. He shut himself up alone, here at Halfont. For weeks together a servant never was allowed to leave his side. What rest he got was in the daytime. At night he had the candles lighted, and sat up, or rather, as Jekyll has since told me, would pace his room for hours and hours together, shuddering and turning white if only a board creaked or a dead leaf beat against the pane. When, at length, he went abroad into the world again, he had so oldened that men scarcely knew him. I wrote, as soon as I had heart to think of the future, and proposed that our family should seek to get possession of Harry's child. It had been his own wish, I said ; Lady Portia was in poor circumstances, did not care for children, and it had been Harry's wish, in the event of his own early death, that his father should take an interest in his child.

"'I forbid you to mention Lady Portia Ffrench to me again,' was Richard's answer—how his fine firm hand writing had broken in these few months ! ' But for his marriage my son would not have gone to ruin. His death, our shame, lie at Lady Portia's door, I will know nothing of her, or of her child !'

"The rest of my story, Portia, can be soon told. When Elliott left the service I returned to England for good, and, as you know, came to Halfont to be Richard's companion. For a great many months I never once mentioned his dead son's name before him. At last, 'twas one April twilight, I remember, as we sat together, we two silent old people over our silent stately dessert, something brought me to speak of my three poor lads, men getting on toward middle age now, away in the colonies.

"'Harry is gone,' said Richard, shortly. ' Don't talk of the others. Harry is gone. I loved him better than them all—I was unjust to him, and he is gone. I can make up for nothing now.'

"I tried upon this to soften him toward his living children. I spoke of Lucy, of his sons, none of them so well off, alas ! as to be beyond the necessity of his help. He scarcely seemed to hear what I was talking of. Harry—Harry was the one he had loved and he was dead, had died in want, in dishonor, by his own hand—your grandfather's face got white as stone—and there was no making up for the past !

"At last I mentioned you.

"'I thought I explained my feelings on that subject before,' said Richard. 'Why recur to it ? What have I to do with Lady Portia Dysart's child ?'

"You have every thing to do with Harry Ffrench's child ! I cried. You talk of making up for the past—make up for it by showing love to her !

"And then I spoke to him, as I had never had courage to speak before, of the details of my visit to Brussels. I told him of Harry's affection for you, and how he had used to have you to sleep at his side when you were a baby, neglected by your mother ; of his wish, too, that we, Richard and I, not Lady Portia, should bring you up in the event of his own early death.

"Richard's face grew whiter and whiter. ' The child can come to Halfont if you choose,' he said, at last. ' Don't distress me with these painful recollections. If the mother will part from her, the child may come, on the express understanding that the two never meet again. But don't say another word to me about it till the day you bring her home.' "

"Upon this grudging permission," said old Miss Jemima, "I acted, and acted promptly. Richard should have no time, I determined, to retract his word. I had already ascertained that Lady Portia still lived in Brussels, and two days after I had had my conversation with your grandfather I arrived there. One of the under waiters at the hotel where I stopped happened to be an Englishman, and, determining to set about my errand the same night, I asked him, as he stood behind my chair at my solitary dinner, if he could get me a directory ? I had come to Brussels in search of an English lady I had known some years ago, but of whose present address I was ignorant.

"The man moved out, with a quick side step, under the gas-light. 'Is the lady's name Ffrench, madam?' he asked, raising his hand respectfully to his head; and in an instant I recognized him—the upright, soldier figure, the close-shorn soldier face—it was Charles. He had been thrown adrift in the world (penniless, I suspect,) at the time of his master's death, and had thankfully accepted the first chance of getting a living that offered itself. Lady Portia Ffrench was in Brussels still—in such a street and number, I have forgotten them long ago—and Miss Baby was well. He hoped I would not be offended; but sometimes, when her ladyship was not at home, he contrived to see Miss Baby still.

"'And I try to talk to her of the Captain, madam,' said Charles, under his voice. 'Poor Miss Baby doesn't get much of what I should call mother-love from her ladyship; and when I take her a bag of sweets, and talk to her of the Captain, the child 'll put her arms round my neck, and say, "take me away, take me away, Lurly, and let me be your little girl, not mamma's." That she will, and she growing a tall young lady already.'

"Lurly!" exclaimed Portia, "is the Charles of your story, Lurly? Why I remember him better than I do my mother—a stiff, tall man, dressed in rusty black, and always smelling of dinner. He used to bring Sophie stuff in a bottle, that she might not tell Lady Portia of his visits, and he gave me sweets, and once, on the sly, he took us both to the play. We sat in the pit, I on Lurly's knee, and ate peppermint lozenges. How I loved him! I don't suppose I could love anybody now as I loved Lurly. But, alas! that attachment was clandestine."

"Portia," cried Miss Jemima, half with temper, "I wonder if you were upon the brink of judgment whether it would be possible to you to be in earnest? Here am I, talking of things that make my heart bleed as I utter them, and you can jest. You are never honestly sorry, you are never honestly glad. You are nothing—"

"But the daughter of Harry Ffrench, who had not the courage to live his life out, and of his wife, a Dysart," said the girl. "Oh, Aunt Jem, if this story of yours teaches us anything, it should be charitable appreciation of my character. Don't you see that I am necessarily nothing?—not a monster of virtues, not a monster of vices, like the people in stories; but a poor, incongruous lump, chance-kneaded, of contradictions? No, you don't see it. Go on with your story, dear Aunt Jem, and I'll try not to interrupt you again. You came to my mother's lodging—that I remember. You came into my room and found me, little vixen that I was, ready to tear you to pieces, because I thought you belonged to her, and took me in your arms. I felt your tears on my face, I know, as you sat and clasped me. What did she say? In what frame of mind was Lady Portia now?"

"Lady Portia," answered Miss Jemima, "was in the only frame of mind in which I ever saw her—supreme indifference to everything on God's earth, save the momentary excitement which helped her to escape from herself. My meal over, I drove straight to her house; it was now between ten and eleven o'clock, and was told by the porter that my lady lived on the second floor, and that to-day, Friday, was my lady's evening of reception. I was dressed just as I left Halfont—the same fashion of bonnet I wear now, Miss Portia, a black stuff gown of sensible length, my travelling-bag in my hand—and so I was ushered into the midst of Lady Portia's guests. The room where they were assem-

bled was small, but finely hung in silk and velvet, and full as it could hold of
ornaments and filigree mirrors and bright color. It smelt like a distiller's shop
—would have been wholesomer, I thought, that warm spring night, for open windows. A couple of whist tables were going on. Near the fireplace, three or
four fashionably-dressed women, none of them in their first youth, stood talking
to some officers in uniform ; on a sofa, a little apart from the rest, sat Lady Portia.
She was playing at cards with a good-looking man, some years younger than
herself, an English clergyman, I could see by his dress, and, as I afterward
found, a constant visitor at her house. The man who eventually became her
second husband—"

"And who made the remainder of her life additionally miserable to her,"
remarked Portia, *en parenthèse*. "It is good to hear grandmamma talk of Mr.
Molyneux. 'The kind of ungowned parson who does prowl about the Continent,' says grandmamma—'The kind of parson who would marry a Lady Portia Ffrench.'"

"Well, for a second or two, the glare of brilliant light, the sight of all
these people confused me. Then—then, Portia, I thought of that darkened,
shame-covered past, which she had been able to forget, and walked straight
across the room to Harry's widow. Whatever surprise, whatever annoyance
she may have felt, Lady Portia's reception of me was perfectly courteous. She
acted nothing, affected nothing ; was not, as a worse-bred woman would have
been, ashamed of me or of my homely dress. I had dined—yes ? Fortunate I
arrived on a Friday, the only evening of the week she was at home. Mr. Molyneux—Miss Jemima Ffrench. If I did not mind, they would just finish this
party at piquet. I understood piquet, of course ? Then she took up her cards
and went on with her game.

"I sat myself down at a little distance," proceeded Miss Jemima, "and
watched her as she played, her fine company, no doubt, watching me. Lady
Portia's face had not grown younger during the past five years. Her cheeks
had fallen, her faded blue eyes told a wearier story than ever of the dissatisfied,
listless soul within ; her arms and neck, profusely bare, glittering with the paste
diamonds, I remembered were the arms and neck of an old woman. Still, as I
looked at her, I knew—knew, how shall I say ? by instinct ?—that she had gone
through no passionate suffering, no ordeal of pain since I saw her last . . .
her eyes had never wept, her lips quivered with anguish over Harry's death, over
Harry's last, irreparable wrong-doing. I knew this, I say, and felt toward her—
God pardon me !—as if she, poor, irresponsible, weak creature that she was,
had been the cause of both.

"When the game was over—Mr. Molyneux won, and something in his whispered remarks, in his manner, as he took up his stakes, made me suspect how
matters stood between them—when the game was over, your mother turned
round to me. 'Portia is grown out of knowledge,' she cried, 'and I am delighted to say, will be a beauty. I wish I had been one. I should not have gone
through such a life as mine. I should not have come to this,' glancing round at
the guests, 'if I had had a nose and mouth like Portia's.'

"Mr. Molyneux bent forward, and murmured something in her ear. 'Nonsense, nonsense,' said your mother, blankly, truthful as ever, and she turned
from him with a look of real sadness on her face. 'I never was beautiful, and
my life has been a failure in consequence. Portia is a Ffrench,' this remark
was addressed to me ; 'outwardly, at least. Her features, and complexion, and
turn of head are all like poor Harry's. She will be able to wear the dark colors

I'm glad Portia will be able to wear the *dark* colors when she comes out. Nothing so foolish as to see a mother and daughter dressed alike.'

"I got up from my chair. 'Where is the child?' I said. 'When your friends are gone I shall be glad of half an hours' talk with you. Till then, if you please, I will stay with the child.'

"And then Lady Portia also rose, and herself showed me the way to your sleeping-room—the room you shared with Sophie, the lady's maid. 'You, dear old soul, to come and find me out,' she said, on the way, perfectly unchilled by my manner, which I know was freezing. 'I've never been able to thank you for the money. I got it quite safe. Dear me, what terrible things have happened since—mind the steps! down two and turn. You must find me aged. I'm sure I feel a hundred or I should never bring myself to do what I am going to do. I'll tell you all about it when these shocking people are gone. There's Portia,' and she pushed open the door. 'Little cat! awake, as usual. For, here's an old friend of mine come to see you.' After which introduction, she nestled away in her flowing silk back to her company, and I walked across the room—child, with what a beating heart, to you!

"You were sitting up in your bed, your black eyes full of curiosity, your whole small figure bristling with defiance. 'Go away,' you cried. 'Don't kiss me, or I'll box you; go away; I want none of her friends here.'

"I am your friend, I cried, and I advanced into the light of the solitary candle, so that you should better see what sort of creature I was. I'm old Aunt Jemima—papa's Aunt Jemima; and I want you to live with me. Charles told me where to find you.

"Portia, whatever trouble you have caused me since, in that moment you paid me, beforehand, for it all. You jumped out of bed—I see you now, with your bare pink feet, in your little white night-dress—ran to me, flung your arms tight round my knees. 'Am I to go away with you?' you cried. 'Am I to live with Lurly? Is my own papa coming back at last?'

"You say that you remember what came next. How I sat holding you in my arms, and how you felt my tears fall upon your face. Well, I stayed there with you long, listening to your baby chatter (baby chatter, intermixed occasionally with such sharp criticisms on your elders as almost took my breath away). At last, tired out, you fell asleep, and I laid you on your pillow. Soon afterward, I heard the footsteps of the departing guests. Mr. Molyneux, I fancied, remaining later than the rest by some minutes, and, by-and-by, your mother came in. She had taken off her glittering necklet and earrings; her evening dress was exchanged for a dressing-gown; she looked fifty years old. 'I know what you think of me,' she cried, as I sat still and watched her. 'I see it on your face. Haven't I aged horribly?'

"I am not thinking of your age at all, I answered her. I am thinking of Harry's child. Her grandfather wishes to see her. Will you let me take her back with me to England.

"'What, will Colonel Ffrench be reconciled?'" cried the poor creature, with a trembling lip. 'Oh, my dear soul, say that is your errand! Mamma gets stingier to me every year. I have scarce enough to keep up even the appearance that you see. Of course I'll let the child visit you. I've been extravagant, I've been everything I oughtn't, but I'll turn over a new leaf. I will, to-morrow, if Colonel Ffrench will only be reconciled, only make me a suitable allowance!'

"And then, Portia, I had to explain to her on what bitter terms she must

give you up, if she consented to the separation at all. And my heart bled for
her while I did so! I don't know how it is, but, whatever people are, if I only
get close enough to them, only hear their own account of themselves, I always
begin to feel I must take their part; at a distance one may call them wicked;
near, one can only see them weak. Lady Portia had not been a good wife to
Harry; she was not even a devoted mother, or she would not have consented
to part from you at all, still I pitied her! Poor, haggard, world-weary woman
that she was, I pitied her!

"'Everything has gone against me,' she cried, sobbing, when I had made
her feel how final the severance must be from you if I once carried you back
with me to Halfont. 'When I was a girl, five-and-twenty years ago, I—I loved
some one, I did indeed. If they had let me marry him, perhaps I should have
been a good woman. Instead of that, what was my life? Put up by mamma
season after season for sale—yes, sale; one year such a bargain falling through,
the next another. At last when all better chances were over, accepted, for my
name's sake, by Colonel Ffrench's spendthrift son. What has my life been
since?'

"Don't tell me, I interrupted. I can imagine what your life has been.
But don't tell me.

"'Oh, I am not going to say anything bad of poor Harry,' said Lady Portia.
'He never loved me, but as men go, he was not a bad husband. Harry was a
man with a *grande passion*. I never believed it till his death, poor fellow, and
then—my dear creature, would you believe it? they found a curl of hair, some
school-girl love notes signed "Amelia" in his breast! You shall have them.
I've had all these sorts of things put by for you, with a paper he wrote on the
morning of his death—my poor Harry! You were always the best relation we
had'—she really said this, Portia—'on either side. If my mother had had a tenth
part of the feeling for me that you had for Harry, should I be what I am now?
Cast off by my husband's family and my own, sinking to the society of such
people as you saw with me to-night, and, for the future, not even allowed to be
a mother. I havn't loved the baby as some mothers do, perhaps,' she went on,
'I never was fond of children, it isn't my nature. But I'd have liked to be
with her when she's grown up and admired. She'll be so handsome, and *I* shall
never see her. Look at her now, look at her little cheek and neck.' . . .
And then she threw herself down, and rested her cheek softly against yours,
and cried over you.

"'I consent to let you have her,' she said, lifting up her face at last, for I
sat silent, letting nature determine for her what she should do. 'And I don't
think I can wonder at Colonel Ffrench's determining to part her from me absolutely. I should never have been a fit companion for her. I haven't an ounce
of good left me. And besides,' the color flamed over her worn face, 'I'm going
to marry Parson Molyneux, and he doesn't like the child. Take her away the
first thing in the morning. I'm saying good-by to her now. It would kill me
to see her happiness at going.'

"She uncovered you upon this, and kissed your little bare feet—God knows
with what thoughts passing through her heart! Then, very gently, covered you
again, and motioned to me to leave the room. That was the last time your
mother ever saw you."

"And so, I suppose, ends the story," said Portia, as Miss Jemima paused.
"I remember all that came next. My joy when I woke and saw Sophie packing up my things, and our breakfast at the hotel, hot little rolls and poor old

Lurly to wait on us, and the journey, and grandpapa's face when we arrived, and how he turned shortly away, and kept to his room for a week afterward. I remember all this, and also how I had to wear crape and try to look solemn, years later, because you told me Lady Portia Molyneux was dead. Aunt Jem," and Portia's face saddened into a look which, could those black eyes but have spoken, would for the moment have been positively tender, " I feel more reconciled than I ever did before to marrying poor Teddy. He is not clever, and he has no nobler qualities than I have myself. Still, money or no money, we like each other, and therefore our best chance, when you consider what stock we come of, is to marry. Don't you think so ? "

" I have always told you that your best chance would be to marry a man you loved," said Miss Jemima. " If love, not money, had been thought of when each was young, the two lives I have been telling you of had not been shipwrecked."

" Let us say so ! " was Portia's answer. " Let us cheat ourselves into the belief that theirs, like all other lives, were not predestined for them. Oh, Aunt Jem," after a minute, " if I *am* fated to marry Teddy, without money, how intensely you ought to pity him, and both of us ! With five thousand a year, my father and mother would probably have lived together contentedly till their lives' end, while poverty . . . but all these things are written," she broke off lightly. " Our best wisdom is to enjoy the hour that we live, and not look forward too keenly to the future. To the day, the evil thereof."

She kissed Miss Jemima as she spoke, and ran away up-stairs with a flush of genuine animation upon her face. Whatever presented life in vivid dramatic contrast before Portia Ffrench, had power, for the instant, to evoke sympathy from her emotion-craving nature. And precisely to this extent Miss Jemima's story had affected her. Poor broken-down, outlawed Harry Ffrench, drugging honor, manhood, conscience, with brandy ; deliberately resolving not to live life out, yet having his baby's nursery beside his own room ; with womanish gentleness tending the child whose whole existence he did not scruple to darken by the act of his own hand ; Lady Portia in her forlorn, haggard middle age, crying over the little daughter who was to have worn the dark colors, yet parting with that daughter that she might herself marry Parson Molyneux; the Brussels lodging ; my lady's receptions ; my lady's paste diamonds—Portia could see it all !

" We go to the bad artistically, if we do nothing else," she thought, looking long at her own handsome face in the glass, when she had reached her room. " Dysart and Ffrench alike, we know how to tread the downhill road with an air, and that is something. Oh Teddy—my poor little Teddy—in ten years' time what story, I wonder, of graceful shame, of picturesque ruin, will have to be recorded of *us !* "

CHAPTER XI

"FOR my part," said Miss Collinson, "I should call a nice brooch set in garnets as suitable a gift as could be made. Susan has not got a garnet brooch, that I know; and garnets can be worn in half mourning—in any mourning short of crape—and they look well by day or candle. I don't see, brother, that you could do better than decide upon the garnet brooch at once."

Tom Collinson was sitting at his breakfast: the late substantial breakfast that cost more than a day's provisions used to cost in Miss Collinson's frugal household; a sporting newspaper on one side of his plateful of cold pie; on the other, carefully outspread on cotton wool, a dozen or so old-fashioned brooches, rings, and lockets. His desire, yesterday afternoon, of making Susan a birthday present had not been a momentary impulse merely: to give comes just as readily as to take to people of Tom Collinson's temperament: and as there did not happen to be any jewellers' shops on Hounslow Heath, the most obvious and natural course in the world was, he felt, to choose whatever trifle Susan might be likely to fancy out of Eliza's trinket-box.

"It will come exactly to the same thing in the end," he had remarked, with Sultan-like generosity, as he ordered his sister to produce her small, long-hoarded stock of treasures. "The next time I go to town I shall bring you back something handsome in my pocket, and so have the pleasure of making two presents instead of one!"

And poor little Miss Collinson, who had never found heart to say "nay" to any male creature in her life, obeyed on the instant. The dearest possession she had, a diamond ring given her once by Mr. Fielding after an illness of Susan's, was safe, she felt. Impossible that Tom even could propose to return the father's gift to the daughter. And her pearl locket, the locket that she had kept and cried over since she was seventeen, and to which so tender a story was attached, surely Tom would never wish her to part with this! From all the rest he might make free choice—the jet cross, or the plain gilt locket, or the brooch set in garnets; Miss Collinson herself inclined, as we have seen, with artful warmth to the many merits of garnets.

"They would suit Susan's complexion nicely," she began anew, "and they are the very best of stones. I got the brooch when Aunt Hannah died. You know all Aunt Hannah's things were good, and—"

"Aunt Hannah be ——," interrupted Collinson, pushing the brooch contemptuously aside. "She left me a chandelier and a pair of plated side-dishes, a nice bequest, wasn't it, to a man without a roof over his head, like me? Out of the lot there are just two things worth giving. This," he raised his left hand, upon the little finger of which he had slipped the diamond ring, "and the locket. Now I'll take whichever you like, Eliza;" and nothing could be more affable than the manner in which he made this concession. "Whichever you like—the ring or the locket."

Miss Collinson blushed up to her eyes. She was a thin, neat-featured woman of eight-and-thirty, or thereabouts, neutral-tinted in her complexion and dress, as in her life and character, with a faded, transitory smile and an apologetic little girlish voice and manner. " The ring, as you know, Tom, was Mr. Fielding's gift to me. He put it on my finger himself. Susan was sitting up for the first time after measles, as white and large-eyed as an owl—she took every sickness she had hard—and he put it on my finger."

" Oh well, I suppose it wouldn't do to give the ring back into the family," interrupted Tom ; " its a very nice stone ; I'll air it for you sometimes, Eliza— so that brings us to the locket. For a girl of Susan's age perhaps the locket is the most suitable. Have you a box for it ? "

" A—a box ? "

" A—a box : " Tom Collinson mimicked his sister's tone with perfect temper, looking up at her with a smile upon his good-looking, impudent face ; "and mo- rocco, if you have one, to look as if it came from the jeweller's. I wish, too, you'd patch up a note—a copy I mean, the note itself must be written in my own ex- quisite fist. Something about birthday wishes and the poorness of the present, and—and my admiration and so on—the usual thing."

Miss Collinson stood for a minute, nervously twitching the frilled edge of her black silk apron ; at last she gathered up all the little courage she possessed and spoke :

" I've had that locket the best part of my life, Tom. I was a girl when it was given me, and—I know it's very foolish, but I like it like a living thing ! I'd rather lend you the money, please, to buy something for Susan Fielding, than give up my locket."

" Money to buy something ! At one of the numerous jewellers' shops be- tween this and Addison Lodge, I suppose ? Now, don't you be a fool, Eliza ; " he proffered this advice with admirable directness and decision. " About the time I was born, and when you were a school-girl, some young donkey—a par- son, wasn't it ? in a fit of spooning gave you this locket. He married some one else, of course, and you didn't marry at all—you didn't marry at all, Eliza ! and now, a quarter of a century later, you pretend to go in for sentiment about this trashy present of a fellow who forgot you in a fortnight ! Go and look for a box and help me write the note to Susan. Don't I tell you I'll bring you something double the locket's value the first time I go to London ? "

Poor Miss Collinson listened to this epitomized account of her youthful romance with shame tingling to her very fingers' ends. In the hazy atmosphere of unmarried, soft-hearted women's lives, the vaguest semblance of love-making is, we know, apt to assume spectral and magnified proportions. Eliza Collinson had never in sober fact received an offer of marriage from any one. But on two occasions of her life, in youth and middle age, she had had kind words spoken, gifts offered to her by men in marriageable positions ; and her heart clung to the remembrance of both with a tenacity highly ludicrous to Tom, who, as you may imagine, relished all the stock jests common to minds of his class on the subject of old maids.

" Say you can't bring yourself to part with the Reverend Jeremiah's gift, and I have done," he cried, as Miss Collinson still stood blushing and silent. " It isn't often I ask a favor of you ; but, if you are so desperately enamored of your locket, say so ! and I can go up to town this afternoon and get what I want. I really thought your last love—the gentleman for whom you still wear weeds—had cut out the Reverend Jeremiah in your affections, or I wouldn't have asked you ! "

He helped himself to another liberal wedge of pie, pushed all the trinkets

aside, and took up his newspaper with the air of a man who looks upon a discussion as ended.

"You—you must let me take out the hair?" said Miss Collinson, after a minute more of burning shame and indecision. "Don't be cross, Tom, I was ill-
natured for a minute, I know, but I've got over it, and you shall have the locket.
I've a nice little morocco box up-stairs, and I'll try to write the kind of note you
mean to Susan."

"You are a brick, Eliza!" cried Tom, all his facile good temper restored.
"See if I don't give you—not a trumpery locket, but something really handsome,
a chain, or a watch, or—or that!" Tom Collinson's promises were vague as
their fulfilment. "Now get a pen and ink at once, and we'll send off the present—the girl can run with it—and, by the way, why shouldn't you ask Susan
Fielding over to dinner this afternoon? I said something about our never seeing her, yesterday, and she seemed ready enough to come if you would invite
her."

Poor Eliza now ran for the morocco box and her writing-case. A lock of
time-dried, whitey-brown hair was taken tenderly from the pearl locket wherein
it had rested more than twenty years; a note written, first in Miss Collinson's
fine governess hand, then in Tom's big scrawling one; and the little packet
made up.

"The girl's trustworthy, I suppose?" inquired Collinson. "I ask because I
know you get them from the Sunday-school. Well, send her off directly, then,
and bid her wait for an answer. Wanted in the house? Nonsense. I'll help
you—answer the bell, and do everything else you like while you are in the
kitchen."

And so it was settled. The small girl of thirteen, Miss Collinson's maid-
of-all-work, was dispatched (walking her slowest, and enjoying her liberty to the
utmost) across the heath, and the brother and sister set about their division of
the morning labors of the household; Tom in an easy-chair, his feet higher than
his head, smoking his pipe and reading his paper at the open parlor window,
Eliza washing the breakfast things, shelling peas, seeing about the stuffed goose
and gooseberry tart for Tom's dinner, in the kitchen. "Poor dear boy," she was
accustomed to say, "Tom liked to have everything nice about him, and no wonder, after such a rough life as his has been. And then he was *inclined* to be wild
—boys have such temptations!—and it was a great thing to make him comfortable at home. Nothing, if a boy was inclined to be wild, like giving him everything nice and comfortable in his own home."

The habit of considering her brother in the light of a boy who must be pet-
ted and indulged, no matter at what cost to herself, was too strong with Eliza
Collinson for her to get cured of it even now that Tom was a man of three-and-
twenty, even after all the bitter experience of the past! When old Mr. Collinson, the Halfont brewer, died, leaving his wife and her infant son destitute,
Eliza, the child of a former marriage, at once found herself, by the most natural
process in the world, in the position of bread winner to the family. "Some one
will really have to do something," said the poor, ailing, fine lady widow, plaintively, "or Tommy and I go to the workhouse." And as Eliza was tolerably
well educated, and there happened to be nothing in the shape of a morning governess in the village, the young woman's life within a month after her father's
death was shaped for her.

"Dear Eliza's duty lies so plainly, so close to her hand," said the widow,
"that we both feel she must accept it without a murmur." And from that time

until the present Miss Collinson had continued to teach; to teach English, French, drawing, piano; all she knew, all she knew not; but conscientiously ever, poor patient soul, not developing any particular ability in her pupils—to do that requires special ability—but never allowing them to skip an observation in grammar, to slur a difficult bar in music, to leave uncorrected a devious line in their drawings. If art, or literature, or music, thus taught could be a source either of use or pleasure hereafter to her pupils was no question for Miss Collinson. Her conscience, like her life, was bounded by a perfectly narrow horizon. She undertook to teach so much, for so many pounds a year, and to the best of her small might she fulfilled her bargain; the pounds all going toward the support of Mrs. Collinson and her son. As time went on the delicate widow ailed and ailed more, then died, Eliza's hard-earned money paying for dainty invalid fare, doctors, nurses, everything. After this came the education and putting out in the world of Tom.

He was educated upon a by no means exceptional feminine system of educating boys; alternate indulgence and injustice, pious kisses and feeble bullyings; and the system bore its accustomed fruits. When he really wanted a whipping—about twelve times a year, this—Tom, by adequate hypocrisy, could at once convert Eliza's wrath into a sermon and tears. When he really wanted to be running wild with the other little lads on the common he was imprisoned, because it was after dusk, or damp, or because his shoes were thin, or because good boys never played of a Sunday evening. The poor woman fretted over him, prayed over him, tormented him, slaved for him, and at last in the middle of a grand scene, was told abruptly that she was an old woman and that Tom, now fifteen years old, would not knock under to her or go to school any more. He was the strongest. He would never obey her again while he lived.

At this juncture Eliza, I need scarcely say, succumbed. Tom *was* too big, she felt sure, for petticoat government any longer—dear spirited fellow! Mr. Mildmay, the curate, must take him seriously in hand for a while; and to Mr. Mildmay the boy, it was settled, should go daily to read. (There might have been an opening, an honest chance of life for him just then, in the firm of the people who succeeded his father in business, but Master Collinson did not consider brewing the occupation of a gentleman, and poor Eliza had visions of sending him to college, and of his ultimately entering the church.) Nothing, it seemed, could be happier than the new arrangement. The forenoon reading and afternoon liberty suited Master Tom to a nicety, and all went on smoothly for the first quarter. Then came abrupt discoveries of the lad being in debt, having bad companions, drinking, smoking, driving up in a tandem on Sunday—horrible climax—to London. He promised amendment; was forgiven; in a month fell into more flagrant disgrace than before. Finally, by everybody's advice, his tutor's most of all, was shipped off to a Scotch sheep-farmer, a distant connection of Mr. Mildmay's, in New Zealand; his sister mortgaging the best part of her coming twelvemonth's income to pay the cost of his passage money and outfit.

The years that followed were perhaps the least troubled ones of Eliza Collinson's life. Instead of wearily journeying, in all weathers, from one farmhouse to another after pupils, she had now sole charge of little Susan Fielding. She had the friendship of Mr. Fielding, with the constant mild stimulus of seeking to convert that friendship into a warmer feeling. And she had good hopes and good news of Tom's colonial life. The healthy out-door employment, the absence of temptation of the New Zealand sheep farm, had, Miss Collinson felt, proved the instruments of her brother's salvation. For a space—that slippery, transitional space over which every boy must tread ere he becomes a man—her hand, she acknowledged humbly, had proved too weak to guide him. Now, far away, alone with Nature and his conscience, were being shown forth those pious dispositions which she had fostered in him from his earliest childhood. At a time when other little lads were wasting their golden hours in the frivolous, oft-times gambling games of marbles and pitch-and-toss, Tom had been committing to memory words of wisdom that should guide him hereafter through the deceitful labyrinth of the world; and now—now the good seed sown was already whitening for harvest! He wrote to her regularly—always wanting money; that was natural, considering the scantiness of his wages, but expressing such beautiful sentiments, such touching contrition over his old wildness, as left no doubt on poor Eliza's mind as to his being a changed, a converted man. At last, some five or six years after he quitted England, he sent a letter to say that his employer—a rattling good fellow, wrote Tom, a fellow who turned all he touched into gold—was about to take him into partnership, and that he Tom, was engaged to be married to his sister. By the time Eliza got the letter he expected he would be a married man; a year later would be the owner of so many thousand sheep, for certain; and if ever his dear sister wanted a home she would know where to find one. With more in the same grand style, and the sisterly love of his intended wife added in a postcript.

After this came a lapse of a great many months without a single letter. An occasional New Zealand paper directed in Tom's hand relieved Miss Collinson from any positive suspense about her brother's fate; but this was all. "He is married now," thought poor Eliza, with half querulous resignation. "Married and prosperous, and I am second in his love. I ought to be happy at his silence. When trouble or trial overtake him again, Tom will write." So she waited and waited, fretting anew every time that the New Zealand mail came in and brought no letter for her; at last, one March evening, found herself, without a minute of warning, in Tom's arms.

It was a day or two after Mr. Fielding's sudden death; and Eliza was sitting drearily alone by her small fire, speculating one moment, with sad tears, as to whether any preparation, any moment's repentance had been granted her friend at the last; wondering, the next, if people would think it "odd" that she should put on mourning for a man who was no relation; also whether, when it was made up, the crape that had lain by since she went out of mourning for her Aunt Hannah, would look brown or black. "For if it looks brown it will be a mockery to wear it," thought Miss Collinson, "and if I buy new every one will know, through Miss Budd, before Sunday comes, and do nothing but talk of me, and say what a fool I am, and how I cared for him. Oh, I did care for him—I did care for him! Nothing's left to me but Tom now, and Tom has forgotten me."

And she started up, hearing the parlor door open, and in the indistinct firelight saw a stranger cross the room to her side. It was Tom—Tom, with a deep man's voice, with whiskers; Tom very nearly in rags, and without a farthing in his pocket. His partner had turned a scoundrel—standing on the hearthrug, his face in shadow, his hand clasped in his sister's, Tom Collinson made fullest confession of his misfortunes during the first ten minutes of their meeting—had speculated with their common savings, failed, and gone off to Melbourne with every farthing he could touch, leaving Collinson a ruined man. No use for him to stop in the colony. The colony was going to the dogs; everybody bankrupt; sheep rotting off by thousands; water failing. He had worked his hardest. No one could say he had not worked ; and after all these years' labor had not got a five pound note in the world. People might talk as they liked, England was a better place for an honest man to get on in than any colony. At all events, he meant to stick to England. Nothing easier than to get employment—in London, anywhere one chose. He rather thought he would take some kind of easy place under government, this time ; and meanwhile all he asked of Eliza was that she would let him look upon her house as home for a few days.

"And your wife ?" faltered Eliza, not without a jealous tremor in her voice.

Tom Collinson was silent for a moment ; then he burst out into a laugh, not a natural one, Eliza thought, though, to be sure, his laugh, like everything else about him, must be altered now that he was a man. His wife ! That was a fine idea. What did he want of a wife ? He had written that he was on the eve of marrying his friend's sister ? . . . Yes, he knew he had ; but writing was a very different thing to acting. One of the family had proved quite enough for him. No, he was *not* married, or thinking of marrying, then—this as his sister continued to hover round the subject—he wished, strengthening the wish by such an expletive as had never startled Miss Collinson's walls or ears before, that she would leave questioning alone. He had been home ten minutes, and already she was at the old work—"the catechizing and cross-questioning that sent me to the devil when I was a boy," said Tom, savagely. "Yes, that sent me to the devil," he repeated, Miss Collinson having interposed a faint expression of horror. "I don't believe I was worse than most boys to start with ; but I became worse—for I became a hypocrite ! Don't you try the pious game with me any more, Eliza. I'm not any honester, perhaps, than other men, now ; but, at least, I've done with snivelling and repentance. Repentance—faugh ! I hate the word. It smells of the Reverend Mr. Mildmay and his New Zealand friends. No doubt that Scotch blackguard who cheated me out of all I had is *repenting* over his misdeeds at his leisure in Melbourne."

And, long before they quitted the parlor fire that night Miss Collinson realized to the full what manner of man the contrite, reformed young brother of her dreams had become ; realized it, and felt that in her inmost heart she did not respect the poor fellow less in consequence. He smoked pipe after pipe of strong tobacco—when he must have seen, too, that the winter curtains were still up ; he ordered her, an hour after he arrived, to send out for brandy ; he used words that almost dislocated her, mentally and bodily, with shocked surprise ; but then—he ruled her, pooh-poohed her attempts at lecturing, bade her ask no questions, pointed out to her, in perfectly clear and forcible language, the boundary line over which he did not choose that she should pass. And this was precisely the kind of treatment that agreed best with Eliza Collinson. Nature designed her, as it designs ninety-nine out of every hundred women, as it designs races, for contented servitude. If Tom had made his appearance heart-stricken, repentant, humble, a hundred to one some of the weakly-tyrannical spirit of old days would have awakened in his sister. Does not a trite maxim tell us that those who are born to obey wear authority badly ? An outspoken bully, he succeeded in impressing her at once with the wholesome sense of her own inferior strength ; and from that first evening onward she had never striven, never wished to free her neck from his yoke. It was not to be denied that Tom was changed, much changed ; but would she wish, said Miss Collinson, to find a man of three-and-twenty a school-boy still ? His language was not, perhaps, at all times what it should be ; but, then, he was such a fine, manly young fellow—hasty-tempered and impetuous certainly, but no hypocrite

—nothing she detested like a hypocrite ! Tom borrowed her money, the hard-got savings of years, and cast it to the winds on his own amusements. He bought smart clothes, flash jewelry, kept bad hours, or, rather, no hours at all ; required hot breakfasts, late dinners, never went to church, did things, not a few, outraging the whole public opinion of Halfont ; and still Eliza bore it all, still no word of rebuke rose to Eliza's lips. The blank that Mr. Fielding's death had left in her quiet, aimless existence had been filled, as if by a miracle, by Tom's return. To hear Tom's cheery voice, singing or swearing, as his humor might prompt, through the small house, to light his pipe for him, brush his clothes, stitch him fine wristbands, cook him savory meats—yes, even to sit up in her night-cap waiting to see Tom walk home unsteadily down the village street at daybreak—all this slavery of affection seemed to lend a new zest, to instil a faint experience of what the dearer servitude of marriage *might* have been, into Miss Collinson's sterile life.

"I feel as if I hadn't really kept house before since father died," she would say when, occasionally, her friends hinted that they hoped poor Mr. Tom would soon get employment, or that it must make a wonderful difference in the week's bills now that poor Mr. Tom was home. "Wish Tom to leave ? Why, I shouldn't know what to do with myself without him. Having Tom's dinner to cook and his linen to see to—yes, and actually having the smell of smoking in the parlor, though it does cling sadly to the curtains, makes me feel as if father was alive again."

And Tom being much too practical a philosopher to fret after work (even an easy place under government) so long as he had the chance of play, it seemed to be growing a settled thing that their present life should continue. Eliza cooking, sewing, giving lessons in her leisure hours, and generally slaving for his benefit ; he eating, drinking, smoking, spending money, and amusing himself. The kind of labor division of which we have just seen an example when Tom's generous birthday gift had been dispatched to Susan Fielding—out of Eliza's trinket case.

Toward two o'clock, and when the young man was beginning to swear and stamp about the room, and deliver himself of pretty strong commentaries on the subject of Sunday-schools and the kind of servant girls foolish women took from them ; the small servant bounced in, her face scarlet, her bonnet hanging down her back. "Miss Fielding's kindest love to Mr. Collinson, please mum, and were much obliged ; and she'll come."

The message gave Tom such a shock of surprised pleasure that he not only forbore to swear at the girl for her long delay, but actually tossed her three half-pence (of Eliza's) off the mantel-shelf. "You young baggage ! how dare you say such a thing ? You've been to the Rose, I can tell it by the color of your face. How dare you say Miss Fielding sent her love to me ?"

"But it was to you, Master Tom ;" poor Eliza still spoke of her brother as "Master Tom," and Betsey followed suit. "Miss Fielding came out in the garden herself 'Give my kindest love to Mr. Collinson,' she says, 'and were much obliged. And she'll come.'" During the two hours in which Betsey had played truant, with another serving-woman of her years, on the heath, she had revolved this message, full stop and all, in her head ; and no judge on the bench could have made her swerve from it by a syllable.

Miss Fielding's kindest love to Mr. Collinson ! Tom walked across to the window, whistled, played an accompanying tattoo with his thick fingers on the glass, then with a well satisfied look on his face ran up to his bedroom, from

THE WALK WITH TOM COLLINSON.—p. 77.

whence he issued forth, later in the afternoon, resplendent: bright flowered waistcoat, polished boots, coral brooch, curry-colored gloves, riding-whip—nothing like a riding-whip for giving one the air of a man of means. He stopped at the kitchen door immediately behind the parlor, and glanced in at Eliza, who with her dress pinned back, her face afire, was basting the goose. "I'm just going out for a turn, Eliza, shall meet Susan Fielding as likely as not, on the common. For God's sake try and cool yourself by then we are back!" he added, considerately. "Nothing more disgusting than to see a woman sit down with a purple blistered face to dinner. Can't Sunday-school look to the dinner?"

And without waiting for an answer Mr. Collinson began to draw on his over-tight gloves, stuck his hat on one side his head, then sauntered forth jauntily from the house. The village clock was striking four; and he turned his steps at once across the heath towards Addison Lodge.

CHAPTER XII.

So when Susan reached her accustomed halting-place on the bridge, she found, to her dismay, Tom Collinson awaiting her. The little girl who yesterday stood on the same spot bemoaning her loneliness, wondering if life could ever bring her another happy hour, was already at a stage of feeling when to be alone is to have the best of all companionship: that first sweetest stage of intoxication in which love, void as yet and without form, itself lends a memory or a hope to every common object in the external world. The sleepy wash of the canal, the wind droning low among the sedges, were the sounds she had heard as she walked by Blake's side last night; this blank white road led to London, where he lived; only last night he had traversed this heath, among whose soft after-noon purples she was to have an hour's walk alone. . . . And now here was Tom Collinson, in gamboge gloves and tawdry jewelry. Tom Collinson, with his terrible atmosphere of bergamot and tobacco, to mar all.

"You have put me in very good spirits, I can tell you, Miss Fielding," he remarked, in his deliberate, self-satisfied voice, and looking full, as he spoke, into Susan's face—the face which the stirring of new emotions had already robbed of half its vacancy. "I haven't felt such a happy man for many a month past, as I did when I got your message."

"My message! why, I never sent a message to you, at all," said Susan. "It was to Miss Collinson—I mean the message about coming to dinner. Of course, though"—the color rose to her cheeks—"I sent my thanks to you for the locket. It is so pretty. See, I have got it on." And she moved away her bonnet strings and showed him his gift, tied with a bit of black ribbon round the whitest little throat in the world.

"I'm glad you like it. I took—I mean I selected what I thought would be your taste. But you can't be so cruel"—and Collinson fully believed that he was making his manner tender—"you can't be so cruel as to tell me the first part of your message was only for Eliza?"

"Oh, but I'm certain it was," answered Susan. "I went in the garden and spoke to Betsey myself. 'Tell Mr. Collinson I am much obliged for his present,' I said, 'and give my kind love to Miss Collinson, and say I'll come'—or something of that sort."

"Ah, something of that sort," said Collinson, "but the 'something' may make all the difference. Now, are you certain "—he was not a man used to be shy with women, but something in the steady gaze of Susan's eyes did discountenance him—" are you quite certain that a little bit of the love wasn't sent to me on the sly ?"

"I am quite certain that messages all mean nothing," said Susan, smiling. "Compliments, or regards, or love—its all the same. How can one send one's love to be delivered by some other person, like a parcel ?"

"But if one could," said Collinson, pertinaciously, "if love could be sent like a parcel, anyhow—wouldn't you have spared a little bit of yours to me ?"

"Oh, when it can will be time enough for me to tell you," said Susan, turning her face aside, "and meanwhile I give you my thanks for the locket. It was very nice and friendly of you to send me a present, and I'll think of you when I wear it."

The awakening of one supreme womanly instinct was calling into action a dozen subordinate ones in this child's heart. Four-and-twenty hours can teach a girl of seventeen so much—of one kind of wisdom ! Dimly she began to suspect a little of the truth as regarded Tom Collinson, and womanlike, ran behind the outwork of friendship for safety.

"Friendly ! as if I cared—as if I wanted to be friendly !" cried the young man, hurriedly ; then he bit his lip, stopped short, and began to whistle. If he said another word at the point to which he had brought the conversation, Tom Collinson had sense enough to know that word would be a declaration ; and from any definite committal of himself he still shrank with a shiver ! He was not a really wicked man, if by the term wicked is meant a capacity for deliberate wrong-doing : such capacity, indeed, mostly belongs to villains of the very grand style of epic poems or tragedy. He was simply bad with the everyday badness that sows the world broadcast with misery ; would play with an ugly temptation till its edges were worn off, till familiarity had shaped dishonor to his conscience ; would vacillate till accident, some chance, unconscious hand, pushed him into its consummation, and afterward cry out against intention and fulfilment alike as a misfortune into which his evil luck had drifted him. He was desperately "gone"—to speak in his own tongue—upon Susan Fielding ; that he knew : and he ought not for a moment to entertain the thought of marrying her ; that also he believed he knew. But the present time—surely, he thought, the present time might be enjoyed without looking forward too nicely into the future. If he got so fond of the girl that he was forced into speaking, or if the poor little thing lost her peace of mind about him, it would be time to worry over troubles that could not be mended—that was to say, if they could not be mended, if there were no middle course by which his own desire could be attained without shame to others or discovery to himself. But at the word "discovery" Tom invariably got hot and uncomfortable, and thrust away the subject from his thoughts, like the thoroughly commonplace happy-go-lucky scoundrel that he was.

"I don't know that I ever deliberately harmed man or woman in my life," he wrote, months afterward, when he believed himself to lie at death's threshold ; his conscience, one may suppose, sharpened upon the whetstone of long sickness, "but I've got into more scrapes than most, and generally managed to drag some one else down with me. I was never one of your cold-blooded, longheaded fellows who can see from the first what line of conduct will turn out profitablest to themselves, and stick to it. I did what looked like best for the moment, and let the future take care of itself. And it did'nt—there's the truth, and there's no accounting for anything." This was Tom's way of disposing of his sins.

He began to whistle; after a minute or so took out his cigar-case, and Susan, with relief, hoped that it was his intention for once to walk by her side without incessant talking. Oh, how pleasant the heath was, in spite of Tom Collinson's society and his unlikeness to Mr. Blake (poor little Susan—already wanting all the world to be cut upon one pattern!) How sweet the air smelt this afternoon of early summer, how warm the sun shone, how loud the wood-pigeons called from their nests in the fir plantation away across the gravel pits! What a pity it would have been to die on one's seventeenth birthday, after all!

"You seem in vastly better spirits than you were when I saw you last," remarked Collinson, suddenly. He had looked stealthily round at her, and detected a suppressed smile at the corners of her lips. "The effect of dissipation, I suppose. Pray, what kind of party did you have at old Dicky Ffrench's last night?"

"A party? oh, none at all," said Susan. "There was no one but Mr. Josselin, Portia's lover, you know, and me—and another person. But it was very pleasant."

"No doubt," answered Collinson. "Big rooms and fine dresses and a real butler to wait, would make any stuck-up party delightful to a woman. I know what Eliza is when she has been to dinner at old Lady Long's. Now, pray, what did you do, Miss Susan, to make this evening at the Manor so superior to all other evenings?"

"We had tea first, and I liked that very much. Portia is so bright and lively, and she and Mr. Josselin talked—you should have heard them talk!—of every subject under the sun, I think. But the pleasantest was to come, for then we went out of doors and strolled by the river; and it was such a delicious evening! We stayed out till the stars shone. Portia and Mr. Josselin together, of course."

"And you?"

"Oh, I was with the—the other person."

"What other person? What are you talking about? Do you mean the old Miss Ffrench."

"I mean—Mr. George Blake." The confession came out with just the slightest little conscious stammer. It was the first time Susan had spoken Blake's name aloud, and she found it lingering on her lips. "A friend of Mr. Josselin's."

"A young man?"

"Not very old; six or seven-and-twenty, I should think."

"And a finical fine gentleman like the other, I'll be sworn."

"I don't believe I know what 'finical' means," said Susan. "Mr. Blake is a fine gentleman, I am sure."

"And you walked alone with this man till the stars shone!" Collinson's face grew orange. "Pray go on. Let me hear the rest. Let me hear the conclusion of this charming evening."

"Oh, well, I don't think there is much more to tell," said Susan, serenely. She was too blind to notice Tom's change of color, and he had managed to hold his voice tolerably under control. "We came in, and had music. Portia played first, then I sang—we sang, rather, Mr. Blake and I." Her companion flung his cigar into the middle of the road. "I dare say you know the duet? a very old one, 'Drink to me only with thine eyes.'"

"Oh, a very old one!" said Collinson. "A very old duet—a very old story." Still he managed not to betray himself by his voice. "After this came more star-gazing, naturally?"

" No," said Susan, "after this came rain. It began to rain, if you remember, about eleven o'clock, and the night turned sultry. That was when I went home."

" Alone ? "

" Mr. Blake saw me home. I was very glad he did. Miss Jemima said, at first, that Jekyll should take me, and I felt so frightened—I always feel frightened of grand men servants."

" But you were not at all afraid of Mr. Blake ? "

" Oh, no."

The "no" with an emphasis that shut up Collinson's lips during the whole remainder of the walk. He was not, it must be remembered, hovering about Susan with mere boyish admiration or idle gallantry. For a good many weeks now his fancy for her had daily been strengthening into very genuine passion— of its kind. And the thought of another man, a man superior in birth and at- tainments to himself, having taken starlit walks, sung love songs with the girl, caused him acutest jealousy. He lit no fresh cigar to succeed the one that he had flung away; neither whistled nor sang; asked no more questions; only walked on at such a pace as made Susan breathless in her attempts to keep up with him, and tortured himself over what he had heard ; tortured himself into a state of acuter misery, probably, than he would have felt for cause so slight had his nature been a more refined one. Those who love coarsely suspect coarsely ; but they suffer on a like hearty scale. Doubtful, if any of the deli- cate hidden suspicions of nobler minds can surpass in positive pain the physical kind of jealousy of a man like Collinson.

And he had to go through plenty of it, to listen to a hundred new hints of that which he hated most to believe, before the evening was over. When they reached home they found Eliza in the parlor, heated and anxious, but trying her best to look as though she had passed the day in elegant idleness ; and the min- ute they sat down to dinner Susan was put through a sharp cross-examination concerning what poor Miss Collinson called the "company rules" at the Manor. Miss Jemima poured out tea herself? Never ! At Lady Long's—what a mouth- ful Miss Collinson contrived to make out of those two short words—at Lady Long's tea was invariably handed round by the page. Were the ladies in high dresses or low ? Who were the guests besides Susan ? What ? gentlemen, both unmarried gentlemen ! And then, again, Susan had to tell of the walk by the river, and of the stars, and the duet, and the rain which obliged Mr. Blake to see her home ; at all of which Miss Collinson, not being in love or jealous, nat- urally made little jokes, such as, " No wonder Susan blushed ! No wonder Su- san was looking in such good spirits this afternoon !" The mildest, silliest little jokes even Miss Collinson was capable of, but which made Tom feel closely inclined to murder her.

He did not, for a long time, interrupt ; neither reminded his sister she was a fool, nor bade her hold her tongue, as was his wont. Some horrible at- traction seemed to exist for him in hearing George Blake's name spoken, in hearing Susan questioned about him, in watching her face color and dimple shyly under Miss Collinson's weak attempts at banter. Only—only as he sat, silently eating his roast goose, the thought which two hours before had been a vague temptation, quickly put aside, rapidly began to take the form of set resolve in Tom Collinson's heart. If no George Blake had appeared upon the scene things might have gone on indefinitely in their present fashion. have gone on (he would say, and believe all this, later) until the girl had left the neighborhood, or till his own fancy for her had cooled. It was the prospect of a rival that

really gave him the final fatal push into all that followed ; and Eliza, for setting
that prospect with such hateful clearness before his eyes, might take to herself
as much credit or as much blame as she chose.

"You are very silent to-day, Mr. Collinson," remarked Susan, when the dinner was nearly over. "I never heard you talk so little before."

"Tom does love a goose so," said Miss Collinson, looking at him with affec-
tionate eyes as he helped himself to a last scraping of stuffing and gravy.
"Father was the same. 'Never expect me to talk,' father used to say, 'when
I've got a goose before me.'"

"And never expect me to talk when I've got a *fool* before me !" roared Collinson, glaring across the table at his sister. "It takes away a man's taste for
talk, I can tell you, Eliza, to hear such stuff as you go on with. And before
the girl too !" Betsey at this moment had clattered off to the kitchen for the
pudding plates. "I wonder a woman of your years isn't ashamed to make such
a ninnyhammer of herself."

The admonition took instant and salutary effect on Miss Collinson. She
knew not in what her offence lay ; but she knew her master was offended ; and
with a meek, "I'm sure I'm very sorry, Tom," lapsed into silence : a condition,
it must be said, of quite as real suffering to her as is a superfluity of foolish
talking to the ears of wisdom.

Susan looked on, shocked and half-frightened, at the little domestic scene.
During her seventeen years of life a coarse, harsh word had never once reached
her ears before, and in her heart she shrank—oh, if he had known how she
shrank !—from Tom Collinson. She would not belong to this man, she thought
—no, not to have the riches of the world—to have Addison Lodge for her own !
And even as she thought this she raised her eyes involuntarily to his face—his
round, red face, choking with anger, or the closeness of the parlor, or roast
goose, or all combined—and remembered George Blake. It was unfortunately
not the last time in Susan Fielding's life when the contrast between these two
men was destined to strike her—to Tom Collinson's detriment.

Directly dinner was over the young man went out into the street to console
himself with tobacco. He had a habit—men often acquire the like on long
voyages—of pacing up and down a space about as limited as a quarter-deck,
while he smoked ; so Miss Collinson and Susan, sitting at the open parlor window, had the benefit of his strong cigar almost as directly at first hand as
though he had remained indoors.

"Poor, dear fellow," said Eliza, under her breath, and looking out at him
with maternal pride. "Tom is a little hasty, as you saw at dinner—and I'm
sure the goose was a fine, tasty bird, and roast to a turn ; I can't think what
upset him—but such a heart ! You wouldn't believe what an excellent heart
Tom's is."

Susan felt the act of faith was beyond her, so kept silence.

"So generous, so outspoken ! All Tom's faults lie on the surface, Susan."

"Do they indeed, ma'am ?" Susan had not got over the old school-room
fashion of addressing Miss Collinson. "I know Mr. Collinson very little, but
I'm sure he seems most—obliging." She would have liked to please Eliza by
some stronger expression, but could not find one ready to her use. "I'm sorry
he should have gone to the expense of this handsome locket for me. I never
wore anything so fine in my life."

Miss Collinson glanced, not without a pang of natural regret, at the locket,
over which so many girlish tears had been shed, so many middle-aged regrets

vainly spent. "My dear," said she, a certain tremor in her voice, "when Tom wishes to make a present he does not think of expense, nor yet, perhaps, at all times, of the fitness of the gift. Nothing is too good for him, nothing too dear. Still, still," said poor Eliza, meekly, "it certainly showed a great deal of nice feeling in him to remember your birthday at all ! "

"But a present a quarter the value would have pleased me just as well," said Susan. "And then to think that your brother should have gone to London on purpose to buy it ! O, Miss Collinson, I'm sure I should feel more comfortable if you would let me give the locket back. I'm sure papa would never have let me keep it ! "

Tom Collinson, who had been listening to every word they said, now stopped short before the window. "What do you say to a walk, Eliza ?" he asked. His cigar seemed to have done him good, for his tone was more than ordinarily amiable toward his sister. "How would it be to have tea early and walk across to Barham Firs ? What do you say, Miss Fielding ? We can stop out there as long as you like, and drop you at Addison Lodge on our way home."

Susan caught at the proposal : a horrible foreboding that she would have to walk home alone across the heath with Tom had been haunting her all the afternoon. "I should like it very much, please. I haven't seen the sun set from Barham yet this summer ; I dare say to-night will be the last time I shall ever go there while I live," she added, with a sigh.

As she spoke she leaned her head out through the open parlor window, and the evening light fell full upon her little crape-clad figure, burnishing her brown curls into bronze, giving lustre to her great blind eyes, shining on the pearls, Tom's gift, that hardly exceeded in whiteness the childish throat wherefrom they depended. Tom Collinson's heart gave a throb of exultation as he looked at her. During the last quarter of an hour he had been steadily bringing himself up to the determination with which he had dallied so long ; had been resolving, cost what it might, to make Susan his. And now, at this moment, the girl in her fresh fairness, so close before him, and all unpleasant things and possibilities so far, he felt almost as one might feel who has gained a painful victory over himself, who, after long vacillation, has elected to do the thing that is right. It *was* right to love anything so absolutely innocent as Susan Fielding ! Loving her, it was right to declare himself like a man and stand boldly by the result. She was friendless, poor, fretting after the old home she was to quit for ever, and he could give her protection, love, home : all she needed. That he happened to be, himself, penniless, was a matter of ridiculous accidental detail. As a married man, it would be advisable to look about for work, certainly ; and in the meantime to have the use of Eliza's house was the next best thing to having a house of one's own. Aye, the matter should be clinched without delay. There should, if he could help it, be no more of these evenings spent at the Manor ; these walks by starlight ; this practising of love-songs with empty-headed London coxcombs. He had spoken already to Eliza about asking Susan to stay with them for a few days while the sale went on at her old home, and to-night this invitation should be made formally. Once under the same roof, and Tom Collinson had too good an opinion of his own charms to doubt that Susan Fielding, that any woman, could be brought to like him. Like him ! Did not a dozen signs—the small coquetry even of wearing his birthday gift—show how frail were the obstacles he had to apprehend on that score ?

He was softer, quieter, less like Tom Collinson, than Susan had ever seen him yet, throughout the remainder of the evening. She began to tolerate him

(During that first rose-flushed stage of feeling through which poor little Susan was passing, human beings are so disposed to charitable toleration of everything—of everybody!) He actually apologized, after his fashion, to Eliza, for having been rude to her at dinner; during the whole course of their walk neither smoked nor talked loud, nor bent down his face to Susan's, as was his wont: he sat quiet, a little apart, and let her enjoy the sunset almost as she used in old days with her father from the Firs; and not until dusk had come, not until they were standing before the gate of Addison Lodge, spoke—in a hesitating voice, a voice oddly unlike his own—about the projected visit.

"Eliza and I have been thinking, Miss Fielding—we have been talking about the sale at Addison Lodge, you know, Eliza, and—"

"And how you really ought to remain on the spot, Susan, or near," chirped Miss Collinson. "Hackitt is an excellent auctioneer; *as* an auctioneer I haven't a word to say against him. Still, when Aunt Hannah's things were sold it was remarked that the fish-kettle, good as new, went for eighteen-pence, and that Mr. Hackitt's sister bought it. The honestest people alive are honester for watching, so what we both think is, that you had better come and spend a few days with us instead of leaving the neighborhood at once, and I or Tom would attend the sale and check Mr. Hackitt off in the corner of the catalogue. You could write to Mr. Goldney about it to-morrow."

Susan hesitated: only yesterday the prospect of going to a strange home far away in France, had revolted her less than the thought of staying under the same roof with Tom Collinson. But during the last twenty-four hours all her opinions, all her prejudices, seemed to be modified. If she accepted Miss Collinson's invitation she would, in reality, be never troubled by Tom; she began to recollect Tom would be away half his time, in London, or elsewhere, and she and Eliza be left peacefully alone. And then she would still be in Halfont Parish, still within a walk of the bridge and the canal, and still, whispered her heart, there would be a chance of seeing Mr. Blake on his road to Portia!

"Come to us, Miss Susan," pleaded Collinson, eagerly. "Don't refuse Eliza, as you did me yesterday. We will do our best to make you comfortable.'

"I don't like to seem so changeable, but if Mr. Goldney says yes. I know, I know I should like to come," said Susan. "You are both very kind to me; I have enjoyed our walk so much," and as she spoke she kissed Miss Collinson, then turned and held out her hand to Tom. "It seems to me the world is getting full of friends!" she told him, softly; and Collinson felt her small hand flutter as he pressed it.

She was thinking of George Blake.

CHAPTER XIII

"Tom," burst out Miss Collinson, when they had got about midway across the heath, "I know you'll be angry with me for what I am going to say, but I must speak, I can't go a step further without speaking."

"Speak out, then," said Collinson, but not in the bullying tone he generally employed toward his sister, "speak out. Your boots pinch you. You know you always will wear them too small."

"Susan Fielding is beginning to care too much for you."

He stopped short; he rested his hand down heavily on Eliza's shoulder

"Are you thinking of what you say?" he asked, almost in a whisper. "Are you talking folly, as you did to her at dinner, or do you mean it?"

"I mean it as solemnly as I ever meant anything in my life," Eliza answered. "I may be a fool in some things, but I do know—every woman knows—something about affairs of the heart. When I saw Susan a week ago she was a child, and now—"

"Now?"

"She is a child no longer. The very expression of her face is changed. She looks twenty times in the glass when before she looked once. She asked me up stairs if I liked her best in a bonnet or a hat. Her grief for her father is —I won't say over—but altogether lightened. Did you hear, more than once, how heartily she laughed?"

"And—and—" Tom Collinson stammered, and felt himself blushing violently in the dark, "you mean to say, then—"

"I mean to say," answered Miss Collinson, with decision, "that Susan is beginning to care for some one better than for herself. I couldn't reason about it, but I know it to be a fact. We must never have her to stay with us, Tom. It all burst upon me as we were crossing the bridge, and I've been turning over in my mind what I ought to do. Susan must never come and stay in our house."

"And why not?" said Tom; but he felt a cold perspiration start thick over his face as he spoke—felt that he drew his breath unevenly. During the last three hours he had been smoothing everything beautifully to his conscience, still he had not bargained for this; for having, without a moment's warning, to commit himself by speech to the thing he meant to do! "Why shouldn't she come and stay with us just the same?"

"You ask me that, brother?"

"Don't you hear that I ask it?"

"Then I should think your own common-sense might give you an answer," Miss Collinson cried, with energy; "but men are like that; men, even the best of them, are like that! A passing gratification to their vanity, and no matter if a woman's happiness has to pay for it! No matter that Susan Fielding should suffer, so long as you were amused for a fortnight, Tom!"

"And suppose"—what a wrench it cost him to bring the words out—"suppose I have no intention that Susan Fielding should suffer! that I care for her as much—that I care for her more, a hundredfold, than she can care for me?"

For once in her life Eliza Collinson stood speechless. From the list of possibilities, virtuous or the reverse, that her heart had ever predicted for Tom, the one possibility of marriage had been rigidly excluded. She had never admitted to herself the actual suspicion of her brother possessing a wife; had never renewed the question so curtly put aside by him on the first night of his arrival. Still (by one of those processes without form or syllogism, through which we are told the feminine intelligence does form conclusions) Eliza Collinson's mind had arrived at the conviction that Tom was not a free man. Mr. Mildmay, the curate, had years ago quitted Halfont for some foreign chaplaincy; she had, therefore, no channel of information, save through Tom himself, as to the past. But the little he did from time to time let fall, the soreness with which he shrank from any allusion to his New Zealand life, had been sufficient to convince her that there was "something wrong" in his relations with the people he had left behind there; some other story of wrong-doing besides that of the man who, according to Tom's own account, had wrought his ruin.

"I'm so surprised I can't get out a word! You—you in love with poor little

Susan Fielding! and here have I been asking her to dinner and everything! People will say I encouraged it—and Mr. Fielding, my best friend, scarce cold in his grave. Oh, I don't think I've deserved this!" And Miss Collinson's voice gave premonition of tears.

"Eliza," exclaimed Tom, harshly, "before you let loose the flood-gates, perhaps you'll have the goodness to tell me what you are making so much noise about? I'll be hanged if I know. Susan Fielding is a pretty girl, and I like her—well, am in love with her, if you choose. What next? Because the women of a family don't marry is no reason that I ever heard of for the men remaining bachelors."

"Marry—you! Do you mean—am I to think that you mean marriage?"

"A pretty question, upon my word!" cried Collinson, with a laugh. "Leave ultra-proper people alone for having ultra-improper thoughts! What the dickens should I mean but marriage, Miss Collinson?"

"Well, you see, I never thought of you as a marrying man! I mean," cried Eliza, with a feeble burst of courage, "I looked upon you so long in my own mind *as* a married man—eighteen months, you must remember—that even now I can scarce believe you have not got a wife, and—"

She was interrupted by an oath from Collinson; an oath not especially loud, but that sounded unpleasantly emphatic in the dead silence of the heath. "And you've been talking to Susan, this way, I'll be sworn! Let me find you trying that game on at your peril! You drove me to the bad with your canting piety, when I was a boy. I told you so the first night I returned, and I repeat it again. You drove me to the bad before I knew what bad was; and now, if you keep that girl from me, you'll finish the work well. What does an old maid like you know of men's lives, of men's temptations? What business have you to interfere in this at all? I love Susan Fielding—you don't know the meaning of the word, still I choose to repeat it to you—I love Susan Fielding, and I mean to marry her, to work for her, to reform for her. If you stand between us, you'll stand between me and my last chance of becoming an altered man. Now, do as you will!"

Having relieved his own uneasy conscience by this small outburst of injustice, Tom Collinson felt better, and marched on along the path, leaving Eliza to follow him or not as she choose. She followed him; overtook him; stole up her hand, not without trembling anticipation of rebuff, under his arm: "I've never said a word of you to Susan but what was good, my dear!" All out of breath the poor woman jerked forth her contrition. "If my influence demoralized you, as you so often tell me it did, when you were young, it was through ignorance. I tried my best. I don't suppose I understood boys' natures—I don't suppose I understand any one's nature. When poor Mr. Fielding's affairs are settled, Susan will have about forty pounds a year, or under, and you have nothing, and I had taken it into my head you were not a marrying man. Forgive me, Tom."

Tom Collinson burst into a laugh. "So—the cat's out of the bag at last, then," he cried. "You are afraid of having to support, not only me, but my wife." The word, this time, came out tolerably glibly. "Set your mind at rest, Eliza. My notion of domestic bliss is not to reside with a spinster sister, I can tell you. When I marry, I'll live in my own house, and be master of it, too; no fear!"

Mr. Collinson did not trouble himself to state where the house should be, neither did he specify by what particular branch of labor he meant to support it;

but he said enough to convince Eliza that on the day of his marriage with Susan Fielding he would be a reformed man. He would abandon brandy-and-water, smoking, extravagance of all kinds ; would take steadfastly to work ; in her declining years, his sister's home (she had had this promise made to her once before) should be under his roof. The prospective generosity to herself Miss Collinson appraised, perhaps, at its true value, but she believed, with all the faith of her upright heart, in the blessing an honorable love might work for Tom ; and by the time she reached home was deep in speculation as to whether her lavender silk, turned, would do to wear at the wedding, also whether they could contrive without a waiter for the breakfast or not !

"I know, of course, this house would not be large enough for a married couple," she remarked before they parted for the night. "Still, I could sleep very comfortably with Betsey, and turn my room into another sitting-room. So just at first, 'till you find anything bigger and get settled, I hope you won't mind staying here ? "

A proposal that Tom instantly and magnanimously accepted. That Susan's voice was still unheard in the matter did not trouble him. He was no diffident or despondent lover. His own mind was made up finally : Eliza won over, any little difficulty regarding Susan's consent would be solved by a week spent together under the same roof ; for Tom, like most persons of his stamp, had unbounded belief in the power of propinquity.

"I'm turning over a new leaf and no mistake," he thought, as he smoked his last pipe on the doorstep, under the clear June night. "Why did I shilly-shally so long. Isn't the past done with as much as if I had lived it out in another world ? It was another world. There are not the same customs and opinions —hang it all ! there are not the same stars even, here in England, as there were in New Zealand ! "

The idea of utter separation conveyed by that difference in the stars was really comforting. At three-and-twenty, Tom Collinson's intellect and moral sense were not very much more advanced than they had been at fifteen. What social obligation *could* exist between a Christian man in England and people who lived at the antipodes ? Did not the weight of the whole globe constitute a burial as final as seven feet of soil in a churchyard ? Was his happiness, was poor little Susan's happiness to be sacrificed because there was one chance in a thousand of a certain ugly ghost not keeping quiet in its grave ? Did not most men, did not the very best men go to the altar with some uncomfortable secret, some lurking memory not altogether suited to a marriage feast ?

Thinking these things Tom took another long look at the consolatory stars ; then went away, whistling the last music-hall air, to his bed—"Poor fellow, beginning early hours already," thought Eliza—and, whatever the sins that ought to have weighed upon his conscience, slept the sleep of a school-boy.

CHAPTER XIV

TOWARD three o'clock next day, and just as Susan was beginning to look out for Tom Collinson's figure between the hollies, a little three-cornered note arrived for her from the Manor.

"MY DEAR SUSAN,—Will you come and see me, and stay to five o'clock tea? Aunt Jemima has gone to town to fight the great fight with grandmamma, and I am alone and unhappy in my mind—I would have asked you to lunch, only grandpapa does not like to be watched as he eats his sage. A heap of the trousseau finery has arrived, perhaps you may care to see it.

"PORTIA.

"I shall give orders for you to be brought up straight to my den, and if you come directly you will not be likely to meet grandpapa."

The postscript was so reassuring that Susan, without a second's delay, ran off to the Manor, where, to her infinite relief, a housemaid, not the dreaded Jekyll, answered her modest single knock at the front door. She was shown up at once to Portia's "den;" a sunny little room on the second floor, containing one luxurious lounging chair, two cheval glasses, a glass above the chimney-piece, and curtains of the exact shade of crimson that suited Portia Ffrench's complexion. No ornaments, no flowers, no work-table; none of the little feminine rubbish by which Susan, if she had the means, would have delighted to surround herself. Warmth, ease, mirrors, becoming drapery against which to test the merit of new dresses, these were necessities to Portia Ffrench, and these she had taken care to secure—nothing beyond. The "den" was characteristic.

She was sitting beside the window, neither reading nor working, a certain anxious flushed look on her handsome face. "Susan, you good little thing to come. I'm bored—bored to death; so I thought I would try if boring some one else would do me any good. Take off your bonnet, child, sit down, and amuse me. I'm sorry I have only one arm chair."

Susan obeyed the first two commands at once. "As to amusing," she remarked, "I shouldn't say talk like mine could ever amuse any one. Certainly not you."

"And why not me, with such an accent?"

"Because you have seen more than I have, and have got more than I have; have got—oh, Miss Portia, I think you have got everything the world can give!"

"I have got," said Portia, "this easy chair; yes, it is legally mine, was given me by Aunt Jemima, I can take it away when I marry, (when I marry! of course you know that the whole thing is problematic, Susan? that I am at this moment waiting to hear whether grandmamma says yes or no?) a case full of not very valuable trinkets; an embroidery frame; a set of tools for wood-carving; every size of tatting needle, and a dozen or so silk dresses; just the sort of collection you see advertised in the exchange department of the Lady's newspaper. With possessions like these what human heart could indeed feel satiety?"

"But I think you have got a great deal more," cried Susan. "I wasn't thinking of dresses and trinkets. You have got—yourself." This was not in the least what she had meant to say; she meant, "you have beauty, you have grace, charm of manner, wit—qualities that can win as many hearts as you choose to conquer!" But something in the mocking expression of Portia's face chilled her, and she stopped short.

"Myself!" repeated Portia with a laugh. "Yes, I have indeed got myself, and fearfully sick I am of the bargain. Susan, has it never occurred to you what a shocking injustice it is to be born a woman? By no fault of one's own to be cramped and whaleboned—I don't mean physically; taught nothing worth knowing, although one's capacities are as good as a man's; given nothing to do, although one's desire for action is as strong as a man's; and then told to be contented! When I was a small child I remember getting hold of an unfortunate bird once, a robin, I think it was. I wasn't very cruel, as children go, and I determined to make his life happy, fitted up an old cage of Aunt Jem's with the tables and chairs out of my doll's house, gave him water, food, a looking-glass even; arranged fresh leaves and flowers over his head. The poor wretch beat his breast passionately for four-and-twenty hours against the bars, then died, happily for himself!"

"But some birds like living in cages," said Susan, diffidently. "Our bullfinch never used to beat himself, and he ate his food hearty, and liked his looking-glass, too. I would ever so much rather be a woman than a man. Everything in women's lives is so nice." (Pardon the school-girl word, reader. It accurately expresses Susan's meaning.) "Women wear prettier clothes than men, and have no hard work, for needle-work and everything about a house is really play, and then they need never go into danger. Think of having to hunt or fight! Think of having to kill people as a duty, think of being cruel to animals as an amusement, and then say if you could wish to be a man!"

"I have said it always, and I shall say and feel it always," answered Portia. "There are birds and birds, as you remark, and I am not a bullfinch. I was not born for a cage."

"And you would like to hunt—to go to battle—to smoke?" cried Susan, with solemn emphasis upon that awful climax.

"Most undoubtedly I would," said Portia. "Fighting is the great natural instinct of rational beings, and when they can't have it in earnest they imitate it by cards or dice, or pursuing the lower creatures. As to smoking, it is really monstrous—monstrous! that woman should be debarred from a means, the only one we know of, by which persons without brains or work can be stupified into enduring the weight of their own existence."

Portia Ffrench, it is just to say, had never tasted the flavor even of a paper cigarette. Her theories were theories only.

Susan's eyes opened wider than usual. "But why should existence be a weight?" she cried. "I know nothing about what men feel or need, but why should a woman want anything who has got home—home and some one to love her and take care of her!"

"Love!" said Portia, with a little curl of the lip. "Such love as falls to a woman's share! Two months of courtship, say; a fortnight's honeymoon; six weeks of waning adoration; and then a kind of pitying friendly toleration, if she is very lucky, 'till the curtain falls. Love is an interlude—a very pretty one, we'll admit—with men. How, with all the wire-drawing in the world, can it be made to spread over the five mortal acts of an ordinary woman's life?"

"I've never been to the play," said Susan, with a humble sense of her own deficiencies, "but I have heard of many women who were made happy for life by marrying the man they loved, even though he had not always been fond of them. There was Rowena, and Rose Bradwardine, and Amelia Booth, if you remember?"

Portia looked hard at the transparent girlish face of Susan Fielding; this daughter of a Brentford bookseller, amid whose prim little stock of humdrum beliefs there lurked a flavor, an intensity, beyond anything that her life, with all its variety, with all its manifest external advantages, could be made to yield. "Rose Bradwardine and Amelia Booth! You read love stories, then? You take an interest in the sentimental agonies, prolonged through three post octavo volumes, of imaginary young ladies and gentlemen?"

"I read nothing else," said Susan. "Except Robinson Crusoe, I don't think I was ever interested in any book that wasn't a love story."

"And I," said Portia, "can read no book in which love is not kept, as it ought to be, well in the background. I'm not intellectual. I can't read, as Aunt Jemima says young women used to do, to inform my mind. When I read, as when I do everything, it is for excitement. And love, as the novelist treats it, is not exciting!"

"Ah, you can afford to say all this," cried Susan, with a half-sigh. "You, who have nothing but love in your own life, don't need to read about it in stories of other people."

"Well—there, perhaps, you hit upon the truth," answered Portia, dryly. "So much love in my own life! Heaven help you, in your innocence, Susan. What love have I got?"

"Mr. Josselin's."

"Poor Teddy! As much as he can like anything that is not Teddy Josselin I do believe he likes me, and I know he will let me have my own way when—if we marry. And then our tastes are the same. We shall run about (together or separate)—that is to say, searching for amusement and spending our money, and not come to a worse end than most people, probably. But love! Ted Josselin's love!"

"Well, then," exclaimed Susan, quickly, "there is Mr. Blake. You can only feel sorry for him, of course, because you know all his devotion is hopeless. Still, it is yours." And having said this, she colored up to the eyes and hung her head.

Portia watched her narrowly. "And you think that all Mr. Blake's devotion, as you call it, is of the slightest value, gives the slightest additional happiness to Portia Ffrench? Mr. Blake goes in for being hopeless and desperate, of set purpose, Susan. It yields him an emotion, an experience that he may use professionally. If I lay in my coffin to-morrow he would go into rhapsodies of grief—gain another experience! write a copy of verses to tell the world what he suffered, and fall in love with a milk-maid, five feet high, next week. No; I may be vain myself, but I am not so foolish as to mistake the symptoms of men's vanity for love. Mr. Blake, in reality, loves Portia Ffrench—just as much as Portia Ffrench loves him."

"That is," said Portia, pausing a little, to prolong the eagerness of her companion's look, "is—oh, why am I so bad at definition, and why are you so much in earnest, Susan? Surely, you have not fallen a victim to Mr. Blake's

melancholy tenor voice and Lara-like sighs? I ought to have guessed there
would be danger the moment you began singing sentimental duets together.
What did he say as he took you home, child? Something very tender and sentimental, I am certain?"

"Please don't laugh at me—please don't say such things," exclaimed Susan,
half ready to cry. "Mr. Blake was good-natured to me because I was your
friend, I suppose. I don't know why he was good-natured to me. I never was
in love with any one; I'm too young to be in love. I hope you'll never joke
me like that again!"

And all the hot shame of a child, whose poor little foolish secrets have been
discovered by mature, superior wisdom, burned on Susan's cheeks.

"Too young to be in love?" said Portia, growing amused. "Why, how old
are you? Within a year or two of my age, for certain, and I—oh, I have been
in and out of love the last five years."

"But I am only seventeen," said Susan, shyly; and then, desperately wanting to get away from the subject of her walk home with Mr. Blake, she added,
"and, if you please, I would much rather we should talk about you—not myself—
Miss Portia. May I see the finery you told me of? I have never seen any
wedding dresses in my life."

"And wedding dresses are quite unlike all others, you know," said Portia.
"Satin, and silks, and laces that are to be worn by a bride are invested with a
dim religious light that distinguishes them from all common apparel! That is
the reason why young ladies flock to gaze and comment upon each other's trousseaux. In the event of my not being married, Susan—very much the most
likely event to happen—mind you tell no one that you saw the wedding garments.
I remember when Alice Long did not marry Charlie Craven, people used to say
forever afterward: 'Ah, here comes another of the wedding dresses. Poor,
dear little Alice, what a trial for her to have to wear out her trousseau under such
altered circumstances!' Now, I don't like to be pitied. Whatever falls to me
I like to bear it by myself, and make no sign."

As she spoke, Portia rose and led Susan into the adjoining bedroom. It was
piled thick in finery. Even at Miss Budd's, the first milliner shop in Brentford,
Susan had never found herself among so many pretty things before. Delicate
silks and muslins, fine embroidery, costly laces, were everywhere.

"It may be very well for people, generally, to suspend marriage expenses
till they know whether a marriage is possible," said Portia. "For me, the most
undoubted wisdom was to obtain all I could while grandpapa was in a humor for
spending—'tis a humor that grows rarer with him every year. Ten to one, Lady
Erroll will laugh at the whole thing; ten to one, Aunt Jemima is here in an
hour's time with word that the engagement is at an end forever. Still, I shall
not be utterly bereft. I shall have my embroidery, my silks, my laces—and it is
something to have brave clothes to wear above a broken heart. Look at them,
Susan, if such things amuse you, and wake me when you have finished."

She sank down with her usual worn-out air upon a sofa beside the window,
and closed her eyes. Dress, as dress, was less than nothing to Portia Ffrench.
She valued it as a means, an auxiliary to her beauty, a passport to her pleasures;
something, like bright smiles or witty talk, to be put on of necessity, while she
played her part in the world, and flung wearily aside the moment she quitted
the foot-lights. Of the feminine instinct that derives pleasure from soft hues
and fabrics, from satin-stitch and Honiton, for themselves, she was simply devoid.
She cared no more for such things than she would have cared for pictures and

flowers and ornaments in a room that no one saw. And Susan possessed this instinct to the fullest extent; Susan, with her village bringing up—whose first little part in life's drama was played but yesterday! So bewilderingly divergent from what you would expect are human characters, the moment you begin to take them in detail.

At the end of another ten minutes—Susan still absorbed in millinery—there came the sound of carriage wheels along the gravel drive. Portia jumped up eagerly. "My fate is hanging in the balance, Susan—don't wonder at my excitement. Now, how does Aunt Jem look? Veil down—that's a bad sign to begin with—and Teddy Josselin with her; a worse one still! To-day is the Rawdons' garden party; Ted would never have absented himself from that without cause. Susan, Susan, I predict the worst! Aunt has thrown up her veil and I can see her face. Our side has lost."

She drew back her head, ran up to the glass and smoothed her untidy hair; then took a knot of scarlet velvet from the dressing-table, and pinned it in her white dress. "No need to look ugly because one is defeated, Susan. If the king is dead, may his successor arise! say I."

"Oh, Portia, I don't understand you," cried Susan. "I don't know how you can have courage to talk lightly at such a time."

"Courage!" said Portia, turning round her dark face with a smile as she left the room. "Oh, whatever my sins may be, cowardice is not one of them. If the worst comes to the worst—follow me to the drawing-room in half an hour and you will know it—if the worst comes to the worst I shall still possess my trousseau. remember, all the silks and laces you admire so much, Susan, and— and one thing more!"

"What is that?" cried Susan, solemn-eyed.

"Mr. Blake's devotion."

Susan's heart stood still!

CHAPTER XV.

FOURTEEN years before the time of which I write, Colonel Ffrench had sworn a bitter oath that his grand-daughter Portia should never hold communication with any member of her mother's family while he lived.

The one natural affection, the one unselfish feeling of Richard Ffrench's heart had, undoubtedly, been his feeling for his eldest son. Harry's ruin, Harry's shameful death, had inflicted upon him a blow under which all his worldly cynical philosophy could offer him no support; and the first instructive self-shielding outcry of his own stricken conscience had been an outcry against the Dysarts. But for their influence he had not been estranged from his son; but for the Dysarts his Harry had lived! They were his murderers. These things Colonel Ffrench spoke in his first excess of grief—that awful, blind grief of a man without belief beyond the hour wherein he grieves—he repeated them in colder blood until he came, not only to regard them as true, but to cling to them with a kind of sullen sense of consolation. Harry's child might be brought under his roof. Let her forget the name of the mother who bore her, let it be an understood thing that she should scarcely know what blood ran in her veins, and Harry's child might be saved from growing up a Dysart. Little as he liked children generally, it seemed to him that he might like, might at least support the presence of this one, could some portion of his hatred of her mother's race be only instilled into her heart! And, as we have seen, Portia came. Came,

and in spite of her grace, her cleverness, her likeness to Harry, her want of affection for her mother, awakened very slight feeling one way or the other in Colonel Ffrench's breast.

During their journey to Halfont good Miss Jemima took due care to tutor
the child into what she should do and say on first seeing her grandfather. "He
is an old gentleman, Portia—nay, never say you don't like old gentlemen; that
is not pretty to say; an old man with his head bowed down low; and you must
run, with your arms held up, and offer to kiss him, and say, 'Grandpapa, love
me for my own papa's sake.'" And Portia, even at six years old being a charming little actress, had carried out these instructions to the letter: the upheld
arms, proffered lips—all.

"She has learned her lesson well," said Colonel Ffrench, turning coldly
away. "Have her kept to the nursery, Jemima. I don't see the likeness you
told me of."

Upon this, Portia, with her baby vanity sore wounded, with confirmed dis-
taste for old gentlemen, was at once hurried from her grandfather's presence,
and from that day until the present had never heard another expansive word
from his lips! He treated her while she was little with a cool, half-sarcastic ci-
vility that would have galled a more sensitive child into positive hatred of him;
as she grew to be a woman, was unvaryingly scrupulously polite to her; no more.
His last flickering capacity for strong feeling had, in very truth, been buried in
Harry's dishonored grave. For Harry's girl he cared nothing; not even enough
to seek to keep up, through her, his enmity toward her mother's family. Years
went on; Colonel Ffrench becoming more and more indifferent to every subject
but gout, and the diet gout involves; and now at one-and-twenty, Portia not only
spent six weeks of every season in her grandmother's house, but was engaged
to marry her first cousin, a Dysart, Colonel Ffrench acquiescent!

In the constitution of some very old men the instincts survive the affections
by a quarter of a century or so. Colonel Ffrench was thus constituted: and
love of rank, worship of titles and of titled people, were really instincts with
him. Harry's bright face belonged to the past, the past in which so many other
fair things, effaced now from the old man's weak memory, had been shipwrecked.
The name of the Dowager Countess of Erroll was still written in the Peerage,
still connected *him* with the world where his treasure, where his heart had been
in his youth. And so the first time that Miss Jemima dared, tremblingly, to
make mention of the Dysart name, a year or so after the death of Lady Portia
Molyneux, she found, to her astonishment, that Richard, then confined to his
sofa with gout, was in just as Christian a frame of mind as she, honest soul, by
stout endeavor—aye, and by earnest prayer, had brought herself.

"The child is of the Dysart blood, as well as of ours, brother," she had
pleaded. "I have had more than one letter from her grandmother inviting Portia to stay with her, but never dared show them you, and now she has written to
me in the same spirit again. There are a few trinkets, it seems, that should
come to Portia from her mother, and these Lady Erroll makes the excuse for
writing. 'Tis her heart—her heart, of course, that yearns to see the child!"
said good Miss Jemima, "and I cannot feel it our duty as Christians to keep
them asunder."

"The Countess of Erroll's heart!" said old Colonel Ffrench, looking up,
with helpless malignity, from his cup of water-gruel. "My dear Jemima, let the
girl go, by all means. She turns her toes in, a London dancing-master will do
her good. But don't let you and me talk nonsense. Old Lady Erroll has no

more heart than she has honesty. Take my word for it, the trinkets will turn out paste."

And they did. On her return home from London, Portia, with infinite disgust, displayed her legacy to Miss Jemima, tossing each article aside with contempt as she showed it. "Paste brilliants, Cairngorm diamonds, miserable garnets, mock pearls ! 'Not things, possibly, of intrinsic worth,' says grandmamma, 'but invaluable as mementos.' As if I cared about mementos ! She is a painted old woman with a peacock voice, Aunt Jem, divides her time equally between squabbling over bills, going to church, and whist—I was reminded of Brussels —and there was *so* little to eat ! Still I amused myself. I went to the theatre four times. I learned to play cards. I heard naughty stories of every one of grandmamma's friends. My cousin, Ted Josselin, taught me to waltz. I amused myself, and I'll go again."

Thus, when Portia was a school girl of sixteen, began the renewal of intercourse between herself and her mother's family. Old Lady Erroll and Colonel Ffrench never met more (in this world), but some kind of half-conciliatory letter passed between them, and at distant intervals, thrice perhaps in two years, Miss Jemima would constrain herself to go up and partake of luncheon—cold in every sense of the word—under the Countess of Erroll's roof. Portia, as I have said, passed some weeks of every season at her grandmother's house. There was still very little to eat at that stately Eaton square table, with its services of plate, and servants in plush and powder ; and grandmamma was still a painted old woman with a peacock voice, dividing her time between rigid economy, her prayerbook, and the odd trick ; nevertheless, Portia found plenty to divert her during her town visits, and took special care to propitiate grandmamma while she paid them. The Countess of Erroll's countenance had been for her the open sesame to the world ; not such a decorous, humdrum world as was comprised in Miss Jemima's visiting list, but the world of London, as London has been any time during the last eight years—quite as piquant a phase of manners, in its way, as was that of the Regency—and with Dysart cousins of all degrees, as her instructors and friends. Play-going, dancing, card-playing, as many flirtations as she could compass, as much excitement as she could live under ; all this, and more, was crowded into a short six weeks, during which Portia annually escaped from Halfont dulness—for her grandmother was anything but an austere or vigilant duenna ; once away from Miss Jemima, once among her "Dysart associates," and Portia did pretty much as she chose with her time and with herself. Nor had her London visits been without serious and tangible results. Four several offers of undeniable settlements had been made to Portia Ffrench since that first season when she came out, a slim girl of eighteen, under the old Countess of Erroll's wing. And each time she had accepted ; played with her new suitor for a week, or a day ; then had a scene with her cousin Teddy, repented, broken off the engagement, and been sent down to Halfont in disgrace.

The last occasion on which this had occurred was during the present spring, just when poor Blake was also falling into captivity—the suitor this time a Glasgow manufacturer, very rich, very plain, very much in love, yet determined to "stand no nonsense" from any woman, earl's granddaughter or no, whom he should honor with his addresses. So, on the second day of his new happiness, the Scotchman thought fit to have an opinion ; found Teddy Josselin helping Portia in an employment they called gardening in the conservatory, and demurred. If Mr. Josselin wished to cut off the leaves of dead geraniums, he

might do so ; but not in such close neighborhood to the lady he—with an emphasis—meant to marry.

"You are jealous, Mr. Macbean," said Portia, with beautiful dignity ; "jealous of my cousin, who is more than a brother to me.   Good-by, and please take
away your ring," drawing a magnificent diamond from her finger.   "It was too
heavy for me from the first.

With a choking heart, but bearing his defeat manfully, the suitor departed.
Then Portia burst into tears.

"It was your fault, Ted ; everything's your fault ! I didn't hate him, not very
much—for a real lover, at least ; and, of course, you oughtn't to have been here."

"Shall I call him back ? " said Teddy, innocently.   "I think I hear his fairy
step still in the hall."

Upon this, Portia's lip quivered, and Teddy put down the scissors, and kissed
her deliberately.

"I don't see the slightest reason why *we* shouldn't be lovers," he said.
"You've been engaged to other fellows, and thrown them over for me.   Now be
engaged to me, and let any other fellow make you throw me over if he can ! "

They went down that moment, hand-in-hand, to the dining-room, where it
was old Lady Erroll's custom to spend her forenoons, looking over accounts—
butcher's, baker's, green-grocer's—detecting a cutlet too much here, a head of
sea-kale she could not remember there ; and Portia told her story bravely.   She
had quarrelled with one suitor more.   She had discarded the Scotchman and his
settlements.   Teddy and herself—a little tremble in her voice—had found out at
last that they liked each other.   Might they be engaged ?

Old Lady Erroll looked up—her finger still marking the place in her account-
book—from one young face to the other. "The last time this kind of folly occurred I was angry," she said, in her shrill old voice. "I'm not angry now.
Old people musn't waste their little residue of life upon useless emotion.   If you
had married Macbean, I would have left you ten thousand pounds in my will.
I told him so last night.   You are so much the richer, Ted."

"Which will come exactly to the same, if I marry Portia," remarked Teddy
Josselin.

"If ! "

This monosyllable, not agreeably uttered, was all the opposition Lady Erroll
offered.   So Portia and Teddy returned to their gardening ridiculously happy—
or perhaps amused might be a juster term ; and in four-and-twenty hours all the
town knew Mr. Macbean was supplanted, and by whom.

Old Lady Erroll received the many-colored remarks of her friends with complete equanimity. "Teddy is a little boy," she would say, placidly ; "is a dozen
years younger in sense and knowledge of the world than my granddaughter.
I don't trouble myself to think about flirtations between cousins.   Teddy might
spend his time worse."

She was unusually affable and obliging in her relations with Portia.   Certainly Mr. Blake might be asked to dinner—any friend of poor little Ted's was
welcome.   Ted knew very well the house and everything in it belonged to him.
To Teddy himself she was charming.   Who, under such circumstances, could
suspect that the good old octogenarian lady meant mischief ?   Well, Portia suspected it, for one ; but then Portia always suspected the worst of everybody.
"If grandmamma's intentions were honorable, she would not be so generous,"
Portia remarked to her lover. "She has given me a real onyx seal, slightly

chipped, and a couple of torn lace lappets. I can't feel easy in my mind with grandmamma in such abnormal dispositions."

But Teddy's peace was untroubled. A sounder philosopher than many wise men, Teddy Josselin never worried himself about any evil whatsoever until it had positively overtaken him. He was really fond of Portia, enjoyed being engaged to her nearly as much as he used to enjoy breaking off her engagements with other people, sincerely thought it would be about the best thing that could happen to him to marry her; at the same time was not a passionate or impatient lover; but content to let everything connected with his engagement shape itself as it would, the subject of money along with the rest. His present means of subsistence were his pay as a lieutenant in the Guards, and five hundred a year allowed him by Lady Erroll. His prospects for the future were from twenty-five thousand to thirty thousand pounds and the house in Eaton square, all dependent upon the will of Lady Erroll. Supposing her to turn refractory, he could thus depend with certainty upon the sum of seven shillings and four pence a day, upon which to maintain his establishment; for Colonel Ffrench had long ago declared that a handsome trousseau and a few hundred pounds in cash would be the only provision he could possibly make for his granddaughter.

Seven shillings and four pence a day—barely enough, with their present habits, to keep Portia and Mr. Josselin in gloves and bouquets. Well, Teddy declared the money part of the matter was not worth disturbing oneself about. See how he managed already! He had five hundred a year nominally; but when by accident he spent twice his allowance, never found any difficulty, to speak of, in getting his debts paid. There were always plenty of people to cash bills and so on, if your prospects were decent; and, besides, grandmamma must consent, in time: no one out of a play ever refused their consent to anything now-a-days. He had sounded her a score of times about his engagement, and her answer was always the same: "You know best, my poor little Teddy, you know best; don't consult me." Of course, if he knew best the thing was settled.

And so Miss Jemima was told that matters were progressing satisfactorily, and Colonel Ffrench's consent gained, for the fifth time, to Portia's approaching marriage; and a wildly-extravagant trousseau ordered by Portia herself before her London visit ended; all without the definite question being mooted as to the means upon which the young couple were to exist.

"We are happy in the present, taking no thought, like lilies," Teddy would say, in his foolish, innocent way, whenever Miss Jemima tried to bring him to business. "The bridesmaids' dresses are decided on, the trousseau is ordered. Now the only thing to think of is Gunter."

And, at last, one fine morning (just two days before the commencement of this story) he told Lady Erroll that she must really begin to see about ordering his wedding breakfast. "Colonel Ffrench is an invalid; and, as you are Portia's grandmamma as well as mine, we thought we would be married in town. A pleasant little party—not more than twenty people, and I'll undertake all trouble about the wine"—the Countess of Erroll's bad wine was proverbial—"I mean I'll undertake to see that we have it nice."

Old Lady Erroll looked, not without genuine compassion, on Teddy's fair, boyish face—the one object left in the world that gave her eyes pleasure to behold. "Teddy, child," said she, "am I to understand that those Ffrench people regard the engagement in any other light than a joke? They do? Ah! now, perhaps, you will tell me what you mean to support Portia Ffrench upon? You

don't know, of course. Very well. Then we old people will talk the matter
over for you. Tell old Jemima Ffrench—you are going there to-morrow, you
say—tell old Jemima Ffrench, with my love, that I shall expect her here to
lunch and to talk over settlements—you will use that word 'settlements'—at one
on Wednesday. Time enough to order the wedding breakfast afterward.'

CHAPTER XVI.

THE message was given duly; and, at the hour and day appointed, Jemima
Ffrench drove up in a cab before the Countess of Erroll's house. The good old
soldier was dressed as usual, in her plain village clothes; but no princess visiting a subject could have held her head higher than did Miss Jemima as she
marched up Lady Erroll's door-steps, and was ushered by a gorgeous six-foot-
high footman into Lady Erroll's dining-room.

The old countess was sitting at her writing table, an open desk at her side,
one or two packets of docketed faded letters upon the table. She rose, gave
Miss Jemima a little curtsy, that had been the mode in the days of George the
Third, and two withered fingers. "How are you, my dear? I haven't seen you
this age. You look pretty well, but people at our time of life don't grow younger
—don't grow younger! How is Colonel Ffrench?"

Miss Jemima seated herself very upright on a chair at some distance from
her hostess, and answered that her brother was in his usual feeble state. He
had not got into the open air three times this summer.

"But keeps his faculties, I trust?" said Lady Erroll. (To no one who
looked at her would it occur to ask a similar question. Seamed with wrinkles
though her face was, you could scarce believe it to be the face of a woman of
eighty. The keenness almost of youth was in her pale eyes; her hair, dressed
in small flat curls, was yellow still; her prominent teeth were still white, and
every one of them her own). "Poor Colonel Ffrench is not, I trust, growing
feeble in his mind," she continued, in her shrill piping voice, "the very worst
affliction we old people have to dread."

"My brother's mind is as strong as it ever was, I thank you," said Miss
Jemima, stiffer than before. "His memory fails him a little at times. That is
all."

Old Lady Erroll took out a gilt bonbon-box from her pocket, opened it, and
helped herself to a lozenge. She ate sweetmeats all day long; before her meals,
after her meals; Portia declared, while her meals were going on. At the kind
of conversational pause in which an old man takes snuff, out, invariably, came
Lady Erroll's bonbon-box. "I did not mean to offend you, my dear Miss
Ffrench, but something my little grandson Josselin told me made one fear poor
Colonel Ffrench must be somewhat enfeebled in his mental state. You can
guess what I mean?"

"Not in the least," said Miss Jemima, but her face turned very red.

"Why, about this love affair—flirtation, I should say—of Portia's and Ted's.
Surely, the boy must have hoaxed me. You can't be taking the thing in earnest,
any of you?"

Miss Jemima's face grew redder. "If we had not taken it in earnest, Mr
Josselin would never have come to our house in the way he has done latterly,"
said she, with energy.

"Oh, dear, dear, how guilty that makes me feel!" said Lady Erroll, with her shrill small laugh. "Why, I had them here together for weeks and weeks, and yet I knew that the whole thing was nonsense. Portia has behaved very foolishly, Miss Ffrench. I hid my annoyance at the time, but I don't know when I have felt more vexed. Macbean was no vulgarer than half the men you meet in society now-a-days, and his offers of settlements were most liberal. Portia may wait long before she meets with as eligible an offer, taking it altogether, as Macbean's."

Indignation, for a moment, held Jemima Ffrench dumb. "Then Portia disliked Mr. Macbean," she cried, hotly. "It made her shudder, she told me, to see him come near her. She detested herself every time she thought of her engagement. Would you have wished her to become the man's wife, with feelings like this?"

"Well, it scarcely matters what I wished," said Lady Erroll. "I am not Portia's guardian or adviser. Remembering who she is, as the child of my poor, unhappy daughter, I certainly should like to see her secured from poverty—married to some man who can keep her in decent comfort, before I die."

The buttons were off the foils; and Miss Jemima's spirits felt relieved. In open warfare she could hold her own against any Dysart of them all. The thrusts and counter-thrusts of preliminary sparring suited her not. "And remembering who she is, as the child of my unhappy nephew, I wish to see Portia marry a man whom she can love," she cried, with spirit, "I don't believe in money. I believe in affection, and affection only, for making the lives of human beings happy."

Old Lady Erroll took another sugar-plum. "It seems to me we are wasting breath on imaginary difficulties, my dear Miss Ffrench. If you believe in poverty as a promoter of happiness, and if Portia believes in it, too, by all means let her marry Teddy Josselin. He has his pay and his debts, and Colonel Ffrench, no doubt, will assist his granddaughter with something more substantial than advice at her starting in life. Still they will be poor, quite poor enough to test the value of your happiness theory. Let them marry, by all means."

"And you, Lady Erroll?" said Miss Jemima, point-blank. "What assistance are they to look for from you? I suppose we may as well talk the matter plainly over."

"Nay," said the old countess, still with suspicious urbanity, "do you tell me the intentions of the lady's friends first. What allowance does Colonel Ffrench propose to make to his granddaughter?"

Miss Jemima's honest eyes fell. If she had possessed a fortune, she would in that moment have settled every shilling of it upon her Harry's child; but she had, remaining in the world, exactly two thousand pounds, the greater part of the income from which was scrupulously received by Colonel Ffrench half yearly as Jemima's "share" in the expenses of Halfont Manor.

"My brother Richard, as you know, is a comparatively poor man. His habits are expensive, rendered more so by his ill health, and every year a narrower margin is left over and above his own personal expenditure. Except a few hundred pounds in ready money, it will not be in Richard's power to assist Portia when she marries."

"And after his death? What certain settlement can be made upon her after his death?"

"My brother's income dies with him, Lady Erroll. The little that remained of his former fortune was sunk by him, years ago, in an annuity. Halfont came to him with his second wife, and failing children of hers, reverts by settlement, as you are aware, on Richard's death, to her family."

"Aye," exclaimed Lady Erroll, a quick expression of anger lighting up her old face, impassive till now. "As I am aware! You do well to use that expression, Miss Ffrench. Before Portia married Harry Ffrench, do you know what your brother told me about that Halfont property? I can show it you—here—in black and white!" She touched, with her withered hand, one of the packets of letters that lay beside her. "When you came I had just been refreshing my memory by reading an old note or two of your brother's. He was considered one of the acutest letter-writers of his day, Miss Ffrench. Men used to say Talleyrand could scarce surpass Richard Ffrench in the art with which he could mislead others, yet leave himself uncompromised. Hear what he wrote me, a week before my daughter's marriage!" She took up a sheet of note paper, yellow with time, unfolded it and, without spectacles, read aloud: "'Settlements, you know, I have always held in detestation. They are needful only in certain exceptional cases, never where marriage begins under such fair auspices as with that of our children! My dear Portia will, I trust, look upon Halfont as her home, now and hereafter, just as certainly as if a dozen lawyers had been at work to secure it to her on parchment!' Would you like to read the letter yourself? You know your brother's hand."

Then Miss Jemima raised her eyes steadily to Lady Erroll's. "I wish to hear nothing of the past. I wish, if I can, to forget it, with its shame and errors on both sides. I loved Harry as well, perhaps, as you loved your daughter, and have mourned for him as deeply." (Old Lady Erroll went to a rout three weeks after Lady Portia's funeral). "All that is over. I came here to talk of Portia. The girl is brimful of faults. She is extravagant, vain, giddy, I don't rightly know how much Portia could love! But she is young—at one-and-twenty everything is possible! Let her marry this Mr. Josselin, because she cares for him, and he for her. Old animosities, old letters, old wrongs—yes, for I will allow that you were wronged—let all be forgotten in the happiness of these two children," and then Jemima Ffrench's full heart overflowed; her voice choked.

Old Lady Erroll looked at her with a smile of cool curiosity. "You are an enthusiast, Miss Ffrench," she remarked, after a minute's silence; "and I am as completely matter-of-fact as Portia herself. I could say nothing stronger. In the case of two unworldly, hot-hearted, hot-headed young people—such young people as one reads of in old romances—I will admit, for argument's sake, that a marriage begun in poverty might brace character, stimulate honorable ambition. But what are these two lovers—my granddaughter and my grandson—whose cause you plead?"

"They are young, and they love each other!" cried Miss Jemima, quite unconscious that she was saying anything ridiculous.

"They are," said old Lady Erroll, "exact representatives of their class and of their period. Teddy, to begin with. I don't say he is vicious, as men used to be when you and I were young. He neither drinks nor gambles, nor commits public scandal of any kind, after the robuster fashion of fifty years ago; but he hasn't an ounce of ballast in his composition. I allow him, nominally, five hundred a year; he spends double that sum, at least—on what? Bouquets, opera stalls, the bills of his men-milliners—who shall say? I, for my part, never ask. I like the boy. He's all that is left to me—Sarah's only child; and Sarah was a good, a creditable daughter to me, Miss Ffrench. If Ted can meet with a suitable wife, a woman with money and position, he may do pretty well. As long as he remains single, he won't go very far astray. If he marries into poverty, marries a woman like his cousin Portia—he is ruined. Simply that. No need to pile up words where one expresses everything so accurately."

"But I don't see why marrying Portia need be marrying into poverty," urged Miss Jemima. "Young people can surely begin life on five or six hundred a year. To my mind, such an income, even with a family, is a handsome one. I will, on my part, do everything I can to help them at starting, and—"

"And where is the income you speak of to come from?" interrupted old Lady Erroll, but with great politeness. "Teddy's pay is seven shillings and four pence a day. Colonel Ffrench, you tell me, can give Portia no other assistance than a certain small sum on her wedding day. Where are they to look for the remaining four or five hundred a year of which you speak?"

"From you, Lady Erroll," said Miss Jemima. "You would surely continue the same allowance to Mr. Josselin after his marriage as you make him now?"

"From the day on which Ted Josselin marries Portia Ffrench," said the old countess, "I never allow him one shilling while I live; not—one—shilling!" dwelling upon each syllable with cruel emphasis. "At my death, as I have really no other relation in whom I take interest, I shall leave my money to a charity. I have nothing to say against Portia, personally. I know no better company than my granddaughter, when she chooses; and she is handsome, too, considering her dark skin. I have done what I could for her. Portia might have married well, four times over, if she had chosen; and through me. I would have settled ten thousand pounds on her at my death, if she had married Macbean. But to be Teddy's wife—no! a hundred times, no. She would ruin him in six months—ruin him first, and disgrace him afterward. Don't interrupt me"—for Miss Jemima's eyes flashed fire. "The girl is no worse than all the rest of her generation. With a new dress a day, with an establishment, with diamonds, equipages, Portia would be a good wife, no doubt, as wives go. For Ted, I would a great deal sooner see him—"

"Lady Erroll," said Miss Jemima, rising from her chair and standing erect— very dignified she looked in her rusty black silk, and with her fine, outspoken old face—"it seems to me that, on this subject, there is nothing more for you to say or for me to hear. Portia is your granddaughter, but she is my Harry's child, and I will not listen to her vilification. What you say of young men and women of the world may be true. I thank God I know little of what you call the world, and I can't bring myself to believe it. I think there is much more good than evil in every young heart. I think a marriage of inclination, not of greed, is the best chance for my great-niece, Portia. I pray that she may make such a one. Of course, I shall tell them, word for word, what you have said. Mr. Josselin meets me, by appointment, when I leave your house, and I shall take him down with me to Halfont. My advice to them both will be to look into their own hearts, to weigh all this well, and—not to give each other up! People can live with little money; but life, as you and I have seen to our cost, is not worth holding without love."

A deep color came over Lady Erroll's wrinkled face, then faded, leaving it almost livid white. "In the marriage you speak of," said she, "there was neither love nor money. It was a marriage that began in deception, that was lived out in misery, that ended in shame and dishonor! And yet it is with such blood as *that* in her veins that you will counsel Harry Ffrench's daughter to marry into beggary."

"I will counsel Harry Ffrench's daughter to keep true, if she can, to the best thing in her nature," said Miss Jemima, staunchly and quietly. " If she loves Teddy Josselin enough to brave poverty for his sake, I shall have better hope for her than if she had married Macbean, with all his settlements."

" Aye, if she does ! " said old Lady Erroll, her good humor beginning to return. " Depend upon it, my dear Miss Ffrench, we are both working ourselves into tragedy quite unnecessarily. Let Ted and Portia know, for certain, that by marrying they will become paupers, and I think you will find them quite disposed to shake hands and lapse back into cousins. Going? No, no, I can't think of it. You must stay to lunch. Don't let two old women like you and me quarrel because a silly boy and girl have chosen to play at falling in love."

But Miss Jemima was determined. Food would choke her in her present state of feeling, she said, bluntly. She wished to quarrel with no one, but her heart was sore ; she must be alone. And then briefly declining Lady Erroll's offer of sending for a cab, she started forth alone on foot from the great Eaton square house, which an hour ago she had thought was one day to be Portia's home.

Jemima Ffrench's honest heart was sore, yet, as she walked onward with her steady long step, her head well erect, through the London streets, an expression almost of youthful energy was on her fresh old face. If, as she still hoped, love won the day against wisdom, *something*, she determined, should be done by which Portia and Portia's husband might live. She would sell out two hundred pounds for them when they married ; two hundred pounds would furnish a small house modestly ; Teddy must exchange the Guards for a public office, Portia be taught housekeeping, and Colonel Ffrench forced into helping them. Nay, after a time, for Miss Jemima could believe positive and abiding evil of no one, would not old Lady Erroll herself be forced to relent ?

" A poor, good, enthusiastic simpleton ! " thought Lady Erroll, as she put away her letters, the cherished relics, not like Miss Jemima's, of dead love, but of dead hatreds, of frustrated ambition. " Ted Josselin fling thirty thousand pounds to a hospital ! Portia Ffrench marry any man for the sake of his handsome blue eyes ! I shall have them both here to-morrow begging dear grandmamma's pardon, and vowing they never meant the thing to be taken in earnest."

Then she sat down to her solitary lunch, and calculated, not without satisfaction, how much chicken and sherry had been saved by Jemima Ffrench's losing her temper.

CHAPTER XVII.

For a long half-hour Susan Fielding waited, breathless with anxiety, not all unselfish, as to the lovers' fate. Then a light step came flying along the corridor, the door opened quickly, and Portia, her face all alight with animation, looked in.

" Come Susan, child ! The oracle has spoken, our fate is decided. Come and witness the last scene in our poor, ill-fated little love drama."

" What—you are not going to marry Mr. Josselin, then ? " uttered Susan.

" Ah, that is just what you will hear," was Portia's answer. " I have had a hard alternative placed before me, Susan, I can tell you. Teddy Josselin and herbs, a stalled ox and Macbean. But I think, considering my youth and inexperience, I have chosen wisely, as you will hear."

She hurried Susan down stairs, and on the landing, outside the drawing-room, they were joined by Miss Jemima who, after repeating, with conscientious accuracy, Lady Erroll's message, had left the lovers alone to deliberate upon their fate.

"Poor old lady! You are a vast deal more upset by all this than you need be," said Portia, patting Miss Jemima's hand reassuringly. "As I tell Susan, we have, considering all things, decided wisely, and what is more, without a tear. You have been crying, Aunt Jem—don't deny it, I see the marks of tears on your cheeks—while we laughed! Yes, laughed so loud I expected every minute grandpapa would send up a message bidding us not disturb him."

She opened the door as she spoke, and Susan, with as choking a feeling in her throat as though her own destiny were under discussion, followed old Miss Ffrench into the drawing-room. Teddy Josselin rose from a sofa where he was reclining by one of the open windows, and came forward to meet them. He looked even more bewitching, Susan thought, in his morning dress, than he had done the other evening; the frock coat, the delicate tie, the pointed moustache, the lavender gloves—all were faultless. And his blue eyes were just as full of lazy contentment, his handsome boyish face was just as untroubled as ever. Ah, if she had a lover, mused the little girl, she would not choose him to wear mien so careless in this momentous hour on which their whole future happiness might hang! Poor, romantic little Susan.

"How are you, Susan," said Teddy, taking her hand, all cold and trembling with vicarious agitation. "I have been thinking of you ever since, and so has some one else. Did I tell you, 'Tia? Blake soothed me to sleep with praises of Susan's voice and Susan's 'rustic woodland air' all the way back to town. Don't be jealous."

The thorough good humor of Teddy's tone, the familiar "'Tia," (Teddy Josselin was the only living being who ever ventured on a diminutive with Portia) made Miss Jemima augur favorably as to the result of their consultation. "Portia is very likely to be jealous about Mr. Blake, or Mr. any one else to-day," she said, with an inflection of the voice that made the remark a question.

"Poor Portia would be jealous always," said Teddy, looking serious. "There is the leading weakness of her character. She cannot part with her meanest slave without a pang, can you, 'Tia?"

Portia had now come close to her cousin's side, and as he was speaking their eyes met. Surely, thought old Miss Jemima, not unobservant, not wholly unversed in love matters, the lacerated feeling of lovers on the brink of an eternal parting were never transmitted through such a heart-whole glance as that!

"When I am tired I will tell you," answered Portia, lightly. "Up to the present time I have had no experience. What one gives up voluntarily, cannot be spoken of as 'forfeited,' Master Ted."

Teddy made a mock-humble bow. "I never knew you had given George Blake up, Miss Ffrench."

"I was not speaking of George Blake, Mr. Josselin."

And then every body sat down; the lovers at some distance from each other, perfectly cool and collected; old Miss Jemima and Susan waiting in agitated silence for them to begin.

"I think," remarked Teddy, when two or three minutes had gone by in silence, "that the barometer must be higher than yesterday—I mean the thermometer—no, which is it, 'Tia?"

Miss Jemima looked up severely at the ceiling; Portia laughed—that pleas-

ant laugh that, as I said before, would in itself have been enough to found many
an actress's reputation! "What will you do without me at your side to tell you
what you mean, Ted?" cried she.

"Portia!" exclaimed Miss Jemima.

"Ah well, Aunt, painful though it may be to tell the truth, there is no good
in putting it off," said Portia, with a business-like air. Susan is in our confi-
dence, and I am sure you are both dying to hear what we have decided on. As
well tell them at once, Ted?"

"I suppose so," began Teddy—then Miss Jemima chancing to look at him
full and suddenly, his blue eyes sank. "Only, do you say it all, Portia," he
added. "You know you get over that sort of thing so much neater than
I do."

"Thanks!" said Portia, gaily. "I accept the compliment at its fullest
worth. Mr. Josselin wishing me to be the speaker, Aunt Jem, I have to announce that—we do not mean to sacrifice ourselves."

"As I guessed, as I foretold," said Miss Jemima, half to herself. "So much
for Lady Erroll's knowledge of human nature."

"We are young, we may be foolish—"

"But not wholly corrupt!" put in Teddy.

"And we cannot give up what to us is simply life itself."

Miss Jemima coughed to keep down her emotion; the tears started to her
eyes.

"Dissipation, excitement, dresses by Worth, coats by Bond street tailors,
French gloves, French wines. What, in very truth, are all these things?"

A shake of the head from Miss Jemima said, "What, indeed?"

"Superfluities to many people, doubtless. To us, necessities of life."

"Portia!"

"Since I was eighteen, have I ever, in one year, spent less than a hundred
and thirty pounds on my dress, Aunt Jem? the precise sum on which grandmamma suggests we should live. Well, we will say that when I was married I
spent half—though the whole calculation is absurd—and Teddy the other half.
Sixty-five pounds a year each on dress. What would this leave over for wine
bills and travelling, and all those incidental expenses? Not a farthing. We
should not be in the least ashamed to beg, but we could not work, either of us,
and the only remaining alternative would be—starvation. Teddy," she turned
round to her lover, with the brightest smile in the world, "we can't make up our
minds to starve, can we?"

"I could make up my mind to anything," said Teddy, "as long as I shared
it with you. If you wanted money, 'Tia, you should have remained faithful to
the Scotchman."

"If my niece wished it, in short," said Miss Jemima, looking searchingly at
the young man's face, "if Portia Ffrench would remain true to her word you
would remain true to her. Is that what I am to understand, Mr. Josselin?"

"If Portia will marry me to-morrow I shall be the happiest man in England," said Teddy Josselin, lifting his blue eyes to Miss Jemima's—honest blue
eyes they were, with all their sleepiness, all their want of intellect. "I've never
taken thought for the morrow yet, and never come to very bad grief, that I remember. The natural tendency of things is—is to fall upon one's legs. I don't
know why you laugh, Portia?"

"A slight confusion of tenses, Ted. Go on. It was the fault of the meta-
phor."

"To fall upon one's legs. I'm put out, Miss Ffrench. Portia knows so well how to put me out. If she would quarrel with grandmamma and marry me to-morrow—"

"You would be doubtfully happy for a week, and decidedly repentant for the remainder of your life!" interrupted Portia, in the sort of admonitory tone in which one puts down a child's impending folly. "We can't afford to quarrel with grandmamma, either of us—I the least. She doesn't love me very much, poor grandmamma, our feelings to each other are about equal, but she really means me to make a good marriage, and I mean to do so, too—in my own way, not a Mr. Macbean. From the first year I saw her, grandmamma and I have been playing a kind of game of chess of our own. Who knows yet which will be checkmated?"

"You have been playing a game which I neither understand nor wish to understand," cried Miss Jemima, indignantly. "I have been always lenient to you hitherto, Portia. When you have led on and discarded suitor after suitor, I have been lenient to you, for I have thought your worst sin was girlish levity, and that in your heart—I may say it now—you cared for your cousin. I was mistaken. You have no heart, You care for nothing. You believe nothing. You regret nothing. I congratulate you, Mr. Josselin, I congratulate you heartily on my niece, Portia Ffrench, having at length made up her mind!"

Teddy smoothed his moustache into finer points, and gave one quickly-averted glance at Portia's face. "All congratulations are the mischief to answer," he remarked. "I remember when my cousin Adolphus was going to be married, old Linkwater congratulated him. I've often told you that story, 'Tia?"

"Very often. You surely have no idea of telling it us now?"

"Oh, not at all, only—you know what Adolphus said is pretty nearly what I feel. All these things are leaps in the dark," this to Miss Jemima; "and it would take a wiser man than me to know, till a year and a day afterward, whether he has drawn a prize or a blank. But I am extremely obliged to you for what you said, just the same."

His unruffled fatuity, the lurking smile round Portia's lips, were too much for Miss Jemima's temper. "I congratulate both of you," she cried, rising from her chair; "and I congratulate the people belonging to you on being spared from seeing two such—" a strong word was in the old soldier's mouth, but she swallowed it—"two such babies married. Lady Erroll was right. She does understand human nature—such human nature as yours—better than I do. You will yourself explain the rupture of your *last* engagement to your grandfather, Portia; that task I decline; and the next time, please, that you have wedding preparations to make, make them without consulting me. I assist at no more trousseaux."

And Miss Jemima crossed over to a table where afternoon tea was already laid, poured herself out a cup and drank it, standing, in short, disdainful gulps, and not turning her eyes again toward the culprits. A stranger looking in at the picture at that moment would assuredly never have guessed that Teddy and Portia were lovers, sternly refusing consent to their own marriage; that this incensed old lady's was the heart that bled at seeing generous, youthful folly degenerate into the miserable wisdom of expediency, and of the world!

Teddy was the first to follow her. "Don't be angry with us," he said, humbly offering Miss Jemima a plate of bread and butter. "Bad though we are, we are not responsible for the sins of our ancestors; everything is forced upon us by grandmamma."

He looked so handsome and so much in earnest as he made his little speech that Jemima Ffrench could not but soften. " I'm angry with myself for having taken so much interest in you, that's the truth, Mr. Josselin. I made he mistake of thinking of you both as of responsible beings, who would help themselves, and whom it would be my duty to help. I see you as you are—children, not knowing the meaning of the words responsibility or duty."

"And who, therefore, must make their way by childish obedience to their elders' dictates," cried Portia, coming up and putting her arm round Miss Jemima's shoulders. "Now, I insist upon your eating, old lady. You know you told me you had not swallowed a mouthful since you started. Take a lesson from us Don't quarrel with your bread and butter."

So peace was made. Shocked though good Miss Jemima might be b the lover's frivolity, it was impossible to remain seriously angry with any two human beings for refusing voluntarily to encounter starvation. She had been a fou., she confessed, and they—had proved themselves philosophers. The world was too old for romantic sacrifice. Let Mr. Josselin look for an heiress, with Lady Erroll's assistance, and Portia, if she could, find another Mr. Macbean.

"You, both of you, suffer so little that I won't go through the pretence ot pitying you," she remarked, as Teddy Josselin took his leave. "But this I do say," and Miss Jemima pressed the young man's hand with honest kindness, "I can't help feeling sorry that we have seen the last of you at Halfont. Some day, perhaps, a long time hence, you will look back, and wish you had decided differently."

"And some day, perhaps, not a very long time hence, you will look back and say that we decided like oracles," said Teddy. "As to having seen the last of me at Halfont, the thing is—is—" Teddy stammered and looked pleasant—"we-diculous. Because 'Tia and I leave oft being lovers is no reason that we should not continue—"

"To be cousins," interrupted Portia. "You shall come again in three months, Ted. Not a day sooner ; the world would talk. Whatever we wish, whatever we think right, do not let us run a risk of making the world talk ! "

She went with him to the top of the stairs, then running back to one of the drawing-room windows, kissed the tips of her fingers as the carriage that was taking him to the station drove away. Could any woman discard, in this light fashion, the man she had once loved ? Susan, to whose simple heart the situation was one of vitalest interest, asked herself this question as she watched Portia's face. Had the whole engagement been idle child's play, as Miss Jemima said, or—a blind. Was Portia's heart indeed occupied by some absent lover—a lover far worthier, nobler, thought Susan, than poor Teddy Josselin, with his lavender gloves, and curled love-locks, and boyish, effeminate beauty.

Portia sank down into a chair and told Miss Jemima to ring for some fresh tea, then in wildly high spirits began to discuss the change in her prospects that the last few hours had brought about. Usually she flagged the moment that a scene, that an excitement, however trivial, was past ; no such reaction seemed to set in after her final rupture with the man she had professed to love. She would go to town to-morrow. Every worldly hope she had was in grandmamma. Suicidal to run the chance of any fresh family feud ! She would get presented at the next drawing-room. She would send her photograph to Macbean. He was vulgar, he lived in Glasgow, was ugly, demoniacal of temper ; but, at the present ebb of affairs, not a chance must be lost. Could a young lady approaching twenty-two, and whose fifth engagement had just ended tragically, afford to be critical ?

So she rattled on, Miss Jemima listening, grimly sorrowful. At last, when Susan rose to go, Portia offered to walk with her as far as the lodge gates, and as soon as the two girls were alone together, out of doors, her mood changed. " You think me a monster of heartlessness, don't you, Susan ? " Oh, I can see you do by your face. Don't accuse me too harshly. Remember you only see half—the outside half that tells so little of the truth."

" I know that very well," cried Susan, half impatiently, "and I have no right of course to accuse any one. It all seems hard on—poor Mr. Josselin, but I believe I can guess why *you* are in such good spirits ! "

" Then you must be a much shrewder person than I take you for," said Portia. " Don't judge by what you would do or feel under the same circumstances, child. Think of something that you would consider wildly, utterly impossible, and you will be likeliest to arrive at the truth about me. Not that I want you to arrive at the truth, Susan ! " Singularly bright was Portia's face, singularly soft her voice. " I should just like to make you say one thing. Aunt Jem congratulated Teddy on my having found out my own mind at last, will you congratulate me ? I'm superstitious, I want good wishes to-day. Give me yours."

The poor child's tell-tale face reddened. I do not say that, after spending one evening in the society of a stranger, a girl's heart can be affected to any passionate or lasting extent. But I do say that a spasm of sharpest pain contracted Susan Fielding's heart at this moment. Love's twin sister, we must remember, arrives so much more rapidly at maturity than does love himself ! " I congratulate you, Miss Portia," but her voice was unsteady as she said this. " As you say, I can't judge of you or of your actions rightly, but I know enough to feel that you are happier than you ever were in your life before, and I'm glad —I mean I try to be glad of it. I wish you joy, you and—the person you mean to marry."

Portia broke out into a laugh, a heartier, louder one than most people had ever heard from her lips. " That is well-wishing with a vengeance ! Well-wishing, not to the living only, but to people who, as likely as not, will never exist. Aunt Jemima often says I shall end by being an old maid, and that she and I will live together in lodgings at Cheltenham, Susan. I shall be just a little more discontented than I am now, thin, blue-nosed, a district visitor, and holding rigid opinions about women's emancipation. Good-by—what ! won't you give me a kiss after congratulating me so prettily ? "

And then, with buoyant steps, she tripped back along the Manor avenue, and Susan, heavy-hearted, went on her way alone toward Addison Lodge.

CHAPTER XVIII

BETIMES next morning Portia was off to London.

"Let grandmamma and me play out our match of chess unaided," she said, when Miss Jemima would have remonstrated on the indelicacy of thus throwing herself in Teddy Josselin's way, the want of proper pride that she evinced in her quick forgiveness of Lady Erroll. "Grandmamma has played the great move of her game, and I must put forward my modest little pawn in reply. As to no proper pride, I have none. If grandmamma invites me I will go and stay with her to-morrow. Dear Aunt Jem, remember that I am a pauper, a pauper with at least four hundred pounds' worth of silk attire and no possible opportunity of wearing it, unless I make an effort for myself!"

The meeting between her and her grandmother was perfect, in its way. Old Lady Erroll extended her little withered hand coldly, Portia stooped, much against her taste and habit, and kissed the still more withered cheek.

"I have to thank you, grandmamma. You have taught poor Ted and me wisdom. We felt a little sore at first," Portia's eyes fell, "then reconciled ourselves to our fate. Everything is for the best."

"And you don't want to lose the world for love, either of you?" said Lady Erroll, scrutinizing the girl's face sharply.

"Grandmamma!"

"Oh well, your Aunt Ffrench thought that you would—I did not. She is a better woman than you and I, Portia, but a simpleton. Pity you were not wise enough to ask my opinion a little sooner. You have bought a great many expensive clothes, Ted Josselin tells me. What do you mean to do with your trousseau now?"

"Put it carefully away, grandmamma, and send my photograph to Mr. Macbean. I think he really did like me, a little bit, and if it hadn't been for Ted I might not have disliked him. I don't know that he was worse than other people's husbands—when you didn't look at him!"

So unaffectedly good-humored was Portia that Lady Erroll could not keep from being propitiated; by-and-by, as Portia intended she should do, invited her granddaughter to come up and spend a few days in town.

"Not to assist you in getting over your disappointment—your face tells me how much you have felt that! but, to prevent the world from saying that you are disappointed. I treated the thing as a joke from the first, and now, if you and Ted are seen together as usual, it will pass off without scandal. You have had love-affairs enough, Portia. In a first or even second season these things don't matter. No girl, with her twenty-second birthday looking her in the face, can afford to entangle herself as you do. The next flirtation you have must end in marriage, do you hear?"

"I hear, and please heaven, mean to profit," said Portia meekly. "I am quite as tired, quite as humiliated as you can be, grandmamma, and quite as resolved to have done with my present life!" she added, with a sigh brimful of obedience and pious contrition.

They took luncheon together; Portia constraining herself to eat little and drink nothing but water, as she always did when she wanted specially to please her grandmother. Between two and three o'clock Teddy Josselin came in. Old Lady Erroll was dressing at the time, for her afternoon drive, and when Teddy ran up, unannounced, into the drawing-room, he found Portia there alone. She turned her head quickly at the sound of his footstep and put her finger to her lip. Teddy closed the door softly, looked well round both drawing-rooms, then came up to Portia's side.

Their greeting, I am bound to say, was still conducted in the fashion of affianced lovers; but the moment it was over, Portia, with a rapid side-movement, ran across to the window—thus putting half the space of the room between them. "We meet and we are to be seen in public together, Mr. Josselin," her tone was low, but purposely distinct; any chance listener outside the door might have heard every word. "The world shall not have it in its power to make merry over Portia Ffrench's last disappointment! Grandmamma has asked me to stay with her—I am to come to-morrow—and remain a week or ten days, and you will be seen with us just as usual, sir, grandmamma says so."

"A week—and then?" cried Teddy, eagerly.

"Then, if Aunt Jem will give me leave, I shall go down and stay with the Gordons at Worthing," said Portia, "that is, if nothing of importance happens meanwhile. I am thinking of sending my photograph to a Scotch friend of ours, Mr. Josselin, a friend whose regard for me, I believe, was real. Who shall say what the result will be?"

Mr. Josselin replied by crossing the room, taking firm hold of both Portia's hands, and looking steadily in her face. "'Tia," said he, "I forbid you to send Sandy your photograph. You hear me? I forbid it."

"Teddy, for heaven's sake don't be a goose! Grandmamma may come in—Condy may be listening. You are making red marks on my wrists. See!"

"You shall not send Sandy—you shall not send any man your photograph. There's scarcely a fellow in the service but has got it already."

"Mr. Josselin—"

"Ah, but its true. 'Tis sickening, sickening, on my word, to look in all the different fellows' books and forever see Portia Ffrench's figure in this attitude and that, and then listen to their explanation of how they came by it."

"But Mr. Macbean is not in the service. If I have given my photograph to every officer in the British army, it surely can't matter giving one more to a poor Glasgow manufacturer whose heart I have broken?"

Ted's answer was conveyed in a whisper, a whisper that made the color leap into Portia's dark cheek. "You silly little boy," she began; then lifting her black eyes suddenly—"Oh Ted, do you care for me so much," she cried.

Upon this Ted kissed her—the coachman on Lady Erroll's carriage box might have witnessed the kiss if he had chanced to look up just at that moment at one of the drawing-room windows—and then a rustle of silk was to be heard descending the stairs, and Teddy Josselin started guiltily back, five yards at least away, and old Lady Erroll herself came in.

She glanced suspiciously first at one cousin, then the other. Portia was not, as a rule, wanting in self-control, yet was Teddy's, at this moment, by far the most innocent face of the two.

"You here!" said the old woman, looking at him coldly. "It might have been in better taste, perhaps, if you had stayed away till you were sent for. Portia, my dear, are you ready? The carriage is at the door."

"And I am just in time to escort you," cried Teddy Josselyn, with his most ingenuous smile. "I don't see that you need forbid me your house, grandmamma, because you have blighted my hopes of happiness. If Portia and I are to be only cousins, let us be that—at least till Portia is married."

"Which she never will be so long as Teddy Josselin is her shadow," said Lady Erroll, grimly. "Yes, you may come to the house, sir. You may come out shopping with us now. But understand your position thoroughly. If you get Portia into any more mischief, if one other engagement is broken off through you, I never speak to you again."

"Oh, I understand my position accurately," said Teddy, with a certain bitterness, real or mock, in his tone. "A tame cat, to be stroked when no better plaything is at hand, and not turn when it is trodden upon—"

"That's the worm, Ted," cried Portia. "When will you abandon the allegorical style?"

"Then some fine morning find myself standing at St. George's, best man at Portia's wedding, for my reward."

"I trust so, I am sure," said Lady Erroll, cordially, "and the sooner the better. Portia and I have been having a long talk, and we agree—don't we Portia, child?—we quite agree in our opinions. Well for you, Ted Josselin, if you had as much brains in your head as your cousin Portia has."

"Ah, I must look out for a clever wife," cried Teddy; he was handing Lady Erroll down stairs as he said this, and looked back over his shoulder at Portia. "Will you help me in my search, Cousin Portia? I'm not a genius."

"You are not, indeed!"

"But, I'm a good-looking fellow, and easy to live with. A young woman inclined to be vixenish could scarcely meet with a better husband than Ted Josselin."

Portia's reply was conveyed through a cunningly swift pull of one of Master Ted's love locks; for these cousins—lovers—under whatever name you choose to rank them, were still much on the same terms as they had been in the days when Teddy first taught Portia, a school-girl of sixteen, to waltz, in Lady Erroll's back drawing-room.

"You would be a good husband for a woman with five thousand a year, strictly settled on herself," croaked the old countess. "Miss Minters is still disengaged; I know it on the best authority. She is a sensible, well-principled girl—"

"Aged thirty-one, and of West Indian ancestry," finished Teddy. "The ancestral pedigree emblazoned on her face. What a pity we can't make up a double wedding for the same day! 'Tia and Sandy, I and the octoroon. Arrange it for us, grandmamma, if you can, and without courtship. Name the day and amount of settlements, and Portia and I will be there to be legally made over to our purchasers."

They now drove away eastward for shopping, Lady Erroll in so benign a humor that in a certain shop in Oxford street she presented her granddaughter with a five-and-six-penny glove box (Portia shows it still); afterward to the Waterloo station, from whence it was arranged that Portia should start by the five o'clock train. Here, loitering about the platform, a sketch-book and color-box in his hand, they came across George Blake.

"Just the man we want," said Teddy; Lady Erroll was waiting in her carriage outside and Mr. Josselin was commissioned to see Portia into her place, a duty, it would seem, involving long and whispered conversation in its fulfilment. "You are going to Halfont, of course? Then you will escort my cousin home. Nothing could be better."

"Mr. Blake does not seem to see it," remarked Portia, offering him her hand with even more than her accustomed friendship. "Would it really be a very great trouble to you to escort me home, Mr. Blake? There will be no carriage waiting for me at the station, and we shall have very nearly two miles to walk, mind."

Before Blake had time to answer, the bell rang, and they had to hurry into the first carriage they could find. Teddy stood, a picture of dandy laziness, of unruffled composure, among the crowd of porters on the platform, and kissed the tips of his delicately-gloved fingers to his cousin as the train moved away. Portia put her head through the window and gave him one last smile—a smile that made George Blake groan in the spirit..

"Now, are you really going to Halfont, Mr. Blake? What a blessing to have a carriage to ourselves! I am very pleased to have your escort, still I would not be so selfish as to take you out of your way."

"I am really going to Halfont," answered Blake. "Where else could I be going? Not to trouble you, though," he added quickly. "I have my tools with me, as you see. I want to study a sunset effect by the canal, and—"

"And you can give me that long-promised lesson at last, then?" said Portia, as he hesitated. "No dinner is going on at home to-day. Grandpapa is poorly, and he and Aunt Jem were to dine off boiled whiting, at two o'clock, so we shall be independent—able to paint and enjoy ourselves as much as we like. What a lucky chance that we met! I always find it so hard to live through a long evening at home when I have been in town during the day."

"A lucky chance for me!" said Blake. "When I saw you with Josselin I never thought I should be so fortunate as to be your escort, alone."

"Ah," said Portia, "Mr. Josselin does not come to Halfont at present, of course."

She threw down her eyes, and trifled with the string and paper infolding Lady Erroll's glove-box. George Blake evidently knew nothing. She was to have the pleasure, always a keen one to her, of enacting a new little part; of watching, of playing with the poor fellow's first surprise on learning she was free.

"Josselin does not go to Halfont?" exclaimed Blake. "Why, he was there the day before yesterday."

"And yesterday," added Portia, "but for the last time. Mr. Blake, you know us both so well, in talking to you I feel I am talking to that rare thing. a friend; and so I can tell the plain truth. The fact is"—here she blushed, and hung her head, "everything is over. Grandmamma will not hear of it, and Teddy has got back his liberty. It is all for the best, no doubt, only I wish we had been told sooner. It is very well for old people, who have forgotten what feeling means, to be so wise about money; but just the least hard on us who are foolish and who suffer."

The blush, the down-bent face, the faltering voice, set Blake's impulsive heart aflame. It was the first moment since he had known her in which he had seen Portia Ffrench thoroughly unbend, thoroughly a woman. "And you have let old heads get the better of young hearts?" he exclaimed. "Josselin has let worldly interest of any kind reconcile him to *such* a loss?"

He stopped; and Portia's eyes sank lower beneath his. "The submission was mine, not Teddy's, Mr. Blake. He would have faced poverty with better courage than I—perhaps could not realize as I could what poverty for people like us would be. I am wiser than my years entitle me to be. I have the bitter experience of my own childhood to show me what men and women come to who cannot work, and do not wish to starve."

"All that may be very admirably reasoned," said Blake, still watching her face; "yet, had I been Josselin, I would rather have listened to worse logic from your lips."

"You would rather have listened to some etherial 'tall talk' about devotion and unselfishness, and the sweets of a life supported on seven-and-fourpence a day; then have awaked a year later to the solid fact of being in the poorhouse?"

"Do you give me leave to answer that question honestly?"

"Certainly I do."

"I would rather you had held to me, in spite of all the grandmothers in the world, and leave the future in my hands. We should not have been in the poorhouse in a year, Miss Ffrench, depend upon it."

A quickly-repressed smile came round the corners of Portia's lips. "*You* can make money," said she; "*you* can paint pictures and write books. My cousin and I belong to the lumber of the earth. We toil not, neither do we spin. Creatures who take no thought of the morrow, like lilies, as poor Teddy used to say. We have no prospects, no hopes, but in the riches of others; and grandmamma has cut out our future for us beautifully. Teddy is to marry Miss Minters—you have heard of the rich Miss Minters?"

"And you?" interrupted George, warmly. "What stall in Vanity Fair is to be tenanted by you?"

"I must wait for the first vacancy," said Portia, with a demure little sigh. "Can girls without money choose? Can a canary tell into which particular cage it will be sold?"

"And you can admit of no other alternative? You cannot even believe in the possibility of a marriage that should not be one of buying and selling?"

"Another day I will answer that question, Mr. Blake. My brain at present is in a whirl of matrimonial arithmetic. I have just spent four hours with grandmamma, remember. So many thousand pounds well invested yield so much income. A man with a given fortune must make such a settlement. Oh, the meanness, the stupidity of it all! Oh, if human beings could be independent of a London house, a carriage, diamonds, and think only of making the best and highest out of their own lives."

The aspiration was not absolutely novel; but what speech can ever sound commonplace from a beautiful girl who blushes as she speaks, and whose voice softens, and whose whole manner gives the listener to understand that his, and his alone, is the ear into which these nobler longings of the soul are poured forth? In the game of chess which she was playing (and playing to win) a London house, a carriage, diamonds, were the very stakes Portia Ffrench had sworn in her heart to carry away. And George Blake knew pretty well that it was so; knew that *he* had about as much chance of winning her hand as though she had been a royal princess. And still the voice of the charmer charmed him, still vanity, subtly flattered, whispered that Portia's inmost maiden heart was still unmoved. She had liked Josselin as a cousin, a playmate; had encouraged her other suitors up to the point at which love was expected from her, then found that she had no love to give. Had she ever made confession like this to any man but himself? Had she not said that she looked upon him as that rare thing, a friend? And did not her voice falter, her eyes sink, as she told him the story of her recovered freedom?

"Of all human vanity, commend me to the vanity of a clever man," thought Portia, leaning back in her corner of the carriage, and glancing at Blake from beneath her eyelashes. "I talk a single sentence of nonsense about not wanting to be rich, and his highness thinks it is meant for him—speculates, at this moment, whether he shall give me a chance of working out my theory or not. Oh, you poor, dear, foolish, credulous genius! Teddy, with all his silliness, is wiser in his generation. I should like to see Ted deceived by the prettiest piece of claptrap that could be put together!"

It would be hard to find a pleasanter walk than the mile and a half of winding road that leads from Eltham Station to Halfont. Middlesex has not a romantic sound; neither does an absolutely flat and highly-cultivated country accord with ordinary ideas of the picturesque in scenery. But in travelling over the world I have never found greener lanes, or sweeter pastures, or finer trees, than I can remember within fourteen miles west of Hyde Park Corner. To George Blake, after London and two days' absence from Portia, every sight, and smell, and sound was simply delicious. Summer had come early this year, and trees and hedges were already in fullest leafage. Eglantines, dog-roses, honeysuckles were in great masses of blossom; the lanes were redolent with the smell of new-mown hay. Portia took off her hat and sauntered, bareheaded—meek, for the nonce, as Ruth among the corn—at Blake's side; her dark face now in sunshine, now in shadow; her black hair warmed into richer lustre by the light that fell on it in quivering emerald shafts through the branches overhead. Just so much of art-instinct was in this girl as made her always externally correct in her adaptation of her moods to those of nature. Flitting in her white dress about the twilight lawn at Halfont, walking bareheaded, with rustic gipsy grace, through the lanes, Portia Ffrench seemed still to harmonize as fitly with the surroundings as she harmonized, in silks and jewels, with a London ball-room or opera box. And to a man like Blake, prone, at all times, to be conquered through his senses mainly, this faculty of being picturesque at will is about the most potent charm a woman can possess. In Portia's case it was, one may say, but a higher kind of millinery instinct—the instinct of an actress, at best. With nature, as nature, she never pretended to hold sympathy; could not, by any effort of imagination, have seen a picture without the central figure—Portia Ffrench—in the foreground; the moment she came indoors, forgot all the trees and blossoms in the world, except, perhaps, one trailing branch of roses that might serve as a framework for Portia Ffrench's face in an open window. But Blake was not likely to be sensible of this, or any other hidden want, in an hour like this. In his saner moments—reasoning on marriage for a friend, for instance—he would say that what a working man's life needed was a companion, a heart to feel with him, a mind to understand him, clever hands to cook him a dinner. In Portia's company all he felt was, that he wanted her!—beauty, grace, picturesqueness—forever at his right hand. If you look round at the wives of the artists, or men of artistic temperament, whom you know, you will see examples enough of the kind of inspiration that guides such men in their choice of wives. Alas, they find out, most of them, at forty, what they ought to have fallen in love with—but did not—at twenty-five!

Colonel Ffrench was in his own apartments, and Miss Jemima abroad on village errands when they arrived at Halfont; so Portia had to entertain George

Blake alone, and a delightful entertainment he found it. Substantial tea, with the addition of strawberries and cream, brought out under the cedars, and Portia as handmaid; Portia running in herself with the teapot for hot water, laughing, eating bread and butter and strawberries as if she had been a Sunday-school child. Could this be a woman, he asked himself again and again, whose heart regretted the lost lover of yesterday?

Time fled so rosily that the sun was already nearing the, horizon before the artist remembered the sunset effect which he had come fourteen miles to study. "It is entirely my fault if you are too late," said Portia, "but never mind. All effects are much the same. Canal scene after sunset—canal scene before sunset —wouldn't one sound just as well as the other in a catalogue?"

And when at last they got to the desired spot, just beyond the disputed willow fence, and close to the garden gate of Addison Lodge; when at last Blake's brushes were in his hand, Portia's influence was on him still, and he could not work. To say that she was frivolous would quite inadequately describe her; indeed, the very grain and texture of Portia's nature were not frivolous, but she was marvellously, absolutely self-engrossed—self-engrossed to an extent that paralyzed every effort you might make to get away from the one charmed circle of her own good looks, her own discontents, her fortunes and misfortunes. Thus when Blake had painted about five minutes. Would he remember, please, that this was to be a lesson to her, not a study for himself? Dabbling in that yellow and red seemed easy enough—let her try it. And she tried it, and immediately spoiled one leaf of his sketching-block—manipulating body color with a heavy hand, just where the shadow in the canal was to have been kept cool and transparent. Spoiled his canvas and argued the point! very charmingly, though the sun would not linger in his course to listen. "Why should shadows be transparent and lights opaque? It was quite different in nature. See, the light was transparent, the shadows black there. Now if any one was drawing *her*, which would be opaque, her complexion, or her eyes? By-the-by, as the sketch was spoiled, would Mr. Blake like to draw her? He had often asked her to sit for him, and this evening she was in the mood—if he liked it!"

And Blake liked it, of course; and turning his eyes from the willows, fixed them on Portia Ffrench; but finding this occupation pleasanter than working (and Portia presently declaring she was in the mood for talking not sitting), the sketching materials were put aside, and at Portia's request the artist took out a cigar, and all further thought of work was over—the precise result which fifty times before, in different ways, Portia's "inspiration" had wrought for him.

They watched the sunset: they watched the midsummer after-glow bathe river and bank and overhanging trees in its soft effulgence; and then Blake's cigar was flung away, unfinished, and his voice began to grow tender, and he managed to lessen by a foot or two the space between himself and Portia. The conversation, wonderful to say, had, by this time turned, not upon her interests but his; upon the hopes, the fears, the hitherto thwarted ambition of his life. At last, abruptly, he told her of the one thing, the one best inspiration, that was wanting to him. "I am mad," he said, "I confess my madness, but I must speak. That which I covet is so far above my reach that it seems idle to speak of hope, yet if I could hear one word from your lips, Miss Ffrench, I should feel that I had something to live, something to strive for."

"And that word?" asked Portia, a little absently; she had been yawning in the spirit ever since George Blake began to talk about himself; "What is this magical word I am to say?"

" Tell me that I need not absolutely despair ! I ask no more. I have not the right, perhaps, to ask that. Only let me hear you say those words—' Do not despair,' and I shall try to be content."

" I—I don't see why you need despair," said Portia, examining the cipher on her handkerchief. " You have energy, ambition. You can make of your life what you will."

" I am not speaking of that. I am speaking of something dearer, sweeter than all ambition."

" Nothing should be dearer to a man than ambition."

" Do you tell me to despair ? Yes or no ? "

" I should be sorry to think of any one despairing, Mr. Blake."

" Miss Ffrench—Portia—"

He came closer, he would have taken her hand—but at that moment the garden gate of Addison Lodge opened close beside them, and a small black-clad figure appeared upon the bank.

" I wish she was at Jericho ! " thought Blake, starting back.

" Thank Heaven *that* little difficulty is taken off my hands ! " thought Portia Ffrench.

So seldom, even when they are love-making, do two human beings feel precisely the same in any given emergency.

CHAPTER XIX.

THE intruder, meantime, sauntered slowly on, a book in her hand, the dreamy uncounscious look of one who knows himself to be alone, on her face. At last, after standing still awhile, intently gazing at the river, she seated herself on the bank, not half a dozen paces from George Blake and Portia, who were watching her in silence.

There was light enough still in heaven to see to read, but Susan's book lay unopened at her side. The book was " Ixion "—a dogs-eared copy that she had procured over-night from the Hounslow library, and the reading of which had proved a terribly hard day's labor to her, in spite of all her predilection for the writer !

Walter Scott, Susan could understand ; and Fielding, interpreted by the light of her own innocent heart ; and Goldsmith. Mr. George Blake was beyond her. The piled-up word painting, the spasmodic leaps of this clever young writer—too fatally convinced of his own cleverness to trouble himself about his reader's interest—rendered " Ixion " difficult as a lesson-book to a child accustomed to the unvarnished style, the honest, straightforward story-telling of the great masters. Whenever a tolerably intelligent piece of narrative came in, Susan had followed it thankfully ; had pursued it with patience (through scenes bearing about the same relation to the plot as do variations to some tortured air set for the flute) ; when, at length, a proper name she knew reappeared, had snatched at it eagerly, trusting ever and in vain that she had at length got some human form in hand for good ; but—she had not been amused. She was now in the middle of the third volume, and she let the daylight go without reading it ; did not want to know whether guilt should triumph, in the last chapter, or virtue ; did not want to know " what became " of anybody !

The exceeding ability of the author had impressed itself upon her throughout, with force ; with greater force, I dare say, than would have been the case had she understood his book. So many French words, so many passages that sounded to her like nonsense, so much knowledge of high life and the wickedness thereof. What a genius, what a consummate man of the world was this great writer who had condescended to her foolish society during a whole summer's evening ! Susan sat thinking of George Blake's powers, in a perfect bewilderment of admiration ; although to the fate of his good young gentleman, and his wicked young gentleman, and the various ladies connected with the destiny of each she was so cruelly indifferent. Then, as she watched the dark flow of the canal, and listened to the dull clank of the distant mill, gradually her thoughts wandered away from " Ixion " altogether, and came round to the deeper interests of her own small life-drama ; to the chances of George Blake having, by this time, forgotten her ; to Portia's superior fortune ; to the almost certainty, as things stood now, of Portia one day becoming George Blake's wife.

She gave a long-drawn sigh when she got thus far, gazing with her blind eyes straight in the direction of the two persons who occupied her thoughts ; and then Portia whispered to her companion, and under his voice Blake began to sing :

Drink to me only with thine eyes.

Susan gave a cry of surprise ; and Portia rose, and moving up the bank, seated herself good humoredly at her side. Portia Ffrench was in a mood to feel good-humored with every one in the world to day. Inaction, and the tedium inaction brings with it to a nature at once restless and indolent like hers, was over. She was playing her game, was fighting her battle in earnest, and could afford to be generous to her unconscious fellow actors—or victims, as the sequel might prove.

"We have been watching you for the last half hour, Susan. I hope you know that you have been telling all your thoughts aloud ? Oh, I forgot ; you won't know whom ' we ' means. Take out your spectacles and you will see Mr. Blake down among the bulrushes. We have been sketching."

Susan felt as though in that moment she got older by a dozen years. The light happiness of Portia's tone, the familiar " we," the spot, the hour in which she had come upon them together and alone, all told her the truth—the truth she had known, but never absolutely realized till now. A sensation like that of suddenly plunging into cold water seemed for a movement well-nigh to suffocate her ; then it passed, and instinct told her she must control her voice and lips, and be a woman, and let this other woman, who watched her, guess nothing of her suffering or her jealousy.

" If I talked aloud you had to listen chiefly to secrets about packing-cases and portmanteaus," she said. " You know that I'm going to leave home to-morrow for ever ? The auctioneer wants to set the house ready for the sale at once, and I am going to stay with Miss Collinson."

Susan's voice trembled ; not, it must be conceded, from emotion wholly connected with Addison Lodge, and Blake, forgetting that a minute ago he had wished her at Jericho, felt all his first liking for the little girl return. " You have not been telling us any of your secrets, my dear. Don't let Miss Ffrench frighten you. It is we who have been talking instead of working—talking nonsense and losing all the daylight. Now there is just enough left, Susan, for me to sketch you and Por—and Miss Ffrench, if you will both remain precisely in your present attitude for ten minutes. I should like to carry away some memento of this evening ! " He glanced at Portia as he spoke.

Without seeming to move a muscle, Portia fell, on the instant, into a graceful position. Sitting for her portrait was a sort of inborn talent with her—an art-instinct of the same purely egotistical and millinery order as that by which she adapted her outward moods to those of nature. The quick blood leaped into Susan Fielding's cheek. She was only to be brought in as a foil, a back-ground to Portia, of course; still George Blake thought her face worth drawing, wanted to possess some remembrance of this evening, and of meeting her. And then, all at once, she remembered the compliment Teddy Josselyn had paid her on Blake's behalf, and the blush deepened, and her great eyes dilated, as grey eyes have a trick of doing when any new feeling stirs their possessor, and Susan looked bewitching!

A dear little unsophisticated child of nature, thought Blake, as he sketched the outline of her soft round face; the face which, despite its present baby "vacancy" never failed to stir your imagination by the possibilities of emotion it contained. Portia Ffrench was a woman to possess whom a man would risk life and more than life. This was a child to inspire—never passion, perhaps, but the tender familiar love one has for a sister; a sweet, confiding, clinging little soul whom he would like to have to live in his house, if he were married to Portia; a child to tease and caress alternately, just for the pleasure of watching those flexible lips quiver, those dilating eyes change hue; a dear little thing who would run for his slippers, and light his pipe, and serve as a model for all the Mignons and Clärchens he might want to paint.

If Susan—for the matter of that, if Portia—could have read his thoughts!

"And so you have been reading 'Ixion'?" remarked Portia, taking up the book which lay at Susan's side. "I suppose our lips, at least, may move, Mr. Blake? Well, how do you like it? Mr. Blake has no literary vanity. Criticise freely."

"I like it very well, thank you, Miss Portia," said Susan, with caution.

"Very well! That is what Aunt Jem's school-children all say when I ask them, after one of my annual bun orgies, how they have enjoyed themselves. 'Very well, thank you, Miss Portia.' Have you no special criticism to make? Do you like the humor best, or the sentiment, or the asides of the author?—pretty numerous, these last!"

"I like the beginning of the book best, as far as I've gone," said Susan. "All the part where Eustace is at school, and how he steals the master's custards, and falls in love with old Miss Burchell. You see I understand anything of a story best," she added, apologetically; "whenever it comes to opinions and descriptions, and—and all the really fine parts of a book I get out of my depth."

"And you have not got to the end, then?" said Portia. "You have been able to lay down this enthralling novel unfinished, as favorable critics in the little bits you see quoted in advertisements, always declare they were unable to do!"

"I read to where Eustace goes to dine with the Marquis—I mean the prime minister—I don't remember the grand people's names! And they all talk politics—oh, a great many pages of politics, and just then it got dark, and I shall finish it to-morrow. I'm sure," remembering George Blake's feelings, "'Ixion' is a book very few people indeed could have written."

"And that still fewer people could read," cried out the author, with his hearty laugh. "Susan, you are the acutest critic I have had. The first half of the first volume is not such trash as the rest, simply because I knew, or thought I knew, what I meant when I wrote it. I really was at school once, and I did steal custards, and I did fall in love with an old Miss Burchell. About all the rest—prime minister, marquises and politics, I know and care as much as you do, Susan!"

"And shall you ever write another novel, sir?"

"Never," answered Blake, with emphasis. "All great men mistake their vocation once. I have got over my mistake, and shall be a painter, and a painter only, till my life's end. Oh, don't bend down your head, Susan—the eyes higher—no, don't look at the clouds—look at me. What a pity we haven't time for color! How can eyes like Susan's be given in dull black and white?"

The sketch in another few minutes was finished and handed up to the two girls for approval. Portia examined it first, a well-contented smile on her face. Blake had drawn her in profile, as he knew she loved to be drawn; the nose and upper lip and cheek faultlessly statuesque, the head poised like a Greek goddess's, every line in the drooping, graceful figure, a flattery. An orthodox stereotyped design for a "beauty heroine," in short; not very much more characteristic than those Blake used to draw on his copy-book covers as the Maid of Athens, or Haidee, when he was still a schoolboy, and had never seen Portia Ffrench.

Of Susan Fielding he had, not seeking to idealize, made a little sketch full of individuality and life—plainer than the girl was, perhaps, for in determining to get a likeness he had exaggerated the peculiarities of her face; given to the eyes a more startled look, to the full lips more fulness, to the wildly curling hair more curliness—but a portrait, a human being, not a heroine!

"They are both excellent," said Portia. "Susan's the *least* bit of a caricature, perhaps; but a capital likeness. Who is it so like? Mr. Blake, who is your sketch of Susan like? Shelley, I think, as one always sees him in the frontispiece of his poems."

Susan on hearing herself compared to a poet, put out her hand, shyly, yet hopefully, for the drawing. All the author's portraits she had seen in her father's books, were good-looking, oval-faced gentlemen, with pretty mouths, and languishing eyes—and foreheads as smooth and marble-like as fine line engraving could make them.

"It is a caricature, I must allow," said Portia, considerately, and keeping back the sketch a moment before she gave it into Susan's hands. "But coloring on the cheeks and hair would make such a difference!"

Poor little Susan held up the sketch within two inches of her nose, and scrutinized it without speaking a word. At last—"And am I like this?" she exclaimed. "Oh, I never knew before I was so hideous. 'Tis like a witch, a negress—such lips—such eyes! and being by the side of Portia makes it worse."

Blake by this time had collected his sketching materials and clambered up the bank. He knelt down at Susan's side, and put his arm jestingly round her slim child's waist.

"The vanity of children! Why, the face is a regular Sir Joshua, Susan. You don't understand its artistic beauty," stooping to look over the drawing with her, and so close that her soft short curls touched his cheek. "You will hang on the walls of the R. A. some day, little Susan, in the same picture with Miss Ffrench, unless I am mistaken."

Susan's breath came and went tumultuously. She forgot Portia, forgot her own shyness, forgot everything in the universe save the burning, intolerable sense of humiliation that overwhelmed her. "Let me go," she cried, breaking from him with force. "You are unkind. What right have you to laugh at me?

I don't know who Sir Joshua is; I don't know what you mean by 'arc, ch!'
But I know I'll *never* be painted in any picture as a background for some one
else's beauty."

And before George Blake could guess her intention she had torn her sketch
into pieces, and flung it in the canal. Then she started up to her feet, trembling
with such vehemence of passion as in her whole life she had never felt till this
moment.

Portia broke into one of her pleasantest thrilling laughs.

"It really was a caricature, Mr. Blake. If you had drawn such a sketch of
me I would have been as cross myself. But you shouldn't have destroyed it,
Susan, my dear. By the time it was colored it would have looked very—nice, I
dare say. Mr. Blake only wanted the rough idea of your face."

"Mr. Blake can find plenty of ideas elsewhere," said Susan, with quivering
indignation. "No need to go far for the model of such a face as that," pointing
to the torn fragments of the sketch, as they eddied slowly down the canal.

"If I could command every model in London I should never get one like
that again," said Blake. "However, you have done no mischief, Miss Fielding,"
he added. "The sketch is gone, but the original face is quite safe in my recollection—the face with a new expression on it." And he rose, and fixed his eyes
steadily on Susan. "It shall be the principal figure, not the background of the
picture, now."

"And I shall have to retire to the background," remarked Portia, quietly.

Blake looked foolish. I will not hazard the opinion that he or any man could
be the very least in love with more than one object at a time. But, speaking of
him simply as an artist, I assert that he would have found it hard to choose at
this moment between the dark, Titian-like beauty of Portia's face, as she looked
up at him with half audacious, half-appealing glance, and the delicate Greuze-
like charm of Susan's—the cheeks all aflush, the lips parted, the fire of latent
passion, almost of latent fierceness, in the great, dove-like eyes.

"Ah, I see that I shall have to take the second place," said Portia, mock-
indignant. "Susan is to wear the white satin, and I must content myself in
white lawn. All I can do is to abdicate gracefully. I think you might have
spared the part of the sketch that held me, Susan. I could have shown it about
the world, as the ideal Mr. Blake *once* had of my face."

Without answering a syllable, Susan took up her book from the bank and
turned away. The poor child's conscience was in a very tumult of shame and
repentance already, and she was silent, not through sullenness, but because, if
she had spoken, she must infallibly have burst into tears.

"All little light green-eyed women have that sort of peppery temper," gen-
eralized Portia, cheerfully, as the small figure moved away. "A pity, perhaps,
that you made the sketch such a terrible caricature?"

"A pity that the child should be really pained by such nonsense," said kind-
hearted Blake. "She must never go away without forgiving me. I'll run after
her, and make it all up in a minute."

And before Portia could laugh him out of his intention he had carried it into
effect.

Susan reached the garden-door, entered; locked it on the inside.

"Miss Fielding?"

No answer.

"Susan, I have something to say to you."

"I can" (voice thick and indistinct) "hear it from this side, sir."

"But I can't say it from this side. Open the door at once."

"I would rather not, I thank you."

"And I would rather that you did. To please me, open the door, my dear little Susan?"

The key turned in a second; the door stood open.

"I have come to reason seriously with you, Susan. You know nothing about Art. Any painter would have told you that the idea of my sketch was beautiful, much more beautiful," added Blake, with the baseness of his sex, "than any studied, insipid copy of regular features; item, a straight nose; item, a small mouth, et cetera. Your ignorance, not my pencil, was to blame, my dear."

"I'm sorry I tore it, Mr. Blake; I believe I was never in such a rage before. I don't know what possessed me."

"The demon of vanity, child; neither more nor less. I drew you, not with a perfect Grecian profile, but with the dear little imperfect English face that you have, and you detested me."

"Oh, no—not you!"

"Who, then?"

"I—I hope I detest no one." And Susan drooped her face, and played with a tiny leaf which, as they talked, had drifted down upon the volume of 'Ixion' in her hand. Behind her fair head rose a whole background of pleasant dusk-subdued color—the prim beds with their borders of midsummer flowers, the old-fashioned espalier fruit trees, which had been the pride and glory of Fielding's life.

Blake thought of the garden scene in Faust.

"And do you forgive me, my dear—that is what I want to know?" he asked.

In his conversation of an hour ago with Portia his voice had not sank to half so soft, so pleading a tone as it took now.

"I think it is me to beg pardon, and you to forgive, Mr. Blake."

"For what?"

"Oh, for having destroyed a drawing you valued—a drawing of Portia. It was very wicked of me, but I scarce knew what I did, you had hurt me so."

"Hurt you, again! and yet I have told you that the idea of my sketch was beautiful—a thousand times more beautiful, really, than—Susan, Susan, who would have thought a little village girl's head could be so full of vanity?"

He took both her hands—"Ixion" falling to the ground, and drew her to him close.

"I don't mean to let you go until you have confessed that I am right and you are wrong. Now repeat after me—'It was all my vanity—'"

"I'll never say that, sir. I am not vain. I was angry because—because—"

"Go on, my dear."

"Because of Portia. She has so much, has everything she chooses, and I have nothing. I was a jest for you both. You, who have each other, what should you think of my being pained or not?"

Blake let her hands go in a moment; his face became suddenly grave. He was not a coxcomb—was, at least, no vainer than the majority of men; but he had the insight born of sympathy that belongs to all people of his temperament; and something in the sound of Susan's untutored voice did make him feel that this little scene might as well have been left unacted. Ah, could Portia Ffrench's well-controlled voice ever quicken, even vibrate, with a sound like that?

"You were angry, in short, Susan, because you were angry." He tried his best to make his own manner fraternal and unconscious. "The only logical

reason that can ever be given in such matters. Well, I suppose I must be
going "—for the girl stood silent and confused, not helping him out by a word—
" I have to leave by the half-past nine train. Good night, Susan."

" Good night, sir."

" And we are friends, are we not? That is right. The next time we meet
you will sit for me again."

" There'll be no next time," said Susan, turning sorrowfully away. " This
is good-by, not good-night."

And so they parted.

Portia was frank and gracious beyond her wont when Blake rejoined her, and
yet how was it? All her frankness, all her graciousness, could not cause the
thread of their discourse to reunite precisely at the point at which Susan's appearance had broken it off. She never said a word about the torn sketch or the
length of time Blake had been absent. All that occupied her mind was plaintive
regret that he must leave so soon. Nine o'clock only—was he indeed obliged to
go by the next train? How quickly had the evening passed; how kindly, how
considerately had Mr. Blake cheered her on this first day of her altered prospects! She would see him in Eaton square to-morrow? unless, indeed, he were
busied upon more important matters than paying nonsense visits. If he would
come round between four and five o'clock she would contrive to be at home, and
they would make out as many pleasant plans as possible for the coming week.
Of course, she might get him an invitation for Lady Blank's ball and Mrs. Dash's
concert—for everything that should be going on during her own few days in London?

" You know I bade you not despair," she cried, when George Blake had
already turned to depart, " and I meant what I said. Now I must do my best,
practically, to help you 'drive dull care away.' At the end of this week I hope
you will tell me that my prescription is taking effect."

The words, and still more the tone in which they were spoken, admitted of
an interpretation dangerously flattering to a man as much in love as Blake ; and
still, for once, Portia Ffrench had overshot her mark. The ring of a voice with
nature, with passion in it, was too fresh on his memory for the very prettiest art
to impress him as it might have done an hour and a half ago. " I will go wherever you are good enough to bid me go," was his answer. " But I am afraid, if
my cure could be worked by means of balls and concerts, it would be such a cure
as I don't wish to think of—a cure worse than the disease."

Over which answer Portia pondered seriously, as she stood and watched the
young man's figure disappear in the twilight. She was about to make the grand
knight's move—tortuous, but decisive—of her game : not a time. surely, to waste
regret over the loss of an inefficient little pawn or two! " Still—still," mused
Richard Ffrench's granddaughter, " many a well-fought match has been lost for
want of a pawn in the end. In the superior game of chess called life, give up
nothing until the sacrifice becomes a duty, and even then—pause."

CHAPTER XX.

NEXT day was the one to which Susan had looked forward as the most certainly miserable turning point of her life—the last day she was to spend in the
old home. And the dreaded hour of parting came, and she found herself travelling in the hired fly toward Miss Collinson's, without being able to shed a tear

—nay, without being able to realize that Addison Lodge and all the household gods that it contained were, indeed, already things of the past.

"Like her age, Mr. Hackitt," moralized old Nancy Wicks to the auctioneer, as he ticketed the chairs and tables for the sale. "A week ago, little Miss were fretting herself to a skeleton at the thoughts of living among strangers, far away from Halfont churchyard; and off she goes to-day as blithe as a lark, and never so much as shed a tear when Jim Simmons carried out her pa's fiddle-case, nor nothing." (The poor little girl had cried herself, with bitterest tears, to sleep the night before; then dreamed a dream of a certain artist painting her portrait on a golden summer noon, under over-arching trees, while sketches of Portia Ffrench —like, but with wild eyes, with angry lips—were constantly floating by along a dark river at their feet—a perfectly delicious dream, the flavor of which clung too pertinaciously to her lips next morning for any reality to have quite its right taste, even the sorrowful reality of leaving home forever.) "Some young gentleman at the bottom of it all, take my word, Mr. Hackitt. There's young Collinson—and a gay, good-for-nothing fellow, too, they do say—been here every afternoon for the last five days, to my own knowledge."

Tom Collinson was standing on the door steps of his sister's house, ready to receive Susan as she got out of the fly. His short, square figure was decked out in his smartest suit and necktie; his naturally florid face was crimson with excitement; a ridiculous minglement of exultation and sheepishness was in his whole demeanor. He helped the driver to carry Susan's boxes up stairs, then led her into the parlor; made her sit down on the sofa; stared at her; circled round and round her, rubbing his hands, as men do to whom hands are an embarrassment; tried to make a pretty speech about her feeling herself at home under Eliza's roof; failed; and expressed his hopes suddenly that she was fond of calf's head and brains.

"Eliza is a good old soul, and not a bad cook, pastry especially, but no more idea of a change than a cat, she'd give one the same dish for a fortnight and think because you had liked it once you must like it always. So she said to me this morning, 'Tom,' she said, 'what'll be a nice thing for Susan,' she always calls you Susan, 'a nice thing for Susan the first day she dines here? A loin of pork, and a pudding baked under?' Now I like pork, and I like a pudding baked under," said Tom, "but I don't like it every day of my life, and we've had it twice this week already. So I said calf's head. I hope you really do like a calf's head and brains?"

To this lover-like appeal Susan was able to reply satisfactorily. She did like calf's head—well, yes, better perhaps (on being pressed) than pork with pudding under. And then they came to another full stop. Susan was never great at originating conversation; and Mr. Collinson, now that he had absolutely made up his mind to be in love, felt his tongue cleave to the roof of his mouth every time he tried to address her.

"Mourning's very becoming—to some people," he jerked out at last.

"Do you think so?" said Susan.

And then this subject, too, fell to the ground. Collinson tried to pick it up a minute later, having stared harder than ever at Susan meantime, by repeating, "Yes, to some people!" But Susan had forgotten what he was talking of, and made no answer.

"Eliza's out," this after a longer pause than the last. "I thought you might fancy a cucumber"—cowcumber, Tom called it—"and Eliza's gone for one."

"Is she?"

"Yes, but I hope—*I hope*—Miss Susan, that you don't mind finding yourself alone with me?"

"Mind! why should I, Mr. Collinson?"

"Oh no, not at all, only I thought perhaps, ah—um—oh, Miss Susan," bringing up his courage with a run, "how long the time has seemed since I saw you last!"

He stopped in his walk, looked at her sentimentally, then sighed. Tom Collinson's was not a face or figure which accorded well with sentiment, and Susan laughed. He felt this was encouraging.

"You know that I called at Addison Lodge yesterday?"

"Yes, I was packing—I mean Nancy was packing and I was looking on, reading."

"And the day before?"

"I was at the Manor. I was there all the afternoon."

"You are always at the Manor, always with Portia Ffrench. I suppose you know this about her cousin Josselin being off with her? He has proved himself not such a fool as he looks, after all."

Susan did not answer.

"And I suppose you know that she is on already with the singing fellow—Blake, don't they call him? They say she was out with him in the lanes at I don't know what o'clock last night."

Susan's face flamed. "A pity 'they' are not better employed than to spy other people's doings and then spread mean stories about them afterward!" she cried, with less accuracy of syntax, than energy of voice and manner.

Collinson watched her jealously. "You are a very warm defender of Portia Ffrench," he remarked, "I wonder whether she'd speak up so hot for you if you got yourself talked about! It isn't my business, I know, to comment on the manners of my betters," went on Tom, "but, to my way of thinking, for a girl to break off with one sweetheart in the morning, and take on another before night is disgusting, neither more nor less. I'm sure you wouldn't act so, Miss Susan?"

He did his utmost to throw tender meaning into this question.

"When the temptation comes, I shall be able to answer," said Susan, in her stiffest little Quakeress tone. "I know nothing about sweethearts, Mr. Collinson, and I wish to know nothing about them."

"You—you can't be so cruel as to mean that?" interrupted Tom, edging himself a little nearer; then just as he felt the ice was beginning to break, Miss Collinson inopportunely ran up the front steps, the cucumber in her hand; and his chance, for this time, was over.

"Still, I have got on a good bit," he soliloquized mentally, glancing at himself in the dingy glass above the mantel-shelf. "'Who talks of love makes it,' I know I've read that somewhere. If I go on gaining ground like this we shall be engaged in no time."

And throughout the remainder of the day he continued to gain ground of the same kind; to hover fatuitously round Susan, to gaze at her askance, to stammer out the beginning of complimentary speeches which he had not courage to finish, to get curt answers which he tried to persuade himself were the flattering result of maiden bashfulness. When night came, and he was at last left alone in the parlor with his sister, he broke out abruptly:

"And pray, what is your opinion of Susan now, Eliza?"

Miss Collinson looked up from the book in which she was going through her accustomed evening exercises, with thoughts undisturbed by love or lovers. "Susan? well, I really think she's getting hearty. She took two helps at dinner, I remarked, but calf's head is just one of those things a delicate person can always enjoy. Three weeks before his death, I remember poor father said—"

"For the Lord's sake don't tell me!" groaned Tom. "Who's talking of delicacy and calf's-head and what our blessed old father used to say! Do you think that she—do you judge from her manner—dash it all, have you still the same opinion about the girl as you had the other night when we were walking across the heath?"

"I don't remember exactly what my opinion was, my dear."

Collinson strode angrily away from the room and from the house, but returned long before midnight; he had altogether given up bad hours during the last few days; and next morning his courtship, such courtship as it was, went on again. He was a man coarse alike by temperament and the life that he had led, a man self-confident through ignorance, and who had never hitherto experienced difficulty in making known his feelings to any of the women with whom he had been thrown. But now in the presence of Susan Fielding, in the presence of this shrinking little girl of seventeen, his whole loud audacious nature seemed to collapse. The most brilliant men do not invariably shine in the position of lovers; Tom Collinson thus situated became absolutely, idiotically taciturn. Every hour found him deeper in love, every hour found him dumber! If he could only once break the ice, he would think, only get as far as the first word of a declaration, he would back himself to find plenty to say for ever afterward. Meanwhile, little as he guessed it, his silence effected more for him than any speech would have done with Susan; reconciled her unconsciously, day by day, to his presence. She was too short-sighted to be much annoyed by the demonstrativeness of his looks, and as he would sit blankly staring at her for hours together without relieving his feelings by a single sentimental speech, the girl grew gradually to think of him as a harmless kindly creature, toward whom she had once cherished a groundless repugnance, and whose worse fault was stupidity. Of course he was utterly unlike Mr. Blake—alas! was it her lot to be thrown with men like Mr. Blake? But he was kind and open-hearted, in his way, did twenty things a day to give her pleasure; and Susan was grateful. More than that, at the end of a very short time, began to feel that she really liked poor ignorant Tom a great deal better than she liked Elizabeth, with all her superior principles, all her superior culture.

Whatever his graver, more positive faults—and one sums them up easiest by saying that he had not a single positive virtue—Tom possessed the negative merit of a sunshiny temperament. He was too thoroughly fond of his own comfort even to be long sullen, too self-satisfied to know the meaning of moral or mental depression. If the small servant had transgressed, Miss Collinson, worthy woman, would address her meekly, admonishingly, yet with a vein of mild sourness—"naggling," Betsy called it—running through the admonition, that would make the child sob her heart out for the remainder of the day. Tom's vengeance, on the other hand, was swift and sharp—an oath, a box on the ear; then, ten minutes afterward, a joking word, or two-pence (from Eliza's coppers) that at once restored the smile to poor Betsy's face. And this difference between them was an essential one—a difference of race. The first Mrs. Collinson had been a sterling, over-scrupulous, melancholy-minded woman, capable of doing everything for her husband and children save making their lives happy. The second was a lazy, selfish, extravagant drone; always expecting and finding other people to perform her duties ; thoroughly ungrateful ; thoroughly without principle ; but easy of temper, pleasant to live with. And her son was like her.

Nothing could be heartier, more confidence-inspiring than Tom Collinson's shake of the hand : Eliza, diffident good soul, extended to you a fish-like palm, through which not a throb of human sympathy was discernible—nothing franker than the look with which his well-opened eyes met yours : Eliza's, from purely physical timidity, sank to the ground every time she was spoken to. And Susan Fielding's was just the temperament upon which this gift of heartiness, animal spirits—call it by what name you will—operates like magnetism. Quiet, dreamy, sensitive herself, the subdued melancholy of Eliza Collinson affected her spirits like a day of drizzling rain, of unbroken cloud. What she imperatively needed in a companion was brightness ; and Tom, despite his want of brains, was bright—yes, even in the present taciturnity engendered in him by love.

Miss Collinson had a score of the little ghostly habits unmarried women con- tract through long years of solitude and economy ; such as when she returned from a walk, taking off her boots in the passage, and creeping up-stairs in her stockings ; wearing list slippers about the house ; sitting without lights in the dark, " unless any one really wanted to employ their minds." Tom's thick boots were to be heard everywhere—was life long enough to think about the effect of mud on stair-carpets ? He whistled reprobate airs from morning till night, Sun- days included. He taught the pious old cockatoo the forgotten blasphemies of her youth. He skirmished from attic to cellar after Betsy. He woke the two cats, neutral enemies for years, into active combat. He made the house alive, in short ; and Susan, child as she was, grew, after four days, to be a little sorry when he went out, a little glad when he returned.

Proper heroines of romance like one human being, and one only, during the course of their mortal lives. In recording Susan's commonplace story it seems I shall be forced into confessing she liked every good-looking young man she came across. And so, I think, with very different degrees of liking, she did. Teddy Josselin for his grace, and dress, and refinement, and handsome face ; George Blake—ah, George Blake for everything ! and now poor, brainless, vul- gar Tom, for his animal school-boy spirits, and good nature to herself. Have not most women—heroines apart—been subject at this chrysalis stage of their existence, to the like chronic but perfectly safe disorder of inconstancy ?

A week passed by, and the Tuesday on which the sale was to take place at Addison Lodge arrived. Tom, ever ready to shirk anything in the shape of dis- agreeable employment, declared that it was necessary for him to go up to town for the day, " on the look-out for employment." He would have attended the sale if his presence there could have profited Susan's interests, but what-possi- ble good, said Tom, could be got by bullying a man like Hackitt ? If you didn't let an auctioneer cheat you in one way he would in another, you might be quite sure. And so Miss Collinson, book in hand, had to start alone on her self-im- posed duty of " checking off" Mr. Hackitt's accounts, and Susan was left at home to get through the day as she could.

It was a terribly heavy day to her ; heavier far than the one on which, upheld in spirit by the remembrance of her dream, she had bidden home good-by. Young people, as a rule, part lightly with external objects. The affection born of habit that clings to an arm-chair, a writing-table, the paper on the wall, is quite an affection of later years. But Susan, not a little from the fact of her short-sightedness, shrank almost as old people do from the unknown ; held with sorrowful eagerness to the thought of every material link that bound her to the past. When eleven o'clock had struck, the hour at which the sale began, it seemed to her that at every ten minutes a sort of death-knell tolled. Once, long ago, she had been with Miss Collinson to a sale in the village, and she remembered the old auctioneer pompously descanting, with flowers of professional rhetoric, on the merits of every table and chair, then remorselessly knocking it down. " A giving of this valuable article away—a robbing of my employer ! " was Mr. Hackitt's formula—" to the highest bidder."

" Going—going—gone ! " All through the forenoon she sat, unable to work or read, with that word " gone " ringing in her heart ; then, unable to bear the weight of her own thoughts longer, put on her bonnet and started for a lonely walk across the heath. It was a perfect June day, the blue sky lightly flecked with clouds, a strong warm wind blowing from the south-west, and after a quarter of an hour's slow walking Susan turned off from the high road upon one of the few portions of the heath that still remained uninclosed, and where, a dozen yards or so from the path, a group of lichened stones formed a pleasant halting-place for idle or footsore wayfarers. These stones had always been a favorite haunt of Fielding and his little girl ; and taking out her glasses, Susan looked long and wistfully around at the familiar landmarks, which till now had bounded the vista of her narrow life. Behind her, Harrow-on-the-Hill ; far away, in the opposite direction, a dim blue spot which she knew to be Epsom Grand Stand ; the dull grey smoke of London to the left ; the heath with its solitary clump of firs, its quick gradations of hue, as the passing clouds threw patch after patch into purple shade or yellow sunlight, filling up all the foreground and middle distance.

Susan had not been here long before she heard a measured, soldier-like step passing in the direction of the village ; in another minute, a figure passed between her and the sun, and, looking up, she saw Miss Jemima Ffrench. Miss Jemima, in the accustomed thick shoes and sensible bonnet in which she paid her cottage visits, a well-filled basket on her arm, the smile which in itself seemed to be a sort of June sunshine upon her kind old face.

She shook hands with the little girl, seated herself at her side, and did *not* begin to talk about the sale. Perfect good-heartedness, you will remark, always begets the very finest good-breeding. " You are just the person I wanted to meet, my dear. I have had a letter from Portia, containing all sorts of messages to you. She seems to be enjoying herself more than usual, and is not coming back for the next ten days."

Susan felt acutely, miserably jealous on the instant. What cause but one could account either for Portia's enjoyment or the extension of her stay in town ?

" I am terribly stupid at remembering messages," went on Miss Jemima ; " but there was something about a sketch, I know. Stay, I believe I have the letter in my pocket—no, yes ; then you may read it for yourself. My niece and I have no very important secrets just at present, and I know Portia would like me to tell you all she is doing and seeing." And, saying this, Miss Jemima drew two closely-written sheets of note paper from an envelope, and gave them to Susan.

Portia Ffrench wrote a thoroughly picturesque hand : bold, unfaltering, full of originality, a hand with really only one fault to speak of—it was illegible. Long habit, the patience of great affection, had broken Miss Jemima in to the task of deciphering her letters ; to the rest of the world they were a blank. " Lucky I am not the kind of person to write love letters," Portia would say of herself. "The man does not live who would take the trouble to read them through." Susan looked down one page, then another, then turned back hopelessly to the first.

"I can't make out a single line," said she. "All I see is that Mr. Blake's name comes very often."

"Very often," repeated Miss Jemima, shaking her head with meaning. "The fact is, my dear, I know that you are fond of Portia, and I know that I can trust you with a secret, so I'll make you my confidante—the fact is, a very strong suspicion has come into my mind to-day, Susan."

"Has it, ma'am?"

"A suspicion about Portia and Mr. Blake."

"Ah."

"I may be wrong, as I have been before. If I am, Portia can laugh at me for my last piece of romantic folly, as she will call it; and yet I don't think I am mistaken this time. I will read you the letter first, and you shall see."

And Miss Jemima took out her spectacles and read, Susan resigning herself to hear what she knew beforehand would be the final deathblow to every hope she had cherished, every dream she had dreamed.

"DEAR AUNT JEM: I haven't ten minutes to write, for we are just going off to the Zoo' "—on Sunday, I am sorry to say, Susan. "Mr. Blake and I, grandmamma, and poor Teddy. Mr. Blake to walk with me, Teddy to give grandmamma his arm, and listen to unqualified praises of Miss Minters, the heiress, and qualified abuse of Portia Ffrench, the pauper. He has been on this kind of duty the whole past week. Wherever we have been, and we have been everywhere, grandmamma has insisted on Teddy accompanying us. To show the world, she says, that he cares nothing, and that I care nothing about the breaking off of our engagement. It would be very detrimental to me, grandmamma says, if I were suspected of having had a *real* attachment to my cousin (I should have thought it wonderfully to my advantage to suppose that I, Portia Ffrench, could have had a real attachment for anything). Oh, how I have been amusing myself! I don't think I ever "—mark this, Susan—"felt the meaning of really wild spirits till now. When we sit at dinner, or walk about in our party of four—Ted and grandmamma, Mr. Blake and I—'tis as much as I can do to keep from singing aloud. We have had two delightful balls, Lady"—Claptrap, it looks like—"and Mrs."—no, I must leave out the proper names. "I wore my mauve satin at the first, my white silk with black flounces at the last. Both of them, alas! trousseau dresses. Mr. Blake, I need not say, was at these balls. He doesn't dance, you know. I did not dance. I feel my advancing years, and prefer sitting out and talking with a *rational* companion. Grandmamma is wonderfully, impertinently civil to Mr. Blake; tries to do art-talk for his benefit—a condescension resulting in much the kind of tone she would use to one of the young men at Howell & James's, if she were talking about shawls. He doesn't mind. He minds nothing. He, too, I think, seems thoroughly happy. By the way, tell Susan"—ah, to be sure, this is the message—"tell Susan Fielding not to regret having torn the sketch. Mr. Blake has done a much better one—of me, I mean. It is colored and half-length. I will steal it for you, Aunt Jem. So the poor little thing is really staying with the Collinsons! Tell her not to let that terrible young Collinson fall in love with her"—you must not mind, my dear; you know Portia's jesting way—"also, that I shall hope to see her before she leaves for France. The Smiths—charming people, I forget whether you know them—have asked me to run down to Brighton for a day or two when I leave grandmamma; and, as I shall be in the neighborhood, I think I may as well go and see the Gordons at Worthing. You *must* remember all about the Gordons? I shall take the Browns at Guilford as I return. All these moves are so uncertain that I can't tell you where to write; but I shall console myself with your favorite saying of no news being good news. Mr. Blake, who, as usual, is sketching my unhappy profile "—sketching, too, on a Sunday! "desires kindest remembrances, and I am your affectionate.

"PORTIA."

"And now, Susan," Miss Jemima folded the letter, and returned it to her pocket, "what do *you* divine from all this?"

"That Portia has very soon got over her regret about Mr. Josselin," said Susan.

"What next?"

"I really don't know, ma'am, except that she has been enjoying herself a good deal, and has worn a mauve satin dress at one ball and a white silk trimmed with black lace at another."

"And what about this *rational* companion, whose conversation she prefers to dancing?"

"Oh, that is quite an old affair," said Susan, doing her best to look easy and unconcerned. "I should say Mr. Blake and Portia came to an understanding long ago about the charm of each other's conversation—it is no news to me.'

"What," exclaimed old Miss Jemima, "has Portia told you?"

"Portia has told me nothing," interrupted Susan, quickly. "But I watched them together—that evening I drank tea with you on my birthday, and another evening a week ago, the day after Portia's engagement was broken off. It was a thing no one could mistake about," said poor little Susan, as decisively as if she had had fifty years' experience in the usages of love and lovers.

Miss Jemima kept silent for a minute; then—"My opinion is confirmed," she said, with a well-pleased face. "Young ladies of your age are wonderfully acute judges, Miss Susan. Yes, yes; the whole thing is pretty plain. And I have accused my dear Portia of being heartless, worldly; never guessing that an honorable attachment to this young man might be at the bottom of all her seeming inconstancy. I see it now; a hundred words of the poor child's come back to me. She was too honorable to break off her engagement to her cousin; but she accepted her release thankfully. Portia's is a fine nature, Susan."

"Yes—I hope so."

"There are faults without number, of which I would wish to see her cured; but they are all faults of her generation rather than of her own. This independence, for instance. Running down to the 'Smiths at Brighton,' the 'Gordons at Worthing'—people her grandfather and myself do not know by name. In olden days, a young woman would have been considered lost who had travelled about the country unescorted. But Portia tells me it is the fashion for girls to be independent—that every one does the same, and so I try to be satisfied."

"And if what you suggest is true, no doubt Mr. Blake will be Portia's escort," remarked Susan.

"H'm! I don't see that that makes it any better, my dear—I mean as regards appearance; for I know Portia too well to suspect her of anything compromising to her personal dignity. However, as matters stand now, all I can do is to keep quiet. Lady Erroll little thinks that, through her instrumentality, my poor Portia may be brought into making a marriage of affection after all." This was more soliloquy than an address to Susan. "She is civil to Blake, because it is convenient for the world to see some man who is not Teddy Josselin at Portia's side, and in the end may find that she has played her adversary's game. You will not speak, Susan—I know you will not speak to any one of what is going on?"

Susan, with a heavy heart, promised secrecy; and Miss Jemima, after a little more talk—all of Portia and Portia's supposed love affairs—went on her way.

"So ends that dream, that exquisite piece of folly," thought Susan, gazing blankly round her at the heath—purple shadow and gleaming sunlight all blurred and indistinct through fast-rising tears. "Was I mad enough to think, with Portia by, that he would look at *me*, feel anything for me but pity? I've been loved once by papa, as a child is loved. The other love is for girls like Portia—girls with beauty, position, wit; yet my heart is worth more than hers. She may marry Mr. Blake—she will never care for him as I could have done. Oh, I hope they'll never see my face again—never be able to look at me with pity, guessing my secret.

Something in the last thought stirred Susan's pride; as much pride as her very unheroic character could be said to possess; and she rose, and walked back, with a brisker step, to the Collinsons' house. She had still some hours to pass alone, and with no other means of distraction than the contents of Eliza's book-shelves—concordances, treaties on home-brewing, knitting-books, and such like dreary odds and ends of literature. It had been arranged that there should be no regular dinner that day, but a cold six o'clock meal to which Eliza gave the name of a "meat-tea." It was seven o'clock, however, before either of the Collinsons made their appearance; and Susan was just beginning to feel not only very unhappy, but very hungry, when Eliza Collinson, heated, limp, brow-beaten, walked in, closely followed by her brother. Alas! Susan felt she had never been so glad to see him as at this moment!

Mr. Collinson seemed to be in higher spirits than usual and had brought a huge lobster in his hand, as an addition to the tea-table. Tea? not for him. Let Betsy run and fetch a bottle of Bass from the Rose—and stay, it would be just as well to get a pint of sherry, too; Miss Eliza was not looking well. "I've good news to tell you, Eliza," he said, turning to his sister. "What, in the name of fortune, makes you look so lachrymose? wouldn't old Hackitt let you get the blacking-brushes for nothing, or what? I've heard of a situation at last."

"You've heard of a great many," said Miss Collinson, in a flat voice. "Have you got one?"

"You are a hopeful, cheery spirit, Eliza, on my word!" said Tom, looking round with a good-humored smile from the side-table, where he was breaking his lobster limb from limb, preparatory to salad. "If there *is* a pleasant doubt to be thrown on any subject, you know so well where to put it in. No, I've not got a situation, Miss Collinson, but I can have one to-morrow if I choose."

And he drew a morning paper from his pocket, and threw it across into his sister's lap. "You'll see it somewhere in the first column. 'Eligible investment for a gentleman of means and spirit.'"

Miss Collinson held the paper at arm's length, as ladies do who are just too young for glasses, and passed her finger down the columns. "A catch-penny piece of rubbish!" she exclaimed, after a minute. "You may see a score such in any paper you take up. 'A new company requiring a secretary with eight hundred pounds capital.' Eight hundred pounds—for them to put into their pockets! Besides, supposing it all to be *bony fidy*,"—Miss Collinson loved to air these marks of superior culture—"supposing it to be *bony fidy*, how could it possibly suit you? 'a gentleman of good address'—referring to the paper—'industry, business habits, and a spare capital of eight hundred or a thousand pounds.' You have no capital, you have no business habits—"

"And no good address," interrupted Tom, still with thorough sweet temper. "Very well, my dear. You will keep to your opinion, I to mine, and mine is that I shall have that situation, value three hundred per annum, before another fortnight is over."

The return of Betsy, a bottle, well-frothed, under each arm, put an end to the discussion. Miss Collinson unloosed the strings of her bonnet, tilted it a little back on her head, and so sat down to the tea-table. Whenever she had been unusually disturbed in her mind, Eliza Collinson seemed to derive mysterious consolation in sitting down to some meal in her bonnet. "Thank you, Susan, I think I should be obliged if you would pour out the tea, for once. My hand shakes like an aspen. Never, while I live, will I enter another sale. It was a heart-rending sight, I can tell you, Tom. The stair Kidderminster, as good as new, knocked down for one and four—not the price of the rods."

"The stair-carpet?" said Susan, who knew as much about money as a baby. "What, all the stair-carpet for one and four pence. Well, that was cheap."

"One and four pence a yard, child. What are you talking of? and the parlor window-blinds ten pence each. I could have cried to see it! Still, there were other things that fetched a ridiculous price. Now the scrapers—I remember your dear father paid eight shillings for them new—and old Miss Budd, bidding against Mrs. Bolt, ran them up to nine-and-six. But I have remarked all my life, scrapers do well, somehow!" Miss Collinson looked hard at Tom, then at Susan, as she hazarded this reminiscence with an air of subdued melancholy.

"And was the sale a good or a bad one on the whole?" cried Tom, his mouth full of lobster. "Susan don't want to hear all this bosh about scrapers and window blinds. One thing with another, did the property realize what was expected?"

"The property," said Miss Collinson, drawing forth her note-book and looking up and down its straggling labyrinths of weak pencil figures, "the property realized (ah, no; eight pence must come off the blue and yellow jug, Hackitt did his best, but Miss Budd had two witnesses to swear that 'twas cracked when he put it up) well, in round numbers, one hundred and seventy-four pounds. From this deduct Hackitt's commission, catalogues, et cetera, and you will bring it down eighteen pounds, good. As near as I can say, one hundred and fifty-six pounds will be paid to your account, Susan."

"It won't do me any particular good," said Susan.

"It would go a long way toward furnishing another house," said Tom.

Miss Collinson coughed, and drank her tea.

"I'm afraid you must have found the day long, all by yourself, my dear Susan. Just when we were in the middle of the sale I remembered I had locked up the pickles, and there was nothing but the end of cold beef for your lunch."

"Oh, I did not want the pickles," said Susan, with a faint attempt at a smile. "I wasn't hungry. It made me sick to think of all our things being handled by strangers. I don't think I ever spent such a miserable day in my life."

Tom gave her a tender glance. "Do take some lobster," he pleaded, drawing his chair a little nearer hers. "Oh, I know you have had veal pie, but you haven't eat half enough. Now do finish with lobster. I bought it on purpose for you, and its as fresh as fresh!"

The kindness of his voice, the boyish eagerness with which he jumped up for a clean plate, then piled it to overflowing with lobster salad, made Susan feel as if she must cry. Never was a heart more in the state of rebound in which the old adage says so many hearts are caught, than Susan's to-night. Tom watched her face, and drew his own conclusions from what he read there. He had made up his mind, come what might, to speak definitely to Susan this evening ; and a wiser man than Tom might have drawn flattering augury from the expression with which the poor little thing's sad eyes sank down beneath his.

"Arn't you ever going to take off your bonnet, Eliza ?" he asked, when the tea things had been cleared away, and Miss Collinson still held her place at the table, going, half aloud, over item after item in her account-book. "Nothing gives me the fidgets like seeing you with your bonnet perched up on your head, as if you had put it there for a cock-shy. Put it on properly or take it off. I should say, myself, take it off."

After tendering which advice, Tom came behind his sister's chair, raised her by the elbows, and holding her firmly in a like manner, propelled her across the small parlor to the door. He put her in the passage, counselling her, kindly, to go to her own room and lie down for an hour, then returned to Susan.

"Eliza's a good, well-meaning soul, but tiring," he remarked, stopping about two yards distant from her and putting his hands behind him. "I saw you were tired to death with all that stupid talk about the sale, and so I sent her away. Oh, Miss Fielding "—the pint of sherry Tom had taken was beginning to inspire him with eloquence—"I can't think what it is that makes you look so pale and cast-down—upon my word I can't ! If I could be of any use to you, if you would only look upon me as—as—"

His face got scarlet. But Susan, happily, was looking away through the window by which she sat, not at him.

"There's nothing more than usual to cast me down, Mr. Collinson." She was thinking at that instant of Blake and Portia, so made the assertion with spirit. "I can't help being upset a little about the sale. I shall be all right to-morrow."

"But you are never all right," persisted Tom. "You are never in really good spirits. Don't you think I watch you, sitting by the window here, as if you expected to see some one pass, from morning till night, and never a smile on your face ? There's something on your mind, Miss Susan ; I know that very well."

"Indeed, there is not," cried Susan, all in a flutter of indignant denial. "You never made a greater mistake. I'm sorry to leave the old home, and to have to live so far away among strangers ; but that's all. Pray, what other trouble do you suppose I could have on my mind ? It's very unfeeling of you to say so."

"Unfeeling !" an opening had come for him in that word ; and Tom made the best of it, manfully. "You think I could be unfeeling, you think I could say a word to offend you "—here he managed to edge a step nearer—"when I think of you the first moment my eyes are open—all the night before last I lay awake as miserable—Oh, Susan "—he fell down on his knees—"I know I haven't much in the way of prospects to offer ; but I'd work my life out for you, if you'd have me !" And he put up his arm round her waist.

As far as coherence goes, the proposal was, perhaps, not quite up to the average mark of proposals. Still, Tom was so thoroughly in earnest, so brimming over with emotion—such emotion as it was—that his deficiencies of language did not make themselves as obvious to Susan's perceptions as they do to yours and mine.

"Don't be silly," she cried, but not very forcibly. "I—I'll tell your sister of you, sir. Oh, dear, suppose Betsy was to come in !"

"Suppose she was—suppose every Betsy in the world was to come in !" said

Tom, carried altogether away; "what should I care? Do you think I'd be ashamed to be found on my knees before you?"

"I know that I should be ashamed for you," said Susan, beginning to laugh. "Do remember the windows are open. People will think we are acting a charade."

Something in her tone made Tom start up to his feet. "You treat me like a boy!" he exclaimed. "You pretend to think it a joke. Acting a charade, indeed! And I tell you that I'm miserable about you, that all my happiness depends on what you say to me!"

The muscles round his mouth twitched; his voice got husky. Susan felt terribly sorry for him.

"Do come here, out of sight of the road, and—and tell me the worst," went on Tom. "I'll try to bear it, if you'll only say you don't care for any other fellow, and if you *won't* laugh at me."

He stood behind the window curtain, extending his arms to her. Susan jumped up, not knowing whether to laugh or cry. She half moved to him; then stopped.

"This is all nonsense, you know, Mr. Collinson."

"It's life or death to me," said Tom. "But, of course, if you hate me—"

"Hate you? I think I should be very wicked if I did!"

"And I have no fine house to offer you. I'll try to get this situation, and work my best; but I couldn't give you a fine house and servants, like the Ffrenches."

"What should I want with a fine house and servants?"

"Susan, do you like me—don't answer! for God's sake, don't answer so quick—do you like me just a little?"

"You know I do; but—"

"Yes, yes. The rest would come in time. I should be content to wait. Now, only one more word. Say you don't refuse me?"

Susan stood irresolute. She had really grown to like—well, to tolerate—this poor Tom Collinson; and it went against her very nature to pain him or anybody; and five minutes ago she had felt so desolate; and she did so shudder at the prospect of that far-off home in France; and George Blake had forgotten her—and other friends than the Collinsons she had none. "I wish you hadn't taken me by surprise so," she said, at last.

Tom got hold of her hand and kissed it. Her heart gave one passionate throb as she thought of George Blake, of the night when he left her at the door of Addison Lodge. And then she remembered that George Blake had only trifled with her, only looked upon her as Portia's friend, and that Tom Collinson was in earnest.

"I'm the happiest fellow on earth," he whispered, with lover-like ardor, and again stealing an arm round her waist.

"Oh, please—oh, do let me go!" cried Susan, breaking from him, and returning to the protection of the window. "Here comes Eliza; I know Eliza will treat it all as a joke."

CHAPTER XXI

M ISS COLLINSON entered the room, saw Susan's blushing, bewildered face; saw Tom's exultantly happy one; and knew, before either of them spoke, what had happened.

"You have done with accounts at last?" stammered Susan, vaguely hoping that Tom would keep his own counsel, that the love-scene she had gone through would remain a secret between themselves—the first act in a charade that was to have no sequel.

"I've got good news to tell you, Eliza," cried Tom, running up to his sister, and in his wild excitement actually kissing her. "Susan and me have found out our own minds at last. Now what have you got to say to us?"

"Us." The monosyllable fell with a singularly grating on Susan's ear.

"I hope you won't think badly of me, Miss Collinson. Indeed it was not my fault, but—"

But, before she could finish, Tom was at her side; Tom, right before his sister's eyes, with his arm round her as though he already looked upon her as his own possession !

" No, it was no one's fault—except Susan's, for having the prettiest face in the world, a face that did my business for me the first time I saw it. If I felt apology was wanted, all I should say would be this: 'Look at Susan.' "

The prettiest face in the world ! Not a dear little irregular English face, whose irregularities were charms in artistic eyes, but "pretty"—sweetest word that can be spoken to a girl of seventeen! Susan's eyes fell, the dimples showed in her cheeks.

"You are both very young," said Miss Collinson, in a depressed voice. "I'm sure I hope you know your own minds. Seventeen and twenty-three—dear, dear, your ages together scarce come up to forty."

Tom burst into one of his loud laughs. "And what the dickens does that signify? why add up anything? We are not talking of scrapers and door-mats, now. I thought you were an advocate of early marriages, Eliza? You have told me, times enough, nothing would steady me like a wife."

"But I'm not old enough to be any one's wife," cried Susan. "Miss Collinson is right. We don't know our own minds. The thing is ridiculous."

" I know *my* mind," said Tom Collinson, almost fiercely, and still holding Susan by the waist. "It isn't only during the last ten minutes I've begun to think of all this, as you know, Eliza. I determined long ago to give up every-thing, here and elsewhere, for Susan, if Susan would have me; and to work for her and become an altered sort of fellow altogether. Where the — is the good of talking about age? I shall make a deuced deal steadier husband now than I should five year hence, going on leading such a — — life as mine has been !"

Miss Collinson ranged herself at once on Tom's side, as she always did when his voice waxed loud, and oaths began to fly about. "I said nothing against early marriages, Tom. I only said I hoped you knew your own minds,

and alluded, as a matter of curiosity, to the rather low figure of your united ages.
If Susan's guardian will consent, and if you succeed in getting employment, I'm
sure I don't even see why your courtship should be a long one. You might
make your home here, if it was any use to you, at first.

Their courtship. It was considered a matter of settled fact then, already!
Susan's spirits sank to zero when they all sat down, Tom close beside her on
the sofa, and the brother and sister began to talk over the business part of this
engagement into which she had allowed herself to be entrapped. Tom's plan, it
seemed, was to set about investigating the advertisement at once, and if the
affair promised well, to invest in it the required eight hundred pounds. He did
not happen to have the requisite cash in hand, for the moment; but Susan's
guardian, no doubt, would advance it to him on his own personal security, and
the proceeds of the Addison Lodge sale would suffice to furnish them a small
house in whatever part of London his duties should require him to live. The
eight hundred pounds were, according to the advertisement, to yield twenty per
cent.; that made a hundred and sixty; his salary would be three hundred
pounds, the interest of Susan's remaining money, say ten pounds. Altogether—
here he produced a little "horsey" looking book and jotted down the different
items—altogether four hundred and seventy pounds a year. "And if young
people, with modest ideas, can't get along comfortably on four hundred and
seventy pounds a year, the devil's in it!" said Tom. "Especially when the wife
is a dear little domestic home-loving girl, like my Susan."

All his taciturnity, all his diffidence had fled. He was again the self-confident, odiously-familiar Tom Collinson from whom Susan used to recoil in the
early days of their acquaintance; and with a sinking heart she realized—as a
good many women have done before—how easy it is to feel sorry for a man as
long as he continues your friend, and sorry for yourself the minute he becomes
your lover! Inch by inch she managed to edge away out of his reach; at last,
pretending that she must look for her work, escaped from the sofa altogether, and
when she re-seated herself took a chair the other side of Miss Collinson. She
kept close there for the rest of the evening, and when ten o'clock came and
Eliza quitted the room, quitted it with her; yes, clinging tight to her arm, so
horribly afraid was the poor little child of being left alone, even for a moment,
with the man she had engaged herself to marry.

He fidgetted and fumed, at last told Eliza point blank to go away; he had
something very particular indeed to say to Susan. But Susan was not to be
conquered. And so all the parting salutation he got, in his new character of
accepted lover, was a faltering "good-night, Tom;" through sheer importunity
he forced her into calling him by his Christian name: a still more faltering touch
of her little cold hand. It was treatment that did not in the smallest degree
check Tom's ardor. A man either of finer sensibility or acuter judgment
would have been sure to read aright the coldness of such a child of nature as
Susan. Tom viewed it as the mere natural coyness or coquetry any decorously
brought-up girl would be sure to show at first to a lover; coyness, coquetry,
which every day's courtship would infallibly wear away.

He had no chill misgivings as to the reality of Susan's affection for him;
and yet, when he was left to the companionship of his own thoughts, Tom Collinson found himself in far less assured spirits than he would have wished. Glad
though he was, there had already, as I have hinted, been room in his life for a
love episode—on one side a tragically real one! Sitting alone by the open parlor window, his senses full of Susan's fair pure face, of Susan's girlish voice,

memory importunately thrusts before him the reproachful vision of another face, less fair, less pure, but overflowing with honest tenderness for him! he remembers, as he has not done for months past, his own solemnly-plighted oaths, all broken now; remembers his outburst of cowardly anger against the woman he had sworn to love and cherish eternally, when her brother betrayed them both; remembers his last cruel parting from her—her sobs, her violent language, her despair.

"Dash it all—I was a boy, I'm little better than a boy now!" thought Tom, getting up uneasily, and walking about the room, "and she was a woman, old enough and knowing enough to take care of herself. Haven't I decided what was right long ago? Why, a woman with passions like Matty's would bring a man's neck to the halter, here in England. Compare her to Susan, my little shy, cold Susan, with her dimples and her blushes. God, if she should hear of my marriage though—it must never be put in the papers—but, if she should hear of it! I may be on the safe side, as far as law goes, but from—from the other way of looking at it, what am I? And I did love poor Matty once. She was as fine a girl as any in the province—and what pluck, by Jove! that time she rode away to Mackenzie's station for a surgeon for me—that night when she and her brother alone defended the hut against a gang! She shot down two men with her own hand—she'd shoot me as soon as look at me, I believe, if she was here now."

A female figure just at this moment passing along the road (one of the mild old village ladies returning from a tea party) made Tom start with all the cowardice of conscious guilt. He shut down the window, and drew together the curtains with an oath; and, getting out the spirit bottle, mixed himself a glass, " stiff enough "—he made the small joke to himself but did not feel much amused by it—" to set six men's consciences at rest." Then took himself off, the first time for a good many nights that he had done so, to the Rose.

Susan, keeping her first love vigil in her own room, a little dressing closet within Miss Collinson's, was sensible of intense relief when she heard the loud slam of the front door. As long as Tom was in the house it seemed to her now that her very thoughts were scarce her own. She listened to the sound of his retreating steps down the street, then quietly slipped the bolt that insured her against intrusion from Eliza, and took out from the breast of her frock—be lenient to her reader!—a relic; something that during the past week had rested upon her heart and kept it warm; a three-inch bit of lead pencil that had once been Blake's. On her last morning at Addison Lodge, she had run to bid goodby, child fashion, to every square foot of the garden and river bank, and down close to the water where George Blake had sat when he took the memorable sketch, had lighted upon this priceless treasure.

Ah, well, he was going to have Portia for his wife, and she was engaged to Tom Collinson. She must never think of any one but Tom now! And she held the pencil with jealous fondness between her little hands, and wondered if it was a positive moral obligation to destroy it? And then broke out crying noiselessly, kissed it, and hid it away in the pocket of the same memorandum book in which her first impressions of Blake and Teddy Josselin were recorded.

On the day when fate brought Blake to read the one, he found the other; and knew from what tenderest love his passion—no, by that time he termed it his madness—for Portia had kept him!

Thus, in different ways, the lovers spent the first hour or so after their engagement. Next morning, however, with its cheerful sunshine and every-day

nfluences, had the usual dispelling effect of most next mornings upon the clouds
of over night. Tom Collinson's sensitive conscience was pursued by chiding
memories no longer ; Susan Fielding's vain regrets were put away, if not out of
mind out of sight, like the relic that she no longer dared wear upon her heart.
They were openly engaged. By seven in the morning Betsy, with delicious
sense of importance, had told the news to the servant next door. By noon every
soul in the village knew it. Later in the day they walked down the street, by
special command, leaning on Tom's arm, and were congratulated by twenty different tongues on their happiness.

These congratulations seemed to Susan to rivet her fate. The seal of the
inevitable was surely upon her projected marriage, now that Miss Budd and Mrs.
Bott, and the vicar himself had wished her joy ! She was going to spend her
life with Tom Collinson ; to share his thoughts, his pleasures ; to have him for
her highest, wisest friend. This she realized ; with her very strength tried to
love him ; recoiled, shuddering, from the effort ; when night came opened the
hidden place where her bit of lead pencil lay, and cried over it—accurately
gauging her want of love for Collinson by the knowledge of how she could have
loved George Blake.

And next day came the same thing over again ; and the next. And after
this she began to be, at least accustomed to her position and her lover ; " accustomed "—word that has no place in love ! If he would never, never try to
kiss her, she thought, and if Eliza would always keep in the room when he was
by, what should hinder her from growing fond of him in time ? Every wife
must be fond of her own husband, Susan was certain. When they were married, had been married a year, she would be *used* to him, surely ; used to bergamot and stale tobacco smoke and demonstrative affection alike ; and then his
fun and good spirits would amuse her again, as in the days before their engagement, and life flow on smooth and quiet as she could remember the life of her
own father and mother had done when she was a child. So Susan reasoned, so
acquiesced ; had she worried, then and there, would probably have passed
through life acquiescent ; not altogether ignorant that nobler, more passionate
love was possible, yet making the best, womanlike, of her bargain, and atoning
to a coarse, inferior husband largely, by patient gentlest submission for what she
lacked toward him of love.

Fate, however, held a deliverance—I mean a reprieve—in store for her.
One fine morning, the engagement about a week old, Tom Collinson got a letter
from his first forsaken love in New Zealand, and by its contents was thrown into
such a fever of jealousy, remorse and cupidity combined, as ended in his de-
ciding to stick to duty, cost him what it might. The letter, directed in an uned-
ucated but not characterless female hand, to an agent in London, from thence
sent on to Halfont, lay by his plate one morning when he came down to breakfast, and Tom had to read it with his sister's eyes and the eyes of his betrothed
reading his own face.

LONG HATTON, OTAGO PROVINCE.

MY DEAREST TOM : I hope you are well and comfortable, and have thought better
of all you said when you left. You promised to write, but I have had no letter from you
yet. My dear Tom, this has been the Wretchedest time of my life. I have thought of
you day and night, and every one turning from me, along of Phil (for he robbed others
besides you), and little Mat sick, and once I had scarcely bread to put between her lips—
but thank God, the worst is past, for as you will see, I have a Great News to tell you. I
hope you have had no return of the fever, and wear your *flannels, constant.* Dear lad, I

hope all your anger against me is gone, and have got no new sweetheart. I was never to blame. Phil was as big a blackguard as ever walked, and tried all he knew to ruin you, and me too, but I had no more to do with it than little Mat. You had no call to visit it on me. Dear Tom, this is to ask you to come back home. Uncle William is dead at last, down at Dunedin, and has left me three thousand pounds, the share that was to have been Phil's and mine too, "to make up," he said in his will, for all I had been in-jured—of course he meant *by Phil*. If you are not in any good situation in England, I say you had best return at once. There's a tidy little farm down St. Peter's way for sale, that I've a mind would suit us, and can be bought cheap—but if you choose, the child and me 'll come to England instead. Any way, there's the money, safe and sure in the Gov-ernment securities, paying over six per cent. Why, only to let it lie there we could live retired and comfortable, if we chose ; only I don't think I could be happy without a bit of land to look after. Folks say now I'm an Airess, and (if I was free) there'd be *many a young fellow* glad to court me, I can tell you. You know this is only to make you jealous. Some way it don't seem I shall have a letter from you at all. I think directly you get this you'll put up your traps, and I shall see you walk in before Christmas. Mat will say a fine lot of words by then. She's well on her feet again, and a stout bold Maid of her age. She can say " Dada" plain, and takes your picture and kisses it—that I taught her. Now, my dear lad, I have told you my News, and will finish. There has been a dearth of water, but things are looking up pretty promising for the cold weather. Jason's Run is let at last, to a Scotchman, I'm glad to say—a staid well to do young man, *about thirty*, and unmarried. Mat's kisses (here followed five or six scrawling crosses) and the same from your True and loving till death.

MATTY.

This letter, I say, Tom Collinson had to read through, with his sister and Susan Fielding sitting at the table with him. His face kept its color tolerably for a face that was not by constitution the face of a hypocrite. He drank his two cups of tea, managed to swallow sufficient food for appearance's sake, then rose and walked away, not into the street, where it was his habit to smoke his after-breakfast pipe, but into the narrow slip of garden that lay at the back of Miss Collinson's house.

His legs felt unsteady under him, like those of a man recovering from sick-ness ; his hand shook as he tried, making more than one failure over it, to strike a vesuvian ; the taste of his pipe seemed noxious, unconsoling, as in his school-boy days, when the ultimate object of tobacco had been, not consolation, but to anger Eliza. "Three thousand pounds, paying six per cent., in government se-curities." An estate, that meant, of his own, a trusty overseer—poor Matty—to manage it, horses to ride, good animal comfort and plenty of every kind till his life's end. To the forbearance, the generosity, the womanly unselfishness of the letter he had received, Tom's soul was not insensible. He was really touched by this full, frank pardon, accorded to him in *her* hour of success, by the woman he had wronged (though, if one considered it, what more natural than that Matty, that any woman, should wish for the return of a handsome young fellow like him-self?) Neither to little Mat's scrawled kisses, to the account of Mat's walking and talking, was he indifferent. If he had received the same letter, minus the news of Uncle William's legacy, it would have made him thoroughly out of sorts —for the remainder of the day ; have required a thoroughly stiff " conscience quieter " before he could have got comfortably to sleep at night.

But three thousand pounds his—if he stretched his hand out for them ; his in very fact at that moment—what a quickener of natural affection, of remorse, of all a man's better sentiment, was here !

Upon the one hand he saw inclination, the woman he loved and for whom he would have to work—poverty ; upon the other, duty, the woman who loved

and who would work for him—and plenty. Was ever moral dilemma so nicely
equipoised?

During the first five minutes that he paced up and down the garden path, one
unvacillating resolve possessed Tom's mind—he would act like a man of honor;
break off his engagement; return to Matty and her child, and do his duty by
them to his life's end. Then, chancing to look up, he saw Susan's figure for a
minute at the stair window—the girlish figure, the soft, curled head that he loved
to desperation—and with a great oath swore that he would never lose her, never
give her the chance of becoming another man's wife.

Duty—which was duty? Did not his word bind him to Susan Fielding as
much as to Matty? If he were to write to Matty, telling her frankly, nobly,
that as he had discarded her in her time of trouble, so now in her time of pros-
perity she might discard him, would not some other man be sure to make the
poor girl happy in time? She was looked upon as an heiress already; there
was many a smart young fellow ready to court her. A well-to-do unmarried
Scotchman, *she was glad to say*, had taken Jason's Run—

Tom Collinson turned short on his heel, clenched his hand with a more bitter
sense of jealousy than all his love for Susan had had power to awaken in him. Matty, his Matty, untrue! a girl whose rough fidelity had been a by-word through the
province; a girl to whom no man who didn't want to have a bullet through him
would ever have spoken a word of light love. And he was going, cowardly, to
abandon her, to leave her to the temptation that riches must be to any young and
handsome woman in such a position as hers. Riches, yes, and by heaven, that
were his; his as much as though he had a check for the money in his pocket at
this moment.

Money for money's sake was no passion with Tom Collinson; but he was
essentially, practically mercenary, as every human being, coarse or refined, must
be to whom present personal ease is the main object of existence. A man who
regards the acquisition of money as a final end will often be raised above the
temptation of momentary gains; the happy-go-lucky pleasure-lover is forever to
be bought. And so, at this crisis of his life, it really was not so much greed in
the abstract as immediate visions of good eating and drinking, horses, abstinence
from work, that lured Tom back to the path of duty. He could make up his
mind to no final severance from Susan, could not indeed see, when he thought it
calmly over, what harm could be wrought by holding her pledged to him. Nothing simpler than for him to be engaged to one girl in England, yet return to New
Zealand and see how matters stood there with the other—who knows? possibly
arrange some division of property with Matty (considering the amount to which
her brother had robbed him, would this be more than rightful restitution?) then
come back and redeem his word to Susan. Life was uncertain; some one of
the three might die. No need, at all events, to make himself miserable about
cruel contingences until they were actually forced upon him.

Keep quiet all round, decided Tom, when an hour's pacing up and down had
enabled him so far to collect his thoughts. Inflict no premature suffering upon
either of the women who loved him, and trust to Providence to bring everything
straight in the end.

And he ran into the house, his face almost cheerful again, and called up the
stairs to Susan to come out and have a talk with him. He had received a letter
of importance on business, and wanted to ask her advice.

CHAPTER XXII.

THE morning sun warmed Susan's cheek with livelier color than its wont, as she tripped at Tom Collinson's side along the garden path. She smiled up at him more brightly, he thought, than she had ever smiled before since their engagement. "If I part with her I'll be shot!" resolved Tom. "What is a paltry three thousand pounds—what would five thousand pounds, what would the world be to me without Susan?"

"You wanted to ask my advice; you have got something very important to say to me, Tom? What is it? I'm all curiosity."

Tom had led her into what Miss Collinson called the "harbor"—worthy of its name, as far as insects went, when the scarlet runners and nasturtiums grew higher; at present a bare damp corner of the garden, fenced round with trellis-work that screened it artfully from nothing, and containing a bolt-upright rustic chair, a cast of the First Napoleon and a ricketty rustic table. Tom was sitting on the table, Susan on the chair, when she spoke.

"Oh well, it's nothing so very particular," he answered, kicking his feet up and down in the air, to seem at his ease. "You see—the fact is—I've got a letter—"

"From New Zealand," interrupted Susan. "Eliza wants the stamp for little Willy Smithitt."

"Oh, she was fingering my letter before I came down, was she?" cried Tom. "Eliza will get more than she wants some day, preying"—this was Tom's own expression—"preying into other people's letters. What further information did Eliza give you about my affairs, I should like to know?"

"She said, we both said, the hand looked like a lady's hand," said Susan, demurely. "At least, not a lady's exactly, but—not a man's."

The blood rose to Tom Collinson's very temples. "We don't talk so much about 'ladies' out in the Colonies," said he. "A woman is content there to be called a woman, and to do a woman's duties, too."

Susan felt her spirits rise higher at his tone. It was so delightful to find Tom sulky, sarcastic, anything but demonstratively loving to herself. "And it's about this lady who is not ashamed to be called a woman that you want my advice?" she asked. "Better give me the letter to read," holding out her hand. "I will put myself in your place and judge for you."

Tom looked at her hard. Upon her soft, childish face he detected, or his conscience made him believe he detected, an expression he had never seen there before, and from which he slunk ashamed. Something of the absolute white truth of Susan's soul had, perhaps, at that moment pierced to his, and enabled him to realize *what* this scheme was which ten minutes ago had seemed so easy of accomplishment; had enabled him to realize the abhorrence Susan would have of him if, by any evil chance, poor Matty's story should become known to her.

"I never show any one my letters—it's a principle of mine—and you and Eliza were both wrong. The letter is from a man, an old mate of mine in Otago; 'tis about money. I have come into money, Susan, indirectly, and—I don't know but what it will be wise for you to stay here with Eliza while I go back to the colony to see after my own interest."

Susan's heart leaped. "It would certainly be very foolish not to see after it," she cried, without a moment's hesitation.

"Flattering," remarked Tom, a choking feeling at his throat. "You take kindly to the thought of separation."

And he remembered Matty!

"I only agreed with you, Tom. You said it would be wise to see after your own interest, and I say so, too. We have very little money to begin upon, you know. Eliza says no one can keep house *well* on less than a hundred and fifty pounds a year, and we have not got that." The secretaryship had proved the veriest flash in the pan of a bubble company, and Susan's guardian had treated the proposal of her money being made available to a husband's benefit, with the natural contempt of an Englishman and a lawyer. "We have only forty pounds a year, certain, and I am so young—"

"If you are young you are deucedly prudent," exclaimed Tom, with bitterness. "So much excellent sense may well take the place of years. Ah, a girl who loved a man wouldn't calculate about money, and age, and prudence the very moment she heard that he was to go to the Antipodes!"

Susan bent down her face. "You would only have to leave me for a bit, I dare say, Tom." But her voice resolutely refused to take a melancholy tone, try what she would.

"Well, I don't know that it would be for very long—not more than a year, as far as I can see now," said Tom; "still, when two people have once got the world between them there are a hundred chances as to their ever coming together again. One of us might die."

"So we might if we were together," said Susan, persistently hopeful.

"Or—or marry some one else." Tom Collinson could not bring his eyes to look at hers as he said this.

"Oh, if you feel that, it is good to put your fidelity to the proof," said Susan, with a small laugh. "I know that *I* would keep my word to any one in New Zealand just the same as if they were in Halfont."

Tom Collinson jumped down from the table; he caught her hand with vehemence. "Will you swear all that?" he exclaimed; "will you take your oath to be true to me if I go away?"

"I will have nothing to do with swearing," said Susan. "Oh, you hurt me," shrinking from him; "let my hand go! Don't you know that I'm half a Quaker, and that Quakers never swear? If I took an oath I should feel I was doing something wicked, and it would mean no more to my conscience than simple Yes or No."

"Well, simple 'Yes,' then. If I go abroad, if I'm away a year, or two years, will you keep faithful to our engagement?"

"Must all this be settled in a minute, Tom? I should like to ask Eliza."

"And I should like you not to ask Eliza. More wisdom to be got out of the old cockatoo; you can teach her beforehand what to answer. You know your own heart, surely, without wanting any other woman to read it for you. If I go away, will you hold faithfully to your engagement to me?"

"You must have an answer now?"

"Now, directly; and if I don't get it, and in the very words I wish, the money may take care of itself. Never fear I'll give up the certainty of you for the chance of a wretched three or four thousand pounds, Miss Fielding."

"Well, I'll say what you wish, then. What is it?"

"'I promise to remain true to you, and to our engagement—'"

"'I promise to remain true to you, and to our engagement—'"

"'Until the day when you set me free.'"

This also she repeated, not without a little paling of the lips. She was gaining an enormous gain in present liberty; but the words that bound her to Tom Collinson for life could not be spoken without an effort.

"That is good," said Tom, with an air of intense relief. "I can talk matters over with a better heart now. There's only one thing more. I'm a fool, a jealous fool, Susan, where you are concerned; but I can't help it. Promise me you'll never care for any other man while I'm gone?"

A flash of indignant light shot from Susan's eyes. "You ask me this when I have promised to keep engaged to you!" she cried, all the eagerness of half-conscious guilt in her voice.

"I only mentioned it," said Tom, humbly. "I can't help being jealous; it's my nature. I was jealous, and I don't mind saying so, at the thought of that singing fellow, Blake, Miss Ffrench's present lover. Promise me you'll never have another word to say to him?"

"Indeed, I'll promise nothing of the sort, sir! If Mr. Blake is engaged to Portia, I shall certainly have to meet him and be—civil to him. You are not reasonable."

"No," said Tom, humbly still, "I know I'm not, where you are concerned, Susan," the tears rose to his eyes; "how shall I live without you?"

"You have managed to live without me a good many years already."

"Don't flirt with Blake. I'm talking like a fool, but I can't help it. Don't flirt with Blake."

"Have you quite lost your senses, Tom? Likelier than not I shall never see Mr. Blake again."

"Yet a minute ago you said you would certainly have to meet him and be—civil to him. You are prevaricating—I insist upon your not prevaricating. Promise me never to write a letter to that man."

"Tom!"

"Promise," seizing her hand. "Now, this moment, or—"

"Oh, I promise, I promise! I'll never flirt with any one. I'll never write a letter to Mr. Blake."

"Nor sing with him?"

With a dart like a bird Susan flew from Tom's grasp to the path, where the back windows of the whole row of houses protected her. "I'll promise nothing more, thank you, Mr. Collinson," making him a little curtsy. "I'm to be engaged to you till the day you set me free, and I'm to flirt with no one and I'm not to write letters to Mr. Blake. There my obligations end."

"Come back here, my dear, and let me put a ring on your finger."

"What ring? Eliza's diamond? No indeed, I think it very selfish of you to take that diamond from your sister."

"I don't mean the diamond," Tom glanced at it as it shone, many colored, on his broad short hand. "That goes with me abroad for poor Eliza's sake. I've a ring of my own that will just fit your biggest finger—this blood-stone that I wear on my chain. Come, you must have it, you know. All engaged girls wear rings."

Susan, on hearing this, advanced, but not out of sight of the houses, then stretched out a little white hand.

"You are never to take it off, mind! It must stay here till I replace it with a plain gold one," said Tom, his voice was positively pathetic. so much in earnest was he as he unfastened the ring (Matty's love-gift once) from his chain and put it upon Susan's finger. "Promise me you'll never take it off?"

"What, not when I wash my hands, Tom? You are so silly to-day."

He let loose her hand and turned impatiently away. Was the girl half foolish after all, incapable of head and heart as he used to think when he first knew
her, or was this childish lightness of manner a simple honest token that she was
glad to be rid of him? Tom Collinson asked himself these questions pretty
often during the next two days, as he watched the irrepressible brightness of
Susan's face—thrown out in strong relief by the constantly red eyes and tear-
stained checks of Eliza, upon whom the news of her brother's projected absence
had fallen like a thunderbolt. She was friendlier toward him, far, than she had
been yet since their engagement; was ready to help Eliza in preparing his
things for the voyage; did not fly, as she used, from being alone with him;
morning and night submitted her forehead to him with tolerably good grace to
be kissed; was generosity itself in forcing him to accept all the little money over
which she had control toward the expenses of his journey. Yet still—still she
was in better spirits than she had been for weeks! once or twice cried, may-be,
at seeing Eliza cry, and laughed before the tears were dry upon her cheeks;
ran with a lighter step than Tom had ever heard her about the house; got a
heightened color, ate better, showed the truth, in short—that she was, and felt
herself to be, reprieved.

Tom Collinson's jealous heart got heavier and heavier as the hour drew nigh
when he must lose her out of his sight. When the astonishing news of his
New Zealand legacy had first been told, with discreet reservations, to Eliza, it
was decided, not a little against Susan's inclination, that the future sisters-in-
law should live together till his return. But the more Tom Collinson thought
over this scheme the less he liked it. Eliza's house was too near the Ffrenches
for Tom's taste. He did not want his little modest Susan to be intimate with
people so much above their own rank in life. And then there were the chances
of meeting that singing fellow again, and the certainty of the Hounslow cavalry
barracks. How could a girl like Susan walk about unprotected in the neighborhood of cavalry barracks? for Eliza, poor pious goose, had no more knowledge
of the world than Susan herself. Wiser, when one thought it over, that she
should go to her Uncle Adam, in France, as had been decided; lead the se-
cluded life fitted for a young woman in her position; dream of him; live upon
the excitement of getting his letters till his return. And Susan accepted the
change of plans with suspicious cheerfulness. She was no longer a child,
shrinking with childish dread from leaving the scenes amid which her un-
stirred seventeen years of existence had hitherto flowed. Her short, too-sweet
friendship with George Blake, her ten day's engagement to Tom Collinson,
seemed to have broken all the old threads of her life sharply in twain. She had
fathomed disappointment, jealousy, vain hope, passionate regret over lost freedom:—feelings that change a child rapidly enough into a woman—since that afternoon when Collinson found her crying, because "the world was too big for her,"
upon the bridge. Now the prospect of leaving Halfont was not only bearable
but welcome to her. She would better enjoy her year's reprieve, she felt, apart
from all old associations; would at least not be perpetually reminded of Tom
Collinson by his sister's presence; would be spared witnessing the progress of
Portia Ffrench's new engagement.

"Whatever you think best for me, Tom. As I never wrote to Uncle Adam
about—about our meaning to be married, perhaps it would be best to carry out
the old plan; and I shall learn French, and take singing lessons, and be quite an
accomplished lady by the time you return."

"Then I hope you'll learn from women, not men," cried Tom. This conversation took place on the evening before his departure; and they were sitting together, all three, in the dusk. "Eliza, I leave this charge to you. Write to Mrs. Byng and desire that Susan may never take a lesson of any kind from a Frenchman. I don't want you to be accomplished, Susan. I want you to be nothing but what you are—only fonder of me."

At seven next morning he started, the vessel in which his passage was taken sailing from Liverpool that night; so the whole little household had to be up at daybreak—Eliza, indeed, did not go to her bed at all. As the hour for parting approached, Tom Collinson cried like a child. Susan had never seen a man shed tears in her life before, and Tom's shocked her beyond measure. If he had been her brother she would, no doubt, have thrown her arms round his neck, and cried with him, and thought his tears the most natural weakness in the world. But he was not her brother; and at the sight of his swollen eyes and red nose she felt half-disgusted, half-inclined to run out of the room and laugh. Girls of her age judge men so heartlessly in these small matters. And then not Tom only, but Miss Collinson, and the small servant cried! If she had been offered a fortune for a tear, Susan could not have shed one.

She busied herself in every way she could think of, to conceal—that she had no emotion to conceal; would scarcely trust herself to speak for contrition at the steadiness of her voice; when the final moment of leave-taking came, tried with her very might to look and feel agitated, and failed signally. Susan Fielding could no more feign than she could hide emotion. Tom, all this time, watching her with jealous anguish through his tears.

"Do go away for one minute, Eliza," he said, as poor Miss Collinson continued to cling wistfully to his side, babbling in a choking voice about the sandwiches and the brandy-flask, and how he must promise to write regularly, and how she would think of him and pray for him. "Not say good-by to you affectionately? of course I'll say good-by to you affectionately—at the door. Don't you see that Susan and I want to have a few last words together?"

Eliza, on this, went out obediently into the passage and sobbed there, giving broken orders to the driver about luggage as she sobbed: the lovers were left alone, face to face.

Tom opened his arms. "Come here, my love—tell me you're sorry I'm going, Susan? I may never see you again, you know."

Genuine feeling shook his voice as he pleaded, but Susan's heart kept ice cold. "Please don't talk like that, Tom. Of course I'm sorry, of course you'll come back; why shouldn't you?"

"God knows! A hundred things may happen to keep me. There's not much good in me, my dear, never has been—if, some day, I turn out a worse blackguard even than you expected, would you forgive me and love me still, I wonder?"

"You know I should forgive you."

"Forgive, yes! Would you love me—*do* you love me now? Say yes, Susan. Come and kiss me once of your own free will. God knows you have kept me at arm's length enough hitherto!"

She came a step nearer when he said this; she looked up at his face, his flushed wet cheeks, his swollen, quivering lips, and all the little girl's honest soul revolted against doing what he claimed as a right. "I do like—well, love you, Tom; I mean I'll try, and I'll be quite true to what I promised. Don't ask me any more—"

Miss Collinson's knuckles here sounded a tremulous warning at the door ; receiving no answer she opened it a couple of inches and coughed. " Jim Simmons says you'll miss the train if you don't hurry, Tom. You are late as it is." And then Susan found herself locked in a passionate last embrace, heard a broken " God bless you," felt tears fall hot and thick upon her face ; a moment more and Tom had rushed off from the house, breaking impatiently past his sister's outstretched arms on his way.

"And he has my diamond on his finger," said Eliza, as they stood and watched the fly drive down the village street. " Poor boy, I had not the heart to remind him of it at last ! "

All through the remainder of that day Susan felt a wonderful lightness at her heart. She was her own mistress once more. No haunting dread of finding herself alone in a room with Tom Collinson, of seeing Tom Collinson's eyes gazing at her with an affection that made her shudder ; nothing but the bloodstone ring on her finger to remind her that her liberty was forfeited. Miss Collinson could not restrain a little natural acrimony at the sight of the girl's tearless face.

" I am glad to see you have your feelings under such fine control, Susan. When I—when *I* had a lover I was not so philosophical. But the girls of this generation are more luckily constituted ! Far happier for oneself to be overblunt than over-sensitive in feeling."

" I don't think my feelings are blunt always," answered Susan.

The evening post brought her a note from Tom ; a few lines scrawled in pencil in his schoolboy hand, and posted at some station on the way to Liverpool. " My own dear love," he wrote, " I've been gone from you four hours, and it seems an Eturnuty." This was Tom's style of spelling. " If it wasn't for shame's sake I'd turn back and let the money go to the dickens. Love me, my little Susan. Don't forget to think of me every hour in the day, and believe always in the affection of your fond lover, T. C." And then in a postscript, written very big and clear, this reminder : " Don't Flirt with Blake."

" I am glad you can smile, Susan," said Eliza, as she watched first some telltale dimples, then a blush mantle over Susan's face. " Pray what message does my poor brother send me ? "

"Your brother wishes himself back already," said Susan. " It's a very nice little note."

" I suppose I mayn't see it ? "

"Well, don't be vexed, Eliza—but I think Tom wrote it for me only."

This, of course, was as it ought to be. Miss Collinson felt better satisfied.

For the first time since her engagement, Susan did not open her pocket-book that night. When Tom was here to guard his own interests, she had never considered it a duty to abandon the pleasure—exquisitely keen like all the pleasures of first love !—of touching, gazing at, shedding tears over her treasure. She felt herself like a prisoner on parole now ; free, delightfully free from her lover's presence, but bound more stringently than his presence had bound her to be faithful to him. Before putting out her candle she read his note once more. " Don't flirt with Blake." Oh, unnecessary command ! Would she ever see George Blake again ; or, if she did see him, would it not be as Portia's lover ? The first tears that she had shed to-day wetted her pillow at the thought.

CHAPTER XXIII.

It had been arranged that Susan should reach her uncle's house within a week from the present time. She was, however, to stay with her guardian in London before starting on her journey, and so the day succeeding Tom's departure was also her last day in Halfont. The wrench of leave taking had come at last.

Summer during the past fortnight had ripened into full warmth and glory, and when Susan, late in the afternoon, called to say good-by at the Manor House, she found Colonel Ffrench and his sister sunning themselves, on the sheltered western lawn beneath the cedars. Colonel Ffrench's handsome old face was just then looking its wickedest and its blackest (when he turned it round suddenly at the sound of Susan's footsteps, it required all the little girl's self-command not to run, like the village children, from his presence), for Miss Jemima, relying upon the genial influences of open air and sunshine, had just broken to him the news of Portia's rupture with her cousin. He took off his hat to Susan with the air of high-bred gallantry that it had been the habit of his life to pay to all women (save those of his own household), then beckoned his valet, who was in waiting at some yards distance, and leaning on the man's arm, walked feebly toward the house.

" Portia has not returned, my dear," said Miss Jemima, with a sigh of thankfulness at the interruption to the scene. A scene with her brother was the one thing on earth that quelled the brave old soldier's spirit ; and no wonder. Who that had seen Colonel Ffrench's courtier-like salutation of Susan would have guessed at the kind of epithets which a minute before he had been lavishing on Teddy Josselin, on Lady Erroll, on Jemima herself—on any one, every one who had involved him in the expense of a futile trousseau, and left his granddaughter upon his hands still ! " You have come to say good-by, I fear, Susan, but Portia is in London still."

" And I am going there to-morrow—I am to stay a day or two with my guardian before I start for France. Perhaps Portia will let me say good by to her in London, unless, unless—" Susan did not like to add, " unless living in the house of a countess Portia will be too grand to acknowledge me ! "

" I will write to her to-night and bid her call on you, my dear. What is your friend's address ? a hundred and eight Tavistock square ; I shall not forget. I knew Tavistock square well in old days ; a hundred and eight must be the corner house. It will do Portia good to see you. She returned from her different visits yesterday, and wrote me a letter half in wild spirits, half miserable—one of those letters of hers that make me so unhappy. How I wish Portia was married, Susan ! "

" When last you spoke to me about Portia, you were thinking she would very soon be married," said Susan, hiding her face.

" Ah, to Mr. Blake. That was all a dream of mine, I begin to fear—however, I dare say you will see them together in London, and then you will be able to judge for yourself."

Susan's heart gave a throb of sudden hope.

" Nothing but new names were in the letter I got from Portia to-day. Lord This, Sir John That—heaven knows where she has met all these people ! Not a word of Mr. Blake ; not a word even of Teddy Josselin."

" Now that the engagement is broken off, you would not have Portia speak

of her cousin as she used, ma'am? Why, I suppose they are scarcely allowed
to be in each other's company."

"Who shall say? Who shall tell, when Portia is among her Dysart associates, into what company she goes and how much liberty she takes? One
thing in her letter certainly strikes me as suspicious—to say the least of it. After running on with the names of all these new acquaintance, and telling me
about her different visits, and what she has worn every day for dinner, she adds "
—Miss Jemima drew a letter from her pocket—"and after never mentioning
Teddy's name, mind, ' Grandmamma is looking dreadfully healthy, and is icier
in her North Pole of an old heart than ever. She tried to make me swear to-
day that I would never marry a first cousin. I almost believe I did swear it!
Oh, Aunt Jem, if a nice little house in Park Lane could be kept up, and a brougham as well, and if two extravagant people could dress and amuse themselves on
seven and fourpence a day, how happy one might be!' Now, seven and fourpence a day happens to be the exact amount of Mr. Josselin's pay, Susan."

Susan walked back across the heath to Miss Collinson's with the sensation
of treading on air. She had been a fool to put such blind faith in one of good
Miss Jemima's romantic fancies, a fool in the pique of the moment, with suspicion all unratified, to accept Tom Collinson. But George Blake was free, and
there was a possibility that she might see him in London. Not flirt with
him, of course ("Don't flirt with Blake!"—clear as the yellow-lettered deca-
logue above the altar in Halfont church these words stood out before Susan's
mental vision). But see him! perhaps steal her hand within his arm, hear the
pleasant whispers, half-joking, half-tender, of the voice she knew so well, once
more. The long exile in France, the prospect of being Tom Collinson's wife
eventually, were certainties still. But meanwhile George Blake was not engaged
to Portia; and there was a chance, no matter how remote, of seeing him. Who
that has loved but knows with what a sublime disregard of all future years the
prospect of some present ten minutes, some present foolish joy, ever so furtively
snatched, has power to fill one.

Miss Collinson thought Susan's spirits unnaturally good, considering that
this was her last evening in Halfont.

"No one would guess you had parted from a lover six-and-thirty hours ago,
and that you will part from everything else that should be dear to you to-morrow,
Susan," glancing with meaning at Mr. Fielding's portrait, which now hung, and
was to hang until Susan's wedding-day, above her own chimney-piece. "I
should be sorry to say you were growing heartless—"

"Heartless!" exclaimed Susan, guiltily conscious that one new, supreme
feeling *was* absorbing every joy, every sorrow of her old life. "Ah, Eliza, not
that. Something's a little wrong with me, I think. I'm like a person in a trance;
everything goes on round me in the world as usual, and, though I hear and see,
I feel nothing. My heart seems asleep."

"People have to awaken out of such sleep sooner or later," said Miss Collinson, tartly. "Suppose, instead of this kind of light talk, we read a chapter in
the Testament together for the last time."

Next day found Susan in her guardian's house in Tavistock square. Mr.
Goldney was a bachelor of between fifty and sixty; a man with one of those indistinguishable sort of business faces which you may always see in masses, hurry-
ing eastward along the Strand at ten or eleven o'clock in the morning; a man who,
dressed in professional black, breakfasted at eight, dined at six, dozed till nine;
then roused up and looked over law papers till bed-time. Few people ever get

nearer to Mr. Goldney than this. "You must make yourself comfortable, my dear young lady," he said, as he was wishing his guest good-night the first evening of her arrival. "Mrs. White, my housekeeper, has lived with me for twenty years; ask her for everything you want. If I had more time I would have taken you to the play—I mean," suddenly remembering her black frock, "to the Polytechnic. You have no friends in London?"

Susan answered that she had one friend, a granddaughter of Colonel Ffrench's, who was now staying with the Countess of Erroll, in Eaton square; and Mr. Goldney's face brightened; English faces that brighten at nothing else will often be found to do so at the sound of a title connected, by ever such slender or devious links, with themselves. "Your father was one of my oldest friends, my dear Miss Fielding. You must never let me lose sight of you. It was not every one who could get on with Thomas Fielding; but I got on with him. I recognized the real kernel under that outside husk of eccentricity. Yes, yes; I recognized the kernel. Eaton square—some way distant from us; I don't suppose you know the town? but you have only to tell Mrs. White, and she will order round the brougham for you whenever you wish to go out."

Next morning Susan was sitting alone at the window of Mr. Goldney's dining-room, thinking to herself that London was a considerably bigger place than Halfont, and that it might be possible to stay here for a couple of days without running across any particular acquaintance one had—when a Hansom cab stopped before the house. Could it be George Blake? She put up her glasses in breathless haste, and saw the figure of a lady veiled and plainly dressed, coming up the steps. After knocking and ascertaining that Miss Fielding had arrived and was at home, the visitor dismissed her cab (what kotous would not Susan's London friends have lost had Mr. Goldney known that they drove in cabs), then was ushered up-stairs into the lawyer's grand drawing-room, all green damask and stiff rosewood, and heavy chandeliers, and pictures swathed in yellow gauze. Here, a minute later, she was joined by Susan—Susan crimson to the temples, at the thought of encountering a stranger alone.

"I was determined to frighten you," cried Portia Ffrench's voice, "so would not give up my name. I got Aunt Jemima's note this morning, and ran off at once to look you up—for, alas, I return to Halfont to-morrow. Grandmamma invites you to dine with us to-day in Eaton square. Will you come?"

Susan's face dimpled all over. Who but George Blake could be asked to meet her? "I should like to come very much, if you thought my plain black frock would do?"

"To be sure your plain black frock would do, better than anything you could wear. I have a little plan of spending the evening out of doors as soon as we have got rid of grandmamma and Miss Condy. There will be no party, only ourselves and "—the color rose on Portia's cheek. Susan felt sure that George Blake's name was coming—" and my cousin, Teddy."

Susan looked as she felt, a blank.

"I came back from my visits the day before yesterday," went on Portia, "and this is the first time poor Ted and I meet as strangers. We went about together by grandmamma's orders when the engagement was first broken off, and hardly realized then that the whole thing was not play. Now we have to meet as indifferent acquaintance in earnest."

She sat down on the sofa, the only easy resting place the room possessed; took off her hat, and threw it on the floor beside her. "My head aches," she said, passing her hand wearily across her forehead. "I was going to say my heart aches, only I know I haven't got a heart. Susan, my dear—I have made the same remark to you a dozen times before, but I repeat it now—*What* a mistake a woman's life is !"

She was looking pale and harassed ; her eyes heavy, the set lines that fore-tell when a young face is going to age early only too plainly visible around her mouth. "Miss Jemima tells me you have been enjoying your different visits," began Susan—

"Oh, good, dear, single-hearted Aunt Jem," interrupted Portia, quickly. "Susan, I hope you will never have to deceive any one who loves you. It is not, believe me—even I, who have no conscience, say this—it is not pleasant work ! Talking of loving, what is all this absurd story about you and young Collinson ?"

"I—I am engaged to Tom Collinson," said Susan, burning with shame, as she made the confession. "I was to have been married to him at once, but something about money has taken him back to New Zealand, and so—"

"You are free to change your mind !" cried Portia. "What a little goose you must have been—for I need hardly ask if you like such a person ?"

"He is very good-hearted," stammered Susan, "and it was very kind of him to ask me."

"And still kinder to return from whence he came," said Portia. "I can see exactly how it happened—Mr. Collinson proposed because you chanced to be under the same roof one wet day, and you accepted him for the same reason. You don't write to him I hope ?"

'I haven't written yet ; I shall, of course."

"Then, of course, do nothing of the kind, my dear. As long as people write nothing they are committed to nothing. I am experienced in such mat-ters, little Susan."

"But no writing could bind me faster than I am bound," said Susan. "I have promised to marry Tom Collinson. Whenever he comes back and claims me I shall marry him."

"Why ?"

"I have promised."

"And you like him ?'

"Oh, I don't know," blushing furiously, and looking down, "please don't ask me. I—I shall be sure to like him some day."

"Ah, I see." After a minute. "I had a kind of fancy once that you were getting to care for George Blake," said Portia, carelessly.

At this direct accusation a sudden desperate courage seemed to enter Su-san's heart. "And I, and Miss Jemima, too, rather thought that you had got to care for George Blake," she exclaimed. "That last evening that I saw you and him together on the river bank—"

"When he drew our portraits, Susan ?"

"When he drew our portraits and when I was so angry—on that evening I felt sure that you and Mr. Blake understood each other. It looked like it, you must allow, Portia ?"

"Ah," answered Portia with a smile, "but then things so often look like what they are not. Now I wonder when you see us together whether you will say Mr. Josselin and I 'look like' understanding each other ?"

"I'll tell you that to-morrow. After all that is past, doesn't it go against your heart sometimes to have to call your cousin ' Mr. Josselin ?'"

"A great many things go against one's heart," was Portia's answer. "When

I look forward, as far as I can look, I see nothing else but trouble and weariness and vexation of spirit. Do you know grandmamma's age? Seventy-nine. Well, I was looking at her this morning and I decided she would keep above ground another ten years at least. She is fearfully and wonderfully vital."

"And you wish her in her grave?"

"Susan, my dear, that is the kind of incisive question never asked between people of delicate feeling. Yes, then! To you, reading me through and through with those big eyes and asking the honest truth, I will give, for the only time on record, an honest answer. I do wish her in her grave, devoutly."

Susan looked perplexed rather than shocked. "It doesn't seem right to wish anyone dead," said she, with the ready casuistry of her age. "Yet what can people have to live for at seventy-nine? Loving matters more than living, and if Lady Erroll's death would enable you and Mr. Josselin to be happy—"

"Ah, but you must know I have given a solemn promise not to be happy with Mr. Josselin," interrupted Portia, gayly. "I see Aunt Jem has been telling you part of my secrets, so I may as well tell you the rest. Imagine my position, Susan. I came back from my—from my round of visits the day before yesterday, and almost the first words grandmamma greeted me with were these—oh, the expression of her face as she spoke! "You and Ted are seeing each other still. Now I know all. I insist upon your confessing. You and Ted are seeing each other still?'

"'I looked—as I am sure I felt—the embodiment of simplicity. 'And if we do see each other still, grandmamma! Did my cousin and I ever promise to shut our eyes when we met each other in the street?'

"''I will have none of this flippancy, Portia. You and your cousin meet clandestinely—clandestinely!' Grandmamma evidently enjoyed the flavor of that naughty word. 'During the last ten days that you have been paying these visits, where has Teddy Josselin been? Answer me that?'

"''I should think Teddy Josselin had better be made to account for himself,' said I, with the most delicious good-temper. (Grandmamma's face and voice of conviction were a whole comedy in one act, Susan. Nothing diverts me more than to see people who have got hold of a corner, just a poor little corner, of the truth, hug themselves over their own sharpsightedness). 'If you suspect that Teddy has been running after me, write, please, to any one of the people I have been staying with, and make inquiries, as one does about a housemaid, as to the number of my followers.'"

"And did your grandmamma write?" asked Susan, full of eager interest.

"Well, no," said Portia. "Grandmamma, on thinking matters over, grew pacified—for that time, as she took pains to impress on me, only that time!" A comic expression came into Portia's black eyes. "To set her mind at rest for the future, however, and relying, she was pleased to say, upon my not breaking a solemnly-given word, she extracted from me, on the spot, a promise that I would never—It was a promise she had no right to demand, you know, Susan!"

And Portia stopped; the least in the world disconcerted, it may be, by the crystal-clear eyes that watched her so earnestly.

"And if the promise required you to be untrue to your own heart you did not make it?" cried Susan. "I need not ask you that!"

"Oh," said Portia, with a bitter little curl of the lip. "I had no choice. If I did not promise, I knew I should never have a chance of meeting Mr. Josselin, even as an acquaintance. I was to be banished from grandmamma's house

—as likely as not should have ruined all poor Teddy's prospects for the future. 'As well try to get a promise from a butterfly as from my grand-nephew, Josse-lin,' said grandmamma. 'You have sense, the sense of worldly interest at least; and for his sake, as well as your own, you had best do as I bid you.' And so I promised; life is too short to waste it in contests over trifles, and after all it was but a trifle that I promised! Grandmamma's horrible old companion was called in—imagine if that made my feelings softer—as a witness, and—"

"You promised never to marry Mr. Josselin?" cried Susan. "Oh Portia, and yet in your heart I know you like him!"

"Like him!" repeated Portia. Her whole face softened, for a moment she looked quite another woman to Portia Ffrench. "Well, yes, I don't mind con-fessing so much to you, Susan. These things can't be forgotten in a day. I do like Teddy—a very little, and for that precise reason had no choice left me but to take the oath grandmamma chose to administer. I repeated the words after her—that horrible old hypocrite Condy pretending to cry, as if she had been witnessing a touching religious ceremony.

"'I swear,' promise, grandmamma said, was not strong enough, 'I swear that I will never, directly or indirectly, renew my engagement with my cousin, Edward Josselin, without the consent of his grandmother, Lady Erroll!' The wording was grandmamma's own, I proposed no alteration. I simply repeated, in a perfectly firm voice, what I was told to say.

"Grandmamma looked relieved. 'You will not object to my acquainting Teddy with this?' she asked.

"'Not in the least,' said I, 'the promise is made. Let the whole world know of it, if you choose.'

"And so then, as a child gets a spoonful of jam after its powder, I was told that Ted should actually be invited to dinner once before I left town. He dines with us to day, Susan. You will see with what kind of nerve we manage to meet."

Susan asked at what hour she should come.

"Oh don't be a minute later than half-past seven," said Portia. "We dine at eight, but I particularly want you to be there when Teddy Josselin arrives. Grandmamma's eyes fixed on us when we meet would be more than I could stand, unless supported by some fourth person's presence. And come in your bonnet and morning dress. I told you—did I not?—that I had a plan for going to—to some gardens that they say are pleasant of a summer's night. As soon as we can dispatch grandmamma to her own evening's dissipation we mean to be off."

"Gardens!" repeated Susan, opening her eyes. "Why, I never knew that there were gardens in London."

"Oh, yes there are—numbers." As she spoke, Portia turned her face aside, then rose and busied herself in putting on her hat. "These particular ones are—down Chelsea way, I believe, and every one in London goes there. Why should they not? You hear good bands of music and stroll about by lamplight or moonlight (we shall have moonlight to-night) and see crowds of people more or less well-dressed, and come home when we choose. We are to go in a party, undeniably chaperoned, and mean to amuse ourselves if we can. At least it will be a change, an evening spent not quite upon the usual humdrum pattern of London pleasure."

"And you are sure it is not too gay a place for me to go to in my deep black?"

"Oh, as for that, the gayety or seriousness of any amusement depends upon the spirit in which one enters on it!" said Portia, evasively. "Susan, my dear, I want you to come! Don't put difficulties in the way. It is a chance you may never have again of seeing life. Are you your own mistress? Is any one looking after you?"

"Only my guardian, and he is engaged to dine out to-day. Unless you had invited me I should have spent the evening alone."

"Then I look upon everything as settled," cried Portia, moving across to the door. "Be at grandmamma's house at half-past seven, and don't order a carriage to come for you. I will promise to see you home. We shall not be late."

"And are you going to walk to Eaton square now?" asked Susan. "I thought from what Mr. Goldney said, young ladies could never walk alone in London."

"Oh, all those old canons of propriety belong to a fossil age," answered Portia. "There are no Lovelaces to run away with anybody now—'tis Lovelace, in these days, who dreads being run away with! Thickly veiled," as she spoke, she drew a little mask of black lace from her pocket, "thickly veiled and plainly dressed, a young lady with common-sense in her head can go wherever she thinks fit. I don't know the neighborhood, but I suppose I shall find a cabstand somewhere near, and if I make haste I shall be home just in time for lunch. Be sure to come early, and mind," she returned a step or two to whisper this, "not a word about the Chelsea Gardens before grandmamma."

CHAPTER XXIV

AT half-past seven, precisely, Mr. Goldney's heavy, old-fashioned brougham drove, for the first time, probably, since it was built, into Eaton Square. A minute later, and Susan, to the full as frightened as on the memorable evening when she drank tea at the Manor, found herself following a butler more awful, even, than the great Jekyll himself, up the staircase of Lady Erroll's house. She was shown into a drawing-room, full of mirrors and amber light and artistic color, but not magnificently stately as Susan had thought everything belonging to a countess must be ; a drawing-room, indeed, looking more as if human beings lived in it than the one in Tavistock Square. She stopped short at the door, dropping her little village curtsey to Lady Erroll's possible presence ; and Portia, in a simple muslin dress, made high to the throat, ran forward to meet her.

"Take off your hat and jacket, Susan ; oh, throw them down anywhere—on the sofa, if you choose. I would take you up to my room, only I am afraid of being away when Ted—I mean when Mr. Josselin arrives. Listen, there is his knock. Poor little Ted. How good of him to be punctual ! "

And Portia's face glowed with an expression of such sweetness as it had certainly never worn in the days when Teddy Josselin was her lawful and acknowledged lover. Was it necessary, before learning to love, that one must be convinced of the impossibility of marrying. Susan speculated, not wholly unmindful of her own personal experience.

The door opened and closed, and Teddy, unannounced, walked in. The two girls were standing together before the chimney-piece, in the front drawing-room, Susan's small figure concealed for the moment by Portia's superior statue and flowing muslin dress, and Teddy, who had ascertained that Lady Erroll was still in her dressing-room, came up to his cousin, with his accustomed loitering and worn-out air, but with both hands outstretched.

"Well, my dar— " he was beginning.

"Mr. Josselin !" cried Portia, crimsoning, and drawing back. "Don't you remember Susan—Susan Fielding? Don't you remember that evening at Halfont when you and she listened to the nightingales ? "

"And when you were jealous, and would take me off to a place where they made gunpowder. To be sure, I remember everything, Susan," shaking her little girl's hand affectionately. "The last time we met you behaved very badly to me—threw me over for Blake. I hope that fellow won't be here to-night, Portia ? "

"No one will be here but you and Susan."

"That is right. I shall have a chance of Susan looking at me this time—and, by the way, Tia, it would be very much to the purpose that Susan should look a good deal at me. Grandmamma is an old lady of singular discernment, Susan. She sees the hopeless state of poor Portia's affections, but does not approve, on theological grounds, of first cousins marrying, so—ah, I forget, you were present that day when we decided upon sacrificing ourselves to Moloch—that saves me the trouble of telling the story. Susan, do you know that I shall feel it my duty to pay you devoted attention all this evening?"

"Pay *me* attention, sir!"

"Yes, I shall, indeed. In the first place, because Portia—well, never mind that; in the second, because grandmamma's fears may as well be set at rest. You agree with me, Miss Ffrench?"

"Act in every way as your superior wisdom dictates, Mr. Josselin."

She moved across the room as she spoke, her face in the air. Teddy Josselin followed her, and managed to get possession of her hand. Evidently, Susan's presence was a circumstance of trifling moment to him.

"So you have put on the dress I told you to wear, after all—and your hair worn plain and small again, not in those atrocious French balloons. Ah, I shall make you have taste in time."

"*You* make *me* have taste!" repeated Portia, with cool contempt, but a smile at the corners of her lips.

"Yes, me make you have taste," repeated Teddy, who never troubled himself about grammar, "and in other things than dress, I hope. I don't deny that you have a tolerable eye for color and effect generally, but then you are not neat enough. See here!"

Without the slightest ceremony he adjusted the little ruffle of lace that his cousin wore round her throat, and Susan began to wish herself back in Tavistock Square.

Portia drew herself away with dignity. "Mr. Josselin!" she exclaimed.

"Miss Ffrench!" said Teddy, looking innocently into her eyes.

And then Portia's face all at once flushed rosy red, and she returned across the room to Susan. "What are the other things in which my taste is to be corrected?" she asked, looking back at Teddy.

"The other things are legion," said Mr. Josselin. "The one under immediate consideration being moonlight drives. I hope you have changed your mind about to-night, Portia?"

"I have done nothing of the kind," said Portia. "It is all very easy for men to be so particular as to what one ought and ought not to do; men who are tired of everything in the shape of excitement under the sun. Why are women never to see, never to learn anything of life, I want to know?"

"It strikes me that women see and learn just as much as they choose," answered Teddy, lazily. "At all events, you will learn nothing very edifying by going to—"

"The gardens at Chelsea," interrupted Portia, with a glance at Susan.

"Oh—to the gardens at Chelsea—agreed! I object, you understand, not on the score of morality," added Teddy, "but because I know how bored we shall be. The same old crowd of shop-boys, same old fireworks, same old wearying tunes—"

"Same old stars, same old moon and sky," interrupted Portia. "If one comes to that, all life is the same, only we forever try to call things by new names. I mean to go, at all events; you can do as you like. Hush," and now she moved to Susan's other side. "I hear grandmamma—not a word about moonlight drives before grandmamma, mind you, Susan!"

Upon this the door opened, and Susan, all eagerness to behold a living countess, saw a tiny, very old woman, with prominent, pale eyes, a sharp, ferret-face, and curious little yellow curls, totter in. "So, you can find your way here again,

now, Master Ted," a cold, little reverence bestowed upon Susan, as Portia introduced her.   "Pray, why did you never come near me all the time that your
cousin was away?"

"I was away, too," said Teddy, ingenuously; and, crossing the room, he
stooped and kissed Lady Erroll's withered, most unkissable face.   "I couldn't
come to see you when I was ever so many miles away from England, could I,
grandmamma?"

"What were you doing ever so many miles away from England?"

"Enjoying myself and spending money," answered Teddy, promptly.

"Where?"

"In Paris."

"Ah, Paris, indeed—I dare say!"   And there for the present the cross-
examination stopped.   Portia, while it lasted, had stood very upright, and with
unchanging color, her lips set like marble.

"You got the letter from me, I conclude?" asked Lady Erroll, presently.
"The letter posted last night."

"Yes, I got a letter," said Teddy, with his placid smile. This was the letter
informing him of the oath that had been administered to Portia.

"We have all come to our senses at last, you perceive?" remarked Lady
Erroll, tartly.

"I wish I had," said Teddy.   "Oh, grandmamma, if you knew the sums I
have been spending in Paris."

Grandmamma's face brightened—If such a term can be used in speaking of
such a face. Never could bachelor folly of Teddy's, even though her purse
must bleed, be more venial in her sight than now. Did not bachelor folly be-
speak delectable indifference to love matches, to virtuous poverty, to Portia?

"If you have spent so much money, I suppose you have brought your cousin
a pretty Paris present?" she said, almost pleasantly.

Teddy shook his head.   "I always think that, where spending money is concerned, Portia can shift for herself," he answered.   "Look at her now." Portia
wore a necklet and ear-rings of rubies set in fine, plain gold.   "Both those bits
of finery are new, I know, since I dined here last."

"When I was young, it was not considered good taste for girls to wear the
same jewels as married women," said Lady Erroll.   "Does your aunt, Miss
Ffrench, sanction all the money you spend on trinkets, Portia?"

"Aunt Jemima sanctions my taking presents whenever they are offered me,"
said Portia.   "Think of all the jewelry I have had from you, grandmamma!
This poor little set was given me by a friend, the dearest friend I have in the
world, a day or two ago, and I accepted it thankfully. A pauper like me can't
be above the temptation of baubles, especially when they suit the complexion as
well as rubies suit mine."

Dinner was announced, and Teddy gave his arm to old Lady Erroll, the two
girls following.   In the dining-room was a little, old woman—twenty or thirty
years younger than Lady Erroll, but still old; dressed in the scantiest of lavender silks, with a "front" dating from some by-gone period, blonde cap and black
velvet bands cunningly disposed at the junction of the head-dress with the forehead.   This was Miss Condy, Lady Erroll's salaried friend and confidante, and
who, when only the family were present, retained her place at the dinner-table.
She purred and curtsied and looked glad to see Teddy Josselin, who gave her a
kindly shake of the hand, asked a kindly word or two about her neuralgia, then

13

seated himself on the side of the table with Susan. By this arrangement, Portia and Miss Condy sat together.

They had been deadly foes from the day when Portia, a girl of sixteen, paid her first visit to Eaton Square. Miss Condy's perquisites, never numerous, had become perceptibly less as soon as Lady Erroll had a granddaughter upon whom to bestow the *disjecta membra* of her toilet-table, and Portia, little as she valued broken fans, torn bits of lace, faded ribbons, or chipped onyx seals for their own sakes, had always felt a malicious amusement in witnessing and augmenting Miss Condy's rage at being despoiled of them.

Every human creature she was thrown with must minister either to Portia's vanity, convenience, or diversion. She was not devoid of pity toward picturesque objects of pity. You could no more have brought her to feel sympathy for the grotesque, the ugly, the morally deformed, than you could bring a child to sympathize with the sad inner life of the clown and harlequin who turn somersaults for his amusement. Miss Condy, of her kind, was not a really bad old woman. Poverty had forced her to be a sycophant, had forced her to spend her life in bearing whims and bad tempers as if she liked them. Instinct taught the poor old creature the wisdom of lining her nest—if it were only with faded silks and shreds of torn lace—before the day when Lady Erroll's death should leave her homeless. She did not speak truth ; would truth have served in her profession ? neither did it jar on Condy's sense of honor to be occasionally employed as a spy. And still, under all veneer of forced or artificial vice, a great deal of natural good resided in the poor soul still. She maintained a sister, older than herself, out of her pittance ; and she was intensely grateful for kindness, would have gone round the world for Teddy Josselin, because he always remembered to ask after her neuralgia ; because once, years ago, he had sent her a valentine ; because, in fine, Teddy treated her as though she were a human being (to desolate people do such paltry favors seem cause for gratitude !) But Portia saw nothing of this ; Portia looked no deeper than the surface; and on the surface was sufficient crustiness, envy, mean smallness of all kinds to afford *her* diversion whenever a wet day, or a headache after a ball threw her, perforce, into Condy's society.

"I could no more bully poor old Condy than I could bully Arno," Teddy would say, in expostulation, when some of Portia's well-applied sarcasms or monkey tricks had sent Condy, in tears of rage, from the room.

"But I delight to bully Arno, too," was Portia's answer. Arno was a grim old Italian greyhound, a broken-down, shivering wreck of a dog, whose scarlet coat and blood-red eyes were always to be seen at the windows of Lady Erroll's carriage. "If it were not that Arno has still a fang or too left in his vicious head I would torment him just as much as I do Condy. I don't teaze nice, finenatured old women, or honest, wholesome dogs, do I ? Can creatures of as low organization as Condy and Arno have feelings ?"

They had memory, for certain. Arno would curl his lip and roll his miserable old eyes if Portia held up her finger to him across the room ; and Condy— well, the future was to prove whether Condy could not only remember, but retaliate. As dinner progressed, and Teddy, warming to the part he had set himself, became more and more devoted to the little girl at his side, the pleasanter grew the faces and remarks of old Lady Erroll and of Miss Condy. For once, perhaps for the sole time in her life, Portia had to drink the cup of humiliation in their presence. No matter that she felt herself, in very fact, the conqueror ; that the rubies on her throat were Teddy's gift ; that every word he spoke had a hidden, tender meaning for her ear; that he cared, that Portia knew he cared, no more for Susan than he *must* care for every pretty girl to whom he talked. Vanity was the most vulnerable point at which Portia Ffrench's spirit could be assailed, and she was destined to have vanity wounded to the very quick to-night. "You are not looking at all the brighter for your change of air, my dear Miss Ffrench," says old Condy, compassionately. And then, "Why, Portia, where are your spirits to-day?" from grandmamma. And then amiable looks, encouraging words from both to Susan—unconscious little Susan, blushing and dimpling at Teddy's complimentary speeches, and feeling that to dine with a countess was not half so awful as she had imagined, yet all the time wishing in her heart that nine o'clock had come, and that they were on their road to the Chelsea Gardens; the gardens to which "every one in London" went, and where she could, of course, scarcely fail of meeting George Blake among the crowd.

"Not at midday, thanks," answered Teddy, "I am engaged to two or three other places to-night, I believe, and may look in at the Wycherley's later, not at this hour."

"You can tell Short where he shall drop you then. It would be a pity for you not to make use of the carriage."

"I only thought I might stop for a quarter of an hour, and walk in the square by moonlight with Miss Fielding and my cousin," suggested Teddy.

"Miss Fielding and your cousin have their own engagements, thank you,' said Portia, quickly. "We are going round for an hour or two to the Wynne's, and Laura and I will see Susan home. We planned it this morning."

"You call Mrs. Wynne by her Christian name still?" remarked Lady Erroll.

Miss Condy rubbed her mittened hands together, and shook her head sorrowfully.

"Certainly I call Mrs. Wynne by her Christian name," said Portia, with an air of surprise. "She deserves a Christian name as much as most people, does she not?"

"Difficult, indeed to say *what* name Mrs. Wynne deserves," said Lady Erroll.

"Ah, indeed! a very true observation, my Lady!" echoed Condy, solemnly.

"I should think the name she lost when she married Dolly Wynne sums up her character pretty fitly," said Portia. "Never let us forget that poor Laura was a Dysart. Mrs. Wynne is a cousin once removed, is she not, Miss Condy? I know you remember all these chronological matters."

But Miss Condy's memory did not in this instance assist her. She believed Mrs. Wynne's mother was—that is to say, she thought—then, meeting Lady Erroll's eye, was not sure, my Lady, as to Mrs. Wynne's being a blood relation of the family at all.

"A very wise observation, my Lady," cried Portia. "When people's reputations tarnish, never remember whether they are blood relations or not. If we Dysarts did that always we should not own very many relations, by the way."

"Miss Condy," said Teddy, in his gentle, unmoved voice, "what wine shall I give you?" He was passing the decanters away from himself, as long experience had taught him to do at Lady Erroll's table.

"Well, the least little tiny drop of port," said Condy, for Lady Erroll retained the fashions of her youth, and fluids labelled port, sherry and madeira were placed on the bare mahogany with dessert. "Oh thank you, thank you! You have given me more than enough," this as Teddy poured her out a generous bumper. It was a thing understood, even by the butler, in Lady Erroll's household, that Miss Condy did not care for wine.

"And some fruit," cried Portia, good-humoredly. "Now, Miss Condy, I know you are fond of peaches. Here is a beauty."

And before there was time for expostulation a fine early peach, the crowning glory of the centre-dish of the table, lay on Condy's plate. The poor old woman looked green with annoyance. It was another understood thing that Miss Condy did not partake of dessert, save of such dead-sea fruits as were unfit to appear upon the table again. And the family apothecary was to dine with Lady Erroll to-morrow; and the centre-dish, but for Portia's sacrilegious raid upon it, would not have required one sixpenny worth of replenishment.

"I have dined, I thank you, Miss Ffrench. I want nothing more." Pushing the peach apologetically to one side of her plate.

"Oh, but peaches have nothing to do with dining" cried Portia. "Let me help you to some sugar. Grandmamma, I think that is the finest peach I have seen this year."

"Early peaches are extremely scarce this year," said Lady Erroll, with dry acerbity. "Extremely scarce, Miss Condy."

"And I care so little for the forced fruits," said poor Condy. "Would not your Ladyship be prevailed upon to try it? Mr. Josselin, may I ask you to hand the peach to her Ladyship?"

"May I ask you to finish your dessert, Miss Condy?" said her Ladyship, waving back the offer with her tiny, shrivelled hand. "The carriage will be here before I leave the table."

And now Condy had no choice but to obey. The peach merited all that had been said of it. It was large, it was juicy, and the sight of Condy gobbling it down—the human nature of her enjoying the unwonted flavor of the fruit, the sense of being under Lady Erroll's eyes almost choking her at every mouthful—went far toward restoring Portia Ffrench's equanimity. She was not really, deliberately cruel of nature; she would no more have inflicted positive injury on old Condy than on Arno—would have shrunk with disgust, indeed, from seeing either Condy or Arno in physical pain. She simply liked to torture, as she liked to do everything, for the distraction of the minute—simply required as much suffering from her victim as should serve to amuse herself. As to the feelings of the victim: well, if we could fathom a cat's sentiments toward the schoolboys who have set her adrift on ice, with walnut-shells for skates, we should, I dare say, guage pretty accurately those of Miss Condy, as, sitting in her lonely bedroom up stairs, she remembers her peach, and prays that the hour may come when she can repay Portia for this dessert, sugar and all, of which she has been forced to partake!

Coffee was served in the drawing-room; and presently Lady Erroll went away, looking, thought Susan, exactly like the wicked fairy in the story-book, in her gold and crimson opera-cloak, and carrying off Teddy Josselin with her. He shook hands warmly with Susan, then parted from his cousin with frigid ceremony.

"And Mr. Josselin is not going with us to the gardens?" cried Susan, as soon as the door was closed. I thought—"

"Hush," interrupted Portia, putting up a finger to her lips. "In this house, walls (and Miss Condy) have ears; think nothing, and what you see forget as soon as you have seen it. Are you in spirits, Susan? do you feel as if you could enjoy yourself? I don't. I feel as if I had had no dinner; I always have that feeling in ninety-nine Eaton Square. We have attendants in plush and powder, and undeniable Sevres and Dresden. We have also solid silver dish-covers, as you may have remarked, but we have nothing to speak of underneath. One of Aunt Jem's good heartsome dinners of roast and boiled would supply material for a week in Eaton Square. And then the wine! What is life worth when you stay with people who give bad wine?"

"I never know whether wine is bad or good," said Susan. "I drank what Mr. Josselin gave me, and it was very sweet and nice."

"That was what grandmamma and her wine merchant call port. Oh, Susan! if things would only taste sweet and nice to me as they do to you, what a happy woman I might be!"

"I should think you are happier than most people, as it is," remarked Susan. "You always talk as if you cared for nothing, and yet—I dare say I'm saying a stupid thing—but it seems to me no one could take so much trouble about amusement as you do who felt amusement to be beyond their reach."

"Badly reasoned," said Portia. " It is just when we feel a thing to be beyond our reach that we stand on tiptoe to get at it. For every five minutes that a woman of twenty spends before her glass does not a woman of thirty spend an hour? It's not an illustration—I'm getting like Teddy Josselin in my style of eloquence, I think—but I know what I mean. Talking of women of thirty reminds me of our chaperon, who will be here directly. She is so objectionable, little Susan. When I look at Mrs. Wynne I shudder. Is that what Portia Ffrench will be in another dozen years, I ask myself?"

"I thought Mrs. Wynne was your friend!" cried Susan. "You were very generous in defending her an hour ago."

"I defended her because grandmamma and Miss Condy abused her—the vileness and yet the wisdom of Condy in pretending to forget whether poor Laura was a Dysart! Yes, Mrs. Wynne is my friend. We chaperon each other by turns: I make her parties go off: Laura gets me invitations to houses grand-mamma would not enter. We feel rather more pleasure in taking away each other's partners than the partners of other people; and, on the score of mutual criticism, confine ourselves chiefly to pity. 'A pity poor dear Portia Ffrench does not marry.' 'A pity poor dear Laura Wynne can never remember the number of years she has lived upon the earth.' Yes, we are friends; and (just to the extent that honor can exist among thieves) would not betray each other's counsels."

Almost before Portia ceased speaking a carriage drove up before the house, and, through the open drawing-room windows, ascended the sound of a shrill resonant voice—a true Dysart tone—inquiring if Miss Ffrench were ready.

"Brilliant trained silk, no veil, white bonnet." cried Portia, peeping behind the window curtains. "The very last kind of dress, of course, that she should have worn—poor Laura's accustomed taste! And Dolly looking—oh, how sulky! Susan, I regret to say you will have an extremely stupid, extremely sulky married man for your companion the whole evening. You don't mind? I thought not. Very likely you will find Dolly Wynne sweet and nice, like grandmamma's port. Now come up to my room and we will adorn ourselves, or rather lay aside our adornments. In going to—to this kind of public places, I believe it is wise to look as much like a shop-girl after hours as possible.'"

CHAPTER XXV.

PORTIA'S room was a closet, indifferently furnished with air and light, at the extreme top of the house. It was a whim of Lady Erroll's that, while half a dozen stately chambers stood vacant, her granddaughter should sleep in a garret upon a camp bedstead, and where the thermometer seldom, at this season, declined below ninety, under the slates. Susan's memory carried away from ninety-nine Eaton Square (the only aristocratic mansion she ever entered) two ineffaceable pictures: one of Lady Erroll watching Miss Condy eat her peach; the other of Portia, as she stood in her miserably-appointed little garret, before the looking-glass, dressing for the "Chelsea Gardens."

It was now close upon ten o'clock, and the last flush of summer twilight had died above the wilderness of roofs at the back of Eaton Square. The moon, however, by this time rode high in the East, wonderfully bright and clear for a London moon; and by its light alone Portia dressed. The ruby necklet and ear-rings were laid aside—a heavy black-lace mantilla nearly reaching to the hem of her dress, an unpretending little black-lace hat was all her costume. Nothing could have suited her better, or disguised her less. To a doubtfully pretty woman, the absence of fashionable adornment may be a travesty; to a really handsome one, never. In a muslin dress and plain, black shawl, Portia Ffrench, instead of looking like a shop-girl after hours, looked more like Portia Ffrench than ever. The fine line of shoulder and throat, the small head, with its simply-braided, jetty hair, did but challenge the eye with greater distinctness because no glitter of trinkets, no inartistic flutter of ribbons or laces, was there to distract attention from their grace.

"Well, that will do, I suppose," she cried, as Susan, who had put on her own things in the drawing-room, stood at her side, and watched her. "Masked like this," she took up the veil she had worn in the morning from her dressing-table, and held it across her face; "masked like this, and not speaking beyond a whisper, I don't suppose it will be possible for any one to recognize me—and if they do—well, if they do, they do! After all, there would be no particular zest in going, if there was not the risk of being found out. Now let us start, Susan. Tread softly, and pray the gods old Condy be not upon the watch."

Upon this, silently and with light steps, they both ran down the staircase of the great, unlighted house. Economy reigned in every department of Lady Erroll's establishment. When her ladyship was out of an evening, no gas was lighted above the basement floor. Then, unattended by butler or page, Portia noiselessly lifted the latch of the front door, and they were free.

"I breathe!" said Portia, when they had taken their places in Mrs. Wynne's carriage. "We are safe from Condy this time. Great heavens!" she broke off, as they turned the corner of the square, "can that be Condy herself?" A female figure was at this moment stepping into a four-wheeled cab, drawn close up to the pavement. "It looks like her, and yet, no—the idea is ridiculous—what could Condy be doing out at this hour? Oh, I have not introduced anybody. Laura, this is Susan. Mrs. Wynne, Miss Fielding."

Mrs. Wynne was a small, very over-dressed woman, of about six-and-thirty; a woman who laughed much and loud, and talked much and loud, and who possessed little wit, and less beauty. As this is her first and last appearance in Susan's story, I don't know that I need lose space by speaking of her at greater length. The escapade she was engaged in to-night may, of itself, I think, be taken as sufficient exposition of her character. Mrs. Wynne's husband, Dolly, was a big, fair young man, some years younger than his wife ; a man of very few words, and ideas to correspond ; at the present moment prodigiously bored by being taken from his own amusements, and put on duty as a chaperon.

"Charming night, Mr. Wynne, is it not?" cries Portia, in her pleasantest voice. "I think Laura and I deserve great credit for this bright idea."

"Ah !" says Dolly Wynne, folding his arms sulkily, and looking up at the moon. They are driving in an open barouche, and Susan, who is beside him, can watch his face.

"'Ah !' isn't that 'ah' like Dolly?" cries Mrs. Wynne, with her shrill laughter. "Would you believe it, Portia, when I first asked him he refused to come. Said some other fellow would take just as good care of us as he would. Didn't you, Dol ?"

"I think the whole thing in bad taste," cried Dolly, "in deuced bad taste, and—and a deuced bore."

Susan remembered Teddy Josselin. Evidently these Chelsea Gardens were not as favorite a resort with gentlemen as with ladies. The thought depressed her ; lessened her hope of meeting George Blake among the crowd !

"Oh, Mr. Wynne, that's so unkind to us," said Portia, pleadingly, and leaning her beautiful face across in the moonlight. It was one of the conditions of their friendship, that Portia should occasionally cajole dear Laura's husband into submission. "I am going back to Halfont for ten months to-morrow, and Susan has never been out of Halfont in her life. This one evening's amusement is a great deal to us, remember ; and you ought to sacrifice yourself with a better grace. Now, won't you be nice and good-tempered if I ask you ?"

"Tell me how I'm to be nice ?" growled Dolly, but in a softening tone ; what man could Portia Ffrench not soften ? "If you will promise to let me take care of you all the evening, I will be as nice as I can."

Portia bit her lips to repress a smile. "Of course you are going to take care of me all the evening—of me and Susan, too."

Dolly Wynne now turned his head, and for the first time gave Susan a long stare. The result was not satisfactory. The first reason Mr. Wynne could find for any woman's existence, a certain amount of good looks pre-supposed, was —that she should be capable of amusing Dolly Wynne ! Shy simplicity, modest grace, "the violet by the mossy stone," were not by any means the kind of charms poor Dolly could appreciate.

"It's a great mistake going to these places at all," he remarked, going back, as men of few ideas do, to his original proposition, "a deuced mistake, and a deuced bore, too."

"It can't be a mistake, as far as I am concerned," said Portia. "I could meet grandmamma and Miss Condy face to face, without the slightest fear of their recognizing me ;" and she took out her "mask" from her pocket, and tied it over her hat. "Laura, dear, surely you have had the prudence to bring a veil ? "

"I have brought Dolly," said Laura, with the calm of conscious rectitude. "I am not ashamed of being seen. No need of disguise when one has a husband with one, my dear Portia."

"Then I need hardly ask if you mean to keep at Mr. Wynne's side all the evening, my dearest Laura ? Little Lord Dormer is not to meet us, I suppose, as you planned ?"

"At these places one cannot have too strong an escort of gentlemen," said Mrs. Wynne "As Lord Dormer was so anxious to join the party, I thought it just as well he should come—about Mr. Josselin I need not ask? and then the best thing we can do is all to keep together. As you think a veil so necessary, why did you not persuade Miss Fielding to wear one?"

"Because Susan's face is better than any veil," said Portia. "Susan doesn't know a creature in London. Besides, what does a child of her age need of disguise?"

"Ah, I understand, *ingénue* of the party." Mrs. Wynne was very fond of French words, but pronounced them indifferently. "Not a bad notion."

Now, most of this conversation might as well have been held in Syriac, for any meaning it conveyed to Susan's intelligence. Escorts; disguises; Dolly and a Shetland veil being used apparently as convertible terms. Susan understood nothing of what it all meant; understood only that Mr. Wynne was destined to be her companion, and that a monosyllable every five minutes would be as much as they would have to say to each other. "Still," thought the child of seventeen, "I shall hear the music, and see all the gay London people, and *perhaps* Mr. Blake. Ah, if I meet him, even Dolly wouldn't be able to take my pleasure quite away from me!"

At the end of another quarter of an hour, the carriage drove up before some kind of entrance-gate, of which Susan's blind eyes could only dimly make out the details. Crowds of people were entering from all directions. It was evidently some kind of gala-night, Susan decided, at these Chelsea Gardens. And no one wearing thick veils, she thought, looking round her, when they had left the carriage. Mrs. Wynne was right. There was no more need to disguise in Chelsea than elsewhere. Before they entered the gardens, Teddy Josselin had joined them (as he did so, a head stealthily looked out from a four-wheeled cab that was drawn up, twenty or thirty yards distant), and Portia put her hand within his arm, as a matter of course, nor quitted it again during the evening.

"You have come, in spite of your engagements, then, Ted?" she whispered.

"Not very likely I should let you be here without me," Susan heard him answer.

"I hope the rest of our party will not miss us," cried Mrs. Wynne, with undisguised anxiety. "Mr. Josselin, have you seen anything of Lord Dormer? Impossible to walk about in these places without a strong escort of gentlemen."

"You have got me, my dear child," said Dolly. "Nothing like a husband's protection, you know. Do you take one arm and Miss Fielding the other, and see if we have not had enough of it all in half an hour."

"Better let the carriage wait, certainly," said Mrs. Wynne, with a sudden sharpness of tone, "and then, if we don't amuse ourselves, we can come away. Portia, I must really forbid you to be out of my sight for an instant."

With the chaperon of the party, in these stern and virtuous dispositions, they now moved on with the crowd into the gardens. Happily for Mrs. Wynne's temper, Lord Dormer had arrived, and was waiting for them. He was an unwholesome, wearied-looking little lad of nineteen or twenty; an infant who had already forestalled one fortune in the purchase of toys suited to his nonage, and who, under Mrs. Wynne's auspices, was at present doing his best to get rid of another—for it was a fact that Laura Wynne, without youth, wit or beauty, had helped to dissipate as much money as any woman of her world in London. "An awkward, ugly school-boy," Susan thought as she looked at him one moment through her glasses. Stupid little Susan! not aware that Lord Dormer was twentieth Baron of Throgmorton, that diamonds and rubies were no more to Lord Dormer than bouquets and opera boxes to other men. "Is it possible that a staid lady like Mrs. Wynne would sooner accept this boy's escort than her own husband's?"

It was evidently quite possible. Looking round, and gaily warning Dolly to be sure to keep close, Laura put her hand within Lord Dormer's arm, and before another minute had elapsed was lost from sight. Susan was as absolutely dependent on Dolly Wynne as if they had been alone together in Robinson Crusoe's island!

"Oughtn't we to walk quicker?" she suggested. "I have lost sight of Mrs. Wynne now, and Portia and Mr. Josselin seem to have gone altogether."

It was the first remark she had made to Mr. Wynne, and she made it excessively shyly, and without raising her eyes to his.

"Well—yes," said Dolly with languid good temper. He had felt the natural indignation of a man and a husband at being put on chaperoning duty at all; but now that he was here, and now that Laura was happily disposed of, seemed ready to resign himself to his fate. "Portia and Mr. Josselin are gone altogether, and we have lost sight for good of Mrs. Wynne. So all we can do is to think of ourselves. Ever been here before?"

"No sir."

"Ah—won't ever want to come here again, I should say?"

"I don't know about that," said Susan, whose feet were already going in time to the distant music. "It seems a very nice sort of place I think."

Dolly Wynne put up his eye-glass, and looked down hard on Susan's face. "I don't generally trouble myself about ladies' motives," he remarked, after reading, to the best of his capacity, what was written there; "above all, where Portia Ffrench and my wife are concerned. But I *should* like to know what they brought you along with them here to-night for?"

"For my own amusement of course," answered Susan. "Portia said it was a chance I might never have again of seeing life."

"Seeing life! Yes, that's just the silly jargon women all talk now. As if they can't see life enough in their proper place without forever insisting upon going where men don't want them! Now, I am not talking about Mrs. Wynne or Miss Ffrench. They have their own business to mind. But you—my dear little girl," Dolly's tone got quite paternal; the creature, of his kind, was honest—"wouldn't you be a great deal better off at home than you are here?"

"No, indeed; I like being here," persisted Susan, obstinately. "It is a treat to me to see all these fine-dressed people—we never were sure at Halfont whether the town ladies wore trains or round skirts—now I know; and I like the music, and look—*oh* look!" her little fingers closing tight on Dolly's arm as a gorgeous outbreak of colored fire burst forth at some hundred yards' distance against the pale, moonlit sky.

The crowd, at this abrupt commencement of the fireworks, began, as crowds do under all sudden excitement, to rush senselessly forward, and Susan and her protector were borne along with the tide. "Hold my arm fast," whispered Dolly, "and at the first turning we will get away. There's a nice sheltered little side-path close here to the left."

Accordingly, when the nice sheltered little path was reached they turned into it; Dolly Wynne and Susan *tête-à-tête* in the moonlight; the colored lamps shining with fantastic stage effect through the trees; the distant band playing deliciously; the star-covered blue sky overhead! Susan began to think the Chelsea Gardens charming They wandered on slowly, and at last Dolly Wynne's arm pressed closer on the slim, girlish hand that rested there, and he began to talk nonsense—what else was there for him to do in this absurd position into which his wife's folly had forced him? Dolly Wynne talked nonsense; and Susan, secure in the knowledge that her companion was a married man, and at no times quick at suspecting evil, was looking up, all simplicity and good faith, at his down-bent face, when, fortunately or unfortunately, a party of four or five people met them full; and Mr. Wynne, dim though the light in this side-alley was, found himself recognized.

"What, Dolly Wynne here!" Susan heard a voice exclaim just as they passed.

Mr. Wynne looked back quickly over his shoulder. "Hallo, is that you?" he exclaimed. Then turning to Susan, "Just wait for me one minute," he whispered. "Walk slowly on, and I'll catch you up directly. I want to speak to a friend of mine, a college friend I have not seen for ages."

And, before Susan had time to reply, or even to think, she found herself alone.

She walked slowly on, as she had been told; but Mr. Wynne's minute proved a long one: he had evidently much to say to his college friend. They had already nearly reached the point at which the path rejoined one of the main thoroughfares of the gardens; groups of people were passing and repassing on all sides; and looking round, Susan found, with a beating heart, that she had lost sight of her protector. Should she wait for him or return? While she hesitated, a knot of young men brushed by, and one of them turned and spoke to her. What he said Susan knew not. An access of blind terror overcame her; she gave a little stifled cry of entreaty; then, too frightened to know which path she took, began to run.

A minute later, and she was once more in the thick of the crowd; this time alone.

CHAPTER XXVI.

WAS I right, Portia? Is it at all livelier to listen to "Tommy Dodd" out of doors than to the "Belle Helène" in a ball-room? Are the London apprentice and his sweetheart less boring than one's own acquaintance when you come to spend an evening in their society?"

Teddy Josselin and Portia were sitting alone in one of the remote quarters of the garden: Portia, closely veiled still, Teddy smoking a cigarette: neither of them in spirits.

"Every place would be stupid to people in such tempers as ours," said Portia. "I *could* enjoy it all very much under different circumstances."

"Oh, under different circumstances you might, but not with me," remarked Teddy, quietly. "Very likely, Mrs. Wynne is amusing herself—I'll wager poor Dormer isn't though!"

"Do you mean to compare me to Laura Wynne, sir?"

"Eh?"

"Do you mean to compare me to Laura Wynne? The question surely does not entail so hard a strain on the reflective faculties but that you may answer it!"

"I don't think you are much like her now."

"But will be some day?"

"You will always be a far handsomer woman, my dear Portia."

"I am not thinking of that any more than you are, Mr. Josselin. Do you mean that I shall ever be—the same kind of woman Laura Wynne is now?"

"I think there is a family likeness between all women of fashion, if I must speak the impartial truth," said Teddy.

A dead silence.

"What a vexation and disappointment everything in life is!" came at length from Portia's lips; a wreath of blue smoke at the same instant from Teddy's. "I wish to heaven I were back at Halfont."

"Well, I must say I like Halfont on a moonlit night, myself." Teddy made this remark almost cheerfully.

"And I wish to heaven I had never left Halfont," went on Portia. "Every step I take seems to bring me to greater grief than the last. I should have done better, by far, to hold to poor Mr. Macbean. *He* had ballast, common-sense, principle."

"Yes; I doubt if Sandy would have done what I am doing to-night," assented Teddy. "Fancy old Macbean at—"

"I should have been able to respect him, at all events," interrupted Portia. "He was not a man to let me have my own way in every ridiculous folly, and then—"

"Then sit quietly and be bullied because you did not amuse yourself," said Teddy. "No; I don't think he was."

"I wonder whether I hate you, sir! I'm sure I feel as if I do."

"Nothing of the kind, my dear child. No woman ever hated me. You are out of temper with yourself, Portia, nothing more."

"Is there any particular object in our sitting in one place the whole evening? As, unfortunately, I have come here, mayn't I as well walk about and try to be amused?"

"Try if possible to be recognized by some man who can float the new scandal about Portia Ffrench through the clubs to-morrow?"

"Recognized—with this mask on!"

"Recognized—with Portia Ffrench's walk and shoulders!"

"Once and for all, it must be confessed, Mr. Josselin, that you are of a thoroughly jealous, exacting, selfish temperament."

"Jealous?"

"Yes, jealous. Don't you know the meaning of the word?"

"I think so. I ought, I am sure! No; I am not jealous, at least I never was yet, of any one."

"Then why used you to be so angry at my distributing my photograph over all the mess-tables, as you were pleased to say, 'in the Kingdom'? Why are you in such a bad temper to-night—so dreadfully afraid of any one recognizing Portia Ffrench's walk and shoulders?"

Teddy took his cigarette from his lips, held it delicately poised between two fingers, and gazed up at the moon. "I'm not good at definitions," he remarked, shaking his handsome little head over a sense of his own deficiency, "however, I'll try for once, to say what I mean. Portia, you see Dolly Wynne?"

"Thank heaven I do not, at this moment."

"Well, if I was Dolly Wynne, Mrs. Wynne would keep up an establishment of her own. You understand?"

Not a word in reply from Portia.

"I'm not particularly straight-laced, that I know of, and I should like my wife to amuse herself honestly, if she could (why can't women amuse themselves honestly?) and I'd let her have her own way in everything, as you have had yours now, up to a certain point."

"And that point?"

"Would be a good deal this side of Mrs. Wynne's latitude," said Teddy, incoherent, but thoroughly in earnest. "I don't believe I am jealous; but I know I should never love any woman who made a fool of herself. And it would bore me to live with a woman I didn't love. And I never mean to bore myself. Those are my principles."

And he put back his cigarette between his lips.

"Well, this is edifying!" cried Portia, with a small scornful laugh. "I have heard of sermons in stones. I never thought though to hear sermons from Ted Josselin and in—a place like this! I am going back to Halfont to-morrow. I make a poor little attempt at one evening's amusement, escorted by you—and people much better than me go everywhere now—to Evan's, to the Alhambra, everywhere; you have told me so yourself—and this is the result! If it is the slightest gratification to you, let me say that I never enjoyed myself so little as I have to-night. My dreadful crime has brought its own punishment."

"I am glad to hear it," answered Teddy. "You will not want to try the same experiment again."

"Not under the same circumstances, you may be very sure," retorted Portia.

This is how two of the party were taking their pleasure. Susan, meanwhile, her cheeks on fire, her heart beating till she could hear its beats, was wandering continually more and more astray in the crowd (for with the adventures of Mrs. Wynne, as with those of Dolly, this story has no concern). She made her way on for forty or fifty paces, vaguely hoping that she was going in the same direction Portia and Teddy Josselin had taken. Then some one spoke to her again; asked her, for she could hear the words clear this time, if she was looking for any one, and would like to be assisted in the search?

"I have lost my friends," said the little girl, half crying. "I don't know where I am. I was never at Chelsea before."

Susan looked up timidly, as she spoke, at the face of her interlocutor, a swarthy Jewish face, with black, evil-glancing eyes, and on the instant was seized with terror so sickening that, forgetting the crowd was now her best protector, she ran off, as hard as she could run, down an alley, lighted by the moon alone, that turned sharply away to the left. At first, she thought she heard steps as of some one in pursuit, and the idea of again seeing the man who had spoken to her gave her power to fly. Then, gradually, all became silent; and panting, faint with affright, Susan sank down on one of the rustic benches that bordered the path.

The moon quivered fitfully upon her face through the branches of a laburnum bush overhead, and a man who had approached alone from the other end of the alley, was able, standing in deep shadow himself, to watch her a good minute or more unobserved. Then he came forward and spoke:

"Susan."

The poor little girl jumped up, ready for flight, half expecting to see her persecutor at her side, and saw—George Blake. She caught hold of his hand, of his arm:

"Don't leave me, don't ever leave me any more!" she exclaimed, then burst out a-crying. "I came with Portia, sir," she said, as Blake stood silent, gravely watching her, "with Portia and Mr. Josselin, and the Wynnes; and Lord Dormer met us here. You know these people?"

"I know who they are—yes."

"Mr. Wynne—Dolly they call him—was to take care of me ; but he met a college friend he wanted to speak to, and I lost him, and got among the crowd —and a man with a horrible face spoke to me—and then I ran away here. Don't leave me, Mr. Blake! I shall die with terror if I lose *you !* "

Blake took her fluttering hand, and drew it within his arm. "I might have known what kind of influence brought you here," said he. "But, for a minute —for one whole minute, Susan—my heart stood still as I watched you! Now, don't be silly," she was trembling yet with agitation, "don't cry, and don't be frightened; I'll take care of you. If you don't see these vigilant friends of yours any more, I'll take you home. Did you come from Halfont to-day?"

"I have left Halfont forever, sir; I'm staying with my guardian in Bruns-wick Square ; and Portia asked me to dine at Lady Erroll's to-day, and we came to these gardens to finish the evening. And I liked coming, and I was enjoy-ing myself—oh, so much, till I got lost," added Susan, with her irrepressible truthfulness.

"Enjoying yourself with Dolly Wynne?"

"Yes. He didn't like being brought here, at first, he said ; but he was very good-natured to me. And he took me along such a pretty path, with overhang-ing trees, and we were listening to the music, and just going to look at the fire-works—and then this friend of his passed, and Dolly bade me walk on a moment, and I got lost. What a fool I was to cry !" She brushed the big tears still resting on her cheeks. "As if anyone would have hurt me ! Now I am with you, I feel as brave as a lion again." And, as she vaunted her courage, Susan's small fingers unconsciously closed tighter upon the young man's arm.

"Do you remember the last evening you and I saw each other, my dear?" he whispered. "You told me then there was to be no next time. Have you forgotten what you told me, Susan?"

Susan hung her head. Ah, that last evening on which she had definitely made up her mind that she liked George Blake, and that her liking was hope-less ! Would that she could forget it ! Would that all she had passed through since had only been a bad dream ! "A great deal has happened since then," she cried, at last. "I feel, I don't know how many years, older since that night when you drew my portrait, and I threw it in the river."

"Indeed," said Blake, "and what has there been to make you grow old? Look at me, Susan. Let me see what wrinkles and gray hairs have become suddenly visible."

They had walked farther and farther from the crowd, while they talked, and were now alone in the clear moonlight ; not a figure, not a shadow which could conceal a figure, within many yards of them.

Susan lifted her face full up to Blake. "I have had a dozen things, at least, to make me feel old," she said. "I don't know why you should laugh at me. I have left Halfont forever, and I'm going away to people I've never seen, in France, and—and—" she had to struggle with herself before she could bring out the confession—"and I've got engaged !" she cried,' with a little resolute jerk.

"Have done what?" asked Blake, not without a smile.

"I've got engaged."

"Engaged—as what?"

"Engaged to be married; but Tom Collinson has had to return to New Zealand to settle some money business, so it won't be for a year. I shall spend that year at Uncle Adam's."

"And who is Tom Collinson—and do you mean to say you are really fond of him? Oh, Susan, Susan! This is a blow to me!"

The child's foolish heart throbbed with an ecstasy of pleasure. "A blow?" she stammered. "Oh, Mr. Blake, how can it matter to you what I do and who I care for?" Susan's mind could never master the accusative case while she lived.

"It matters everything," answered Blake, not, I fear without undue tenderness of manner; the hour, the distant music, the moonlight, all conspiring against his wisdom, as such influences are apt to conspire against men's wisdom at five-and-twenty. "But, for the existence of this miserable man, Collinson, how can I tell you would not some day have looked at me?"

He stooped; he laid his hand upon the small fingers that held his arm so closely. "Don't be cruel enough to tell me that you love Tom Collinson in earnest?" he whispered.

"Love—oh, I don't know anything about that," stammered Susan, her breath coming short and tremulous. "Tom Collinson and Eliza were kind to me when I had no one else, and he wanted me to says 'yes,' and I said it. It was one day—I had been walking, very miserable indeed, on the common—and—and I first thought, for certain, that you and Portia were engaged, sir."

"Oh—I see," said Blake in a somewhat altered tone. "The day you thought for certain that Portia Ffrench and I were engaged you accepted Mr. Collinson?"

"Yes."

"Who told you the news of—of my engagement?"

"I don't know whether it would be right for me to say."

"It is right for you to say everything to me, my dear."

"Well, I was staying at the Collinson's, and old Miss Ffrench met me on the heath. It was the day of the sale—I'm sure I was wretched enough, already—and we began to talk about Portia and her engagement being over with Mr. Josselin—"

"Go on Susan. Don't mind me."

"And we thought she could never take it so lightly unless in her heart she cared a little for some one else, and of course we knew you liked her, and—oh why do you make me say all this?—I felt there wasn't a doubt you understood each other at last."

"And went home and engaged yourself to Tom Collinson?"

"Yes, Mr. Blake."

Blake stood silent, revolving many things in his mind; at last—"And you have found out your mistake by this time?" he asked, but without looking in Susan's face. "You know pretty well how much Portia Ffrench cares for me now?"

Ah, how his voice had changed! Foolish little mock, lover-like speeches, tender hand pressures, might be for her, in the moonshine—Portia not by. His heart—easy to see that—his heart was Portia's still. Susan instantly felt it was her duty to be dignified and freezing, and, as a preliminary step, snatched her hand away from beneath Blake's.

"It is not likely I can judge of Portia's feelings, sir. If I gave an opinion—"

"Well, if you gave an opinion?"

"I should say she likes Mr. Josselin still."

"Of course she likes Mr. Josselin still. How is she looking to-night, Susan?"

"Oh, handsomer than ever. She is dressed very plainly; a muslin dress, a black shawl; Mr. Josselin's choice, I heard him say. It suits her.

Susan would not have trodden on a garden-worm for anything you could have offered her; yet would she pitilessly torture the man she loved—yes, and enjoy the sight of his pain. Have you not remarked this crookedness of spirit in the very softest-natured women you know?

"What do you mean by her dress being Josselin's choice? Do they talk of muslins and laces before Lady Erroll?"

"Oh, no. It was before Lady Erroll came in."

"Susan, you are a dear, kind-hearted little girl. Tell me exactly what they said, both of them."

"About the dress?"

"No, yes—about everything."

"Portia pretended to be a little cross at some nonsense of his—you know a way she has of pretending when she likes—and walked away as though she would never speak to him again; and then Mr. Josselin followed, and said how well her hair was done, and that he would make her have taste in more things than dress in time. This was a joke, of course. I think Portia has the most perfect taste in the world. And then they began to discuss about coming here to-night. Mr. Josselin did not want to come; but Portia would have her own way, and then—"

"Then?"

"Old Lady Erroll came in, and Mr. Josselin talked most to me for the rest of the evening."

"And came away with you both from Lady Erroll's house?"

"Oh no. He made believe to say good-by to us in Lady Erroll's presence, and met us here, outside the gates."

"And Portia—Miss Ffrench is with him now?"

"I suppose so. I have not seen them since."

"Thank you. For administering a moral tonic, strong, bitter, undisguised, commend me Susan, to a little girl of your age! No trembling of the hand, no mawkish attempt to disguise the taste of the salutary draught by sugar! You hit straight, my dear—drive the nail well home, as it ought to be driven. Now, just take my arm again—so! and let us return to what we were talking about. What were you telling me, Susan? That you are engaged, too? That's all absurd nonsense. I forbid the banns. A poor little thing like you to talk of being engaged—and to Tom Collinson, too!"

"No; but I can imagine him. He's not good enough for you, Susan. Don't you feel in your heart that Tom Collinson is not good enough for you?"

"I feel that I shall marry him," cried Susan, unhesitatingly. "It's a regular engagement, I can tell you. Look, this is his ring that I wear on my finger."

"And you think he is good enough for you?"

"I—I don't see why he shouldn't be. He has got faults. Every one has got faults."

"And what are Mr. Collinson's special ones?"

"He smokes too much."

"Venial; very venial, Susan."

"And he can drink ever so many glasses of brandy and water."

"Afterward?"

"Oh, Mr. Blake, he is so jealous! I think that's the very worst fault he has."

"Jealous—the plot thickens!" said Blake. "When I saw you last—a fortnight ago, isn't it?—you were a good, unsophisticated little country girl, Susan. And now you have got a lover, and the lover has got a rival—a rival or rivals, which?"

"Tom would be jealous of the air, if he could think of nothing else," said Susan, shirking this direct question. "He was jealous of people he had never seen, and he likes me to go and live with Uncle Adam, at St. Sauveur, just because I shall have no one to speak to there. And I'm not to write to anybody—that I've promised—and—"

"Oh, but all this must be seen to!" interrupted Blake, seriously. "These sort of oaths were never intended to be kept. In the first place, you must write to me."

"Never!" said Susan. "That is the one thing I never *can* do, while Tom is gone."

"What, were you weak enough to give a special promise on that point?"

"I had no choice but to promise. Of course, I couldn't say—as Tom wished—that I would never sing with you or speak to you, because I knew I might see you with Portia; but I thought I might easily obey him about writing. I write shocking letters, Miss Collinson says; when I've put, 'My dear so and so, I am well, and hope you are the same,' I can think of nothing else. You wouldn't care to get them."

"My dear," said Blake, "I should care to get the sheet of paper that your sweet little hand had touched."

And after this they walked on for a space in silence, silence soft and pure as if they had been a hundred miles away from London; even the music (a set of quadrilles, containing such melodies as "Tommy Dodd" and "Champagne Charlie,") becoming refined in its transit across the moonlit gardens; the distant crowd, every belonging of the place, so Blake felt, losing its vulgarity by the fine contact of Susan's presence.

A woman of fashion, if she choose to visit doubtful resorts, assimilates singularly, rapidly, in the minds of her male associates, with her surroundings. The innocence of a little girl like Susan can transmit to the grossest background something of its own whiteness—if the experiment be made but once!

They sauntered leisurely along; and some association of ideas, the juxtaposition of country simplicity, perhaps, with the follies of the town, made Blake's imagination travel back to that summer evening of a hundred and fifty years ago, when the good old knight went down by water to Spring Garden, and listened under the May moon for the nightingale. "There is nothing," said Sir Roger, "there is nothing in the world that pleases a man in love so much as your nightingale." He thought of the buried generations that had masked and wantoned in the years' long dust through these "Mohammedan Paradises;" of the frail dead lips that had kissed and quaffed beneath their shades; of the inexorable next morning—grim ghosts of all the vanished hours which to youth and pleasure had fled so swift.   .   .   .   .

"I do think," said Susan's fresh voice, "that people in town have great ad-

vantages over us in the country. If ever I live in London, I will come to a
place of this kind every moonlit night."

" In a grand trained silk dress, and with company like the people you see
here, I hope ? "

" If I'm only lucky enough ! What can be better than a grand trained silk,
and well-dressed companions, and music, and a garden like this to walk about
in ? "

Blake did not speak. The *capability* for evil in Susan Fielding (capability
of which men and women of the world may detect pathetic forewarnings in
every unknowing word a child utters) was a new idea to him !

" If you don't think places of amusement nice, I wonder you come to them
yourself ! " said she.

" Places of amusement may be ' nice ' for me—not for you, little Susan. Besides, I came here with an object to study light and shade. See, here is my
note-book ; " he touched the breast-pocket of his coat. " I had just been jot-
ting down some details for a moonlit garden-scene I am thinking of painting,
when I ran across you. When do you leave London, my dear ? You have not
told me half enough about yourself."

" To-morrow evening," she sighed, audibly. " Oh, I shall be so sorry to go.
Now that I have had a taste of London, I don't want to live with Uncle Adam."

"And I think to live with Uncle Adam will be just the best thing you can
do. Tom Collinson is right ; I begin to have a higher opinion of Tom Collinson. You will have no dissipations of this kind at St. Sauveur, I take it, Susan ?"

" Uncle Adam says there are balls and concerts at St. Maur, a mile distant
from St. Sauveur ; but they will be nothing to me, I shall never enjoy them—
how should I ? "

" On about the same principle, perhaps, that you have enjoyed yourself to-
night, my dear. Only, we will hope, with Uncle Adam to take care of you, that
the enjoyment will be a little less perilous."

" Perilous ! " cried Susan, " perilous ! And haven't I had you to take care
of me ? "

CHAPTER XXVII

IT was past eleven o'clock when they reached the entrance of the gardens.

"Not much use in waiting for these friends of yours," said Blake, looking at his watch. "In the first place, they have, beyond all question, forgotten you ; in the second, even if they came, we, should be certain to miss them in the crowd. As chaperonage seems to be an institution more honored in the breach than the observance, I think the best plan will be for me to get a hansom and take you home."

Susan had not a doubt upon the subject. To drive alone in a hansom with George Blake, by moonlight, was probably the highest form of terrestrial happiness her imagination could have soared to. "Still," said she, with an effort to be conscientious, "I believe it would be *right* to wait, if it is only a few minutes longer, for the rest. It doesn't matter a bit if we miss Mrs. Wynne ; but I should be sorry for Miss Portia to lose a night's rest through uneasiness about me."

"I don't think you need fear that," said Blake. "Miss Portia has never lost a night's rest, save through ball-going, in her life."

However, he waited, Susan still hanging upon his arm, and began slowly to pace up and down the walk immediately in sight of the entrance. After a couple of turns they came across Portia and Teddy Josselin : Teddy, his hands thrust despondently in the pockets of his light overcoat, Portia veiled close as ever ; neither of them, it seemed, speaking a word. At the moment of meeting, Susan's figure, as it chanced, was in shadow ; Blake's perfectly distinct in the moonlight. He raised his hat and moved slightly aside.

"Ah, how are you, Blake ?" cried Teddy, looking round, but not offering to stop. Portia turned away her head, and quickened her pace perceptibly.

"Portia—Miss Portia !" cried out Susan. "Don't go away, don't let us lose each other again !"

So now no choice was left to Portia Ffrench but to accept her position. She accepted it gracefully, as she accepted most things ; moralized, as she shook hands with Blake, upon the impossibility of committing any crime with impunity ; was duly indignant at Dolly Wynne's desertion of Susan, duly thankful at Mr. Blake's, "like the fairy prince in a burlesque," coming just when he was wanted, to the rescue. "And I hope, Susan, all these thrilling adventures have served to make you pass your time pleasantly," she finished. "For my part, I must confess that this scheme of Laura's has turned out the greatest failure, even in the way of amusement, I ever experienced, and that is using strong language."

Thus saying, she dropped Teddy Josselin's arm, and drew a step nearer to the others. At the instant in which she found herself recognized, she had detected an expression such as she had never seen before on Blake's face ; not so much, she was forced to acknowledge, an expression of indignation, of anger, of jealousy, as of contempt. And the thought was exceeding bitter to her ! No woman living, whatever her theoretic contempt for the world's opinion, but feels poignant pain at the first humiliation, the first descent from her pedestal, in the sight of the man who has loved her !

"Don't you think we had better walk about here till Mrs. Wynne joins us ?" she said—in what a humble tone for Portia Ffrench ! and turning her veiled face up to Blake's.

"As you choose," said he, coldly ; "I had just decided upon getting a cab myself, and taking Miss Fielding home to her friend's house. I resign her into your charge now."

"But you will stop with us until we find the rest of our party ?" pleaded Portia, in a whisper. "Oh, if you knew how, I repent having been drawn into all this foolishness !" She had turned, and was walking slowly back, Blake, of necessity, keeping by her side. "Please tell me you won't think very bad things of me for having met me here ?"

"I don't assume the right of thinking anything," he answered. "You are much the best judge of what is fitting for you to do. A little girl like Susan Fielding might as well have been left out of such an expedition, perhaps."

If he had meant to sting Portia Ffrench to the quick, he succeeded admirably. "Susan Fielding !" she exclaimed. Susan and Teddy Josselin were now some yards distant behind. "Oh, I quite understand you ! A little girl like Susan Fielding might as well have been left out of an act of folly that is seemly and consistent for Portia Ffrench. You are in a complimentary mood this evening."

"I am, I fear, in a sane one," said Blake. "The cure which you foretold for me that last night at Halfont, is wrought at length. Ah, Miss Ffrench, you may remember my saying to you then that the cure would be sharper to bear than the disease !"

And in speaking thus, he spoke the truth. His first fever of infatuation had been cooling longer ago, perhaps, than he himself suspected. But he had lingered, obedient to Portia's will, for some time after his heart had in very fact escaped her thrall. On the evening of the drawing lesson, he would have given up his life to her, had she chosen to accept the sacrifice of his life ; during the week succeeding the rupture of her engagement, he had paraded his allegiance to her in whatever public place it was her pleasure that the world should note it. At this moment—her voice pleading to him as it had never pleaded yet—George Blake knew definitely, finally, half relieved, half with a feeling of exquisite pain, that he was sane—cured; that Portia Ffrench was nothing to him!

She would have retorted, but the words died on her lips. She had never for a moment believed herself in love with the penniless young treasury clerk; had confessed, openly, that vanity on both sides was the sole foundation of their attachment. And her heart was full as it could hold of other hopes; hopes, ambitions, fears, in which Blake had no part. And still she grudged, passionately grudged him his recovered freedom. She had never loved, had never meant to marry Blake; all the love that it was in her to give was at the present time Teddy Josselin's. But she had lost him! The unimportant pawn was off the board; the fish had got back to the river; sufficient vitality left in him to swim away. She could almost have gone upon her knees at this moment, if going upon her knees could have brought him back. For it is curious that wounded self-love will ofttimes push people further than would wounded love for others, in their desire for reconciliation.

"You have become sane again!" she cried, bitterly, after a minute. "Oh, how easy it would be for me to be sane, truthful, upright, everything I ought to be, if my position was not such a false one! Some day I hope I shall be able to convince you that I was not quite as much to blame as you think me now?"

"I don't blame you in the slightest degree," said Blake, stiffly; his stiffness proving to demonstration that he was not utterly indifferent! "Your life is apart from mine in every way, Miss Ffrench. Your life, your associates, your amusements."

"Amusements! Do you pretend to think I came to this shocking place to-night for amusement?"

"I should be sorry to suppose you came here from curiosity," answered Blake.

"And why, pray!" cried Portia, quickly. "What possible danger can there be in ladies going anywhere they choose, properly escorted?"

"Danger—oh, if you argue the question in the abstract, what danger can there be in anything that does not imperil life and limb?"

"Don't hit too hard, Mr. Blake. I really can't bear hard hitting from any one to-night. If you knew how worried I am, what trouble of all sorts lies on my mind, you would be more lenient to me—to me and to my faults!"

She raised her hand with a quick gesture to her forehead, and her veil fell to the ground—by accident or intention, who shall say? In her whole life Portia Ffrench had never looked handsomer than she looked at this moment; her light summer dress, artistically relieved by flowing drapery of black lace, the minglement of lamplight and moonlight shining on her picturesque, Italian-hued face. Never had she looked handsomer; never had her beauty fallen so powerless on George Blake's heart! Fresh from the simple charms of a girl whose every look, whose every tone, was natural, Portia Ffrench with her town-taught air and well-posed attitudes, yes, and with the town-made artistic dress and the veil fluttering exactly at the right moment to the ground—Portia Ffrench, with all her superior breeding, with all her superior grace, struck him—the word must out—as more than half an actress. And Blake had known so many actresses! had been spectator, on and off the stage, at so many a scene of touching contrition and repentance! The comparison of itself was a disillusionment.

He picked up the veil and returned it to her gravely, and without answering a word. At that moment their eyes met, and Portia knew the truth.

"I can't think why it is," she cried, in her lightest tone, "but I am perpetually feeling that we are all acting our parts in a play to-night—the effect of so much music, and lamplight, and colored fire I suppose ; Susan as the ingenuous village heroine, of course, and Ted and I—well, we'll leave that alone—and you, O Mr. Blake, you as the great tragic element of the whole piece. If you could see your face ! Teddy," she paused a minute till her cousin and Susan came up ; then, with the prettiest mock-unconscious air of familiarity, stole her hand under Teddy's arm, "did you ever see any one grown so tragic-looking as Mr. Blake ? Really, Susan, if this is the influence you exercise over people I shall expect to hear of some horrible ending to poor Dolly."

"A pity some horrible ending didn't happen to him earlier in the day," remarked Teddy. "If it had, the widow would have kept at home, at least I suppose she would, for one evening, and we should have been spared the trouble of waiting for her. How much longer do you intend to wait for Mrs. Wynne, Portia ?"

It would be ridiculous to say that Teddy Josselin's lazy voice could ever sound authoritative. In his way of asking this question, however, there lurked just a ring, a suspicion of latent self-assertion. And George Blake's ear detected it in a second. Whatever the avowed rupture of their engagement, the real relations between these two people had not, he felt, grown more distant since he was with them last. Teddy Josselin was already on the verge of having opinions.

"I was proposing, just now, to Susan, that I should take her home in a hansom. Now, if a hansom would only hold four people—"

"But two hansoms would hold each two people," cried Teddy, brightening, "and that makes four. What a splendid fellow you are for ideas, Blake. We'll get two hansoms, if hansoms are to be had, and Blake shall run away with Susan to the east, and I—no, that's where ideas always break down, you can't reduce them to practise. My cousin and I could never drive up to grandmamma's house at midnight."

"Condy looking from a garret-window in her night-cap, and grandmamma probably, at that very moment, stepping out of her carriage," said Portia. "No, we couldn't go to Eaton Square, but we could go to the Wynnes'. We are all invited to finish the evening and have supper there."

"Host and hostess both unavoidably absent," remarked Teddy. "Well, bad though Mrs. Wynne's supper parties are, anything would be better than remaining longer on one's legs. Susan, my dear, take my arm—oh, some one else has taken it—then Blake will bring you."

And off Teddy Josselin walked ; he and Portia speaking never a word the moment they were alone together ; Blake and Susan in the rear.

"To-night's experience has shown you a sample of fashionable pleasure-taking, Susan ?"

"Yes, indeed it has. Such a sample that I wish I was a fashionable person myself. I think, altogether, it has been the pleasantest evening of my life."

"And now, of course, you are looking forward to finishing the night with a gay party at Mrs. Wynne's ?"

"No, Mr. Blake. I am looking forward to our drive home in a hansom."

However, the difficulty Teddy had spoken of regarding putting ideas into practise once more made itself felt. Neither two-wheeled or four-wheeled cabs were to be had for money. After walking a considerable distance down the line

of carriages, they came upon the Wynnes' barouche, close behind it little Lord
Dormer's brougham, the servants chatting together in the moonlight; their
theme, perhaps, the social manners and customs of the class assigned to them by
Providence as masters.

"Thank heaven, one thing at least is open to us," cried Teddy, with relief.
"We can sit down without the London apprentice and his sweetheart treading
every minute on our toes."

And he had just stretched his hand forth to open the door of the Wynnes'
carriage when the unmistakable, shrill tones of a "Dysart voice" made themselves heard, and up came Mrs. Wynne herself, in excellent spirits and humor
with everything, on Lord Dormer's arm.

"And we are all safe and sound!" she cried, not taking sufficient notice of
the man she believed to be her husband to notice that it was some one else.
"No adventures, no runaways?"

"None, except Mr. Wynne," said Portia, lowering her voice. And then the
story of Dolly's base conduct, and of Blake's opportune rescue of Susan had to
be told again; Portia giving whatever slight additional edge the story was capable of receiving by her manner of narration.

Mrs. Wynne burst out laughing. "That *is* so like Dolly!" she cried,
aloud; philosophically indifferent, it seemed, to the presence of the servants.
"Just what he does with me. 'My dear child, there's some one I haven't
seen for a hundred years—wait one minute.' And then off he goes and I never
get a sight of him again. Now, how can we pack? We are very late. I told
Nelly Rawdon to come at eleven. Lord Dormer, you can make room for some
one. Portia, my dear," aside, "introduce me to Mr. Blake."

At the time when Blake's infatuation was at its height, when scarce a night
passed without his haunting Portia Ffrench at some theatre, concert or ball—during that brief taste that Blake had had of fashionable life, he had known Mrs
Wynne well by sight, but had resisted all Portia's endeavors to make them better
acquainted. "A woman with a harsher voice and harsher nature. A woman
without the charm of youth, or the grace of age." This from the first had been
the judgment of the fastidious young treasury clerk upon the "syren" whose
allurements many a girl in her first season, many a wife in the first year of her
marriage, had had cause to acknowledge. His opinion was not likely to be modified by the circumstances under which he met her to-night.

"I hope we are to see you, Mr. Blake?" Portia had now gone through the
ceremony of introduction. "The rest of the party are all coming. We want
supper and champagne, I am sure, to support us after our adventures."

Susan, who was still on Blake's arm, looked up at him eagerly. "Do come!"
that look said, as plain as a look could speak; but to no avail. He had to rise
early, he had given up late hours altogether, he begged of Mrs. Wynne to excuse
him. And so, almost crying with disappointment, Susan had to get into the carriage with Mrs. Wynne and Portia; and Blake, taking off his hat, wished them
all a formal "good-night," and walked away.

He had gone without shaking her hand, without saying a single kind word of
parting, felt Susan, blankly. She turned her face away, thinking how empty and
disappointing a place the world was, and found that Blake had come round to
her side of the carriage. The formal salutation, the cold good-night had **never**
been meant for her at all.

"What time do you start to-morrow, Susan, and from what station?" he
asked, in a whisper; "of course, I am coming to see you off."

"Will you—will you, really? Oh, how nice—I'm so glad! I was afraid, when you took off your hat so grandly, I had seen the last of you." Her face, as she spoke, was within a couple of inches of Blake's, in the moonlight; one of her soft curls brushed his cheek.

"Don't talk of our seeing the last of each other, Susan. I hope that won't happen until—oh well, forty or fifty years hence. What station do you start from?"

"Waterloo Station, sir. Mr. Goldney has written all my journey on a card, and made me learn it by heart. I leave Waterloo at eight thirty-five, Bradshaw."

"Very well. At eight thirty-five, Bradshaw, I shall be on the Waterloo platform. Come in good time, Susan, and if you can leave Mr. Goldney behind you, do."

And then a whispered good-night—a good-night in which the hands met, "and the spirit kissed;" and Blake was gone, and Susan left wondering in a sort of dream how the hours would pass till eight thirty-five, Bradshaw, to-morrow! Of the remaining fifty years or so that she might have to pass in the world without Blake, and with Tom Collinson, nothing. Who that loved ever thought, ever reckoned beyond the next meeting?

> Oh for Friday night!
> Friday at the gloamin'—
> Oh for Friday night!
> Friday's long in comin'.

"And now that the Ursa Major has departed, I suppose we may start," cried Mrs. Wynne. "Portia, my dear, why do you encourage such terrible bears in the shape of men as you do?"

Teddy Josselin, on the plea of wishing to smoke, had gone in Lord Dormer's brougham, and the three ladies were alone.

"I beg your pardon, Laura, dear!" said Portia, sweetly. "What did you ask me?"

She took off her veil as the carriage started, and turned her face round with a smile, to her friend.

"I asked you how you can encourage such fearful creatures in the shape of men as you do, my dear child?"

"I suppose because I have no taste for fearful creatures in the shape of little boys," answered Portia. "That is a taste, like the taste for olives, that belongs to maturer years, my dear Laura."

And after these gentle amenities, the friends lapsed into silence; silence which lasted until the carriage stopped before Mrs. Wynne's house, where the brougham, with little Lord Dormer and Teddy Josselin, arrived a minute or two later.

A young lady, whom Mrs. Wynne saluted with a kiss and addressed as "Nelly dearest," and whom Portia called "Miss Rawdon," and presented with three stiff fingers, was sitting in evening dress in Mrs. Wynne's pretty little drawing-room. A few ornamental figures of the other sex were also dispersed about there, not looking exactly as if they belonged to the place, and yet with something in their appearance that indefinitely suggested to you the idea of the place belonging to them. One of these mirrors of fashion was in an easy-chair on the balcony, smoking; a second reclining on a sofa, languidly interested in the shape of his own nails; another was patiently allowing Nelly Rawdon to flirt with him over a book of photographs. All of them were young, and all very much alike, and all "very pretty gentlemen, indeed," thought Susan, as her shy eyes were raised, during the ceremony of introduction, to their faces.

Nelly Rawdon was a young lady of four or five-and-twenty, Mrs. Wynne's second-best young lady friend and chaperon ; a young lady with very scarlet lips, hair of the same shade hanging loose upon her shoulders (fine shoulders they were, shoulders invariably made the most of !) and quite unlimited command of the kind of language which it is so hard to classify without using the school-boy word, " chaff."

Portia never despised herself so heartily as when she was thrown with Nelly Rawdon in the Wynnes' house. She would go anywhere, she would stoop to any society in quest of excitement ; would sacrifice pride, delicacy, self-respect, so long as she could gratify her thirst for admiration, her restless longing for the diversion of the moment. But refinement of taste, rather than of feeling, was inherent in the granddaughter of Colonel Ffrench ; and Nelly Rawdon's loud voice and louder jests jarred on Portia's sensibilities just as it jarred on her when the poor young woman would insist upon decking her flame-colored hair with crowns of pinkest roses. She knew well enough how men spoke of Nelly ; knew the dozen or more pitiful histories, after being the heroine of which, Nelly, at five-and-twenty, was Nelly Rawdon still. And even while she would not quite give up a house where there was always "something going on"—something to gratify vanity, or at least get rid of the weight of time—never, as I have said, despised her own character so heartily as when she found herself within its walls, with Laura Wynne and Nelly Rawdon for associates.

" It makes one ashamed of being a woman only to look at such women as one meets here," she remarked, when she and Susan had gone to Mrs. Wynne's dressing-room to take off their bonnets. The men are well enough—one expects so little from men of their stamp—but the women ! but Nelly Rawdon ! I don't, of course, mean to question the designs of Providence, but why are women like Nelly Rawdon ever called into existence ? "

Partly, it seemed, to minister to the intellectual solace of men like Teddy Josselin. On returning to the drawing-room, the first thing that greeted Portia's sight was her cousin, lazily nestling in the laziest chair the room contained, with Nelly at his side fanning him ; fanning him and, as Portia with quick resentment felt, amusing him. The unwonted ill-humor that had clouded Ted's face during the evening was gone ; he was laughing, as much as he ever laughed, over some remark of his companion's, while the heightened color on Nelly Rawdon's face, the heightened animation of her voice and manner, told plainly enough that she was interested in her employment. " Poor Nelly's devotion to people might certainly be a little more subdued," Teddy would acknowledge sometimes, when Portia was upbraiding him for his bad taste in being amused by "such a person." " Still, she never bores you—takes the trouble even of laughing at her own jokes off your hands. Few of the fellows I know tell a story as well as Nelly Rawdon." " For their own credits' sake, I should hope few of the fellows you know tell *such* stories ! " Portia would retort, with cold disgust.

She gave them one steady look, quite as steadily returned by Ted's blue eyes, then turned away toward an open window, where Mrs. Wynne and little Lord Dormer were studying astronomy together upon the balcony. And, on the instant, a scheme of perilously-prompt retaliation crossed Portia Ffrench's mind. In her justification I must say that there was much in her present position to make Portia's pride smart. The escapade which, in an evil hour, she had consented to join had, in very truth, originated with Mrs. Wynne. She had allowed herself to be made ignoble use of—a screen behind which to hide Mrs. Wynne's superior folly! And now what had she gained? George Blake's respect forfeited, George Blake's old love for her sullied; a fight for power (their first) going on, with every prospect of her becoming the loser, between herself and Teddy; and now Teddy, in her very presence, encouraging the attentions of a woman whom she detested and despised like Nelly Rawdon!

The blood mounted into Portia's dark cheek, a light shone in her eyes. She moved in the direction of the window, and paused just where Lord Dormer could see her to the greatest possible advantage; her face turned toward him in profile; her hands clasped, and hanging down in an attitude full of pensive grace; her figure, with its rounded lines and perfect youthfulness, presenting a sufficiently marked contrast to the pinched, waspish proportions, from which youth had so long fled, of little Mrs. Wynne.

Before two minutes had passed, Lord Dormer's attention wandered a good deal more than Mrs. Wynne liked, from the stars. He was not an enthusiast on any subject; but at twenty years of age few men are so jaded or so obtuse but that a face like Portia's, its possessor willing, must influence them for the moment. And Portia willed that the influence should extend over very much longer than the moment.

"Do you know anything about the stars, Miss Ffrench?" asks his lordship presently.

Portia, on this, moves a step nearer, hesitates, goes outside the balcony, and lifts her beautiful face to the heavens.

"I know Ursa Major," she answers, gravely. "You will not see it by looking at me, Lord Dormer. Look away to the north, where I point."

And the arm whose soft large curves the muslin sleeve softens, but does not hide, is raised, and Lord Dormer has to correct his standing point, to follow the direction Portia indicates; to make original remarks about the stars seeming a good way off; to wonder if it can be true that there are mountains and volcanoes and all that sort of things in the moon?

"I'm sure I don't know about volcanoes," replies Portia Ffrench. "It would be very nice, I think, to be able to go up to the moon, like Hans Pfaall, and live there, away from everybody."

"Not everybody, surely!" says Lord Dormer, with a fat little sigh.

And then Mrs. Wynne remembers that it is high time to be thinking about supper, and, with a vexed little rustle of her silken skirts, leaves the balcony.

By the time supper was announced Portia had her intended victim well in hand. It did not occur to her to feel humiliated by the part she was playing, the feelings she was gratifying. It was far easier to shock Portia Ffrench's artistic, than her moral sense. Pink roses in scarlet hair, a loud voice, a coarse jest, caused her absolute physical nausea. She saw no ugliness in a woman posing her charms for the brief captivation of an idiot's senses, provided only the charms were posed gracefully. And nothing, it must be admitted, could be fuller of grace than her manner with Lord Dormer. She held him aloof, and yet she drew him closer at every instant; she said no word that the whole world might not have listened to, and yet every tone of her voice, every glance of her eyes flattered his vanity into believing that she was trying to please him, and him alone. He began to wake up; his blood to quicken, not as much, of course, as the last seconds of a race, or cast of the dice at a critical moment in chicken hazard could quicken it, still with a pleasant tingle of oncoming intoxication, very new for him to feel in the society of a lady. His heavy face lightened ; every now and then he originated a remark.

Mrs. Wynne, bearing her defeat with the enforced good-temper in which women of the world excel, laughed longer and louder, and seemed in ever heightening spirits during the whole of supper. But she knew perfectly well that defeat was impending, and listened to each low word that fell from Portia's lips, noted each passing expression of Portia's face, with inward trembling of the spirit. For Lord Dormer himself, Mrs. Wynne cared about as much as did Portia Ffrench. But she had every intention of prolonging Lord Dormer's attentions not only over the end of the London season, but into an autumn at Cowes ; into yachting excursions ; perhaps into next winter and the Mediterranean—was not poor Dolly's throat always delicate about Christmas ? And now here was the rival she most dreaded in the world, her own familiar friend and counsellor, evidently and of set purpose, about to cross her path !

For the wiles of manœuvring mothers, for the lures of marriageable daughters, Mrs. Wynne cared not a straw. She had entered too often into the lists with these legitimate opponents, had too invariably come off victorious, to be afraid of them, above all, when the prize to be won was a Lord Dormer ! But Portia— an instant told her this—Portia no more meant to marry Lord Dormer than she meant to marry him herself. They met as fair foes on equal ground ; only with the superior weapons of youth and beauty, the animus (no trifling advantage this) of invasion upon Portia's side.

Thinking these things, Mrs. Wynne ate her supper, and drank her champagne, and excelled herself in pleasant words and looks for her different guests, and altogether conveyed to Susan's mind an impression of being one of the happiest, best-contented women in existence. Teddy Josselin, meanwhile, still at Nelly Rawdon's side, still encouraging Nelly Rawdon's attentions, ate *his* supper and thought his thoughts—of which we shall know more hereafter.

Midnight had merged into the small hours before any one moved from the table ; and by the time Portia and Susan left the Wynnes' house, a broad, pink flush of daylight stained the sky, cloudless at this hour as though the great city were a hamlet. Portia leaned her face out of the carriage and gave a sweet farewell smile to Lord Dormer as he stood watching to see them drive away. At Teddy, who had brought Susan to the carriage, she scarcely looked. Her eyes were aglow, her cheeks flushed ; her whole face was looking admirably handsome, even after a night's dissipation, even with the cold light of morning resting on it full. Portia Ffrench had found a new excitement, a new peril, almost a new emotion.

"I was so sorry you and Mr. Josselin got divided from each other at supper," said Susan. " You must have found it very tiring work talking so long to that stupid little boy."

" That stupid little boy has more thousands than he knows how to get rid of, my dear," answered Portia. " Never say another word against him in my presence. Isn't St. Sauveur on the sea, Susan ? Well then, Lord Dormer will bring me over in his yacht to pay you a visit—me, Aunt Jem, George Blake—any-one I like."

" Mr. Josselin one of the party, of course," suggested Susan.

"Well no, I think not," answered Portia. "I don't know how it is, but I'm afraid Mr. Josselin and Lord Dormer don't take much to each other's society."

And after this the conversation dropped.

CHAPTER XXVIII.

"GARDENS at Chelsea, gardens at Chelsea!" said Mr. Goldney, next day at breakfast, when Susan was giving him an "eclectic" account of her night's dissipation. "Why, bless my heart—no, no, that could never be—still if they were public gardens!—and who did the party consist of, do you say, my dear Miss Fielding?"

And then Susan had to go through the muster-roll again. Mr. and Mrs. Wynne, distant relations of Lady Erroll's, Miss Ffrench, and her cousin, and Lord Dormer—she forgot, unaccountably, to mention George Blake's name.

Mr. Goldney listened, with a conviction that Joseph Fielding must have been a much nicer fellow than he ever took him for, to this enumeration of Susan's acquaintance. The old gentleman was not a tuft-hunter; indeed, his life had never thrown him into positions where tuft-hunting was possible. He was simply a middle-class Englishman, and felt the natural satisfaction of his race and nation at being brought in contact, no matter how indirectly, with the pleasant little follies of the upper classes. If these Chelsea Gardens turned out to be what Mr. Goldney half suspected, there could be no very great harm in a frolicsome visit paid them from the house of a countess, and with a peer of the realm and minor offshoots of the aristocracy forming the party!

"They were public gardens, I know," said Susan, "and there were fireworks, and crowds of people, all very smartly dressed. If ever I live in London, I mean"—with a sigh this—"when Mr. Collinson comes back, and he and I live in London, those are the sort of places I should like to go to."

Mr. Goldney looked at her over his spectacles. "Ah," said he, "there is another subject, an important subject, my dear young friend, that you and I ought to have a long talk about. But my time is so terribly full! Ten minutes to nine—well, we have just eight minutes left, then ; for I'm afraid I have no chance of returning till dinner. Now, are there—are there," he shifted his glasses so as to regard her through, not over them, "any advantages to speak of in this engagement you have entered upon?"

"I don't quite know what you would call advantages, sir?" said Susan, playing with her teaspoon.

"Well, has Mr. Tomlinson, Collinson, to be sure, Collinson—I was thinking of another case—has Mr. Collinson private means? Very little. Birth—not that it is of the slightest consequence, still, as an old friend of your father's, I like to ask? None. Profession? None. My dear young lady, what *has* Mr. Collinson that, at your age and, you must let me say, with your attractions, you should engage to marry him? I have only a few minutes to spare, but as an old friend of your father's, allow me—dear me, dear me!" taking out his watch, "there is Pancras striking nine! I am four minutes and a half slow, positively!"

And he jumped up, and hastily collecting the papers that lay beside him on the breakfast table, rushed away from the room. "I'm sorry our chat has been so short," turning to Susan, who had followed him, "but I have, unfortunately, business of the highest importance, and that won't wait for me. We will finish it all this evening. Good-bye, my dear—pray think seriously over what I have said."

And away Mr. Goldney hurried, forgetting Susan and Susan's love-affairs before he had turned the corner of the square. A man whose opinions are worth six-and-eightpence each can scarcely be expected to throw away many of them gratuitously; especially on the subject that women weakly regard as the most important business of their lives.

Susan felt relieved at the abrupt ending of the discussion. Little as she loved, impossible as it would ever be for her to love, Tom Collinson, she had given her word to marry him, and to Susan's unsophisticated mind a promise, right or wrong, was absolute. Joseph Fielding (under his outside shell of scepticism, it might be juster to say, of non-conformity with received opinions, a man of austerely-upright conscience) had reared his child in the belief that falsehood of all sins was the most intolerable, the most degrading to character. Some day the casuistry of passion might suggest to her that truth is relative; that while adhering rigidly to truth in the letter, it is possible grossly to violate it in the spirit; that in boldly forfeiting a promise to an unloved lover there may be nobler courage, truer honor, than in adhering to it. Suggestions like these, I say, might be for the future. At present, Susan looked upon herself, beyond all recall, as Tom Collinson's future wife, and she shrank away from any discussion in which her heart but too promptly joined issue against him at the instigation of others. She was to marry Tom Collinson, a year or two years hence—and in the meantime was to see Blake to-night! Opening the dining-room window, the girl leaned her face among the smoky heliotropes and geraniums on the window-sill, and, looking up at as much blue sky as could be seen from Brunswick Square, fell into a day-dream—

Oh for Friday night !
Friday at the gloamin'.—
Oh for Friday night !
Friday's long in comin'.

It had been agreed the evening before that Susan should go to Eaton Square toward the middle of the day, to bid Portia good-bye. "Grandmamma looked queerly at me this morning when I returned from visiting you," Portia had said, "and Miss Condy, I cannot help thinking, is watching me; so I had better, on the last day of my visit, keep myself virtuously under their eyes. Come early, and you will find me in the square, with Condy and Arno. Horrible though the prison walk is, it is better than grandmamma's big drawing-room, and I have something to say that I want no walls to listen to."

Accordingly, when Mr. Goldney's brougham stopped before Lady Erroll's house, Portia, who stood watching at one of the square gates, ran across the road and met Susan as she got out of the carriage. She was looking five years older than she had looked in the first flush and triumph of last night's conquest. Her complexion was pale, with the dead, sickly pallor dark complexions are apt to assume after dissipation; her eyes were heavy, her lips unsmiling.

"I know what you think of my looks," she cried, in answer to the expression of Susan's face. "When I have really amused myself over night, I am always like this—dead, literally dead, till I get some new sensation, bodily or mental, as a 'pick-me-up,' next day. And I was really amused, absolutely excited, last night, little as you may have thought it. Come away as far as we can get from the enemy, and I will tell you my plans for the future—or as many of them as it is good for you to know."

They had now entered the square, and Portia led Susan away toward a tolerably shady seat, twenty or thirty feet distant. Eaton Square was looking as melancholy and aristocratic as square could wish to look. A most noble old gentleman, with a green shade over his eyes, tottering along, supported by his valet, a Lady Adeliza, six months old, in the arms of her attendant, Miss Condy slowly pacing up and down with a large white parasol, under whose shade re-

posed Arno. Dogs on foot were not admitted in the square ; so, as Arno's carriage exercise was not considered sufficient by the physician for his health, it was
a part of Miss Condy's duties thus to air him in the forenoon.

As the two girls walked past her, Portia shook one finger with playful meaning at Arno, and was at once rewarded by a roll of his vindictive Italian eyes, a
wicked display of broken fangs. Miss Condy, at the same instant, looked at her
steadily, Susan thought with a look quite as full of malice as was Arno's snarl.

" The poor creature hates me, would injure me if she could, I believe," said
Portia, when they were out of hearing. " Happily, I am never likely to be in
her power. If she had seen me—tracked us, as for a moment I suspected, last
night—but the thing is impossible ! and yet all this morning I have thought I
saw new animus on old Condy's face. The working of my guilty conscience, I
suppose."

" But there are others in the world to fear as well as Miss Condy," said
Susan. " Are you quite certain of all the people we were with last night keeping silence ? "

" I am quite sure of little Lord Dormer," said Portia. " He will do for the
future as he is bidden. Dolly Wynne is too obtuse to remember anything twelve
hours after it happens, and Laura—oh, well, Laura's friendship is of too old a
date to run the risk of betraying me now. Susan, my dear, sit down here—it is
tolerably sheltered, and tolerably secure from listeners—and tell me what you
think of my latest conquest ? Is not Lord Dormer charming ? We did not half
exhaust the subject last night. That little boy has run through one huge fortune already, and will come into another on his next birth-day, Susan."

" He may be very rich," said Susan ; " but he is horribly ugly, and, I should
say, if you won't be offended, a thorough fool. It may be my ignorance, but I
cannot see Lord Dormer's charm."

" Why, you have specified it to a nicety," said Portia. " Don't you know the
proverb about a fool and his money ? To say of a man that he is enormously
rich and enormously foolish, is to say that he is fair game for everybody, a gold-
en goose, at whose plucking we can all assist. I have some feathers in prospect
already, Susan. That was sober earnest that I told you about the yacht."

" If I was in your place," said Susan, resolutely, " if I was in your place I
would rather give up all the yachts that ever floated than run the chance of of-
fending Mr. Josselin. I know very well now that you and Mr. Josselin care for
each other. How can you be cruel enough to risk hurting his feelings ? "

" Hurting his feelings ! " cried Portia, lightly, and yet her lip gave a quiver.
" My dear Susan, Ted Josselin is not made of the fragile stuff you suppose. As
long as Ted Josselin has good dinners and wines, and a grandmamma to
pay his debts, and a Nelly Rawdon to amuse him, his heart won't break, depend
upon it ! We are paupers, both of us ; we must each push our own interests as
best we can. Make our way, like the son in the old story, honestly if we can,
but make it. I'm quite determined to make my way. Susan, and—"

" Portia, Portia," screamed out a gruff voice, horribly human in its inhuman-
ity, " you will come to grief, Portia—come to grief ! "

Susan started ; Portia turned round her face with a laugh. " Don't be scared
—it's only old Sam, the parrot. If you put on your spectacles, you'll see him in
the sun, at the drawing-room window. Ever since I was sixteen, Ted taught him
to preach me that little sermon, ' You'll come to grief, Portia.' How well I remember the day the poor boy first got him to say it ! I'm sure I don't see what
is to keep us women from coming to grief. Susan, do you know—of course you

don't, though—what it is to feel that everything is going to the bad with you, that circumstances, a great deal stronger than yourself, are drifting you down the stream wherever they choose ?"

"I felt it once," said Susan, guiltily, remembering the night when she had accepted Tom Collinson, the night when she dared not touch or look at her bit of pencil.

"And I feel it at this minute," said Portia. "If Sam never spoke opportunely in his whole reprobate life before, he has done so now. The thing is," putting her head on one side, as a woman will do when she is choosing a new dress or ribbon, "how to come to grief with the best grace ? There are so many ways of arriving at the same end."

I must remark, in justice to Portia Ffrench, that, in saying all this, she was but half in earnest; the consciousness of the perilously-false ground on which she stood, the sense of running a new kind of danger, alluring her, very much as the possibility of losing his balance allures an Alpine climber to the brink of a glacier.

"You know what I said this morning about my paying you a visit," she went on; "Lord Dormer is going to bring his yacht about the world just wherever I bid him, and what I want to speak to you about now is this : Aunt Jem and I are going to have a fortnight's wild dissipation this summer. We have been plotting, and poor old aunt has been saving up for it during the last two years. A number of the rooms at Halfont have got to be whitewashed and the roof made a little water-tight, and we must all clear out. Grandpapa and Jekyll go to Bath—in August; 'if one is forced out of one's own damp house,' says grandpapa, 'additional warmth, not cold, is what one should look for ;' and aunt and I have unconditional leave of absence. Well, Susan, without betraying too many secrets I may say that I want to go to some place where we shall not be too narrowly watched—I mean where Lord Dormer can be as devoted as he likes, unchilled by the gaze of the world—and I think this little French town where your Uncle Adam lives would be quite a fitting Eden for us. I have said nothing to Aunt Jem, but she would go to Kamtchatka if I bade her, and so would—"

A hansom at this moment stopped before Lady Erroll's house, from which descended Teddy Josselin, his fair, boyish face fresh as the moss-rose bud in his button-hole. He walked across the road and leisurely entered the square. Miss Condy was leaving just as he came in, and he stopped and shook hands with her, then patted Arno's head. The hard face of the poor bondswoman lighted ; Arno put up his ears, and half wagged his dislocated old tail.

"Nelly Rawdons, Condys, Arnos, all vile things like Ted Josselin," said Portia, with a curl of the lip. "For the sake of distinction, only, one feels inclined not to like him."

But the flush that deepened on her cheek as he drew near, the flush she had to lower her parasol to hide, did not look much as if this state of distinction were as yet attained by her !

"You are out early to-day, Mr. Josselin !" He had now shaken hands with Susan, and taken his hat off, with distant courtesy to herself

"My usual time," said Ted, placidly. "During the last five years, I believe I have always come to see you at about this hour, whenever you were in town. Can you make room for me, Susan ? ah, I thought you could—thanks."

He sank down on the bench between the two girls, and smiled. In positions where less happily-gifted men would rack their brains in search of fitting remarks, it was Teddy's invariable plan to smile and look handsome, and experience told him that the plan was a wise one. Portia glanced at him coldly, and knew that she had never loved him so well as now, when, for a dozen hours or more, she had been telling herself that she hated him! She had no lofty ideal of men, although, at fitting times and seasons, she could enlarge with great good taste and feeling upon such an ideal. The true child of Lady Portia Dysart, she liked the fair patrician beauty, the refinement, the dandyism of Ted Josselin by instinct—and instinct, as it generally proves, was the safest guide Portia Ffrench possessed. To a rougher, more sterling lover, men like little Lord Dormer might have proved dangerous rivals; in Portia's imagination, at least. Ted Josselin beat them at their own weapons. Whatever their quarrels, whatever his derelictions, Teddy was always the best looking, best appointed, best mannered man Portia knew. It was, consequently more than an injury to her affections, it was a stab to her vanity to lose him even for an hour. She glanced at him coldly; glanced with the slightest increase of warmth half a minute later; then their eyes met, and they were reconciled—began, both of them, to say the most disagreeable things they were capable of. And with lovers whose united ages scarce make up half a century, you may always regard this as a sure sign of reconciliation.

"Susan and I were just talking over our autumn plans. She is going to live at St. Sauveur, in Brittany (Brittany is in France, I must acquaint you, Mr. Josselin), and Aunt Jem and I are going there for a fortnight in August. We shall cross in Lord Dormer's yacht."

"Poor Dormer! You are not a very good sailor, Portia—is Miss Jemima?"

"I am an excellent sailor, when I am in good spirits. Whenever you have seen me at sea I have been in attendance on grandmamma, and there has been no one to amuse me. I am not at all afraid of being ill in the Lily."

"Poor Dormer! The Lily has never been farther than the Solent yet."

"The Lily will go a great deal farther than the Solent this year. I am not at all sure that, after Brittany, I won't go and look up Jack Dysart in Norway.

Teddy Josselin laughed, a mild, good-tempered little laugh; but that irritated Portia more than the bitterest sarcasm could have done.

"You must forgive me for not seeing what amuses you!" she said. "I evidently say my wittiest things by accident."

"Oh, dear, no, there was nothing witty at all," said Teddy, and now he laughed aloud. "It was only the idea of you and Aunt Jemima and Dormer looking up Jack Dysart in Norway! Forgive me for being so foolish, Portia."

"I have forgiven *that*, long ago," said Portia.

And then, Teddy continuing to look imperturbably good-tempered, she abruptly seemed to forget his existence, and began talking across him to Susan. "Yes, Aunt Jemima will go wherever I bid her, and so will—the other person we were speaking of. What I want you to do, Susan, is to find out about lodgings; for we won't spend the very few pounds we possess on hotels—"

"Dormer not spend the very few pounds he possesses on hotels?" interrupted Teddy, looking mystified.

"Three rooms, the size of cupboards, would be enough for us, provided there is one decent looking-glass, and a balcony. I don't mind about shabby chairs and tables, but I must have a balcony—"

"Like last night," put in Ted with his little foolish air.

"And we could go out and dine at *tables d'hôte*, and places—poor, dear, old aunt at *tables d'hôte!* Now will you promise to write directly you get there?"

"And you must look for lodgings for me, too, Susan," said Teddy, when Susan had promised to look diligently for three cupboards, a decent looking-glass, and a balcony. "It is an odd coincidence, but I have made up my mind to go to Saint—Saint—where is it, 'Tia, dear? this autumn."

At the familiar "'Tia, dear," the appeal to her superior intelligence which words of more than three syllables, French or English, invariably called forth from poor Teddy, Portia at first frowned with all her might. Then, in spite of herself, her lips softened, and in another instant the tender look that on rare, too rare occasions made her more than handsome, broke over her face.

"Why, you don't mean to say Nelly Rawdon is going to St. Sauveur?" she remarked.

"I hope not, for my own sake," said Ted gravely. "Susan, if ever you are married—I mean if ever you are going to be married—no, I mean if ever you have a good-looking cousin whom you can't by possibility marry—beware of jealousy. It's a quick-sand—"

"On which people who go down to the sea in yachts are particularly prone to founder," cried Portia, tossing him a little piece of jasmine that she had un-pinned from her waist-belt. "Oh, Ted, when will experience teach you that met-aphor is not your forte?"

"And when will experience teach you that resistance is not yours? that a woman is never so charming as when she knocks under with a good grace? Oh, well, not 'knock under,' then," for Portia's eyes flashed, "but when she confesses she has been in the wrong. You have been in the wrong, my dear child, and you have apologized, in your way, and I accept the apology. Peace is made."

So these two quarrelled, repented, and were reconciled, each playing at "half a love with half a lover;" Miss Condy meanwhile watching them from behind the venetians in the dining-room, and old Sam at intervals screeching out his proph-ecy, "You'll come to grief, Portia—you'll come to grief," from the balcony above. Months afterward, when the game begun in jest had turned to bitterest earnest, on a night spent beside a death-bed, a blankest to-morrow all her prospect, how clearly Portia remembered every detail of that summer noontide scene!

They walked with Susan, a few minutes later, to the brougham. "And be sure you write me at once," said Portia, when they had shaken hands and bidden good-bye. "Three cupboards and a balcony—don't forget."

"And be sure you write to me, too," said Teddy, holding Susan's hand, affec-tionately. "And if you are a very good little girl, perhaps I'll bring a friend of mine with me to St. Sauveur."

"Ah, but Susan's engaged, Susan's affections are another's," cried Portia, as Susan's face dimpled and grew rosy red. "What business have you, sir, to divert people from their lawful allegiance?"

"It is the business you have brought me up to," said Ted with all the inno-cence imaginable.

It was two o'clock when Susan got back to Brunswick Square; six hours and a half before the meeting so sighed for, so "long in coming;" the meeting that was to last five minutes and be the awakening point from the one supreme, delicious dream of her life! How could the interval be better employed than in writing to Tom Collinson? He had begged that there might be a letter await-ing him at a certain address he had given Susan in Dunedin, and some portion of her last day in England ought, she felt, to be consecrated to him—the right-ful owner of all her days, of all her thoughts, now and forever more.

She went at once up to her bedroom, took her writing-desk from her port-manteau, and dutifully set herself to the task of composing her first love-let-ter. " My Dear Tom, I am quite well, and hope you are the same." She was not a good correspondent, as she had told George Blake; had no more nat-ural genius for letter-writing than for any other form of expression, and these opening ideas were not immediately succeeded by a flow of others. So she put down her pen, and began absently rearranging the contents of her desk, hoping thoughts would suggest themselves.

Accidentally, or by the mechanical force of constant habit, her fingers touch the spring of a certain secret drawer in which lies a pocket-book, of which the reader knows, and before she can reflect on what she does, a two-inch end of pencil is in her hand. She lifts it for a moment to her short-sighted eyes, then, pressing one little palm over the other, holds it closely, wistfully for a good many minutes ; the tenderest look you can imagine giving warmth and sweet-ness the while to her whole face. Is this the way to write a love-letter to an absent sweetheart ? With stern resolution, Susan puts the pencil away out of sight, snatches up her pen, and goes on :

" I left Eliza the day before yesterday. I am in London with Mr. Goldney, and last night I went with Portia Ffrench to some gardens at Chelsea. It was very nice. There were fireworks and a band, and a great crowd, and I got lost, which was very terrifying, but luckily I met Mr. Blake. I was all right then, and we walked about a long while, and he is going to see me off to-night, and perhaps—"

A charming letter truly to send to a jealous man like Collinson, a man whose last pathetic injunction, spoken and written, had been, " Don't flirt with Blake." Thoroughly discouraged by the complicated difficulties of writing letters, love-letters especially, Susan here tore up the sheet of paper into a dozen pieces, re-turned her desk to her portmanteau, then finished what still remained to do of her packing, seated herself by the window, and wished anew for eight o'clock. It would be much easier to write to Tom from St. Sauveur, she felt sure. In-teresting for him to hear about the French nation, and Uncle Adam, and her journey ; was it possible that a post or two could make any difference in places as far away as New Zealand ? For she had just got so much out of the narrow path now as to feel that her own conscience needed apologies.

Mr. Goldney did not return home till a quarter to six, and the moment din-ner was over he announced that it was time to start. To Susan's dismay, he also announced his intention of accompanying her to the station.

" Indeed, sir, I don't think you need take that trouble. I believe I have sense enough to buy my ticket and see to my baggage."

" I don't doubt your sense, my dear Miss Fielding," said the old lawyer. " What one has to consider in these matters is, what is right. It is not usual for young ladies of your age to go about London unescorted."

Susan was silenced. Long years of Miss Collinson's moral rule had taught her that, in all arguments about right and wrong, the two words, " not moral," must be regarded as final. And so it was, leaning on Mr. Goldney's arm, that Blake first caught sight of the small figure for which he was watching on the platform at Waterloo Station. Here Susan's blindness for once stood her in good stead. If she had seen her friend she would, infallibly, have stopped to speak to him, and Mr. Goldney as infallibly have felt it his duty to keep guard at her side till the train started. Happily, she did not see him ; and happily a coolish east wind was causing draughts the entire length of the platform. And draughts always gave Mr. Goldney toothache! So, when the ticket was bought, and Susan was fairly in her place, and a guard had told them that there were still ten minutes to wait, the old gentleman, drawing up his coat-collar to his ears, inquired if she would think it very rude of him to run away? Wind in the east, symptoms of his old enemy; alas, Miss Fielding must remember that he was not so young as he was once!

"Oh, pray—pray go," cried Susan, eagerly. "I mean, thank you very much for coming; but pray don't run a risk of taking cold. The wind really is quite sharp."

Mr. Goldney pressed her hand once more, begged her not to lose her ticket, to talk to no one but ladies on her journey, to drink a little brandy and water if she felt sea-sick, and always to look upon his house as her home. Then ran as fast as he could go out of the draught, and back to his comfortable brougham, and in another minute a voice that brought all the blood up into Susan's face was speaking to her.

"You are here, then, after all, Mr. Blake? When we came along the platform, and I couldn't see you, I felt sure you had forgotten me."

"Did you?" The door of the carriage had been shut by Mr. Goldney's care; but, as he spoke, Blake opened it, then stood on the step and bent forward toward Susan. Never had she felt so thoroughly alone with him as at this moment. "Did you care enough about my coming to think whether I had forgotten you or not?"

No answer to this.

"Susan, I have something very especial to tell you. I had better say it at once, before the old gentleman with the coat-collar returns. You must write to me."

"I cannot," said Susan, very low. "Ask me anything but that. I told you before what promise Tom Collinson made me give him."

"Tom Collinson—ah, we will discuss about Tom Collinson another day. Don't write me a letter at all, then. Write your address on a sheet of paper; add some statistics as to the climate and scenery of St. Sauveur, and direct it to George Blake, at the Treasury. You needn't even sign your name."

"Well, I don't see how that could be called a letter!" hesitates Susan, her moral declension proceeding even more rapidly.

"Of course, it could not," says Blake. "The thing is settled. Now, the next subject to consider is—Susan, I have thought of nothing but you during the last twenty-four hours. I don't at all like the thought of losing sight of you—"

"Beg your pardon, sir—room here, ma'am," cries a porter, and an old lady gets into the carriage. She has many wraps and hand-bags; she has questions to ask about her luggage. By the time she settles into her place the second bell rings. They are to have three minutes more of each other in this world.

"You will be gone directly," says Blake; the door is shut, and he can only speak to her distantly through the window. "And I have said nothing that I meant to say. I think it is likely you may see me in St. Sauveur, my dear. My holiday is next month. I have a great mind to come and sketch the Breton peasants, Susan."

"Everyone is coming to St. Sauveur," cries Susan, jealous suspicion aroused in a moment. "Mr. Josselin, Lord Dormer, Portia, and now you. Of course, you didn't know anything about Portia's movements?"

" Nothing in the world—don't let us lose time by talking about other people.
I may come to St. Sauveur, Susan, may I not ? "

At the tone of his voice, every fibre of Susan's heart thrills. She is frightened at what she feels, and gets confused ! " You had much better stay away,
I'm sure. If Tom was to return—"

" Susan, don't waste another moment. Let us talk only of ourselves."

" Well, then, for my sake, you had better keep away."

In this moment Blake knows all her secret !

" Decide as you choose," he says, pretending to be hurt. " I will certainly
not trouble you with my presence unless you bid me come."

The last bell has rung ; the guard glides swiftly along, locking up his prisoners in their carriages.

" Perhaps you are right, little Susan. Give me your hand—let us part
friends, at least !"

She stretches him an ungloved, trembling hand, and Blake grasps it—can
she ever forget that warm, protecting grasp ? " I'll write in the way you told
me," she cries, relentant. " It could never be called a letter, could it ? "

" And though I musn't see you any more, you will not forget me ? "

Their hands are parted ; the train is already in motion.

" Forget !" echoes Susan, drearily. And then Tom Collinson, her engagement, everything in the wide world but the fact of losing Blake, fades from her,
and this poor little daughter of Eve puts her head through the window, and in
her clear, girl's voice, cries, " Come !"

"COME!"—p. 186.

CHAPTER XXIX

ST. SAUVEUR, as the reader who has wandered through Brittany need not be told, is a straggling offshoot, or suburb, of the old garrison town of St. Maur.

Within the gray, sea-girt walls of St. Maur proper, the first thing, I think, which strikes the traveller, winter or summer, is a certain cheerful atmosphere of well-to-do citizen life. In St. Sauveur, the other side of the harbor, he is encountered, for nine months of the year, at least, by the dreariest embodiment of living death possible to conceive of—an English population existing in a foreign watering-place, out of season. An English population, void in purse, void in spirit; people leading lives, to describe which the word "aimless" is inadequate; too broken by adversity even to seek to share their misery in common; whose hopeless faces, when you have once fairly got them before your mind's eye, you would recognize at a glance in Lapland or Arabia. A class of Pariahs, or social castaways, of the like of which no country but our own seems to have the knack of getting rid !

At Spa, Baden, Biarritz, you may, during the dead months, light upon every other specimen—and all are melancholy—of the British Wandering Jew, in search of cheapness—he calls it climate. You must come to one of these smaller Breton watering-places if you would see abject, hungry poverty at its last grim ebb. There were people in St. Sauveur who, hiring a house by the year, and sub-letting it at season prices during July and August, lived, as nearly as possible, upon nothing—vegetables, cider and bread being cheap throughout the province; people, many of them, who had once worn warm clothes and eaten sufficient meat, but who had had to fly from ruin entailed on them by others—or from the consequences of ruin entailed on others by themselves—who shall say ? In a place where every one was so manifestly out of suits with fortune, the past was not a favorite subject. No man liked to talk of himself. Every man liked to talk and surmise the worst of his neighbors; (barely possible, perhaps, to live in St. Sauveur, without becoming more or less of a misanthrope!) The French hotel-keepers and tradespeople looked with the profound distrust of solvent, legitimate robbers upon them all.

When the cheery garrison band played by the harbor side of a Sunday, and the St. Maur citizens would flock forth, with their wives and daughters, upon the quays, a stray English couple might occasionally be distinguished—the man by his threadbare coat and wide-awake, the lady by her unsmiling face and trailing skirts—among the crowd. But as a rule, the English inhabitants of St. Sauveur shunned all such occasions of festive gathering—did it not cost a sou a head to cross to St. Maur by the ferry boat? Only in the Protestant temple where they and their pastor met together to celebrate the Anglican service, had you a chance of seeing them in a mass, and then—Reader, I declare, the spectacle of that sorry flock and shepherd was one to make your heart bleed. Talk of the loud-spoken ill of paupers at home, paupers born and educated to pauperism—ah, one must go to places like St. Sauveur to learn what English *gentility*—silent, decent, wearing shoes on its feet; gentility just, and only just, above starvation line—can live through!

These remarks, however, apply to winter. On the sunny July morning when Susan Fielding first saw the black ramparts and peaked gray roofs of St. Maur growing distinct above the sea, everything was at its brightest; bands playing, Frenchmen drinking their coffee and reading their morning papers outside the Casino, an army of bathing machines down on the sands, French ladies fluttering in gay wrappers from their hotels to the beach. The steamer stopped, for it was high water, close alongside the quay; and Susan, who had as much practical knowledge of travelling as she had of money, was drifting hither and thither among the crowd of custom-house officers, passengers, and sailors, when she heard the welcome sound of an English voice, and looking up, saw a very bent, very poorly-clad old man offering her his hand.

"My niece Susan, is it not? ah, I was sure of it. Thee has thy mother's face. No need of introductory letters. Welcome to Ile-et-Vilaine, Susan. A primitive life we English live here, a primitive life, not the comforts thy father lived in at Halfont; but thee are welcome to it."

Susan's mother, a Quakeress by birth, had, after her marriage with Joseph Fielding, drifted gradually—partly through deference to her husband's opinions, partly through the distance to meeting-house—out of the religion of her youth. Quaker phraseology, however, the soft, ungrammatical "thee and thou" of the society, she had never been able wholly to put aside. And at Adam Byng's first words a dozen tender, long-dormant chords were suddenly touched in Susan's memory.

"And I should have known you by your way of speaking, Uncle Adam. I have never heard any one say thee or thou since my mamma died."

"And would not hear it now if I was a man of stronger will," said Uncle Adam. "The present Mrs. Byng does not hold by Quaker speech, and I have tried my best for fifteen years to abstain from it. But the habit is stronger than I," he shook his head meekly, "the habit is stronger than I. Mrs. Byng is a most superior woman," he added, giving a timid little glance over his shoulder as he spoke. "It will be well, my dear Susan, for thee to seek to please Mrs. Byng from the first. Now, where is thy luggage?"

Susan's luggage, one modest portmanteau and bonnet-box, was at the bottom of the hold, and it was a long hour-and-a-half before it was taken ashore and got through the custom-house. One of the few books the child had brought with her was a little half-crown selection of French poetry, a prize-gift from Miss Collinson, on the first page of which were some verses from the pen of Victor Hugo. With a grand official air a very small custom-house official opened this book, lighted upon the treasonable name. Ah, ah! but here was an affair to be seen into! The little man cocked his hat ferociously at Susan, shook his head over his own suspicions of her dangerous political character, called up another official—they consult, refer to documents, inform Uncle Adam fiercely that a Frenchman, for committing a similar offence, was sent to prison not a week ago, finally confiscate the book, and allow Susan—with a sort of brand against her name, she is sure—to leave the custom-house.

"And so I have had a narrow escape from going to prison—I could understand enough to know that. Oh, Uncle Adam, what dreadful men Frenchmen are! Half-tiger, half-monkey—I read that once and now I know what it means."

"Tiger? not a bit of it, my dear. Jean Poujol, the little fellow with the big voice and the cocked hat, is the kindest-hearted fellow, and best gardener, in the parish. I got a dozen young lobelias from him last week. Madame Poujol chastises him corporeally, the gossips say; but who knows, who knows?" The subject seemed to bring back Adam Byng's saddest expression. "For my own part I believe Madame Poujol to be a most superior woman—too superior perhaps for Poujol. Now, the question to decide is, shall we ride or walk? Our house, the Petit Tambour, is two miles off if we drive round by the causeway—half a mile, if we cross the ferry and then walk. The question is, which will cost least?"

A crowd of human beings, of both sexes, each dirtier, more hideous than the other, now beset Uncle Adam with offers of their service; the men, drivers of carriages, proposing to take him home by land for three francs, the women to carry up the luggage, by way of the ferry, for one franc fifty—for one franc forty—for whatever Monsieur would give to mothers of families for honest labor and the love of the good God!

"Brittany is a loyal district, as thee has seen at the custom-house," remarked Uncle Adam to Susan, "and a pious country as thee may gather from the discourse of these ladies. Now, my friends," speaking in fluent but thoroughly English French, "depart!" He made a step forward, throwing out his arms, and the crowd dispersed in thin air—nothing disperses a French crowd like the sight of a pair of English arms. "Raoul Bertrand, bring thy carriage. Raoul will take us to the Petit Tambour for two francs thirty—counting the ferry we should certainly save forty centimes the other way—but thee are looking pale, child. Better spend the money on carriage hire than have thee laid up."

Uncle Adam said this gravely, conscientiously. The expenditure of forty centimes was not, evidently, in his eyes, an enterprise to be undertaken lightly or wantonly.

After waiting another five minutes (during which interval occurred a fight between some of the bloused, fur-capped savages from the carriage stand; a fight conducted on the usual French system of exchanging everything but blows) Raoul Bertrand brought up his carriage, a huge, springless, indescribably filthy *droscha*, and Susan started for her new home. As long as they were rattling up and down the narrow streets and over the villainous paving-stones of St. Maur, the coachman stood upright, and by yells, execrations and flourishes of his tattered rope harness contrived to keep his two jades of horses—buried, despite a July sun, under blue and crimson sheep-skin—in a gallop. When they emerged from the last postern, and were on a flat, smooth sandy road—the cause-

way connecting St. Maur with the main land—he stopped, began to sing, to
nod at the passers-by; then took out a pipe, lit it, and let the horses go their
own snail's pace the remainder of the journey. So Susan had time to improve
her acquaintance with her new relation before reaching St. Sauveur.

"Thee are surprised at the carriages, I see, Susan. They tell me the carriages of this district belong to the time of Louis XVI., but I have lived in
Brittany till I am accustomed to every thing it contains. Eighteen years altogether, two with my dear wife, sixteen with the present Mrs. Byng. There are
many advantages in St. Sauveur, Susan, as thee will find after a time.
Strangers do not see much in the place at first, but we who live in it feel that
we should be sorry to have to move elsewhere. I don't mean to be buried on
French soil "—a brighter look than Susan had seen it wear yet crossed Adam
Byng's face—" but I am well content to linger out the remainder of my days
here. We have warm sun in summer, and in winter—well, some seasons of the
year are dreary everywhere. There are many advantages in St. Sauveur."

Not external ones, thought Susan, when at length they had quitted the coal
heaps and barge-masts of the St. Maur quays, and were driving up through the
steep and noisome lanes of St. Sauveur. Oh, desolation of desolation, was
your name ever more clearly written than on every squalid wall and building of
this poor town! The word grass-grown could be justly applied to the high
street, the main thoroughfare only. The smaller divergent lanes, mostly inhabit-
ed by English, were grass-*covered*, the gutters alone tracing dark and sinuous
paths, unclothed by verdure. After ascending an unsavory labyrinth of these
streets or lanes, Raoul pulled round his horses with a jerk into a kind of street,
alley or court, gray dilapidated walls towering high on either side, two or three
gaunt dogs prowling about the corners, the air, even on this July day, striking
chill, and laden with a peculiar kind of oily flavor with which Susan was to become better acquainted hereafter.

"The Rue de la Guerre, at last," said Uncle Adam. "To my mind the quiet-
est, pleasantest street in St. Sauveur. Thee can perceive the colza, perhaps?
that building with the blind windows to the left is a colza mill, but 'tis a wholesome odor. I am accustomed to it. Indeed, at this moment I smell only the
roses and carnations from my own garden."

The carriage stopped before a door that had once been painted green—in the
time perhaps of Louis XVI. Uncle Adam got out and rang, very gingerly,
considering that the bell was his own, and after a considerable time the door
opened.

"Wipe your shoes, Mr. Byng," said a voice within, "and bid the man leave
his *sabots* outside. Wipe your shoes again."

Uncle Adam obeyed instantly; meekly rubbing his large feet lengthways,
sideways, on the toes, on the heels, upon the rush mat inside the doorway. Then
he lifted Susan from the carriage, and deposited her opposite an open door a few
steps from the entrance, where Mrs. Byng stood ready to receive her.

She was a spare, elderly woman, of five feet eight or nine inches, frosty-faced,
thin-lipped, awfully clean and neat. She was attired in a black satin dress, and
gold chain, and had blue ribbons in her cap. Her appearance contrasted strongly
with that of Uncle Adam, who wore an old chip hat, a colored shirt, and a
patched gray suit so shrunk with frequent cleaning that his wrists and ankles
were bare, like those of a schoolboy.

"Here is our niece, Susan Fielding," he remarked—the gentlest. most piti-
fully crushed voice you ever heard was Uncle Adam's. "I thought it was well to

ride, my dear," he went on, apologetically. Susan almost trembled at hearing him address this imposing figure as "my dear." "The child looked tired, and my good friend Raoul Bertrand has brought us for two francs thirty."

"The statute fare is two francs. Raoul Bertrand will receive two francs. After a sea voyage, I should have said a brisk walk would have done your niece good. How do you do, Susan Fielding? I cannot say you look healthy." She scrutinized Susan's face with chilly interest. "You don't understand French money? Then take out an English gold piece and your Uncle Adam will settle for you with the driver."

Susan drew half a sovereign from her purse.

"The exchange is twenty-five forty," said Mrs. Byng, addressing her husband. "Ten centimes higher than last week."

"Does thee think Raoul Bertrand knows aught about the exchange, my love?" hesitated Uncle Adam.

"Then put the half sovereign in your pocket and pay him another 'me. You can get twenty-five forty at either of the St. Maur banks. Bertrand," in resonant, hard French, "take off your *sabots*, and bring in no straw with you. The boxes are for the left-hand attic."

And then she motioned to Susan to enter the drawing-room while Uncle Adam and the driver took her luggage up stairs.

The drawing-room, like the polished stairs, like every nook and cranny within the Petit Tambour, looked the very pink of cleanliness—cleanliness the more surprising to Susan's eyes by reason of all the outside ruin through which she had newly travelled. The furniture of the room might, at a liberal estimate, have been worth five pounds. If you sat down with inadvertent weight on a chair, it broke; if you examined the paper narrowly you found so many patches in it that you were thrown into a state of utter scepticism as to which could have been the fundamental pattern: the damask coverings were cobwebs; the muslin curtains had been darned until darns were more frequent in them than the original fabric. And still, by dint of heroic industry, by unflagging carpentering, sewing, pasting, the drawing-room of the Petit Tambour looked fresh and habitable. The oft-darned curtains were white as a French laundress could make them, the bare floors were polished and slippery as ice, spotless muslin covers concealed the faded damask of the chairs and sofa, great bunches of roses, arranged by no inapt hand, were on the mantel-shelf: through the open window came in a very volume of odor and sweetness from the small flower-garden, thirty or forty yards square, that lay at the back of the house.

This garden, Breton fashion, was inclosed by high lichen-stained walls—walls only to picture the dampness of which in winter gave you a shudder! but upon whose southern and western sides, luxuriant yellow and crimson roses, passion-flowers and jessamine now hung festooned, while the north was artfully draped over by such annual creepers as have natures to flourish in the shade. The centre beds were all ablaze with scarlet verbenas and geraniums. Close beside the drawing-room window rose the glossy leaves and waxen white buds of a magnolia; a border entirely filled with purple heliotrope sent up delicious fragrance at its foot. Not a plant in that garden, you could see, but had been artistically chosen for its showy hue or penetrating odor; not a plant save those whose blossoming season came in July and August. Mrs. Byng would no more have allowed Adam to impoverish the ground by cultivating nonsensical flowers for spring or late autumn than she would have hung up the clean curtains or put on her own satin gown before June the first.

On June the first opened the casino, and the *tables-d'hôte* of the principal hotels.   On June the first a placard containing the words "*à louer*" was hung on
the wall of the Petit Tambour, and every morning for the remainder of the
summer, Mrs. Byng, by eleven o'clock, was dressed, her house swept and gar-
nished, ready for exhibition.   There was no necessity for poor old Adam to
dress.   By five o'clock in the morning Adam had to be out and busy, tying up
flowers, cleaning the walks, or working in the kitchen-garden—the products of
which went far toward supporting the household.   During the midday hours,
when house-hunters might be expected to call, the meek old man's principal
duty was, not to show himself.

Long experience of watering-place human nature had taught Mrs. Byng two
things : first, that the poorer you look the harder the bargains others will try to
drive with you ; secondly, that truth-telling, when you have a house to let, is a
virtue about as much in its place as it would be in the selling of a horse.

Adam looked incurably poor, and was incurably truthful.   Though his meat
for the coming winter must depend upon the summer letting of the Petit Tambour, Adam, for instance, never could bring himself to say that the water in the
well was good.   "We use it ourselves without ill result, but thee must be aware
that water near the sea is ever brackish," would be his style of answer in the
days when he was allowed to speak at all to people who had perhaps flown from
Paris or London to escape cholera !   And as this disease of veracity strengthened
rather than diminished with him, as he advanced in life, Mrs. Byng, during the last
four or five years, had steadily excluded him from business transactions of all
kinds, and with the best possible results.

"We are neither the physicians nor the purse-keepers of others," she would
say, when Adam gently expostulated with her sometimes on the results of her
want of conscience.   "Why didn't they taste the water ?   How could I have an
opinion as to whether it would agree with their children ?   Here is my estimate
of the damage they have done the furniture.   If they dispute any item in the
agreement they have the alternative of the law."

Tenants to Mrs. Byng were as the strawberries in July, or pears in October ;
seasonable spoil, of which she, for her part, would gather to the uttermost.   To
Adam Byng, a human being, under every circumstance, was a human being.
Always keep a crotchety man like this out of money transactions if you can.

Susan crossed to the window, and gave an exclamation of surprise.   Greenhouse plants did not come to luxuriance such as she saw here, under the cool
sky, exposed to the cutting winds of Hounslow Heath.   "You must be very
fond of your garden," she said, turning shyly to Mrs. Byng, of whom already she
stood in awe.   "I never saw such flowers out of a hothouse."

"They last like this till the end of September," said Mrs. Byng, "and on
October the first the casino closes.   If you know any one likely to come abroad
this summer you had better write to them about the house.   We stand two hundred feet above the sea level ; on gravel ; we are midway between the railway
station and bathing-place ; five beds, besides servants' ; salon, salle, excellent
kitchen, English range ; the only kitchen in St. Sauveur where you can burn
either coal or charcoal.   Have you any friends you can write to ?"

"There are two ladies in our parish who are thinking of coming here," hesitated Susan, "but they would only want a small apartment, three rooms with a
balcony—"

"I know the place for them," said Mrs. Byng, decisively.   "They must go
to the Hôtel Benjamin, and will be less robbed, more reasonably robbed, I should

say, than in a lodging. You had better write to-night, and at the same time in-close a description of this house—I have cards written out—for them to give to their friends. Now, Susan"—Adam Byng by this time had returned, and stood just within the door, watching his niece's face—"we will, if you please, speak about business. What are your exact means?"

"My—my means, ma'am?" cried Susan, taken thoroughly aback by this commercial question.

"Ma'am!" interrupted Uncle Adam, in his kind voice. "Aunt Isabella, you mean, my dear."

"For heaven's sake, Mr. Byng, don't make your niece waste her breath on so many syllables. She calls you Uncle Adam, let me be Aunt Adam. One name is as good as another. Forty pounds a year, I believe you mentioned, Susan, as your probable income?"

"I believe so, Aunt—Adam. Mr. Goldney tells me I have something like twelve or thirteen hundred pounds."

A light came into Mrs. Byng's cold eyes. "Thirteen hundred pounds yield-ing forty pounds a year! Mr. Byng, this must be seen into. The money, lent in small sums, could be made to yield six—seven per cent., with safety. You are as much Susan's guardian as this other man."

"Well, well, that is for the future," said Uncle Adam. "No need to trouble the child about business to-day. Thee are fond of flowers, Susan? Come out in the garden with me—the other way, I do not cross this floor in my boots—and I will cut thee a bunch."

"And cut them out of sight, and no heliotrope, Mr. Byng," said his wife. "Susan, my dear, I will have a longer talk with you by-and-by. You must look upon us in the light of parents, child. Your interests will be ours."

CHAPTER XXX.

SUSAN, on this, followed Uncle Adam from the salon, then out through the small dining-room, another miracle of threadbare tidiness, into the garden. As soon as he was under the blue sky, among his flowers, and away from his wife, an almost childish expression of serenity came over Adam Byng's worn face.

"The happiest hours of my life are spent with my roses and carnations," he said, making the confession in a whisper, and resting his hand with kindly pres-sure on the little girl's shoulder. "I call them my children—to myself, Susan, to myself—and thee wouldn't credit what it costs me to give them over in their prime to strangers."

"I can quite credit it," said Susan. "Papa used to say it gave him pain like having a tooth drawn, even to see his flowers plucked."

"Ah," said Uncle Adam, looking up dreamily at the sky, as he recalled the past, "Joseph Fielding may have had his faults, as far as his radical opinions went. For my part, I don't much concern myself with men's opinions. I have never seen the equal of Joseph's apples and pears in my life. That last evening, it seems but yesterday, that we spent with him, a few months after his marriage —it was in October, and he had packed me a hamper of as fine Ribstone pippins as thee ever saw, when the quarrel came between him and my poor Martha. She was a woman little given to argument, in a general way, but a staunch churchwoman, and thy father was no friend to any established forms, and so the quarrel came about. Thy mother chanced idly to mention to poor Martha how

'twas said in the village that the foundations of Halfont church were beginning
to totter, that any high wind might bring the old spire down—

"'Aye,' added Joseph, rubbing his hands cheerfully—I can see him now as he
sat beside the fire. 'Aye, sister Martha, before we die, I expect we shall see a
good many spires lying where the tombstones now stand.'

"Thy mother, Susan, and I took the remark as a joke. We of the Society of
Friends have never been quick to heat ourselves over the polemical differences
of others. My wife started up, her face—Ah, 'twas a fair face then !—afire with
indignation.

"'Joseph Fielding,' she cried, 'am I to think that in what you say you express
your true sentiments ?'

"'To the best of my belief I do,' answered thy father, in his dry way.

"'Then the sooner we quit such a house the better,' cried my wife; and
straight out of the room she walked—"

"And for a few foolish words like that you and papa were never friends
again ?" asked Susan.

"I don't think we ever ceased to be friends at heart," said Uncle Adam.
"Still, we never saw each other's faces more. Thy mother and I tried our best
at the time to soften the matter down, but to no avail. Joseph would not unsay
his opinion about church steeples, neither would Martha forgive him—although
supper was already laid upon the table. So the family was broken up, and so I
lost a hamper of the finest Ribstone pippins that were ever grown. Aye, aye,"
went on Uncle Adam, shaking his head, "all that happened close upon twenty
years ago, and none of us are left but me. We lived at Hammersmith in those
days, little Susan, and I kept my horse and chaise, and Martha had two maids
to wait upon her. That was before my riches left me."

He walked on, his head bent down upon his breast, round the small garden, stopping ever and awhile to cut a flower for Susan. At last, when they
were at the farthest point of all from the drawing-room window and Mrs. Byng,
he spoke again.

"Thee knows—thy father has told thee—the story of my losses, Susan ?
No ? Well, half-a-dozen words will tell it. I trusted my money to a friend.
After the crash came—it must have been when thee was a baby—when Ashley's
bank failed, and half the neighborhood with it, I had no choice left me but to
leave England, and luck—my good luck I say now—brought me to St. Sauveur.
Out of all we once possessed we had only a poor three hundred pounds of Martha's remaining, and upon this—not upon the interest, alas! of this—we lived.
St. Sauveur was cheap in those days. Meat five sous a pound, a fine Michael-
mas goose for a franc."

"And Aunt Martha died here ?" said Susan, as the old man paused.

"Martha died here ?" said Uncle Adam, in the calm, soft voice with which
after long years, men grow to speak of their dead. "Her last wish was to
lie in a Protestant country, among Protestants. So I journeyed with her—
I had money enough left for that—to Guernsey. I shall rest there, also, Susan
—the place is left for my name on the stone—in a pleasant little yard where
the sea washes close, and the laurels and ilex are green throughout the year.
Till then I want no change. St. Sauveur has many advantages, and I have everything to be grateful for in my domestic life. My present wife is an admirable
woman "—it seemed as though Uncle Adam must derive some occult support
from the frequent enunciation of this truth—"an admirable woman, and a first-
rate economist. Every one in St. Sauveur is an economist, of necessity; but

Mrs. Byng beats them all. Now, if thee has flowers enough, come with me to the back garden, and I will give thee a peach. We have few luxuries here," added Uncle Adam, with his sad smile, "save those the sun gives us."

"And those are the best luxuries of all," said Susan, in whose present frame of mind the sun meant summer, and summer, George Blake. And then these two—the child of sixty and the child of seventeen—walked away together, hand in hand, under the bright noon sky, to the kitchen garden.

"Thirteen hundred pounds!" thought Mrs. Byng, as she stood watching them, upright and with folded arms, from the drawing-room window. "And if anything happened to the girl, Adam would be her heir. Ah!"

The summing-up of a whole character was in the monosyllable. To delineate any human being as living, moving, and breathing under the exclusive dominion of one passion is, in ninety-nine cases out of a hundred, to draw a caricature. Yet of Mrs. Byng such a picture can be given with absolute truth. Economy up to a certain line is, I suppose, a duty; more or less painful, according to the temperament of him who practises it. At the point at which it becomes an end, not a means, it develops into passion, the only one of our passions from whose vitality time does not take away. And, more years ago than she could count, economy had overstepped this line with Adam Byng's wife.

Why she had ever married the poverty-stricken Quaker widower at all, was a mystery that the united wisdom of the St. Sauveur gossips or motive-mongers had never solved. In part, probably, it was for the sum of forty pounds that still remained to Adam, a year after his first wife's death; in part, that she might become proprietress of an unpaid hewer of wood and drawer of water until her life's end; somewhat, no doubt (even avarice being human), from a feeling of pity or personal regard toward the man himself. Miss Isabella White was, at the time of Adam's great sorrow, a spinster of forty, holding hunger at bay by the precarious means of keeping a St. Sauveur lodging-house; and under her roof Adam's first wife died. What more natural than that the friendless, heart-broken man should fall back upon the first capable arm outheld for his support? On returning from his last sad mission of love, after laying Martha to rest in the little Protestant grave-yard by the sea, Adam, simple as a child, at once gave over the management of his small remaining worldly possessions into Miss White's hands."

"Make the money last for me, while thee can," said he, meekly; "and if there is work about the house for me to do let me do it. It may be that I shall think less so than if I sat with folded hands."

And then, during the long, drear winter months, was to be seen a sight at which the kind-hearted French housewives would glance with wet eyes—Adam Byng, in his black clothes, working in Miss White's garden, chopping wood in Miss White's court-yard, running errands—walking them, I should say, heart had he none to run—for Miss White's lodgers. Before the year was quite out she married him. He had forty pounds still left, thanks to her—the money left in his hands would have melted away in three months—and she had the same. They took the Petit Tambour on lease, furnished it, let it when they could in summer, existed in it in winter, and now, at the end of fifteen years, had saved well on for a couple of hundred pounds. How, Adam himself could not have told. Income they had none: there were years like the present one, in which summer passed without their letting; and still, winter and summer, Mrs. Byng, who knew the market value of respectable appearances, kept a servant, and all the year round Adam was allowed a weak half-tumbler of Hollands and water after his dinner.

No wonder he believed in the advantages of St. Sauveur!

"In any other place on earth I must have starved long ago," the poor old fellow would say. "Where, but in St. Sauveur, could a man with nothing a year live in a good house and have all the comforts of life about him, as I do?"

"The comforts of life!" Well; more, perhaps, than any term we constantly use, is this one relative. If, soberly and philosophically, one set oneself to compare Adam Byng's life with that of men overcome by riches and all that riches bring with them (in the way of servants, public duties, entertainments, friends), it might, I think, be hard to decide on which hand the balance of solid comfort lay. Adam was free to wear unfashionable clothes and old shoes. His food was poor, but admirably cooked—who knew better than Mrs. Byng that the best cooking is the best economy? During eight months of the year a sun that gave real, honest warmth shone over his head. He never went through the misery of party giving. He knew not the meaning of indigestion. One of the conditions of his second marriage had been that he should be buried with the wife of his youth : he had, therefore, no care for the future. Of hope, ambition, interest in anything beyond his roses and carnations, he had no more than had the yellow lichens that grew upon the garden walls ; but then he was contented—passive might, perhaps, be the fitter word—as only a man reduced to an absolutely nugatory or lichen state of existence can ever be.

Adam Byng was passive : long habit, together with the sweetest natural gift of patience, had made him bear his galling domestic fetters unmurmuringly ; and the only alien trial or discomfort of his life was during the eight or nine weeks of summer, when they had succeeded in finding a tenant for the Petit Tambour. Mrs. Byng was far too cautious a woman to leave the place, as was the custom of the other St. Sauveur English, with her property in the possession of strangers ; so, during the bathing season, the hottest time of the year, poor Adam's fate was generally to be carried up to a couple of rooms, three or four stories high, in St. Maur, there to pine for his garden and get rid of the troublesome fact of being alive, as best he might. At such times, Mrs. Byng was in her best spirits. Nothing like the gratification of a genuine passion—a mean passion just the same as a noble one—for enabling men and women to be heroic under petty troubles ! With the knowledge that a revenue of so many hundred francs, without breakages, was being added weekly to her coffers, Mrs. Byng was not only oblivious to personal inconvenience, her hard face would grow almost genial, she would actually lend herself to amusement, go out and listen, in an absent, unenjoying mood, to the band, sit on the beach in the sunshine, nay, had been known to give alms (in all persons with whom avarice is a passion you will find some of a gambler's superstitions) to the poor.

In the present year no such modifying influence was upon her. It was the worst season—an international exhibition going on—that St. Sauveur had experienced for years ; houses close to the sea unlet, the chances for the Petit Tambour lessening daily, Mrs. Byng's humor at its dryest. No wonder that her husband's mood was more than ordinarily crushed, no wonder that a heartfelt "ah" rose to her lips as she watched Susan Fielding and reflected that only a delicate girl's life stood between Adam and the inheritance of thirteen hundred pounds !

I doubt if the imagination of love can be more remorseless than is that of avarice in sweeping away obstacles between itself and what it desires to possess.

CHAPTER XXXI

THE days in the Petit Tambour were alike as beads upon a rosary. At six the big bell tolling from a neighboring convent was the signal for Susan to rise, throw open her window, and let in the scents from the garden, where Uncle Adam at this hour was generally busy with rake or pruning-knife among his flowers. At seven came the first breakfast, of coffee and bread. At twelve the second one—fresh fruit, an omelet, salad, and a small bottle of the smallest claret ever pressed from grapes. At five dinner ; the same kind of fare as breakfast, with the addition of vegetables and one modest plate of meat. Then a walk to St. Maur, or through the fields of colza and buckwheat down to the little river Rance, and to bed at nine.

Days monotonously alike as beads upon a rosary ; but full-flavored, radiant with expectant hope to Susan Fielding. On the evening after her arrival she had written a letter about the St. Maur lodgings, and the merits of the Petit Tambour to Portia Ffrench. Then—because, pleaded heart against conscience, her desk was open ; because she was in a writing mood ; because a promise, however hastily given, should be kept—wrote another one—no, not a letter ; Tom Collinson himself could scarce have cavilled at those few formal lines of "statistics " —and addressed it to the Treasury. By return of post came word that Mr. Blake availed himself of her permission ! " The one kind word," he wrote, " the one kind word you ever spoke to me, Susan, was that word 'come' at parting." She might expect him in a fortnight at furthest.

A fortnight—only fourteen days more, and the present day half gone already ! Susan ran at once to her own room, and scratched thirteen little marks upon the whitewash at the head of her bed, one of which on every succeeding night she effaced—reckoning up the lessening score with rapture. She wrote a love-letter that cost only two hours' heavy labor, to Tom Collinson. She sang her tenderest English love-songs (sweet with all the pathetic sweetness of disuse) to Adam Byng's ears, as they sauntered through the twilight fields or sat together in the pleasant garden shade at noon. Faint pink roses began to grow steadfast in her cheeks ; some new shade of intelligence lit up daily in her eyes.

" I like St. Sauveur, after all, and I don't want to be back at Halfont," she made confession in her diary. " I sing the first thing when I get up, and I sing till I go to bed. Have I grown heartless ; have I forgotten so soon ? Ah, Papa, you would never have been happy, you would never have sung again, if I had died ! " Then, in another place : " I feel, I don't know why, that my spirits can only be for a time, that my grief *must* come back stronger than ever to me some day." And then farther : " I have heard again—half a page longer than last time—from Mr. Blake ; and he is coming on the twentieth, only three days more. Oh, if I should be wrong, if it should be for some one else's sake that he is taking so much trouble." The same post had brought a letter from Portia to say that the Lily now waited her orders at Southampton, that Susan might look any day for their arrival. " I certainly think it a most *unhappy accident* their both coming at the same time. Three days—how shall I live through them ? I will think of poor Tom Collinson. Eliza used to say the only thing to make the time pass quick is the fulfilment of *duty*."

She grew all at once fastidious about her dress ; found out that village-made boots were heavy for walking ; what, in this warm weather, could be nicer than the Paris-fashioned shoes, with rosettes and heels, that the French ladies wore ? She must have her hair frizzed and pyramided ; a bonnet two inches square in-

stead of the honest fabric of silk and crape that Miss Budd had made for her
first mourning ; she must have perfect-fitting gloves, one of those new-shaped
parasols ; would like to be looking " like other people " when the Misses Ffrench
arrived. At all these extravagances, with a sensation of positive bodily pain,
had Mrs. Byng—not yet holding her niece's purse-strings—to look on powerless ;
and still Susan declared her wardrobe incomplete. Still a pair of jet earrings,
a brooch, a bracelet—nothing to make the hand look neat like a bracelet !—was
wanting. Still her jealous child's heart told her she was all unfit to cope with
Portia, with the crowd of finely-dressed fashionable ladies among whom George
Blake's eyes would first see her.

True as the instinct of women may be in most things, it is nearly always at
fault here : they believe men judge them outwardly by a woman's, not a man's,
standard. If the feminine creed on this one point could be set straight, I suppose two-thirds of the leading milliners might shut up their shops. What did
the simple child's face that was haunting Blake's fancy—hour by hour dispossess-
ing Portia Ffrench more utterly from her throne—what did Susan Fielding want,
in his eyes, of adventitious setting or adornment ? To a man who has spent
his life ever since he was a schoolboy, in a great city, what charm can there ever
be in the trite vagaries of fashion—above all, if this man, like Blake, be an artist ?
What should a shy, " Sir Joshua face," a pair of dimpled hands, a girlish white
throat, gain by brooches or earrings, a new shaped parasol, or a two-inch French
bonnet, in his sight ?

Well, women, at least, judge each other by their own or the fashion-book
standard. Portia's first exclamation on seeing Susan Fielding in her altered
Parisian style, was one of approval. Miss Jemima, partly under the influence of
cajolery, partly of force—somewhat swayed, too, by the old dread of Portia's " doing something worse " if she were thwarted—had been led on into accepting th
offer of Lord Dormer's yacht. And one evening, just as dinner was over and Uncle Adam was sipping his Hollands and water in the garden of the Petit Tambour, came a messenger with a note for Susan Fielding telling her that her
friends and the Lily had arrived at St. Maur.

" We have been thirty-six hours crossing from the Needles," wrote Portia,
" and.I can assure you, had come not only to our last idea but to our last powers
of speech when we reached the Hôtel Benjamin. The rooms here are charming,
picturesque with a vengeance—alas, shall we be amused in them ? Come to see us,
if you can, this evening, and hear a piece of rather good news I have got to tell you."

A piece of rather good news—what could it be but that Blake was at this
moment at Portia's side ? To-morrow was the twentieth, the longed-for day on
which he was to reach St. Sauveur ; what more likely than that Portia, at the last,
had persuaded him to join Lord Dormer's party in the yacht ? All in a tremor of
hope and fear, Susan, after a cold permission from Mrs. Byng, ran upstairs to
put on her bonnet, then with Uncle Adam for her escort, started off for the Hôtel Benjamin. To walk round to St. Maur by the mainland took exactly one hour
longer than to cross by the ferry ; but to cross and recross the ferry cost two
sous a head ; and it was a standing injunction laid on Adam years ago by his
wife, never to use the boat save in times of dire emergency. This evening, however, Susan coaxed him out of the path of duty. She had a two-sous piece in her
pocket, of whose weight she would gladly be rid. She was dying to see her English friends. Well, then—these arguments failing—the heat had tired her ; putting on a piteous little expression of weakness. Would Uncle Adam force her
to go all the way round by the causeway when she was almost too tired to stand ?

"Thee are not too tired other evenings," said Uncle Adam, "and I ought not to allow thee to squander thy money. Who knows better than I what careless-ness in money leads to? Still, if thee are bent on it—for once!"

And so Susan had her way, and half an hour after leaving the Petit Tambour, was running, with a heightened color and quick-drawn breath, through the outer court of the Hôtel Benjamin; Uncle Adam, who had business of his own in St. Maur (business that consisted in sipping a glass of sugar water and playing a game of dominoes with Jean Poujol in one of the smaller *cafés*) promising to call for her on his way back to St. Sauveur by nine o'clock.

The staircase leading to the first floor of the Benjamin was outside the house, as one still sees in some of the old, second-class Breton hotels; a granite stair-case with an ancient oaken balustrade, half hidden now by a drapery of purple passion-flowers, and with the lily of France carved by some fifteenth century hand on every pillar. Up this staircase Susan was conducted by Josephine, the head waitress of the hotel, then along a narrow, many-doored passage, still with blue sky overhead, to the western or seaward side of the hotel. Here the waiting-woman knocked loudly at a door built into a kind of recess or archway in the wall, and Miss Jemima's voice, in the most determined of all British ac-cents, called out "*entrez.*"

The room that Portia had selected for her sitting-room was a vast old tapes-. tried chamber—in reality one of the show-rooms of St. Maur—with windows opening to the Channel, and a balcony from whence a flight of perpendicular steps led down across the ramparts to the rocks; a chamber in which the "good Duchess Anne" had once slept, and whose walls, if the St. Maur records spoke true, had witnessed many a scene of love and romance, ages before this prosaic little nineteenth century episode of which I write.

Portia, still in her yachting dress, stood at one of the open windows through which the yellow sunset streamed; her sailor hat lying beside her on the win-dow step, her black hair falling in glossy waves below her waist, a morsel of scarlet ribbon, the necessary spot of becoming color, knotted at the open collar of the blue and white sailor shirt.

She came across the room to meet Susan Fielding, and, as I have said, her first exclamation was one of approval. "Why, Susan, child, what have you done to yourself? I hope French air improves every one in the same way. Crimped hair, short dress, shoes—certainly I must wear shoes and crimp my hair! Aunt, is not Susan improved?"

Miss Jemima was standing, diligently mending a pair of torn gloves, at the other window. Abroad or at home, before or after a journey, the fingers and needle-case of the good old campaigner were never long left idle when Portia was at hand. "Susan has altered herself," she said, pushing up her spectacles, and looking kindly at the little girl who ran to greet her. "But as to improve-ment!—stand so, my dear, let me look at you straight—well, no, I can't say I think her improved. I want time to be sure of that. I can't see that whatever is fashionable is right, as you do, Portia."

"Ah, that is a cut at my dishevelled locks," cried Portia. "Do you admire them, Susan? oh, you must see me with my hat on before you judge." She stooped, picked up her hat, on whose ribbon was the name of Lord Dormer's yacht, and stuck it, the least in the world on one side her head. "Now, give me a candid opinion. Some one for whose taste I have the greatest respect has been telling me incessantly for two days that my sea-going make-up is perfection. Aunt calls it depraved."

While Portia spoke, three little French officers were staring up at her, as only Frenchmen can stare at a pretty woman, from the walk upon the ramparts; and the consciousness even of this audience brought color and life to her face. Never, alas, to Susan's eyes, had she looked so desperately, so unapproachingly handsome! "Whatever you wear suits you best. You always look well," she cried, with such an intense air of conviction, that Portia stooped, the audience more and more interested, and kissed her cheek. "My opinion agrees with that of—of the other person." Then she stopped and hung her head; blushing with shame over her own jealous fears.

"You would agree with him in nothing else, I hope," remarked old Miss Jemima. "Susan, my dear, in the course of your short life has it ever happened to you to be thrown for six-and-thirty hours into the unrelieved company of a fool?"

"Aunt," cried Portia, authoritatively, "I won't let you say these things of Lord Dormer—"

Lord Dormer, only: oh, the one big, joyous throb of Susan's heart!

"I'm sure nothing could be nicer than his manner has been to you. The way he ran about after you with wraps and cushions was most—"

"Thoroughly and painfully ridiculous," said old Miss Jemima. "As if I needed the poor little creature's attentions; as if I even looked upon crossing the Channel in his cockle-shell of a boat as being at sea at all!. I fancy if a storm had come on we should have seen Lord Dormer's yachting qualities tested in earnest! The lad felt sea-sick half the time, Portia. I could tell it by the cadaverous green shade of his skin."

"Cadaverous, indeed! Why, that is his lovely natural hue, the last thing out in complexions. Every young lady I know admires little Lord Dormer's interesting, colorless, dissipated-looking face."

"Except me," cried Susan. "I dare say I should like to go in his yacht and have presents, too, if he asked me, but I think little Lord Dormer hideous."

"And so do I," said Portia, the Frenchmen having at last stared themselves tired, had walked on, and as she spoke she descended from the raised step or dais by the window. "But he does ask me to go in his yacht, and he does give me presents. And I accept everything unblushingly—don't I, Aunt Jem?"

"You do," answered Miss Jemima, drily, "and before very long will, I have not the slightest doubt, accept Lord Dormer himself in the same manner. No need to keep Susan out of the secret, Portia. She was present at the breaking off of your last engagement, and she knows how another, worthier man—ah, well, no need to speak of that! Susan, my dear, Lord Dormer has run through thirty thousand pounds already, and on his twenty-first birth-day will come into fifty thousand pounds more. Never say that he is hideous again. My niece Portia is quite disposed to spend the remainder of her life in his society."

A look of regret, so keen as to be almost one of pain, crossed Portia's face. "Fifty thousand pounds!" she repeated, in a queer, compressed sort of tone. "Oh, how I hate to think of other people having money—how I hate myself for *never*, even by accident, doing the thing that is right! If one could only calculate chances, only look forward—Susan," she interrupted herself hastily, "what is to be seen in St. Maur of an evening? When aunt has finished her work we will sally forth. Our luggage is still on board the yacht, so we must appear before the world in our rags and tatters just as we are. What does every one do, where does every one go?"

"Uncle Adam and I go far away upon the sands, or down through the fields to the river; but the visitors, when they are not at the Casino, walk up and down

on the Place, close to this hotel—I came once with Mrs. Byng to see them—and
a band plays, and an ugly woman on a little stage sings, all out of tune—I stopped
my ears when she sang—and then the people clap their hands and applaud."

"As I shall do," said Portia. "Who cares for discord or ugliness, Susan?
The thing is, whatever happens in life, to clap one's hands with the majority.
Now, Aunt Jem," considerately, "will you come with us, or shall Susan and I go
alone? Remember I have brought you to France to amuse yourself and I'm
not going to have your life made miserable by any ridiculous ideas about propriety, or chaperoning duties."

"I am extremely obliged by the hint," said old Miss Jemima, "and you may
set your mind at rest, my dear. During daylight you shall have as much liberty
as you choose. As you say, we have come to France to enjoy ourselves. After
seven o'clock in the evening we keep together. That is the last vestige of authority in which I mean to clothe myself."

For a moment, down went the corners of Portia's lips; then, "Of course we
will keep together," she cried, good-humoredly; "both before seven o'clock and
after it; though if the truth were told, it is I that am chaperoning you, Aunt, not
you me. Now, run and get ready like a good old lady, and we will start. I can
put on my hat here."

Miss Jemima, thus bidden, went away into the adjoining bed-room, Portia
moved across to the huge old-fashioned fireplace, standing before which on tiptoe
it was just possible to see one's self in a faded, ebony-framed mirror that reached
from chimney-shelf to ceiling. She smoothed back her hair with her hands, put
on her hat, took one of those long, exhaustive looks handsome women love to
give at their own faces in the tarnished glass, then in a whisper called Susan to
her side.

"I am going to let you into my secrets, Susan—not a word to Aunt Jem,
though. All this about my accepting Lord Dormer is nonsense, of course."

"And yet you have come to France in his yacht."

"And yet I have come to France in his yacht. The fact is, I have been
wretchedly unhappy ever since I saw you. That very day you left, Teddy and I
had a horrible scene with grandmamma, as soon as we got back to the house. I
can't exactly say why, but I have an uneasy sense that Condy knows more than
she ought about where we went the evening before. At all events, grandmamma
hinted, as only a Dysart can hint, as to what she was pleased to call the laxity of
my principles. The way I ran after my cousin—Ted standing placidly by, mind
—was, after all that had occurred, shameless."

"Portia!"

"Hard to bear, wasn't it? and so unjust! Well, I looked at Teddy and saw
that in another minute he would say something to ruin both of us. Really, I
never knew till then how handsome the poor little fellow could look—his face
flushed, his blue eyes all alight with anger! It was no time, I knew, for hesitation; and before he was able to speak a word I had got out something—I
scarcely like to think what—about my preference for Lord Dormer—"

"Lord Dormer—oh, how cruel of you!"

"Don't look so shocked, my dear. Do you think I felt no struggle, no com-
punction at going so flat against my conscience? Grandmamma and Condy,
both of them, looked fairly mystified.

"'Am I to think,' stammered grandmamma, 'that Lord Dormer—that Lord
Dormer can be seriously coming forward, after his intimacy with your friend,
Mrs. Wynn, as your suitor.'

"'Think what you like, grandmamma,' said I, with beautiful dignity; 'but for the future have the kindness, please, not to hint any more of these unworthy suspicions—at least in the presence of others.'

"Then I glanced round at Ted. His brief anger had all faded out of his face now. 'My Cousin Portia is so well able to take care of herself that I won't say what, a minute ago, I meant to say,' he remarked. I felt every word of this as he meant that I should feel it: 'Lord Dormer is to be congratulated—that is the only opinion I hold on the subject.' After this he continued for half an hour or more, to talk to Condy and grandmamma on indifferent subjects, then walked placidly away, out of the house."

"And you have not seen him since?'

Portia had the grace to hesitate an instant at this point-blank question. "Seen him? of course not, my dear child. Where is the good of people, placed as we are, seeing each other? I had begun my little fiction about Lord Dormer (rather a bold stroke, considering I had never spoken ten words to him till the night before; still, I felt pretty sure of my ground!) I had begun my fiction, I say; nothing remained for me but to carry it through. I can't say, miserable though I have been at times, that a good deal of the by-play had not diverted me. Poor Aunt Jem's bewilderment when she found Lord Dormer—instead of Ted, instead of George Blake—coming down to Halfont. And grandpapa's amiability! He was glad, at last, to see a young fellow of breeding and wit—Lord Dormer's wit!—at his table. Grandpapa positively kissed me when we came away. And Laura Wynne's face, when I told her gravely that the Lily was at the disposal of my aunt—poor, innocent old Aunt Jem—and myself for the summer.

"And Mr. Josselin?" asked Susan, as Portia again hesitated.

"Oh, Mr. Josselin has been taking care of his own amusements," said Portia, quickly. "Until a day or two ago, he was staying—yes, staying in the house with Nelly Rawdon's detestable people in Essex. But the ugliest woman in Christendom, if she knew how to flatter Ted Josselin's vanity, could command his attention—there is the truth."

"And he is not coming to St. Sauveur, then, after all?"

"Ah, that is my secret, the bit of good news I spoke of," answered Portia, lowering her voice. "Teddy is coming, and you must help me, Susan, like the good little soul you are, in keeping matters quiet. If we had a solitary grain of sense between us, Ted Josselin and I would keep apart; but—I'm sure I don't know how it is "—a momentary gleam of softest tenderness flitted across Portia Firench's face—"I don't know how it is, but we can't. The moment we see each other we fight, are reconciled, fight again; but we can't keep asunder. These things are written, I suppose. From my very heart I despise Ted Josselin for staying with the Rawdons: he despises me quite as sincerely for the part I am forced into playing with Lord Dormer; but still—put your ear closer—by the last train to-morrow evening Teddy and—command yourself, Susan—as likely as not George Blake with him, will arrive at St. Maur, from Paris!"

"And then Lord Dormer and his yacht will have to go away?" cried Susan, hardly knowing what she said, for confusion.

"And then, more imperatively than ever, Lord Dormer and his yacht will have to stay," answered Portia, in her lightest tone. "Because one is unlucky enough to have well-looking cousins, like poor Ted, is no reason why the solid good things of life, the Macbeans and Lord Dormers, should be thrown away. Lord Dormer will stay—"

Enter Miss Jemima, equipped in the village dress and bonnet in which she had travelled. "Talking of Lord Dormer still, I hear, Portia?"

"Of what better should I talk, my dear aunt? Where the heart leads, is it not natural that the tongue should follow? Now," giving a twentieth look at herself in the glass, "supposing we start. I predict that you and I will make a decided sensation among the French people, Aunt Jem. A certain young lady, with fine, frizzed hair and shoe-buckles, they will look-upon s one of themselves, of course."

The open space, or *place*, before the Hôtel Benjamin was thronged with people of every class and degree. Here—for it was still too early for the Casino ball—a group of mature Parisian ladies, ready dressed in the last fashion of short white muslin over colored skirts, like school-girls for the dance; there, a family of good St. Maur citizens, the father drinking a cup of coffee, to insure Madame and the children seats beneath one of the *café* awnings for the evening. On a pasteboard stage, under the trees, the *artiste* of whom Susan spoke was making night hideous with one of Thérèse's songs, heightened in moral tone to suit the soberer taste of the provinces, but sung half a note flat throughout. Grewsome figures of beggars, professional traders in their own deformities, were stretching forth distorted limbs, or exhibiting festering sores, and demanding "Charity, charity—in the name of the good God." Ever and awhile, the black frock of a priest or white robe of Carmelite brother would be seen to stealthily traverse the crowd, then glide away under the shade of the tall, overhanging houses into one of the smaller streets. A German band was playing waltzes and galops, with more noise than melody, in the intervals between the *artiste's* songs; while constantly, the one note of true, pure music to be heard! came the measured wash of the tide—and on this Breton coast you get the long-sustained wave of the Atlantic, not the chopping sea of the Channel—upon the shore, without the ramparts.

The scene, altogether, was an animated one; and Portia, taking her tone of spirits as usual from the color of the background, chattered gaily, and looked her handsomest and brightest as they walked along. The French ladies glanced pitying at her flannel suit, plain sailor hat, and dark, sunburnt face. I don't know how it is, but French ladies always see more to pity than to admire in a thoroughly well-built, handsome English girl. The Frenchmen, on the other hand, were in ecstasies of admiration; four or five little officers, with pretty waists, dangling swords, and long spurs and moustaches, following her about wherever she moved. (Had their eyes not been blinded by Portia's beauty or their own vanity, these officers of the great army must certainly have been mortified by Miss Jemima's demeanor toward them. Not an intention had kindhearted Jemima Ffrench of ever wounding the feelings of mortal creature; but as a Briton and an old soldier, the sight of these small warriors of the Empire was really too much for her. And so she would turn, stand, blandly curious, and watch them, as children watch the dancing figures on an organ; their tight-laced waists, baggy red trousers, diminutive stature, swaggering walk—then shake her head, almost mournfully, and smile. "It makes me think less of the conquests of our army, now that I have seen these people on their own soil!" said Miss Jemima.)

When they had taken two or three turns on the Place, and were again close to the gates of the Hôtel Benjamin, they were joined by little Lord Dormer. It may seem fantastic to assert that an English peer of large means can, under any circumstances, look unlike a gentleman; yet if, not knowing who he was, you had met the twentieth Baron of Throgmorton in his yachting suit, I believe you would have set him down for a sickly young city clerk, taking his season's ten pounds' worth of pleasure under false pretences. A yachtsman worthy of the name has, at least, a weather-tanned face, a look of honest health—*something* in his mien and gait reminding you, however distantly, of a genuine tar. But salt water, in very truth, did not agree with Lord Dormer; a misfortune not unfrequently occurring to wealthy yacht-owners. He had been a good many voyages in the Lily—in the Thames and Solent; also in the Mediterranean, himself crossing France by railway. The open Channel Lord Dormer liked not. And there had been a heavy ground-swell, though no wind, during the last thirty-six hours, and his cadaverous face told only too plainly of suffering that his attachment for Portia had bidden him stifle. The poor little Baron of Throgmorton, in his yachting suit and still under the influence of suppressed sea-sickness, was altogether not beautiful to look upon.

He loitered up to the ladies, with the languid, indifferent step of young England, and made this Chesterfieldian remark: "Well, here we are, then!"

"Yes, here we are again," said Portia, "and here is Miss Fielding. You remember meeting Miss Fielding that evening at Laura's?"

Lord Dormer's memory seemed at fault; however, he raised his hand within an inch or two of his cap.

"Miss Fielding is staying with some friends at St. Sauveur, and has been showing us the lions. Please have chairs brought for us, and we will drink our coffee, like all the rest of the world, out of doors."

"Chairs?" said Lord Dormer, looking round about him with an expression of entire vacancy. "There doesn't seem to be any—does there? *Garçon*," addressing nobody, "*apportez chaises.*"

"If you will wait one minute, Lord Dormer," said Miss Jemima, with marked politeness, "I will go in search of some myself. Nay, my dear Portia, do not move. I am quite equal to the exertion of carrying a light wicker chair or two without help."

And off walked the old soldier to the side door of the hotel, a few yards distant, returning presently with three chairs, which she carried with no more difficulty than she would have carried a parasol.

"I am sorry I could not bring one for you, too," she remarked, addressing Lord Dormer with gravity.

"Oh—ah—thanks!" said his small lordship, coolly, and quite unconscious of ironical emphasis in Miss Jemima's apology. "I dare say some one else will."

And some one else did—in the shape of Josephine, from the hotel. She brought, at the same time, a small marble-topped table, and inquired with what Monsieur and these ladies would wish to be served.

"*Servi?* oh, of course, remember the service," said Lord Dormer, taking out a shilling and tossing it on the table. "Trust to a Frenchwoman for remembering her own pocket."

Josephine took up the coin, held it a minute between her finger and thumb, looking at it curiously; then, with suave politeness, laid it down again, and repeated her question, this time addressing old Miss Ffrench.

"You really should not think every one so mercenary, Lord Dormer," Portia remarked, when Miss Jemima, in her fine Anglo-Gallic, had ordered coffee. "People often fall into mistakes that way. You see Josephine did not think your shilling worth accepting."

"I shall put it into my purse, and keep it as an amulet," said Lord Dormer, returning the shilling to his pocket. "It's the first time in my life I ever offered any one anything and got refused—on my honor, it is, and—and—" tenderly this —"I hope it will be the last, Miss Ffrench." After which somewhat leading remark he seemed all at once to grow afraid of himself, and stopped; and Portia had to go on with the conversation.

She had been out four seasons, and knew perfectly well how to find conversation for young men—of the mental calibre of Lord Dormer, rather than of George Blake. " I enjoy all this foreign scene, Lord Dormer, don't you? And yet," plaintively, " I am half sorry to have left the Lily. If ever I am a rich woman, I shall keep a yacht, and live about in the world, or rather on the waters, independent."

" Well, the sea is a great bore, too, without a pleasant party," was Lord Dormer's response.

" But I was thinking of a pleasant party, of a succession of pleasant parties—oh, what an ear-rending note ! What *do* you think of that poor woman's singing?"

Lord Dormer thought he was sick of all singing women of all nations. This one was a wretched imitation of Thérèse, but without her *chic*. Where's the good of singing of that sort, without *chic !* "

" And pray what is '*chic*," if I may ask ?" said Miss Jemima. " I have just French enough to make myself understood when I ask for a cup of coffee, but I know nothing about these new slang words."

" *Chic ?* " said Lord Dormer, slowly turning his lack-lustre eyes upon Miss Ffrench's fresh old face. " Oh, *chic*, of course, is—is *chic*."

" Thank you. I must try to remember that definition for the future. Portia, my dear," in a whisper, " who is that man who is staring so impertinently at you ? "

"A man staring impertinently ? Really, considering that we are in a crowd of about five hundred Frenchmen, aunt, I think you might make the question a little more definite ! "

But, in spite of her air of indifference, a heightened color had newly risen to Portia's cheek.

" I am not speaking of any Frenchmen at all," said Miss Jemima. " I mean the tall, good-looking man—an Englishman, evidently—who is crossing straight toward us at this instant."

" Well, unless I knew him to be in Norway, I should say that tall, good-looking man was John Dysart," answered Portia. " Do you see the likeness, Lord Dormer? I think I have heard you say you knew Mr. Dysart in Paris."

" I don't see the likeness—I see the man himself," remarked Lord Dormer, epigrammatically. " I was telling Dysart you were here not an hour ago."

Old Miss Jemima, on hearing the terrible word, " Dysart," bent forward, eagerly—" Portia, is that man *the* John Dysart ?" she whispered.

" So Lord Dormer says, Aunt Jem," answered Portia, with a smile.

" Don't recognize him, child, if you possibly can help it. Oh, these Dysarts, these Dysarts—there is no escaping from them !" cried good Miss Jemima, with bitterness.

" Well, happily, whatever their other vices may be, cannibalism is not one of them," said Portia. " John Dysart, if he should happen to remember me, will not eat us. I really don't see of what else one need be afraid. Ah, here he comes," her voice brightening with pleasure. " Poor, dear old Jack, he has not forgotten me after all ! "

CHAPTER XXXII.

FIVE years before the present time, John Dysart had been the moral bugbear, the secret, haunting dread of Jemima Ffrench's life.

From the earliest period of Portia's reconciliation to her mother's family, Teddy Josselin had been her chosen companion and playmate—a playmate who,

as we know, had, later on, stood very seriously in the way of more eligible ad-
mirers. But, until her regular introduction at least, John Dysart had been the
man whose attention the girl, in her inmost heart, most prized. He was a cousin once or twice removed, and, therefore, said Lady Erroll, the fittest attendant
in the world for a child not yet out. By all means, let John Dysart take her for
her morning rides in the park. By all means, let her keep her round dances for
him at the half-grown-up parties to which, for Portia's sake, John Dysart condescended to go. He was not a man of the highest social reputation, Lady Erroll
knew and acknowledged. When Portia was once introduced she must never
waste her time upon any cousin of them all. Meantime, no man better for forming a young girl's manner and taste than John Dysart. His being married, too,
poor fellow, made it so perfectly safe for both of them ! So the intimacy went
on ; and so, to Miss Jemima's horror, she found, when Portia was still under
seventeen, that the girl had already formed a tender, admiring friendship for the
most fascinating and least-principled member of the whole Dysart race.

"Teddy likes me to wear so and so," Portia would say, "and I wear it to
please him ; but Jack Dysart declares that it is not my color, and I know he is
right. They say Jack knows more about dress than all the milliners in London
put together." Or, when she had been to one of the so-called children's parties,
"I might have liked dancing best with Ted Josselin, if he had been there, Aunt
Jem, but fine young guardsmen are much too grand to go to children's parties.
Jack Dysart went for my sake alone, and every girl in the room, from six to sixteen, wanted to dance with him ; and he told me to put him down as often as I
liked on my card, and threw over that detestable little Lady Clementina Vernon for
me twice. Would Ted have done as much ? Besides. he takes me off my feet.
I like to be taken off my feet. When I dance with Ted I have most *real* fun,
but when I dance or walk with my Cousin Dysart I know every one points us
out. I don't, for my own part, think his yellow face and tired, gray eyes so very
handsome ; but he is unlike other people : he is thoroughly good style. Even
grandmamma is obliged to admit that Jack, with all his faults, is the most dis-
tinguished-looking man in London."

And all the arguments Miss Jemima could bring to bear against the intimacy
had unfortunately only served to strengthen it. For instance, Portia was too
young to be aware of John Dysart's evil reputation—

"Not a bit," Portia would interrupt, "I had heard of it long before I saw
him. It was more than half his evil reputation that inclined me to like him."

He was a gambler—

"But an extremely lucky one, and we always bank together at Van John. I
lose nothing that way !" the girl would retort.

A spendthrift—

"Like all nice people, dear Aunt Jem! Have *your* favorites through life
been misers, I should like to know ?"

Last of all, John Dysart was married and living separated from his wife—

"And so, alas ! can never think of me," Portia would say, with a sigh. "He
is to give me away when I marry. and I am always to ask him down for pheas-
ant shooting—for Jack and I have decided I must marry nothing under a country
gentleman and ten thousand a year. Oh dear me, if Jack Dysart was only a
country gentleman with ten thousand a year, and free—I mean, if there was no
Ted Josselin in the world !"

All this was an affair of long ago. During the last three or four years, the
years succeeding Portia's formal introduction, John Dysart had been out of

England, and Jemima Ffrench's peace of mind, as regarded this member of the family, at least, undisturbed. Time had, however, not done much to lessen the old danger. John Dysart was still a gambler—not always as lucky a one as when he and Portia banked together at Van John. He still lived apart from his wife, and still (even Miss Jemima could not but regretfully acknowledge this as he drew near) was about the last man living for whom sentimental, admiring friendship could be felt with impunity!

"Portia," he cried, as Portia started up to greet him—what a pleasant voice Jack had—Dysart though he was! "I should have known you at once, even if Dormer had not told me you were here. This really is being in luck! I never thought you and I were to meet again in this life."

He held both her hands and bent down over her as he spoke, reading, doubtless with natural cousinly interest, the changes that the last four years had wrought in her face; but with a tenderness of manner that Miss Jemima at once judged by a standard of forty years ago, and found unlawful. "Portia, my dear!" she remarked, stiffly, "I think you forget I have not the honor of Mr. John Dysart's acquaintance!"

"No? ah, to be sure not," cried Portia. "All you know of him used to be through my rose-colored descriptions. Let me introduce you—my Aunt Jemima, Mr. Dysart. Oh, Jack, how good it is to see you! I feel young again already. Do you remember our last match at écarté? I never paid you that dozen pair of gloves. What in the world have you been doing all these years? Give an account of yourself."

And thus commanded, John Dysart stood before them, his hat in his hand—his manners belonged to an older school than those of Lord Dormer—and gave an account of himself. Since that last écarté match with his cousin Portia, he had, he confessed, been a miserable wanderer on the face of the earth; picking up a scanty subsistence on the fish and fowl of Norway in summer; living on the fruits of the earth in the south in winter—

"And filling up all odds and ends of time with Paris," interrupted Portia. "I have heard of you, and, what is more, I'm pretty certain I saw you with my own eyes one day in the Champs—"

She stopped short, turned crimson, and bit her lip.

"You saw Mr. Dysart in Paris with your own eyes?" remarked Miss Jemima, but without any great surprise. She was too accustomed to the florid little arabesque of mendacity with which Portia enlivened conversation to be much taken aback by the audacity of this, or any other assertion.

"In my dreams, Aunt Jem, in my dreams. Don't you know I'm a little bit of a clairvoyant? Ah, here comes the incorruptible Josephine. Fancy, Jack! Lord Dormer has had a new experience this evening, has found a human being, and a Frenchwoman, who was above the temptation of the British shilling."

Lord Dormer, from the moment John Dysart appeared, had been looking the very picture of perplexed despondency. He had been uncomfortably, vaguely jealous of Teddy Josselin ever since that night when he first began to forfeit his peace of mind at Mrs. Wynne's supper-party—some miserable instinct of his own counteracting all Portia's pretty acting, all Portia's touching candor on the subject of her forlorn and suitorless condition. And here he had brought the Lily across the Channel, and made himself sick (he more than half suspected ridiculous) only to meet a more dangerous rival still; a cousin again, and one whom Portia had the impertinence to call openly by his Christian name in his very presence! Ah, well, Jack Dysart might be a lady-killer, but he was a mar-

ried man ! Lord Dormer had the advantage of him there. At the first syllable
of serious intentions, of settlements, in what position in the race would the
handsomest man in Europe find himself with a girl like Portia Ffrench ? From
the thought of marriage in the abstract all the strength of Lord Dormer's intellect had hitherto recoiled. If such a sacrifice at any future date were to be
forced upon him by untoward fortune, he had always known pretty well what
kind of an alliance his impoverished estates must bid him seek. And still his
present fancy was ardent enough to carry him up to the very altar rails, beside a
penniless bride ; and his sharp, new-born jealousy of Jack Dysart told him at this
moment that it was so! Had not poor little Lord Dormer good cause to look
despondent and perplexed ?

Josephine ran off to the courtyard for another chair, and by Portia's invitation, John Dysart, who had now been introduced to Susan, joined the party. He
belonged to a class which I believe furnishes the very pleasantest "Joseph Surface" kind of acquaintance in the world ; a class of Englishmen to whom Continental cities are familiar as London, but who, "not changing their country
manners for those of foreign parts," have never degenerated by the smallest detail into Anglicized foreigners or foreign Englishmen. John Dysart's dress and
smooth-shorn face were as ultra English as any model to which a Parisian dandy
could aspire ; he spoke the English language in its integrity ; his breeding was
English ; he professed English opinions. And still there was some undefined
nomadic flavor about him, a certain affluence of disposition, one may say, a capacity of looking at all things and all men with perfectly wide, good-humored tol-
erance, which does not belong, as a rule, to Englishmen who live in England.
You could detect this foreign graft in his nature by the merest of trifles. When the
poor strolling singer had shrieked out her next song, John Dysart cried "*brava*"
with the mechanical kindness of the French crowd at its finish, tossing the
smallest of silver coins to the withered child in rouge and spangles who came
round with her tambourine. He drank the well-chiccoried coffee, over which
Lord Dormer made wry faces, and seemed to find it good. He had desperately
wicked little stories to tell of more than one notability whom he pointed out in
the crowd ; but he told them pleasantly ; none of the edge off the malice, but all
the sub-acrid flavor of pharisaism—without which the true Englishman so seldom tells a story—wanting. (It must be remembered that John Dysart was a
man without any moral standing-point whatever.) And then he was charming to
old Jemima Ffrench—as very few Englishmen are ever charming to old ladies !
talked more to her than to either of the girls, held her coffee-cup, ran into the
hotel for a footstool for her, made her pin her shawl round her throat, "people
who didn't know the Breton climate must take care of themselves after sunset ; "
all this with such simple good faith, such thorough *gallantry*, as Charles Lamb
understood the term, as I must confess caused most of Miss Jemima's prejudices
against him to subside.

"I take a deep, a brotherly interest in Portia," he contrived to whisper to her
at last. "I grew as fond of the child as if she had been my own daughter," John
Dysart was now six-and-thirty, "when I used to see so much of her in Eaton
Square. A wonderfully graceful little creature she was," he went on, his eyes
resting musingly on the fine outline of Portia's figure. "I can remember my
cousin, Harry Ffrench, years and years ago in Brussels. Ah, what a handsome
fellow he was—the very line of face of Portia ! "

At the mention of Harry Ffrench, Miss Jemima's last scruples melted like
snow at noon.

"You will let me come and see you?" said John Dysart, watching her face. "You are staying at the Hôtel Benjamin—when may I call? at what hour shall I have the best chance of finding you alone? So delightful to come upon people one has long wanted to know like this!" he added, almost with effusion.

Miss Jemima, thus pressed, could only answer that at any time before twelve to-morrow she would be in, awaiting Mr. Dysart's visit—Portia, seeking to restore Lord Dormer's temper in honeyed under-tones, heard both request and answer—and then John Dysart rose to depart. He had an engagement with some friends of his, the Ramsays, at the Casino—Portia must recollect Ironside Ramsay who married the little Welsh heiress? Of course his cousin meant to belong to the Casino during their stay at St. Maur?

"I think not," said Miss Jemima, feeling she must make a stand somewhere. "We have come abroad for sea air, not dissipation. Portia has had quite enough of that in London."

"But why not have sea air and dissipation too?" cried Portia. "By all means let us belong to the Casino, to everything that is going on. And so the Ironside Ramsays are here! Is poor Mrs. Ramsay as terribly made up as ever, I wonder!"

"Mrs. Ramsay is—well, Mrs. Ramsay is not younger, perhaps," said John Dysart, a little evasively.

"I never knew her, but I detested her. I hope you are not intimate with those people, Mr. Dysart?"

"Ramsay and I are old friends. He is one of the best-hearted little creatures in the world."

"And Mrs. Ramsay?"

Just at this moment the tall, slouching figure of Adam Byng emerged from the crowd, and in the diversion that followed—old Miss Jemima begging to be introduced to Susan's uncle, Lord Dormer walking away too sulky to take notice of anybody—Portia and John Dysart found themselves for a minute alone.

"And so my cousin Portia has grown clairvoyant!" said Jack, in a whisper. "Ah, you are not so prudent now as you were at sixteen. I never knew you make a slip of the tongue then."

"A slip of the tongue! what are you talking about?" answered Portia, innocently.

"Only about the day when you saw me in the Champs Elysées. My dear child, I must have been clairvoyant, too, for " Jack's lips approached Portia's ear closer, "I recognized you. You had on a thick veil—the poor little thing had done her best—but I knew you in a moment. You, and unless I am very much mistaken, your companion, too. Now what do I deserve for keeping the secret so well?"

For a moment, for once in her life, Portia Ffrench stood speechless. "Don't have anything to do with these horrible Ramsays, and I'll tell you what you deserve," she answered, recovering her self-possession with an effort.

"Portia, my dear," cried Miss Jemima, "Susan is going home. Do you know how late it is?"

Then, after another whisper or two, the cousins bade each other good night, and John Dysart strolled slowly away in the direction of the Casino.

A curious expression came over Portia's face as she watched him depart.

CHAPTER XXXIII

THE St. Maur Casino stands upon the causeway that connects the little sea-girt fortress with the mainland, a couple of hundred yards or so outside the city walls. Lights, voices, the sound of flutes and violins were issuing through its open windows as Susan and Adam Byng approached the gateway; and, at Susan's solicitation, they loitered there awhile to listen to the music and catch what furtive glances they could of the gay company within.

"I don't know what Mrs. Byng will say to us," remarked Adam, when they were walking on their road again. "This has been an evening altogether of d's-sipation. I haven't seen the Casino lighted and the people dancing there these three years."

For a minute or two Susan hesitated; at last—"Uncle Adam," she whispered, stealing up her hand under his arm, "I think, if you don't mind, I should like to subscribe to the Casino." The vision of so many muslin-clad figures, the sound of the dance music, the glitter, the joyousness of the scene, had fired Susan—with the ball fever common to girls of her age? no: but a burning dread of the temptations to forget *her* that were awaiting George Blake! Ah, could not her jealous heart picture him surrounded by enchanting French ladies, with Portia, with all the world smiling on him, and she, in her black frock, standing at Uncle Adam's side in the darkness without? "I should never want to dance, of course, but I should like just to see the fine dresses and hear the music; and the Misses Ffrench would take me."

"The subscription costs twelve francs a month," said Uncle Adam, in a scared voice. "Only two of our resident families belong to the Casino, and they are both moneyed people. Nay, nay, child, thee must moderate thy wishes. We can walk over once or twice during the season and look in, as we have done to-night. What more can thee desire? The moths outside the window are better off than those who burn their wings in the candle little Susan!"

It was a quarter to ten o'clock when they reached the Petit Tambour. Uncle Adam had never once been out late since his marriage, and crept more meekly even than his wont to the dining-room, where Mrs. Byng, by the light of a solitary candle, sat at her needle.

"You crossed by the ferry," she said, in her measured, passionless voice. "Louison saw you. Susan, I request you not to lead your uncle into these extravagances."

"The child felt tired, and it chanced had a two-sous piece in her pocket," pleaded poor old Adam. "It shall not happen again, my dear, I promise you."

"All your acts of folly are never to happen again, Mr. Byng. Yesterday 'twas a brioche, to-day the ferry. Two sous a day squandered are thirty-six francs a year squandered. On what pleasures of my own do I spend thirty-six francs a year?"

"On none, my love, on none. Susan and I were in the wrong, and we confess it. But for all that, I have not lost money on the evening! While Susan was with her friends at the Benjamin, I drank a cup of coffee and played a game of dominoes with Jean Poujol, and won both; and more. See, I make you a present of the stakes."

And Uncle Adam laid down a silver piece of twenty-five centimes before his wife.

"And if you had lost?" she remarked sternly, but putting the money in her pocket.

"Jean Poujol would have taken it out in picotees," returned Adam, with a chuckle of simple exultation over his own shrewdness. "We agreed that before we played. I have more young plants than I know what to do with, and—"

"—Jean Poujol is no fool," interrupted Mrs. Byng. "The picotees are worth a franc a dozen, at least."

Still the heart of the woman was mollified. For Adam to stake flower-roots, otherwise unsalable, against actual hard cash, raised him probably as much as it was possible for him to be raised in his wife's respect. At all events the poor old fellow, with half an inch of candle, was allowed to go up to his bed without farther reprimand. "To you, Susan," said Mrs. Byng, laying a cold hand on the young girl's arm, "I have a few words to speak. They may as well be spoken to-night as another time. Do you know, child, what extravagance means?"

"I'm sure I'm very sorry," stammered Susan, trying to look contrite. "I'll never cross the ferry again unless you give me leave."

"I do not speak of the ferry only. I speak of the way you squander money on trifles, on dress—of which you have already more than sufficient—on your whole plan of life. A rational being when he rises in the morning should say to himself, 'how much can I save to-day?' The first thought of a fool is 'how much can I spend?' What brought your uncle to poverty? Extravagance. Extravagant ideas of comfort, extravagant ideas of human nature—the proof of which was trusting his money in a friend's bank! What has brought all the people you see in this place to poverty? Extravagance—for, mind, I call want of honesty, in its way, extravagance. Now as long as you are under my charge I do not mean that you should waste your money. I mean to do my duty by you."

"Thank you, ma'am," said Susan, faintly.

"I have been setting down different items to-night, and have made out, as near as possible, what you add to our expenses. You don't eat more, I dare say, than other growing girls, but you eat a great deal. You more than double our butcher s bill alone "—Susan's face crimsoned with shame—" and you also eat fruit from morning till night. Altogether your keep—of course I reckon fruit and vegetables at market price—would cost every franc of twenty pounds a year. Well, I propose that you should have another ten pounds, for dress, pocket money, seat in church, collections, laundress, and give me the remaining ten to lay by for you. I could put it out with perfect safety at six per cent., and on the day you are twenty-one you would have saved interest and principal; after that of course the whole of your money will be in your own hands and must be invested anew."

Four years hence—years! unless Tom Collinson returned to marry her, spent in the Petit Tambour! In a dozen words Mrs. Byng had epitomized the story of a youth, with the fairness and odor and keen capacity of youth for enjoyment crushed from it: the best years of a woman's life spent in saving francs and reckoning centimes! Susan's heart sank within her.

"You have not had time to know me yet," went on Mrs. Byng. "Your Uncle Adam picks you his peaches and flowers, and allows you to throw away money on brioches and ferry-boats. Naturally you like him best. I am a person of few words. When you know me better you will find, as Mr. Byng has done, that I am a person of deeds. I have my ideas of duty, and I keep to them. Light your candle, and hold it upright: there were two spots of grease on the stairs this morning. To-morrow our new account begins. You will pay by the quarter, in advance, and I will at once take charge of whatever spare money you have in hand."

Susan crept up the polished stairs of the Petit Tambour, holding her candle upright as she was bidden, and as soon as she reached her own room wiped away the last stroke from the whitewash on the wall, then ran and seated herself before her glass. She was a pretty little girl, decidedly! not faultless of feature, not in any way to compare with Portia, but pretty. (By a single admiring glance, by two or three whispered words, John Dysart had substantiated all the compliments that sounded so dubious from Tom Collinson.) And George Blake was coming to-morrow. And there were people who lived in a world of shillings and half-pence; who looked upon money as anything save a means of buying nice things, of giving pleasure, directly or indirectly, to those one loved. How she pitied Mrs. Byng and poor Uncle Adam: how she pitied everyone to whom to-morrow did not mean the delicious hopes of seventeen! Now, should she put her hair on crimping pins or not? This was momentous. Portia's judgment was all in favor of the new Parisian style: not so Miss Jemima's. Which would George Blake be likeliest to prefer, nature or artifice? She decided promptly in favor of nature; then, when her head had been five minutes on the pillow, veered round; remembered the French ladies in their ball dresses. and how *they* had looked with balloon-spread, decorated heads; rose and by the light of the stars—for Mrs. Byng allowed no lucifer matches throughout the Petit Tambour—put up her soft brown curls on crimping pins. Then, in such tortured positions as crimping pins allow, lay awake, thinking to-morrow—to-morrow—until the soft voice of the convent bell striking midnight told her that to-morrow was already here.

Many a night during the months to come, Susan Fielding lay awake till midnight; but never again from pure, unmixed happiness after to-night!

She was out betimes with Uncle Adam in the kitchen garden next morning; eating peaches—the peaches for which she was to be charged market price! laughing and chattering with the old man over his work; jumping up and down the garden-paths from sheer excess of contentment. By-and-by followed the second breakfast, and in the middle of the meal came the postman's loud ring at the front bell, and a letter for Mademoiselle Fielding, bearing the postmark, "Paris." Susan blushed up to the eyes as she bent over it, recognizing the handwriting.

"You get a great many letters," remarked Mrs. Byng. "*I* never get any. Letters require answers. Nothing fritters money away like postage."

Susan murmured out some utterly wild and foolish remarks about Paris, and old Halfont friends, and no answer being needed ; then put her letter, unopened, into her pocket, and, the moment breakfast was done, ran out into the flower garden to read it.

My dear little Susan,—I am afraid I shall not see you quite as soon as I thought. I find I have more to do in Paris than I expected. I shall certainly not reach Brittany for another three or four days. Till then, good-by. In great haste, your devoted friend,

George Blake.

The letter fell from her hands ; she stared up blankly overhead. When she is an old woman Susan will remember the glaring blueness of the sky at that particular moment, the humming of the bees among Uncle Adam's flowers, the quivering, sunny air, the morning carol of a canary in a neighbor's window—the intolerable apathy of the whole bright, outer world ! "Not reach Brittany for another three or four days." She picked up the letter, re-read it, repeated the words aloud before she could thoroughly bring home to herself the immensity of her disappointment: George Blake not coming, and the last line of her calendar obliterated, the day that she had looked forward to so long already wearing on toward noon ! Boum, boum, went the convent clock, striking ten. Did clock ever strike with such stolid slowness before ? Susan recalled the happiness with which she had counted its beats last at midnight—ah, that contrast was too great ! Tears rushed into her eyes, a suffocating tightness came in her throat; crushing the letter in her hand she ran back into the house, and to her own room, locked the door, flung herself on her knees beside her little bed, and burst into a passion of crying. How could she, how can any thwarted child, look forward to the eternity of three or four days ? She was disappointed now.

"I shall never expect you again—I shall never believe what he writes again," she sobbed to herself. "If it had been poor Tom Collinson. he would have come. Tom Collinson would have cared more for me than for all the *Parises* in the world. I love Tom best—I mean I wish I did love him best. Oh, why did I ever see Mr. Blake ? why does he care so little for me ? And still," holding the letter up close—and with a gesture. rather of forgiveness than of anger—to her near-sighted eyes, "all he says is kind. 'My dear little Susan,' and 'Your devoted friend.' Ah, but does he mean 'devoted?' Is that only how people who know how to *write fine* finish off their letters ?"

In the course of the afternoon the two Misses Ffrench found their way to the Petit Tambour ; Susan was alone in the drawing-room, darning window blinds— her aunt already set her plenty of tasks for odd times—Uncle Adam away in the kitchen garden, Mrs. Byng out of the house.

"And so this is the Petit Tambour !" cried Portia, as she ran to the open window—the lichened walls, and smalt-blue sky. and scarlet masses of geranium-bloom setting forth to perfection the rich tinting of her southern-looking face. "I suppose one would get as tired of picturesqueness as of hideousness in time, but just at first I must say it is pleasant to the eyes to rest on something more

romantic than Hounslow Heath!" She had been running all the morning over
the streets of St. Maur, attended by John Dysart: in every quaint bit of fif-
teenth-century architecture, in every narrow glimpse of green sea, discovering a
new effective background for the graceful central figure of all her thoughts.
"Oh, what high-backed chairs! Susan, my dear, do you really look forward to
living in this Castle of Otranto, winter and summer? Why, what have you done
to yourself? The becoming crimped hair all gone, and the rough Addison Lodge
curls come back again!"

"I crimped my hair last night," said Susan, "and this morning lost heart—
lost heart, Miss Portia, about everything, and washed it with cold water till it
got back to its own old way. A thought came into my mind that perhaps it
wasn't lucky to take so much trouble with one's self beforehand. I've always
heard that the happiest times of life come when one doesn't go out of one's way
to meet them."

"Ah, the copy-books say that," remarked Portia. "I know how much happiness I should get unless I went a very great deal out of my way to meet it. If
I had taken things as fate sent them, where should I be at this moment?"

"In whatever room at Halfont the plasterers are not," said Miss Jemima.
"And as far as I can see, very much better off you would be there than here."

"Because the little French bagman would talk to you at breakfast, Aunt
Jem, or because we have tumbled across Jack Dysart, and you are angry with
yourself for liking him—which?"

"For every reason," answered Miss Jemima. "If I had known in the least
what the tone of these foreign watering places was, you may be sure I would
never have crossed the Channel with you, Portia. French people are not *human!*" went on Miss Jemima, with warmth. "I have lived in India, I have
travelled over half the civilized globe, but I never saw anything so humiliating
to myself as a human being as what I have seen to-day. Old men and women,
fathers and mothers of families, jumping up and down, in yellow sacks, in the sea
together. I hope, my dear little Susan, you have not been on the St. Maur sands
of a morning?"

Susan confessed that she had not. She spent her mornings and afternoons at
the Petit Tambour; had never seen as much of the St. Maur gayeties as she had
seen in front of the Hotel Benjamin last night.

"Well, then, you will have an opportunity of enlarging your experience this
evening," said Portia, "for we are going to take you back with us now. We are
all to dine in a party at the *table-d'hôte*—ourselves, Lord Dormer, and my
cousin (you have made an *immense* impression upon my cousin, I can tell you,
Susan!) and then we will walk round and look at the people in the Casino and
undertake, some of us, to see you home afterwards."

For a minute and a half Susan tried, with real sincerity, to excuse herself;
she was not in good spirits to-day; Mrs. Byng was not at home to give her
leave; ought she to leave Uncle Adam alone? Portia, however, put so much
insistance into her manner that one by one these objections melted away. Impossible not to feel a little pleased that she had made an impression on John
Dysart—in her heart Susan thinks John Dysart charming! And as Mr. Blake
was able to amuse himself in Paris, was it not the wisest thing for her to try and
make time pass pleasantly in St. Sauveur! Reader, did you ever know a girl
of seventeen so much in love as to disdain amusement under an absent lover's
neglect? Susan ran to her room, dressed herself with care, put on her buckled
shoes, her prettiest earrings and bracelet, then ran away to the kitchen garden

where Uncle Adam was trenching out his celery, and acquainted him, with as much assurance as she could master, that she was going to St. Maur with the Misses Ffrench for the evening.

"And I—I am to break this to Mrs. Byng!" said poor old Adam, leaning on his spade and looking frightened, "and likelier than not they will cross by the ferry! Susan, Susan, thee will have thy head turned with so much pleasure."

"But only for ten days, Uncle Adam!" pleaded Susan. "In ten days my friends will be gone, and I shall never want to cross the ferry again all the winter."

Upon which Uncle Adam not only relented, but coming as far as the entrance of the flower garden, cut the choicest bud off his choicest noisette rose for Susan's waist-belt; a bud which, by the most natural process imaginable, found its way to the button-hole of Portia Ffrench's jacket the moment they quitted the door of the Petit Tambour.

It was now half past five, and people were just beginning to issue forth from the lodging-houses toward the *tables-d'hôte*. At the principal thoroughfares stood peasant children, offering bouquets to the gayly-dressed ladies as they passed along; the afternoon sun shone mellow across the dead calm sea; a band was playing in the High street—St. Sauveur altogether looking its brightest. On their road down to the ferry Susan and the Misses Ffrench had to pass the cemetery gates. Three coffins, one large, two small, were being carried in together. A priest walked chanting at their head.

"Ah, that priest's voice—how well I know it!" said Susan. "The cemetery lies between our garden and the river, and I can hear the funerals from morning till night."

"The funerals?" repeated Miss Jemima, looking interested. "Why, what can so many people be dying of in this fine summer weather?"

"Cholera, if you please, ma'am," answered Susan, matter of fact as usual.

"Cholera—good heavens, how disgusting!" said Portia, changing color. "Come away quick, Aunt Jem. Never let us pass up this shocking street again."

"I shouldn't think the street can matter much," said Susan. "The cholera patients are dying everywhere, my Uncle Adam says. I don't suppose cholera can really be catching, for every minute Uncle Adam can spare from the garden he is among them, nursing the dying, stopping beside the dead—doing as much, he says himself, as a man without money can do—and still he takes no harm."

"And I—I, for one, *love* your Uncle Adam!" exclaimed Jemima Ffrench—

"—Has it reached St. Maur?" said Portia uneasily. "Is it known? Why do so many visitors remain in the place?"

"The visitors know nothing at all about it," answered Susan. "Only the very poor are dying, and my aunt says there won't be any stir till some rich person gets carried off. She wouldn't be pleased with me for talking about it. I have heard her tell Uncle Adam never to say a word about cholera before visitors."

"And is it in St. Maur—near the Hotel Benjamin?" repeated Portia, looking scared and white.

"I believe it is everywhere, Miss Portia. There were thirty-six deaths from cholera yesterday; the most we have had in one day yet."

A look, as of some sudden resolve, lighted up Jemima Ffrench's face: "And all these unhappy creatures are poor, you tell me, child?"

"So poor that they not only want bread but water, Uncle Adam says. In many parts of the town water fit to drink can be only got by paying for it. Uncle Adam fetches water for them from the fountain upon the top of the hill, a couple of flasks at a time. In that kind of way he can help them a great deal."

Miss Jemima said nothing further, but the color kindled in her cheek; an expression so warm, so tenderly compassionate as to make that old face beautiful, came round her lips. (A superannuated hunter can no more listen unmoved to the neighboring bay of hounds than could Jemima French to an account of sickness, poverty, or pain!) Portia hastened to shift the conversation.

"I suppose wherever one is there is some kind of revolting disease going on, only generally one is lucky enough not to know it. We must take care to drink champagne instead of claret, and for the future keep ourselves amused and out of sight of all cemeteries. I declare the very sight of those coffins has made me sick and chill."

Lord Dormer and John Dysart were waiting for the ladies in the salle of the Hotel Benjamin, and Portia sat between them at dinner. Little Lord Dormer, guided by Mr. Dysart's superior judgment, ordered the best wines the house afforded; a harp and violin discoursed pleasant, if not classical music beside the fountain in the court-yard; and long before the dinner, with its multitudinous courses, was over, no one but Miss Jemima remembered the three coffins and the priest chanting at their head, and the sorrowful story of those who needed not bread alone but a drink of cold water in their agony!

Lord Dormer's hopes and temper had undergone a decided change for the better since last night. Whatever the terms of friendship arrived at between Portia and John Dysart during their morning's walk, all her attention, all her smiles were Lord Dormer's now. And Mr. Dysart seemed thoroughly acquiescent; ate an excellent dinner, amply justified his own connoisseurship in wine, and also did all he could (not a little, be it said) to turn the head of the blushing, shy-eyed child who sat upon his left hand. Susan's inmost heart was filled, of course, with thoughts of George Blake and of her disappointment, but she could no more help coloring and dimpling and feeling flattered at John Dysart's attentions than a daisy, closed by a shower ten minutes ago, can help reopening its petals to the sun. He helped her to the nicest bits in every dish; made her, for the first time in her life, sip champagne; cut her fruit for her with the silver clasp-knife which long experience of French hotels taught him to carry in his pocket; told her what ought to be her colors; begged her—with a look of his handsome gray eyes that Susan felt sure he never could have given to any woman but herself—to regard him as a brother as long as their acquaintance lasted. Susan blushed and dimpled. Lord Dormer blushed and sighed. All this time Portia and John Dysart were flirting as desperately as they had ever done in the old days in Eaton square. Flirting, as only adepts in the science can; without a look, without a word: every bit of nonsense that each addressed to their unconscious fellow-actors bearing a hidden meaning to the ear for which it was in fact destined.

They had coffee in the court-yard after dinner, and by-and-by strolled round along the sands to the Casino, where Susan Fielding, for the first time in her life, found herself inside a ball-room. The little girl had never regularly learned to dance, modern round dancing being one of the many social subjects on which Joseph Fielding held strong opinions, but Miss Collinson had once, on her birthday shown her the polka step, and instinct told her she could move tunefully to any music that was played. So when Portia and Lord Dormer joined the waltzers—Portia's fine high-bred face held a good two inches above Lord Dormer's head—poor Susan, standing in a corner at Miss Jemima's side, could not help looking at the delights of the scene before her with a good deal of wistful eagerness in her eyes—

John Dysart, who was talking to some people the other side the room, happened to turn just then, and saw her. He came across and offered her his arm. " You are keeping this waltz for me, I hope, Miss Fielding ? "

" Oh, *do* you think I could dance it ? " cried Susan, all in a flutter ! " I should like, but I'm afraid I don't know my steps well enough."

" I can teach you the steps as we go on," said John Dysart, smiling. And in another minute Susan found herself borne swiftly, musically along, in the arms of one of the best dancers in Europe, through the crowd.

She danced, as you will sometimes find children of eight or nine dance, by pure intuition. All the graces of style that can be learned from a dancing master wanting ; but such a flow of natural harmony, of innocent girlish abandonment in her movements as more than atoned for their absence. John Dysart, one of whose few principles it was never to dance but with partners upon whom the world had set its seal of approval—John Dysart would scarcely lose a bar of this waltz ! He complimented Susan till her cheeks tingled at its conclusion, and instead of taking her back at once to Miss Jemima led her out upon the small terrace or plateau of grass which lay between the ball-room and the road.

The moon has risen now, and Susan's excited, flushed face can be seen, plain as if it were noon-day, by two young men—travellers newly arrived by the mail from Paris—who are standing just outside the Casino gates.

" You must give me another dance before the evening is over," remarks John Dysart, bending over her with his tender, fraternal air. " I take great credit to myself for that first waltz."

" Oh, but are you sure I made no wrong steps ? " asks Susan, lifting up her great, serious eyes. " I thought once I should have fallen, my feet seemed flying in the air, but you saved me so beautifully. I hope you didn't think me very stupid, but—I couldn't help clinging to you ! "

John Dysart's answer is conveyed in a whisper, and then Susan laughs—that foolish, sweet little laugh one of the listeners has got so well by heart ! and arm in arm they walk back slowly toward the ball-room.

" So much for taking people unawares, Blake," observes Teddy Josselin, in his languid, good-humored voice. " Old Jack Dysart, too, of all men living, to have turned up here ! I told you no one would die of grief if we did keep away another eight-and-forty-hours. Now, let us see what other surprises are in store for us. Aunt Jemima, by Jove—look in through that open window—Aunt Jemima, under the mask of écarté, coquetting shamefully with half a dozen Frenchmen at a time. My poor friend, let us make our way boldly in at once, and know the worst ! "

CHAPTER XXXIV.

" Is it possible that Miss Fielding is without a partner for this dance ? "

A quadrille had begun, and Susan, hemmed in by strangers on either side, stood watching the dancers.

Among all the onerous duties of a soldier's life, Jemima Ffrench had be enexempt from those of a ball-room chaperon. She was, in consequence, profoundly ignorant of ball-room customs and moralities. If young ladies were capable of protecting themselves while a waltz was going on, Miss Jemima could no more

see why they needed protection when it was over than she could see why old
ladies should not move about in places of entertainment just as unconcernedly
as old men, if they were so minded. As soon, therefore, as both her charges
were off her hands, she had walked away, unescorted, to the card-room, and finding the faces of the écarté players a more entertaining study than those of the
dancers, had remained there. Susan was thus left alone.

"Is it possible that Miss Fielding is without a partner for this dance?" asked
a voice suddenly, at her side.

She turned round with a start, got crimson, got white. "You—you have
kept your promise after all, then?" she stammered, with trembling lips. If
Blake had not already known Susan Fielding's secret, surely that changing color,
those trembling lips must have betrayed it to him!

"Yes, I have kept my promise. When the time came I found I could not
stay away. Josselin was in Paris with me, and when I wrote to you we had decided to remain there together for another two or three days; but, Susan, I was
rash enough to think some one in St. Sauveur would be disappointed, and started
and—which was a great deal more difficult—made Josselin start, by the mail this
morning. What a good dancer you are, my dear! What enviable enjoyment
that last dance afforded you, I needn't have feared your life would be dull—even
in Brittany."

Now Susan had not wisdom to know, as an older woman would have known,
what an enormous advance in regard was shown by Blake's semi-bitter tone.
She felt herself tacitly arraigned for want of feeling, for inconstancy, and put
herself on the defensive. "You may think what you like, but I was never more
disappointed in my life than when I opened your letter. I felt I had got a blow.
I felt I could never believe you or any one else again."

"And to drown these cynical feelings resolved to finish the day with
dancing?"

"Portia and Miss Jemima asked me to dine with them, and to come to this
place afterwards, and I was glad to come. I thought—if *other people* could
amuse themselves in Paris, why, I would try to amuse myself in St. Sauveur."

"And have succeeded?"

"I can't help liking waltzing—rather. Did you watch me dance that last
waltz? My partner was Mr. Dysart, a cousin of Miss Portia's. I don't know
whether I did the step well or ill, but I couldn't help liking it. I know now I've
danced in my heart all my life. Dancing and music are very much the same,
really, you know."

The great short-sighted eyes stole up to Blake as Susan delivered herself of
this wise platitude: every dimple in her face was telling its story of absolute contentment at seeing him.

"Take my arm, my dear;" her hand obeyed him on the instant—"you and I
can't quarrel if we try, little Susan—and show me all the wickedness of the place.
We got a glimpse just now of Miss Ffrench, of old Miss Ffrench, I mean.
Portia is here, I suppose?" Even yet Portia's name came with a slight want of
fluency from Blake's lips.

"Portia must be with Lord Dormer," said Susan. "They danced the waltz
together, I know, but I don't see them in the ball-room."

"Lord Dormer? ah, yes, Josselin mentioned that he was in St. Maur, too."

"He brought Miss Jemima and Portia across in his yacht, and he has invited me to go on board some day, but I don't mean to go. I want to see nothing belonging to him. I don't care for Lord Dormer."

"Which shows that you are an ignorant little girl, Lord Dormer being rich and unappropriated. Why, even Portia Ffrench, I dare say, manages to endure him?"

"Oh, Portia can afford to endure stupid people because she is clever herself."

"And is Mr. Dysart clever?"

"He seems clever against me, sir."

"'Clever against me, sir!' Now we are back at Halfont, on the river bank. What a pleasant night that was, Susan! Do you remember our long talk under the trees, my dear, and our duet—"

"And how you and Portia went away to the window and forgot me as soon as ever I had sung it? Yes; I remember quite well."

"And how I took you home afterwards? The nightingales sung deliciously—"

"It was only frogs, Mr. Blake."

"And the stars shone—"

"No, sir; it rained. Don't you remember Miss Jemima threatened me with Jekyll and an umbrella?"

"Susan, you hard little child, you have not an ounce of sentiment in your composition! You don't soften a bit at the recollection of that evening which to me—" et cetera.

Odd that in all these matters the one who feels deepest is never the one who is able to say the pretty things. Blake had a talent, quite as marked as any of of his artistic ones, for love-making—Susan Fielding had a genius for loving. Wide difference between the two!

"I'm sure I thought you had forgotten long ago," she answered, a perfectly choking sensation of pleasure at her heart. "I have had nothing to put it all out of my mind."

"What, not the engagement with Tom Collinson?"

Susan was silent.

They quitted the ball-room and after taking a few turns outside came across Ted Josselin, composedly enjoying the sea air as he leaned up against one of the pilasters of the balcony—the very picture of contentment.

"Well, Josselin, have you met with any old friends yet?" asked Blake, touching his shoulder.

Teddy turned his head about an inch and a half. "Ah, is it you? Cruel to interrupt a man who has strung his energies up to the delicious point of not thinking. I have seen no one. I have looked for no one. I was speculating, until I got beyond thought, upon the happiness of being a limpet. Ah, Susan?" holding out his hand, "you have done waltzing! and you never wrote to tell me about lodgings, as you promised!"

He sauntered along with them, on Susan's other side, through the "gardens" belonging to the Casino; half an acre or so of sand, neatly laid out with rustic baskets, plaster of Paris goddesses, and wire-work archways, but no flowers. At the end nearest the shore a bend in the walk brought them suddenly upon John Dysart and Portia. John Dysart, who was leaning with considerable earnestness of manner over his companion, had his head turned aside. Portia's face—the beautiful, discontented face which even at this moment Blake could not help crediting with so much more emotion than its owner was capable of feeling—was distinctly outlined against the opal background of still sea.

"Weary and dissatisfied with everything! You used to tell me just the same story when you were sixteen," said John Dysart's fluent, low voice. "My dear child, shall I tell you why you are dissatisfied? You ask too much from life. You have not learned to live for the minute ; to expunge the words 'to-morrow' and 'yesterday' from your vocabulary."

"Yes, if the follies of yesterday could be expunged!" said Portia, in a tone half of penitence, half regret.

"And which particular folly are you speaking of, my dear little cousin? The folly of being found out, or—"

"What sort of *écrevisses* does one get down here, Susan?" asked Teddy, in his laziest manner. "Almost the last remaining weakness life has left in me is for *écrevisses*, and some one in Paris said St. Maur was the place for them."

Portia started round with a gesture in which, for once, there was no self-consciousness, no acting. Her companion's cool face remained imperturbable. Impossible, perhaps, for John Dysart to be surprised by anything more in this world. She came forward and spoke to Blake first. "Who would have thought of seeing you in these wilds, Mr. Blake?—but really, St. Maur is the oddest place for coming across people! Ah, Mr. Josselin, I did not see you for the moment. You remember John Dysart?"

"Very well indeed," answered Teddy quietly. "How are you, Dysart?" The cousins shook hands sufficiently cordially. "Been here any time? then you are just the fellow I want. You can answer me an important question." Teddy laid his hand on the other's arm and looked tremendously in earnest. "Is it true that *écrevisses* are the specialty of this coast?"

On every point connected with the table John Dysart was an authority. He was in a position to assure Teddy Josselin that his hopes had not been misdirected. The bay they saw before them supplied half the markets in Paris with crayfish. Such a hotel in St. Maur was the proper house to eat them at. Why shouldn't he and Ted breakfast there together to-morrow? "I call you Ted as in the old days, just as I call Portia, Portia;" he remarked, with pleasant candor. "I can't bring myself to look upon you as anything but children still."

The quadrille had been over some minutes, and just now sounded the first notes of another waltz. "Dear me, I'm afraid I am engaged for this," said John Dysart, making a pretence of examining his card (so he was engaged : to Portia). I suppose I must go and look for my partner. Portia, what dance is there a possibility of your being able to spare me by-and-by?"

"Whatever you ask me for," she answered, coldly. Portia Ffrench had pride, of its kind : and she recoiled from this secret, tacit understanding which John Dysart, by a word, had contrived to establish between them. "I am engaged for the next to Lord Dormer. After that, if we don't go away—"

"Very well. Make use of me, or throw me over, just as you like—my old fate!" And away John Dysart took himself, half humming the air of the waltz aloud as he walked.

For a minute there was a slightly awkward silence: then, Susan uttering some commonplace little note of admiration about the beauty of the moonlight, Blake considerately began to walk with her in the direction of the sea, and Teddy Josselin and Portia were left alone.

"What are you doing, here?" said Teddy: authority rather than displeasure in his voice.

"Doing?—Teddy! I don't know what you mean! Is this the way you meet me after all this horrible separation?"

"Grandmamma told me about Dormer bringing you over in his yacht—"

"An accident, forced upon me, as you know."

"Well, accident or not, the poor old lady seems a good deal pleased about it. What are you doing with Jack Dysart?"

"Sir?"

"Oh, I don't mind. If you don't like to tell me, don't. It was another accidental meeting, doubtless."

"How cruel, how unjust you are!" cried Portia, the tears rushing to her eyes. "I hadn't the faintest idea of ever seeing Jack Dysart again. He came up last night as we were sitting outside our hotel, and I was glad—yes, I don't mind saying I was glad, very, to see him. If there was any harm in our friendship for each other would I have been talking to him at the exact time when I expected you?"

"—Having had a letter in the morning to say I should keep safely in Paris a couple of days longer! Well, never mind. We won't quarrel during the first five minutes of meeting, if we can help it."

"Certainly not about poor old Jack Dysart! Oh, Ted, what do you think?" She glanced round her, then drew close and whispered a few words in Teddy's ear. "Now, what was I to do? Wasn't it my *duty* to try and keep John Dysart my friend?"

The blood rushed over Ted Josselin's face. "And you acknowledged to John Dysart—to any man—that such a suspicion was correct, and stopped there? Portia, if you have done this we will have the whole play over at once—don't interrupt me, I say it shall be over. I will never see you placed in such a position!"

"And grandmamma?"

"We must take our chance of all that. Money's very well, but it isn't everything—"

"It can imitate everything quite nearly enough for me!"

"—Besides grandmamma is ill. Condy told me herself she didn't think grandmamma would last long. A poor old woman with the grave before her could never behave badly to anybody at the last."

"Couldn't she?" exclaimed Portia, with energy. "Well I, for my part, believe old women are never too near their graves to behave badly. I believe if grandmamma were to discover on her death-bed that—that it was not possible for you to throw me over, the discovery would give her sufficient strength to leave her money to the Foundling."

"Then the Foundling stands every chance of making a good thing of it," said Teddy. "I shall invent no more facts, I'm not clever at that sort of thing. If grandmamma wants the truth from me now when she is dying, she shall have it—"

"Old Bloxam standing by her pillow ready with pen and ink and the new will? May her end be a mercifully sudden one, then!" The wish only flashed through Portia Ffrench's heart: aloud, "Ted," said she, tenderly, "is it fated that you and I shall never meet and continue friends? Why decide what you will do and say *when* grandmamma is dying, or what it would be your duty to do *if* I had made certain senseless admissions to John Dysart? I laughed in his face, simply. I in Paris! I, who had never been out of England since I was six years old! If you had seen, if you had heard me, you would not accuse me of the folly of betraying my own counsel."

"Well," answered Teddy, a little dryly." I certainly believe you are capable of holding your own in that kind of way. Only you see, my dear child, there is a slight contradiction. If your cleverness threw John Dysart so well off the scent, why is it your absolute duty to conciliate him now as a friend?"

"Because he is a Dysart," cried Portia, promptly. "Because he may correspond with people who know grandmamma. Because, properly advised, his letters will mention Lord Dormer's rather than Teddy Josselin's name in connection with that of Portia Ffrench."

Either Teddy's thoughts were not brisk enough to note how dexterously and thoroughly Portia had shifted her ground, or he was too indifferent to the subject to care to prolong it. Jealousy, save on the largest scale of all, was not a vice to which Ted Josselin was prone.

"You are looking your best, 'Tia—I forgot to tell you so before. Perhaps I think so because I've been seeing the faces of Frenchwomen during the last three days—"

"Or perhaps because you have been staying with the Rawdons. Is Nelly as charming as ever?"

"Quite."

"Has she made you a declaration yet?"

"My dear Portia, do I ask these embarrassing questions about Dormer?"

Lord Dormer just at this moment came up to claim his dance. "Why Josselin! you here! Where have you sprung from?" he exclaimed, rather more surprise than is consistent with delicate breeding in his voice.

"Mr. Josselin has arisen unexpectedly from the sea," said Portia, before Teddy could answer. "I was walking about in the moonlight with my Cousin John, and suddenly Mr. Josselin's apparition rose before us from nowhere. It seems my fate to be surrounded by cousins. I wonder whether it is quite certain that you are no relation, Lord Dormer?

She had taken Lord Dormer's arm the moment he joined them, and without giving the young man time to exchange a word, walked away with him toward the building. By the time they reached the ball-room Lord Dormer had collected his scattered faculties sufficiently to answer her last remark.

"There are—ties, Miss Ffrench—I mean, without being related a man may hope—er—ties nearer and—and all that sort of thing."

Not very coherent; but leading: *how* leading, Portia Ffrench probably knew far better than the youthful lover himself! And a pang of exceeding bitterness contracted her heart. Fortune, title—the prizes she coveted most on earth—placed within her very grasp, and her fingers not daring to close upon either by an inch!

"You were not offended with me for what I said?" he asked presently, in one of the breathing spaces of the waltz.

"Not offended, but—surprised," answered Portia, looking down with a charming little air of bashfulness. Whatever happened, time, she felt, must be gained with Lord Dormer. A single too discouraging word and he would probably leave with the first tide that could float the Lily out of the St. Maur harbor.

"Surprised? Well, I'm sure I thought every one must have seen what was coming—I mean, I thought *you* were sharp enough to see it! I'm miserable, miserable, with all these fellows lounging after you, one after another! I haven't had a happy hour since we landed."

"Lord Dormer, will you take me to Miss Ffrench, please. I cannot listen to you when you talk like this."

Lord Dormer stood aghast. Was he being refused? Josephine's rejection of the British shilling enacted over again : the thing rejected, a British peer: the rejecter an ambitious girl like Portia Ffrench!

"You—you won't even listen to me?" he gasped.

"When you talk sentimental nonsense, most certainly I will not."

It was a grand opening for him had he wished to draw back from his danger; but he did not. He had been in a fever of jealousy of John Dysart during the last twenty-four hours, was in a fever of jealousy of Teddy Josselin now. Although accident rather than premeditation had propelled him into the thick of a serious declaration, it seemed to Lord Dormer as though all that could make life sweet, zestful, worth holding, depended on Portia's answer at this instant.

"In short, I have been making a fool of myself," said he, turning very red. "For you know, as well as I do, that I am not talking 'sentimental nonsense.'"

"I know that you are talking on the spur of the moment," said Portia, with a sigh. "You are much younger than I, Lord Dormer—oh, I don't mean in years only, but in knowledge of the world, of life, of everything! It would be ungenerous of me to take what you have said in earnest; besides, I must have time—time," she added, with a half-smile, "to think over—such a terribly serious matter as this. For the present, we may continue as good friends as ever, mayn't we?"

"And when do you give me leave to speak again?" whispered Lord Dormer, touched to the quick by so much modest good feeling. "I'll not say another word till you bid me! I'll not be jealous—if you won't have any more cousins! I'll—" his emotions grew too much for him to make any more promises. "When may I come to you for a final answer?" he pleaded.

"Answer? oh, on this day year—well, on this day week, then," said Portia, too embarrassed still to look higher than the floor. "And please, in the meantime, let us forget that all this has been said. Now, are we going to dance, or shall we look out for Aunt Jemima?"

"To dance, of course!" whispered Lord Dormer, with fervor; and his fat little arm gave ever so slight a pressure to the cool, firm hand that rested on it."

Portia, looking up at last, saw Teddy Josselin in the doorway, steadily watching her face. If she did not love herself, guess how much she loved Lord Dormer at that moment!

But Lord Dormer was happy.

Teddy Josselin was joined, before the dance was done, by Blake and Susan. Almost before the last notes sounded, Portia came up to them upon Lord Dormer's arm, and said that it was time to think of leaving. She was not going to dance another step—"No, Lord Dormer, not *even* with you;" had no notion of making Aunt Jem, who had come abroad for pleasure, perform the duties of a hardened, ball-going chaperon.

"If you had meant to dance again, Miss Ffrench, I should have asked for one quadrille," remarked Teddy Josselin. "Only to look at people waltzing"— with a glance at Lord Dormer's heated face—"is too much exertion for me in this hot weather."

Portia's head rose a couple of inches at the impertinence.

"Miss Jemima, after watching game after game of dominoes, écarté, and whist, had seated herself in an arm-chair, beside one of the open windows of the card room, and was in her first sound beauty-sleep when Portia touched her arm, "If you can tear yourself from these scenes of dissipation, aunt, Susan and I are ready to go."

The old soldier was wide awake and on her feet, ready to march in a second. "I was just saying to myself it was time to look for you," she began, then caught sight of George Blake, and then of Ted Josselin, for Teddy was loitering a step or two in the rear of the others, much as you will see a married man do when his wife's last partner is conducting her to her carriage from a ball-room.

Jemima Ffrench's face was a study.

"How do you do, Mr. Blake, how do you do," bestowing on them both a frigidly-distant bow. "*You*, too, in St. Maur, Mr. Josselin? This is an unexpected meeting, I must confess."

"An unexpected pleasure," said Teddy, taking Miss Jemima's hand whether she would or no, and shaking and re-shaking it. "St. Maur is a wonderful place for meeting all one's acquaintance. Yourselves, Susan, old Jack Dysart, and now, in the distance, I see the Ironside Ramsays. We shall get on capitally here for a week or two."

"And pray what made you think of visiting St. Maur at all?"

"Ask Blake. I came across Blake in Paris, and nothing would content him but bringing me off here post haste. It really seemed to me," said Ted, with an air of perfect innocence, "that Blake must have correspondents somewhere in these parts."

Susan, on hearing this, grew as red as peony, and hung her head. Miss Jemima looked at her severely.

"I do not like to suspect evil of any one," she remarked to Portia, as soon they found themselves alone in their room at the Benjamin. "But it looks to me as though these young men must have received encouragement to come to Brittany."

"Which young men, dear Aunt Jem?" cried Portia, suppressing a yawn and sinking down exhausted, the excitement of the day over, on the first chair that came to hand. "John Dysart? Lord Dormer?"

"You know as well as I do, child." Miss Jemima held aloft a solitary taper, whose feeble circle of yellow light seemed only to make the darkness of the big room darker, and looked down searchingly at her niece's face. "Portia, how is all this going to end? I will not speak of John Dysart. He is a married man—"

"Very little married, Aunt Jem!"

"But the other two—Teddy—Lord Dormer! Is it delicate, is it womanly for you, standing on such terms as you now stand with Lord Dormer, to permit your cousin, your lover of three weeks ago, to be again at your side?"

Portia's dark cheek flamed. "I am not the controller of my cousin's actions," she answered, shortly. "As long as I live, whatever becomes of me, you may be sure I shall never turn aside when I meet poor Teddy Josselin."

"In your heart, Portia, you care for Teddy Josselin still?"

"Oh—not as you think! My heart is a very elastic organ, if, indeed, I have a heart at all. Teddy suits me. I suit him. We shall see each other, we shall like each other, God willing, till the end of the chapter."

"When you are Lord Dormer's wife, you mean."

"Aunt, dear old lady, don't be prophetic! It is past eleven o'clock."

"You will continue to see Ted Josselin, and to like him, when you are Lord Dormer's wife?"

"Certainly; and Jack Dysart and George Blake—everybody. La la, la lira," under her breath she hummed the air of the last waltz. "Whoever becomes Lord Dormer's wife will enjoy one blessed immunity—she need never waltz with Lord Dormer again! My chin rested on the top of his head; he kicked me, he trod upon me; I had to repeat 'fifty thousand pounds, fifty thousand pounds' to keep myself up to my work at all. How plain Susan looked again, poor child! Her improved looks were only the result of shoe-buckles and crimping-pins."

"Mr. John Dysart does not seem to think her plain."

"Oh, Jack puts on that manner with every one. Now, if you had said George Blake!—do you know that Susan and George Blake are walking home together in the moonlight."

"Yes; if matters stood differently I should have my suspicions," said good, sincere Miss Jemima. "It crossed my mind for a momennt, just from some look on her face, that she might have written—but no; I am sure Susan is too well-principled a little girl to do anything indecorous."

"Indecorous? Writing a letter indecorous?"

"Susan is engaged, Portia. She was talking to me very prettily of Tom Collinson on the way to the Casino. Susan is too well-principled a girl to forget an absent lover."

"But at the same time she might remember a present one!" answered Portia Ffrench.

CHAPTER XXXV.

An artificial world of harlequin-hued tinsel gayety: a horribly real one of gaunt hunger, noisome disease, grim death! In the squares and promenades, bands of music, singers of Parisian love songs, ladies to whom life were insupportable without five or six changes of dress a day; in the by-streets and alleys of the town, Pestilence!—her list of victims swelling hourly. The parish priests are worn out with shriving the dying, burying the dead (yesterday a priest himself was buried). One or two cholera cases, quickly hushed up by hotel-keepers and others in authority, have already occurred among the better classes.

Such is the state of things in the gay little watering-place, St. Maur, at this moment; and, at the end of another two days, Miss Jemima and Portia have gravitated each into her natural and appointed sphere of action.

It would be unjust to say that Portia Ffrench's heart was an absolutely hard one. In a showy, impulsive way, Portia had often, at home, performed acts of charity toward the poor; mostly toward the cleanly, good-looking ones, and in the absence of infectious disease. She was not inaccessible to compassion, as an abstract feeling, and under the most favorable circumstances. Dirt, disease, the foul air, the fouler sights that they must encounter who carry compassion into practice, were simply invincibly repugnant to her. There were human beings, doubtless, created for such work. She was not. It was a fault, she confessed, of her organization. Were there not people so constituted as to turn faint at certain odors, at being in the presence of certain animals? Well, she also had inborn repugnances of temperament; repugnances which were too plainly laws of nature for her ever to feel it a duty to rebel against them.

"A horrible creeping instinct tells me that you have been among the cholera haunts," she remarked to Miss Jemima, four-and-twenty hours after their meeting with the coffins outside the cemetery gates. "If you have—don't tell me! I'm sure life is not so sweet that one need fret at leaving it, but not"—turning away with a shiver—"not by such a disgusting road as that."

"It's a very short road, my dear," said old Miss Jemima, calmly. "At the point where all roads meet, I fancy 'twill matter little by which particular one we shall have travelled."

And from this moment forward there seemed to be a tacit understanding between them that there should be perfect liberty and few questionings as to the manner in which each filled up her days.

Into the dancing and dressing section of the world of which I spoke there might be some difficulty to penetrate. Even Portia had to subdue her pride and seek Mrs. Ironside Ramsay's acquaintance, then court introductions to one after

another of the small potentates of the hour, before she could find herself included in "the" set of visitors who led the fashion and governed their fellow
butterflies in the quest of pleasure. But in the section of the world toward which
Jemima Ffrench's tastes inclined no introductions were needed. Crazy doors
stood wide open, emaciated hands were upheld, glazed eyes upturned to whom-
soever would enter, Protestant or Catholic, priest or layman, and give help!

Of sickness of all kinds Jemima Ffrench had had the experience of a camp
surgeon: the sight of men wanting bread was not unknown to her. Of the two
together, sickness and starvation hand in hand, she had never seen the like as
now she saw in this prosperous little watering place of the great empire. The
lack of clean water was, of itself, a thing to make your heart sore. Pure water,
aye, it might be got from the fountain on the hill up yonder, but who was to fetch
it? With the mother or father, or both, of some miserable family down on the
clay floor that was to be their death-pillow, who was to think of such details as
wholesome water for the children or for the sick? "If they are to die they are
to die," say the neighbors, crossing themselves. "The Lord knows his own work
best. His will be d ne." Every Sun lay in his sermon the good curé—who was not
afraid it seemed, for one, of frightening away visitors—told the people that they
must bestir themselves, or perish as their fathers had done during the last cholera
visitation. Impiety to speak of the Lord's will, yet make no effort to cleanse
their houses and courts, or walk a poor little mile uphill for water that might be
the water of life for their children! And still no one cleansed anything, and no
one fetched water, and steadily, steadily increased the number of funerals each
day (in the garden of the Petit Tambour the drone of the priest's voice was constant as the hum of bees among the flowers), and Jemima Ffrench, instead of
spending her forenoons only, began to spend her entire days from breakfast till
dinner time, in the houses of the sick and dying.

She met the priests there, and the Sisters of Mercy of the parish, and Adam
Byng: and soon between all these people—the rigid Breton Catholics, the strict
Anglo-Protestant, the latitudinarian old Quaker—a kind of freemasonry of charity
was established. Between Adam Byng and Miss Jemima arose a friendship: a
very taciturn one! Adam was not a man of many words, neither in these lowly
chambers of death was there occasion for much speech; but still a genuine
friendship, born of the sympathy of kin natures, not chance. Portia, it is remarked, cares little now to speak of the companions whose pleasures she shared
during her stay in Brittany. Miss Jemima will love to recall the gray, stooping
figure of Adam Byng while she lives.

Six days had passed since the arrival of Teddy and George Blake in St. Maur.
To-morrow little Lord Dormer was to get a final answer to his suit. He was
more in love than ever; he was also a thousand times more doubtful as to his
fate. During the first day or two of his probation, Portia Ffrench had given him
as much encouragement as a man under such circumstances could hope for,
Teddy Jossilin standing by; the spectator, it seemed, of a play in which he was
indifferently interested. Then her mood changed: cruelly, incomprehensibly, to
Lord Dormer, who was too obtuse to discern the wires by which a character like
Portia's is set in motion: and John Dysart, to whom since the Casino dance she
had scarcely spoken, came again into favor. In vain Lord Dormer chafed, in
vain Miss Jemima expostulated. "What are you afraid of, my dear aunt?"
Portia would say to the latter. "As I used to tell you when I was a girl, Jack
is married. There can be no danger for either of us. Besides, what am I to do?

Ted Josselin I am forbidden to look at, George Blake is nowhere—or teaching Susan Fielding to paint buttercups—"

"And Lord Dormer? After coming here in the poor little man's yacht?"

"Ah, that is just the reason why I have nothing to say to him now. After being bored by Lord Dormer in a yacht at sea, is it to be expected that I am to be bored by Lord Dormer on dry land? The fact is, when one has no serious intentions (and I have none), the first thing one desires in people is that they should be outwardly creditable. Jack Dysart is always creditable. You admit yourself how good-looking he is, how well he dresses, how well he talks. If Lord Dormer would have the amount of his wealth, or even his pedigree legibly written, and hung as a placard around his neck, it might be different. Till then I really must prefer one of nature's bankrupt noblemen like poor old Jack."

And, as far as it went, this explanation was a sincere one. Few people better understood the value of self-confession than Portia Ffrench; stopping short always at a certain discreet point of reservation. She did like John Dysart, as she had done when she was sixteen, because of his handsome person, his good air, the attention they called forth—"the two handsomest people in the place" she was wont to say, whenever they appeared in public together. But his attentions had, in truth, a value, his society a fascination, quite apart from all this. Lord Dormer's homage to her was undisputed: John Dysart owed, or Portia believed him to owe, another allegiance. She was not only holding him captive at her side, she was winning him from the side of another woman. And for his good, poor dear fellow, for his good—

"The Ramsays are the worst possible kind of friends for you, Jack," she would say; Portia Ffrench assuming an elder sister's tone with John Dysart! "Of Mrs. Ramsay we won't speak. It is certain the honorable Ironside gets money out of you at écarté."

"Never," answers John Dysart, with perfect truth. "Ironside Ramsay is an out and out good fellow, and—extremely unlucky at cards! You are prejudiced, Portia."

"And you consider Mrs. Ramsay good style?"

"I thought we decided not to speak of Mrs. Ramsay?"

"I can't imagine why you give them so little of your society! You came with them, I suppose you mean to go away with them. Why are you so much with me in the interval? Impossible that any one who admires Blanche Ramsay can admire Portia Ffrench."

"Are you in earnest, Portia? Do you tell me to spend more of my time with the Ramsays?"

"I tell you to spend your time with the people you really care for, Mr. Dysart. If you care for me, stay with me."

To most women of one-and-twenty this would have been playing with terribly edged tools; but Portia felt herself beyond the reach of danger; and the knowledge that she did so gave John Dysart redoubled zest in her society. For whom did this girl of one-and-twenty care? for what stakes was she playing? She had been able to guard her own secrets, he knew. Would she be able to guard her heart, if heart she possessed, as successfully. Her courage, her mendacity, the vein of weary non-enjoyment that ran through even her lightest moods piqued his curiosity. On the day when he came to understand her, the main interest of the flirtation would probably be over. Meantime, he put the game unreservedly into her hands, just as in the old days when they used to bank together at Van John. A face like Portia's was a decidedly pleasant object to

have at one's side during these long summer days ; his friendship with the Ironside Ramsays was not seriously endangered by the intimacy: he had as many
dinners and breakfasts as he liked at Teddy Josselin's hotel and expense, and at
little odd moments had already won over thirty pounds of Teddy Josselin's
money. Cousins like these, Jack felt, were manifestations of providence too
beautiful and too rare to be neglected.

Pleasant, penniless, easy-tempered creatures who toss about the world, a new
acquaintance for every day of the year, are seldom, alas, very noble or disinterested
in their motives ! If a pretty woman would smile on him, if a man would ask him
to dinner and back his own play at écarté afterwards, Jack Dysart was contented.
Beyond to-morrow he seldom looked ; and if, by any chance, an embarrassing
to-morrow dawned, why, the first train up to Paris, or out of Paris, as the case
might be, was his ordinary *deus ex machina* for setting things straight. I don't
know, capital companion though he was, that Jack was a very desirable kind of
antagonist at any game. Principles are abstract things ; and a man leading the
life Mr. John Dysart led, has really scarcely time to deal with abstractions ; besides, people with nothing to lose fall sometimes into a kind of knack of winning
that is curious.

Six days, as I said, had passed by. It was Thursday evening again, the evening of the weekly dress-ball at the Casino. " Not the slightest necessity for you
to be a victim, Aunt Jem," said Portia, looking compassionately at Miss Jemima's
tired face, when the time for starting came. " Much better let me go with the
De Miremonts ; " the De Miremonts were a youthful bride and bridegroom,
spending their honeymoon at the Hotel Benjamin. " Let me run at once and
bid little Madame de Miremont wait for me."

But Miss Jemima had made up her mind to be a victim, to let Portia go out
under other charge than her own no more. Making her way back from some
narrow alley through the Paroisse, or High street of St. Maur, this afternoon,
she had come suddenly upon Mr. John Dysart in attendance on her niece ; and
something in the face and manner of both had aroused all the smouldering Dysart terror ever ready to burst forth in Jemima Ffrench's heart ! "As long as
we remain in France, Portia—not many days more, thank heaven ! I shall feel it
my duty to watch you," she remarked, as they walked along the narrow open
gallery (Portia a picture, in her floating muslin skirts, her head uncovered, for
the night was intensely hot, a single white rose in her jetty hair : Miss Jemima
erect in her black moiré, that had been her best dress for fifteen years, a master-
piece of Miss Budd's in the way of head-dress). If I only look as I feel I know
how out of place I shall be in any scene of gayety to-night. But I will keep
my post, I will keep to my post. You and Mr. John Dysart will meet each other no more, except in my presence."

Portia turned round short. " And you will not go near those disgusting
cholera people again? My dear Aunt Jem, only say that and our compact is
made—you know I haven't dared kiss you for a week past ! say you won't enter
any of those horrible dens of infection again ? "

" After to-morrow, no," said Miss Jemima, a little sadly. " I feel my strength
failing ; I cannot waste that, with the thought of Richard wanting me at home ;
and my money is gone."

" What, the seven pounds that was to have bought you a new black silk ? "

" In such company as I have been amongst, child, one does not remember
silk dresses."

Miss Jemima walked gravely on, and Portia could not but remark that the fine old soldier's step was heavy, that her head stooped a little as she walked. The natural results, as Portia had always foreseen, of these Quixotic ideas of nursing miserable foreigners who had, or ought to have, their own friends to look after them! Money gone, spirits gone, health weakened. Any darker misgiving, the possibility of Death leaving the "horrible dens of infection" and showing his ill-bred face among the upper classes, did not at present cross her mind.

It was the brightest, fullest ball of the whole summer; Portia Ffrench and little Madame de Miremont, a rose and white wax doll of seventeen, the acknowledged beauties. Wherever Portia went she felt, rather than heard, a murmur of admiration; to her the most delicious music that the world could yield! She knew that Mrs. Ramsay's costly Pompadour silk, fresh yesterday from Worth's, was eclipsed by her plain white muslin whose outside value was twenty francs; knew that John Dysart, for the first time since the renewal of their intimacy, was beginning to lose his head a little; that Teddy Josselin's eyes followed her wherever she moved; Lord Dormer's condition was, of course, too patent to every one to take into account. The certainty that her reign was limited, that not one of these men whom she held in fetters to-night but might free himself or insist upon the others obtaining their freedom on the morrow, only added the last keen gambler's edge to her enjoyment. "I dance as the prisoners during the French Revolution used to dance," she whispered once to Teddy, who stood beside her and John Dysart in the intervals of a waltz. "Pleasure to-night; to-morrow the guillotine—or grandmamma, or some dreadful explanation of some kind. This kind of thing won't go on for ever."

"That it most certainly will not," replied Teddy, a good deal of meaning in his voice: then sauntered coolly away to join old Miss Jemima in the card-room.

"Capital little fellow, our cousin Ted," remarked John Dysart, looking after him. "I don't know how it is, but in spite of all you say, Portia, I can never get it out of my head that little Ted Josselin is your destiny."

"I try to like all my relations," answered Portia, demurely, "I consider it a duty."

"You don't like me a quarter as well as you do Ted—don't tell stories, Portia, I know it! If I were to tell you how many times I chose you to dance or sit out with any one partner, would you obey me?"

"I have never obeyed any one in my life yet," said Portia.

"And you are not in the least under orders to-night? Come, confess! You know, my dear child, you can't say 'no' without blushing."

"But I do say 'no;'" looking at him straight; "and I certainly don't feel as if I blushed. If the number of times I dance, or do not dance with any one here is as completely unimportant to Ted Josselin as it is to myself his peace of mind will be untroubled."

She had never given one of John Dysart's half-tender speeches so decisive a counter-thrust before. He looked at the black eyes that met his own so coldly, and asked himself whether, in the long run Blanche Ramsay would not be a very much pleasanter kind of woman to get on with than Portia Ffrench? In the long run, yes: but in the short one—for the present? Well, for the present John Dysart had never so thoroughly made up his mind as he did at this moment to decipher the enigma of his cousin Portia's heart!

A boating excursion had already been planned, much against Miss Jemima's wish, for to-morrow afternoon, Madame de Miremont to be the chaperon. Portia and Susan Fielding the young ladies of the party; the gentlemen, John Dysart, Teddy Josselin and George Blake. Little Lord Dormer, by Portia's special request, to hear nothing of the expedition till it was over.

"And now I have a great mind to say the thing shall not take place," remarked Miss Jemima to Teddy, when he joined her in the card-room. "I am
not easy about Portia, I mean the weather is too hot to trust her out till evening.
Oh dear, that man again!" Miss Jemima had taken up her post at an angle
which commanded not only a distant view of the ball-room but of the door
through which the dancers defiled in and out to the veranda. "That dreadful
man again!"

"What man?" said Teddy, looking about him guilelessly.

"Why, John Dysart. Mr. Josselin, will you let me talk to you for one minute, seriously?"

Teddy seated himself at Miss Jemima's side, and inclined his ear to listen.

"After all that has passed I cannot, of course, expect you and my niece Portia
to have very much to say to each other. As far as the world's opinion goes it
might, indeed, have been as well that we had not come across you here."

"You mustn't say that," interrupted Teddy. "Putting Portia aside, you know
what pleasure it gives me to come across you."

"Don't pay compliments, sir, John Dysart paid compliments the first night I
spoke to him, and I believe I was fool enough to be pleased by them. I wish
that man was—in Norway! from my heart I do!"

"John Dysart? Why, he's one of the best fellows living," said Teddy. "I
thought everyone liked John Dysart."

"I do not," said Miss Jemima, "or, which comes to the same thing, I don't
like to see my niece Portia like him as she does."

A faint little flush rose to Teddy's face. "Portia does well to amuse herself,"
he answered, quietly. "John Dysart is the best-looking fellow and the best
waltzer here. Besides, Portia always was fond of him."

"I know it," said Miss Jemima. "That is precisely why I blame myself for
having allowed a renewal of the intimacy. Good heavens, *again!* the third
dance! No, they have gone out under the balcony. I shall follow."

Teddy Josselin laid his hand on Miss Jemima's. "Aunt Jemima," he began
soothingly—"I beg pardon, but you know I had got so into the habit of calling
you Aunt Jemima—it is quite unnecessary, believe me, for you to annoy yourself
about Portia. Let us have a game at piquet, half-franc points, do! Jolly for us
old chaperons to gamble while the young ones flirt. I know Portia is all right,
and—"

"And I," cried Miss Jemima, energetically, "say that Portia is all wrong.
This is a light matter to you, of course."

("Very, indeed," said Teddy, stroking his moustache.)

"The time is over when you had a right to take umbrage at your cousin's
conduct. It is no light matter to me. I have seen little or nothing of her during the last five days; there I reproach myself. I have thought of strangers
while I should have minded the duty that lay to my hand; and now I see the
progress that John Dysart—dangerous, bad man that he is—has made in her
regard. Look at them at this moment!"

The two figures were slowly pacing up and down in the moonlight, not many
yards away from the open window by which Miss Jemima sat.

"They are a fine-looking couple," said Teddy, approvingly. "I should be
glad if Portia would leave off dancing with Dormer. It doesn't become her."

"I would rather see Portia dance all her life—aye, all her life—with Lord
Dormer than go on as she does now with John Dysart!" said Miss Jemima.
"If you had the good, kindly heart I once gave you credit for, Teddy Josselin,
ou would feel a little more as I do."

Teddy seated himself upright, and looked thoughtful. "Are you really in earnest, Aunt Jemima?" he asked. "Does it really vex you that Portia should try her small weapon on John Dysart's battered old heart?"

"You—you seem to forget that John Dysart has a wife already," said Miss Jemima, a blush like a girl's rising on her honest cheek. "What weapons can Portia, can any girl seek to bring against a married man's heart?"

"Ah, I never thought of it in that light," said Teddy; "but the fact is, one forgets at times who is married and who is not. Now, would you really like Portia to have less to say to John Dysart?"

"It isn't a question of what *I* like," answered Miss Jemima, shaking her head.

"Yes, but it is," said Teddy. "I'm not going to have you cut up like this for all the Jack Dysarts in creation. The thing must be seen to."

He rose, tried to look stern, then, catching sight of himself in a mirror just opposite, smiled; took a pair of cream-colored gloves from his pocket, drew them on with the care that a very exact fit, even of Jouvin's, requires, and passed on into the ball-room.

The room, as it happened, was nearly cleared. It was the interval between two round dances, and the dancers had all thronged out to breathe whatever cool air might be obtained under the veranda outside. In a corner, talking with depressed cheerfulness, as women do in seasons of neglect, to some old lady at her side, was Mrs. Ironside Ramsay. The weapons of reprisal lay ready to Ted Josselin's hand. Blanche Ramsay was at a time of life when, partnerless at a ball, a woman may say with dignity, "Ah, my dancing days are over; all I look for now is some one nice to come and talk to me!" and yet, if she is invited to dance, feel young enough to accept with grace, and prove a dangerous rival to half the girls in the room. A flush of well-pleased surprise rose to her face when Teddy Josselin crossed the room and asked her, as if all his happiness depended upon it, for the next waltz.

"Why, Mr. Josselin, we shall see Ironside waltzing next. I thought you never danced?"

"Almost never," said Teddy, looking his handsomest, and throwing the most pleading look of which he was master into his blue eyes. "Won't you be the exception?"

Not grammar, I admit; but flattery no amount of Lindley Murray could have improved in the eyes of a woman of four-and-thirty, whose accustomed faithful attendant was at this moment walking in the moonlight with a rival a dozen years younger than herself. The first bars of the waltz strike up, and Blanche Ramsay's hand steals under Ted Josselin's arm—they float away together, pause, and Teddy begins to whisper soft nothings into his partner's ear; when the dance is over, stations himself at her side in one of the most conspicuous places in the ball-room, and asks leave to fan her.

Coming in from the garden with Jack Dysart, this was the little picture on which Portia's eyes rested. For a moment she could scarce believe what she saw. Teddy presuming to dance! and with Blanche Ramsay! Then it *could* only be an accident, thought Portia, lifting her head in the air. Blanche Ramsay, of course, had waylaid him, and Teddy, with his usual laziness, had thought it less exertion to dance than to resist. But when a galop began, and they danced together again, and when more fanning went on afterward, and, finally, not a look for any but his partner, when Teddy led Mrs. Ramsay out under the veranda, the smiles, the brightness began to fade ominously from Portia's face.

"You don't hear a word I am saying," remarked John Dysart, who was watch ing all the by-play attentively. "I never knew before, my dear Portia, that your face could look so—"

"Ill tempered—use the right word," cried Portia, recovering herself. "If you had such martyrdom in the shape of lancers before you as I have, I don't suppose you would look pleasant."

As she spoke, little Lord Dormer advanced to claim her.

"Remember your promise about to-morrow," whispered John Dysart, before she quitted his arm. "Let no Destiny interfere."

"Of course not," answered Portia, but without meeting his eyes. "Don't I always remember my promises? Oh, dear, dear," turning to Lord Dormer, "do you really think there will be breathing space for us? Wouldn't it be much nicer to go to Aunt Jemima and look on?"

But, after waiting in miserable impatience half the evening, Lord Dormer was not going to be cheated, even out of a set of lancers. There was plenty of breathing space if they went to the other end of the room, and he had already engaged two couples for their set—only their own *vis-à-vis* wanting. Just then Teddy and Mrs. Ramsay passed along.

"Will you be our *vis-à-vis*, Mr. Josselin?" asked Portia.

"What for? Lancers?" said Teddy, languidly. "Thanks; no—I never work out geometrical puzzles for amusement."

"But your partner, no doubt, would help you through the figures," remarked Portia.

As she said this her eyes met his; and Teddy knew that there was an entreaty in them.

"Would you mind dancing a square dance with me," he whispered, turning with his soft, petitioning air to Mrs. Ramsay. "I am half ashamed to ask you."

But Mrs. Ramsay, it seemed, liked square dances; philosophically forestalling the time, she said, gayly, the not far-distant time when square dances would be the only ones left her. And so Portia and Teddy Josselin found themselves bowing, "setting," touching the tips of each other's fingers, and going through all the other evolutions of the lancers with great coldness and ceremony; both apparently engrossed in their partner's conversation during the comparatively lucid intervals of the performance.

Once, and once only, they spoke. It was in the zigzag round of hand shaking that takes place in the final figure. "Your next dance is with me, sir!" whispered Portia, fixing her eyes steadily on her cousin's face.

"What—to dance it?" returned Teddy, looking the picture of surprise.

"I am indifferent about that. No; not to dance it would please me best. I want to talk to you. Do you refuse?"

"Do I ever refuse you anything?"

The interchange of these few words had thrown the whole figure into a state of chaos. Lord Dormer grew fever-hot with irritation. "How glad I *shall* be when to-morrow comes," he remarked a minute or two later, as Portia was walking round the room on his arm. "I never felt so nervous in my life, Miss Ffrench; no, not on the evening before the Derby. I'm sure I didn't."

It was the most enthusiastic compliment Lord Dormer could have offered to any woman.

"Nervous—what about?" said Portia, suppressing a smile. "Oh, I think I know what you mean. Who would have believed that at your age you could remember anything so long!"

"At my age! Why, I shall be twenty-one in October. My own master,

Miss Ffrench," looking at her meaningly; "able to do as I please with myself, and all I possess."

"Can't you do as you please now?"

"With myself, of course. I don't know about—ah—er—a minor making settlements."

"The doubt is a most important one," said Portia, gravely.

She refused, point-blank, to walk with Lord Dormer under the veranda, declaring that she had had enough of moonlight—"yes, and of sentiment and everything else that goes with moonlight"—to last her her life. Teddy Josselin and his partner, accidentally no doubt, remained also in the ball-room. The next dance was a cotillon lead by John Dysart and the charming little bride, Madame de Miremont. "I never could remember the figures of a cotillon in my life, but if *you* would teach me, Miss Ffrench, make allowance for my ignorance?" whispered Lord Dormer, tenderly.

"Unfortunately I am engaged already," answered Portia. "That is to say," with a glance at Teddy, who still kept beside Mrs. Ramsay in a corner, "if my partner remembers to claim me."

"I shouldn't have thought Miss Ffrench would wait for any man," remarked Lord Dormer, who had followed the direction of her eyes.

"Nor would she unless the air were at a temperature that makes waiting more pleasant than exertion!" said Portia.

However, when the first few bars had been played, Ted Josselin rose, hovered a moment or two by Mrs. Ramsay's side, then, still keeping possession of her fan, came across the room to Portia. "Our dance, I think, Miss Ffrench?"

She took his arm without a word, leaving Lord Dormer alone to study the figure of the cotillon. "Take me outside, Teddy, the air of this place is stifling—no, not this way, we will go out by the other door. You have to return Mrs. Ramsay's fan."

"I think not. She has been good-natured enough to lend it to me."

"Teddy," a tremble in her voice, "will you return that woman's fan or not?"

"Suppose I say not!"

"You would not be so unkind. You know I don't like Mrs. Ramsay, Teddy—dearest—give her back her fan!"

"Do you know, Portia, that you are the most unreasonable woman living?"

"Certainly, I know it, and I also know all that you have in your heart to say to me: You like to have Jack Dysart, Lord Dormer, every man in the room, at your feet, and I am to talk to Aunt Jemima, play écarté, keep quiet any way I choose and watch you! Ted, it is true! I confess myself I have no right to ask you anything, only—only I do ask it! Take Mrs. Ramsay back her fan?"

"To-morrow, my dear. She has promised to lend it me till to-morrow morning."

"What! you visit the Ramsays at their hotel? Oh Teddy, how mean-spirited, how deceitful of you!"

"An act of simple justice; *you* have taken away Jack Dysart. Besides, I really am fond of Mrs. Ramsay. She's the right height for me. I like her step. I like the way she looks up at one with those sleepy hazel eyes."

They went out into the yellow moonlight, the fan still between Teddy's hands, and walked, without exchanging a word, to an angle in the path at the farther end of the grounds: the very spot where Teddy had come upon Portia and Jack Dysart on the night of his arrival.

Then Portia stopped abruptly. "And how—how is all this going to end?" broke, with an accent almost of genuine passion, from her lips.

CHAPTER XXXVI

SHE quitted his arm and moved a pace or two from his side. "How is all this to end?" she repeated, impetuously.

"To end? why, how do all cotillons end?" said Teddy Josselin. "I don't quite remember the order of the figures myself, but—"

"—Talk sense, sir, if you please. You are not talking to Mrs. Ramsay now. How is all this to end between you and me?"

"Oh! I understand. You are cleverer than I, Portia, you can answer the question best. Besides, the solution is in your own hands."

"In mine?"

"In yours. I've seen a good deal of this kind of grief in my life," said Teddy, with the air of a sexagenarian philosopher, "and have always remarked that one side is to blame—not the man's side. Men, in such things, follow pretty much where they are led." Teddy smiled just enough to show his even white teeth, and looked up at the moon.

"Grief—for I know enough of your language to guess what you mean—grief! You mean to say," Portia's voice trembled, "that you and I have come to grief already?"

"Not quite, but a remarkably close imitation of it," said Teddy Josselin. "You must know that just as well as I do, my dear Portia."

"I know that you are unkind, ungenerous!" broke forth Portia. "You take your own way in everything (look how you went to stay with the Rawdons, in spite of all that I have said about your intimacy with that person!) and deny me the right—well I won't even talk about *liberty*—but of the commonest amusement. You forget what my position is—"

"Never. You take very good care I should not."

"You forget that half of what you are pleased to consider my crimes are acts of policy, undertaken for your sake."

"Coming to France in Dormer's yacht, for instance?"

"Most undoubtedly. Does not grandmamma take it for granted that I shall be twentieth baroness of Throgmorton? What object but your good could I have had in wearying myself with such a man?"

"And Jack Dysart?"

"Jack Dysart relieves me from the trouble of Lord Dormer."

"And the next comer from the trouble of Jack Dysart. I understand. You must always remember, my dear, that I have not complained. I've given Jack breakfasts and dinners, and lost my money to him at écarté because you bid me, and come here of an evening and drank sugar-water over penny whist with the Frenchmen, and never made myself intrusive or disagreeable in any way. It's only when you ask me how things are likely to end that I speak at all."

"And then, your answer is—"

"That it rests altogether with yourself. In these days," went on Teddy, warming into unwonted eloquence, "I don't suppose fellows are ever frantically jealous—nothing of the Othello sort of fire in fellows now. But a man knows the opinions of his set and acts up to them. I'm not in the set of—of Dolly Wynne, let us say. The men I call my friends are—it sounds like the speech of a prig, but I can't help it: you make me speak—are men of honor, my dear child."

"Honor!" stammered Portia, her face turning white. "Why, of course they are. Who is talking of honor? What do you mean by mentioning such a word to me?"

"It does seem rather ill-timed," answered Teddy, unconscious of sarcasm "but you see, one must have a standing-point somewhere, and I make mine there."

"And my actions are—that I should speak the words!—are not to your—"

"If they went much farther they would be neither to your honor nor to mine," said Teddy, helping her; "and if you will listen to my advice 'Tia, you'll make a dead stand now. I was never the kind of fellow to watch and suspect and keep guard over a woman, I haven't the energy. Besides, to my mind, anything that wanted so much looking after would be too great a bore to be worth keeping. But, as far as I can, you know, I shall do my duty to you; to you and to myself, too."

Duty. Out of the mouth of Teddy Josselin—Teddy Josselin whom she had ever held to be lighter, shallower even than herself—had come this word, which practically was without a place in Portia's vocabulary! Her eyes filled; a choking sensation rose in her throat. To the superior endowment of a *heart*—endowment which, in spite of all his frivolity, raised Teddy's nature into so different a class to hers—she was blind. To recognize the existence of a heart you must probably possess one; and, as I have remarked, Portia was at all times easier to reach through her intellect than through her feelings. Still the woman lives not but will bow down before, even while she outwardly resents, the first show of superior moral strength in the man she loves, and Portia French admired, respected Teddy Josselin as she had never done in her life before, while he spoke. Difficult, indeed, to say how far the future of that contradictory, impressionable, unemotional character of hers was influenced by the attitude taken, in all simplicity, by poor little Teddy Josselin at this moment.

—"And you'll come to-morrow, Ted? Yes, yes, I'm going to turn over a new leaf. I'm never going to flirt again, and I'll send Lord Dormer back to England and Jack Dysart to the Ramsays—after to-morrow! The party is made up. The De Miremonts have accepted, and I sent notes to Susan Fielding and Mr. Blake this evening. It would be worse than imprudent, it would be ridiculous, to put it off because I have talked to you for half an hour in the moonlight. You know that Jack Dysart has suspicions as it is."

They were walking slowly back together across the garden; the cotillon was over; everybody preparing to leave the Casino. "Do you refuse me, Ted? Will you oblige me to set people talking by breaking up the party at the last?"

"There won't be wind enough to get us out of the harbor," said Teddy, lazily. "We shall all have sunstrokes, or worse. I read in "Galignani" to-day that the people are dying here of cholera by hundreds."

"But this is on shore, not on sea. Now, sir! I'm sure I've given up enough for you—"

"Prospectively!"

"Make this sacrifice for me. You will have Madame de Miremont to talk to, and Susan Fielding, not counting me. I promise you, you won't be bored We are to meet Susan at the St. Sauveur pier at five, and not return till quite late, in the cool of the evening. Now say yes?"

"Well, yes, then; if I happen not to have died of cholera meantime."

They reached the veranda of the Casino as Teddy spoke, and found Miss Jemima and John Dysart side by side. Lord Dormer, desperate with jealousy at Portia's prolonged absence, had gone back some hours ago to his hotel.

"They are putting out the lights," remarked Miss Jemima, sententiously: in escaping from the Scylla of Jack Dysart, she by no means intended Portia to fall back upon the Charybdis of Teddy Josselin. "Five minutes more and—"

"Five minutes more, and everything in our lives would be changed," cried Portia. "I never can get pathetic about accidents that would have happened if something else had only happened first. The De Miremonts are here still, I see—ah, you too, Mr. Dysart? All the nicest people left to the last."

"The nicest people may as well walk back in each other's society," remarked John Dysart, addressing Miss Jemima. "To my mind this is the most enjoyable part of the whole evening."

And accordingly, a minute or two later, they were all returning in a party toward the town; Madame de Miremont leaning on her young husband's arm—a bewitching little picture, with her white satin hood inclosing her baby pink and white face; John Dysart resolutely attentive to old Miss Jemima; Teddy Josselin and Portia following last.

The night seemed at each instant to grow hotter. The sea was quivering like a sheet of molten copper under the waning yellow moon; the air so intensely still that the lungs labored to draw breath: a curious bluish haze veiled all the suburb of St. Sauveur across the harbor. "Delicious night, real southern temperature, is it not?" said John Dysart. He had taken off his opera-hat, and was sauntering along bare-headed by Miss Jemima's side. "Not often we get such weather at this here in the north."

"It is the weather of death," answered Jemima Ffrench, looking slowly round her. "There will be a score more funerals than usual to-morrow morning. I have seen that blue mist too often in my life to be mistaken about its meaning."

Just at the entrance of the town a ghastly sight greeted them; four coffins borne aloft on men's shoulders into one house, a house not a hundred yards distant from the Hotel Benjamin.

"But Albert—my friend—what are the men doing? Monsieur Dysart, for what are those black boxes?" cried the little bride, stopping short, and holding closer to her husband's arm.

The St. Maur cholera statistics had reached "Galignani," but not the fashionable visitors of St. Maur itself.

"They *look* a little like coffins, madame," said John Dysart, in his pleasant voice.

"If an average of fifty deaths occur daily from cholera, the coffin people must be well employed," remarked Teddy; for now they all stood together in a knot.

"Coffins—cholera—people are dying here of cholera? Take me away, Albert, take me away! I shall die if I stay here another night!" shrieked the poor little French girl, clinging to her Albert. "Oh, my God, that I ever left Paris and mamma! Take me to mamma by the first train to-morrow."

"Oh, but our boating party is to-morrow," said Portia Ffrench. "I have known about the cholera for ages, Madame de Miremont. It is not a bit worse now than it was a week ago, and only the common people die."

"And thou hast thy boating costume all ready—thy boating costume from Paugat, my angel," whispered De Miremont, tenderly, in his wife's ear. "Would'st thou return to Paris without having worn it once?"

"That argument was the potent one, depend upon it," remarked Portia, as the bride and bridegroom entered the hotel gates. "What Frenchwoman would not brave cholera to wear a new costume? Our party has been threatened by many shocks, but has withstood everything, even the fear of death itself."

"And your promise stands good, remember!" whispered John Dysart: Teddy Josselin was bidding Miss Jemima good-night, a few paces away. "If all the other people fall off, you will go with me?"

"There is no chance of the other people falling off," said Portia, evasively.

"Oh, come, that won't do! I must have a more decided answer. The Ramsays want me to go to a picnic up the river, to-morrow, but I have left the engagement open. If the other people stay away, do you still promise to go alone with me, or—has destiny interfered?"

"Destiny! I should have thought you were the last man living to believe in destiny!" said Portia, but without lifting her eyes to his face.

"And the promise holds good?"

"It is a ridiculous one. There are five other people, at least, certain to go."

"And if they do not?"

"Well, if anything so utterly, wildly unlikely should happen, I suppose I should have no choice but to keep to what I said."

And upon this they bade each other good-night and parted.

CHAPTER XXXVII.

THE same scorching sun, the same breathless, livid heat as yesterday: the carnations and heliotropes smelling their richest in the garden of the Petit Tambour, the geraniums and verbenas almost too dazzlingly vivid for the eye to bear their blaze; the drone of the colza mill at the back of the house mingling with the voice of the priest in the burying-ground midway down the hill; in the odorous shade of Uncle Adam's summer-house two people, around whom, not merely a few scores of human creatures, but whole empires might go to dissolution without brushing the bloom off their paradise—George Blake and Susan.

While death during the past week has been busy at his work in the by-alleys, and fashion busy at hers in the thoroughfares, these two have been enacting a part older than fashion, older than death, in the great human drama. And still (this is why I speak of them as in paradise yet) not a word savoring of a warmer feeling than friendship has been spoken by either. At this instant, did you question them, Blake would tell you his madness for Portia is but indifferently cured, and Susan that she is the affianced wife of Tom Collinson. Their love is just at the final, sweetest stage of immaturity—the rosy breathing space before sunrise, the breaking point of the wave, the last sparkle of the uplifted glass of champagne !

"This boating party is a mistake, Susan, depend upon it. We have had nothing to do with other people and gay parties hitherto, why should we begin to-day ? Which would be pleasantest—to broil for hours in the St. Maur roads, listening to the talk of people for whom we care nothing, or go up to the Falaise and finish our picture alone ? Now, the truth ?"

The Falaise was a certain heathy knoll, about a mile distant from the Petit Tambour, a knoll overshadowed through all the hot hours of the day by a group of silver beeches, and from whence spread a broad view of sea and coast, with the purple windings of the little river for foreground. "Not much doubt as to which would be pleasantest," answered Susan, "only you see I have promised to go. I sent my note back last night by the messenger who brought Miss Portia's. She complains that they have never seen anything of me since you came, I mean during the last six days."

"The last six days !" repeated Blake. "Susan, do you remember that night when you made the time fly so quickly upon the river bank, and I told you you were a witch ? There is witchcraft about you still, I'm afraid. Surely it can't be six days since I first saw you, flirting with Mr. Dysart, at the Casino."

"You have a sketch to show for every day, sir," said Susan, demurely, "and I never flirted with Mr. Dysart, I—" she bit her lips and looked down—"I am under orders never to flirt with any one."

Just then the door leading from the kitchen to the flower-garden opened, and Adam Byng walked slowly up to the summer-house. His tall figure was more bowed than usual, his quiet old face, grayer. It was evident that he had to lean on the garden-hoe he held in his hand for support.

"Uncle Adam," said Susan, running to meet him, "I want you to do me a favor. Don't go among the sick people to-day. You are looking so pale, I'm sure you want rest. Don't go farther than the garden this afternoon. You know I have you in my care now." Mrs. Byng during the last few days had been absent on business, seeing with her own eyes—she never trusted agents—into the worth of a small peasant farm six or eight leagues distant, a farm on which she was negotiating to advance some few hundred francs. "What would Aunt Adam say if she were to return to-night and find you ill ?"

"Say—what we must all say when the hour comes !" answered Adam, with his patient smile, and laying his hand on the girl's soft curls. "Nay, nay, Susan, there is no fear for me, whatever there may be for younger people ; and that brings to my mind that I have something to say to thee, child. Thee must not go lower in the town than the Place Dauphin, for the present. If Friend Blake will take thee with him into the country this afternoon, go—breathe the purest air thee can ! I have business of my own that will keep me abroad for some hours, but old Louison will watch the house till we return."

For Adam Byng knew nothing of conventionalities, even after living sixteen years in the land of rigid conventionality. George Blake's hearty voice and honest face had won Uncle Adam's sympathy from the first morning when the young man called at the Petit Tambour ; and nothing seemed more natural to his simple mind than that this English friend of Susan's should be the companion of her walks during Mrs. Byng's absence.

"Not lower than the Place Dauphin?" cried Susan. "Oh, Uncle Adam, but you must let me break through the rule to-day. I am invited to a boating party, there will be six or seven of us, Miss Portia says, all young people, and we take our dinner with us, and—"

"And I say thee shall not go," said Uncle Adam, decisively. "This is the hottest day we have had this year (though signs on the horizon already foreshadow change) and the cholera cases since yesterday have increased by a third in the lower parts of the town. I ask thy opinion, Friend Blake, will not my Susan be better on the cool hill-side than exposed to the burning sun in an open boat?"

"Infinitely better on the hill-side," said Blake, treacherously. "I was just telling her the same thing, sir, when you joined us."

And so it was settled; Susan, after some difficulty, obtaining leave to walk down under Blake's charge to the water-side and make her excuses, personally, to Portia Ffrench. It was now close upon four o'clock; the hour at which the party was to assemble was five; there was therefore little time to lose, for, by Uncle Adam's order, they were to take the longer but more shaded route, and not walk beyond a snail's pace at their peril. The old man came with them to the door of the Petit Tambour; he kissed Susan twice, held her hand in his, seemed wistfully unwilling to lose sight of her. "Take care of her, Friend Blake, take care of her. I trust her in thy hands." Those were the last words they heard Adam Byng speak.

The heat, as long as they kept to the close, pent-in streets of St. Sauveur, was suffocating; but the moment they reached the open Place Dauphin, from whence a narrow lane led down to the water side, a gust of fresher air blew suddenly in their faces. The mist was clearing on the horizon; for the first time for weeks a few small cloud-flecks were visible far away in the west. "Uncle Adam might just as well have let me go," said Susan. "It is getting cool already—ah, we are only just in time, here come some of the party up from the ferry, and we shall be saved going down the hill."

The arrivals were Portia and John Dysart. Portia's manner showed unmistakable signs of satisfaction at meeting Susan and Blake. "Can you imagine anything so unfortunate? The De Miremonts are not coming. Madame, ill—sheer fright, I believe, little goose, because she saw a coffin or two last night! However," turning with one of her old smiles to Blake, "we shall be a charming little party of four by ourselves, shall we not?"

And now Susan had to begin her own story of excuses: the heat, the cholera, Uncle Adam's fears for her. Could not the expedition be put off till a cooler day?

"I have never put off anything in my life," interrupted Portia, coldly. "I am neither afraid of sun, tempest, nor pestilence, and if no one else goes, I go alone."

"Cousins counting for nothing," put in Jack Dysart.

"Cousins!" a solitary cousin, you should say." answered Portia. "Mr Josselin has not thought fit to appear—the sun too hot for his delicate state of health, no doubt. Yes, a cousin counts for a great deal, Jack. But for you I should have been deserted altogether."

"We must take care not to miss the tide," said Jack, looking at his watch. "It is quite time for us to be getting on towards the pier."

Still Portia hesitated. "A formidable thing to go boating, unchaperoned," she remarked. "Lucky Aunt Jem was out when the news came of Madame de Miremont's illness, or I should never have been allowed to start at all! Vain to ask you to come, I suppose, Mr. Blake? I have had no answer to my note, but I relied upon *you* not proving faithless!"

"I only got the note late last night," said Blake, and until an hour ago looked forward with pleasure to joining the party. But Miss Fielding is in my charge, and—"

"And Miss Ffrench is in nobody's," cried Portia, with a somewhat forced laugh. "I fully expect you will leave me in the lurch at the last, Jack."

"Much more likely that my evil destiny will leave me there," said Jack Dysart.

And then they started; followed by one of the servants from the Benjamin, bearing a basket of provisions, down the hill.

"I don't like Mr. Dysart," said Susan, looking after them, "no, I oughtn't to say that, for I am sure I did like him immensely the one time he paid attention to me; but I don't trust him. I wish Miss Portia had put the party off. It would have been very pleasant to turn it into a picnic at the Falaise."

"Very pleasant," said Blake. "You would have had Mr. Dysart's pretty speeches to listen to, and I could have fallen back upon my old employment—"

"Your old employment?" cried Susan, with a start of jealousy.

"Of drawing Portia Ffrench's profile. Still I'm not sure, my dear, but that we shall find it as pleasant by ourselves."

"Upon their road to the Falaise they called at the Petit Tambour for a color-box left there by Blake in the forenoon. Uncle Adam had gone out; old Louison was busy talking to two or three of her gossips over the garden wall; the solemn ticking of the great clock on the stairs was the only sound that broke the quiet of the sultry, darkened house. Blake and Susan went together into the salon—for during Mrs. Byng's absence considerable laxity in domestic rule prevailed: polished floors were trodden with as much levity as though beeswax were not three sous a pound. It was deliciously cool and shaded, redolent of the scent of the magnolias outside; the piano stood invitingly open.

"We have a long evening before us," said Blake, "and I must have the shadows at a certain level before I can finish my sketch. Let us have one song before we go."

He seated himself at the instrument, and Susan drew to his side.

"Take off your hat, my child, I want to see your face as I saw it on that first evening we ever sang together. That is right," giving a long look at the soft face, more exquisitely soft than ever in this half light, and with the curls pushed back disordered from the young white forehead. "What were we talking of? Oh, of that first evening at Halfont and the song we sang. We will sing it now, Susan. 'Drink to me only with thine eyes.'"

He struck a few chords of prelude and the two voices trembled forth together upon the silent air. Will the walls of the Petit Tambour ever vibrate again, I wonder, to voices of youth, to words of passionate music, while they stand? At the conclusion of the last stanza, Blake's quickly-wrought feelings were on fire. "If life could only be spent in singing love-songs!" he remarked, a good deal of tender meaning in his voice.

"One would get tired of it, I dare say," said Susan, appositely. "And Aunt Adam says it puts a piano out of tune to be forever playing on it. I shall have no time for singing after Aunt Adam comes back. We are to set about the moreen curtains for the dining-room at once."

And yet, notwithstanding the prosaic answer, was she more swayed in very fact by the music than her companion ; swayed so that the blood was tingling in her finger-ends, her heart beating till her fear was he must hear its beats. For here was just one of the subtle unlikenesses that fitted them for each other so admirably : Susan could feel, Blake express. "The piano out of tune ! moreen curtains ! Miss Fielding, I've sometimes wondered if *anything* could exorcise the common-sense out of that wise head of yours ! If your own singing can't, I'm afraid the case is hopeless."

"Exorcise my common-sense ? Mr. Blake, I don't know what you mean," lowering her great lucid eyes to his face. "Music works on me—ah, if you could feel my heart beat—works on me till I don't know whether what I feel is pain or pleasure, but what I said about the window curtains is quite true. You see Aunt Adam always takes down the muslin ones on the first of October."

Blake looked at her with a sigh of regret. He had few faults to find with Susan Fielding, or with the delight her simple society yielded him ; still if a child loving and sweet as this had but the faculty of comprehension, nay, if she had but the faculty, like Portia Ffrench, of seeming to comprehend—would it be possible for her to suit him better ? He asked himself the question with a start.

They sang another song, and another ; then remembered that their shortest path to the Falaise lay through the kitchen-garden, at the farther end of which a wicket-gate opened into one of the meadows overhanging the river. The cool green and blue shadows of the old garden looked deliciously tempting : tempting was the smell of peaches, and nectarines and plums. By the time they reached the Falaise it was past six o'clock. The air by this time had grown actually fresh ; a stiff breeze was blowing from the south-west ; the upturned beech-leaves glinted white against an iron-purple sky.

"If we had only a picnic and a few jovial friends, how enjoyable this would be," suggested Blake, as he put Susan in position for his foreground figure. "Imagine Mr. Dysart on your side here, Portia Ffrench by mine—"

"I will imagine nothing of the kind," interrupted Susan. "This is my last day's happiness—oh, but I know it ! All day long I seem to hear those words, 'the last, the last,' ringing in my ears. I won't spoil it by thinking of anything but what I have got. We couldn't be better off than we are now."

"I am not so sure of that," said George Blake.

After an hour's quiet work the sketch was finished : a dream of blue sea and sky, with the mist-softened harbor and town of St. Maur in the middle distance ; in the foreground, the figure of a young girl with rough brown hair, with a baby face, with large eyes fixed on the vision of an absent lover—or on vacancy. And now Susan, her duties as a model over, pulled a handful of such pale wild-flowers as still survived the heat upon the parched hill-side, and came and sat down by the artist's side.

"How well curly hair looks in a picture," said she, regretfully.

"How well curly hair surrounding a certain face looks always," said George Blake.

"When I first came to Uncle Adam's and saw how stylish the French ladies looked with crimped hair puffed up all over their heads, I tried it. You don't know how different I looked. Portia Ffrench said I looked better, and I am nearly sure I did."

"Really ! I wonder you had strength of mind to give up such a becoming fashion."

"Well, you see, crimped hair brought bad luck," said Susan, gravely. "The most miserable—no, not that—the most disappointed moment of all my life was when my hair was crimped."

And having got thus far she colored up to her eyes and shrank away.

" The most disappointed moment? I must have an explanation of all this. What was the most disappointed moment of your life? "

"I can't tell you. Nothing. I'll *never* tell you, Mr. Blake."

" Your confusion is sufficient answer, Miss Fielding. The most disappointed moment of your life was brought about, in some way or another, by John Dysart."

It was on Mr. Blake's lips to say " by Tom Collinson," but he hesitated opportunely. With the absent legitimate lover as clear forgotten as though he had never been, it were poor policy in the present lover to recall a sense of his existence.

" Mr. Dysart—oh, what things you think of me ! It was you, then, since you make me say it. I had heard from you to say you were coming, and then at breakfast that morning, when I felt as sure of it as that the sun shone, came your dreadful letter. I took it out in the garden. The sky was blue and the flowers were smelling sweet, and the canary singing at the Le Bruns' window—I shall never forget it all —and I opened the letter and—and you were going to stay in Paris ! "

" And what has this got to do with crimped hair ? "

" Oh, mine was on crimping-pins at that moment. Miss Portia had said it made me look so much less plain, and of course I wanted to look my best, and when I read the letter I thought luck was against me, and I went to my room and wetted my hair and let it have its own way. I shall always let it have its own way for the future."

" Always let everything have its own way," said Blake. " Its the best guide of life I know of. Ah," after gazing a minute at her down-bent face ; (had he quite forgotten the evening when he gazed as intently at Portia's and wished Susan Fielding at Jericho ?) " and so you thought luck was against you that day. Would it have cost you anything if I had stayed in Paris altogether, Susan ? "

" I think I have told you quite enough, sir, I knew you wouldn't stop in Paris altogether, with Portia Ffrench in St. Maur."

She began to arrange her flowers, one by one, on her lap.

" Portia Ffrench, indeed ! Susan," coming an inch or two nearer, "let us talk sense. Don't let all our time be wasted on frivolity. Give me a lesson in botany. What are the names of your flowers."

" As if you don't know ! This is stone-crop, and this is a bit of heather—"

" And these yellow things ? "

" How foolish you are to pretend ! As if every one doesn't know those are ox-eyes, the commonest flower that grows. The children at home used to find out whether you liked butter with them."

" Indeed ? Show me how."

" Oh, it is only children's play. I hold one of them—well then you hold it—so—and if it throws up a yellow light on my chin it shows I like butter."

Blake held the flower as he was bidden close to the delicate round throat : at that moment a ray of sunshine broke out between the clouds and lit up all the girlish figure of Susan Fielding with radiance. " My love." he whispered, "don't let you and me deceive each other any more. I love you. I have loved you pretty nearly since the day I saw you first."

He flung the flower away, put both his arms around the child and kissed her

Curiously enough, she never thought of Tom Collinson.

If Mr. Blake had asked her formally to be his wife, or to be engaged to him, something in the very sound of the words would, I am sure, have recalled her to her sense of duty, to the remembrance of her affianced love. As it was—reader, as it was, at the first clasp of Blake's arms, at his first unexpected kiss, the poor little girl was at once transported into a world wherefrom "the pedant reflection is barred out;" a world in which neither place nor people, loyalty nor disloyalty exist. She was loved. What should her consciousness take in but those words: words only a minute old and yet that seemed already to shed back divinest sound and fragrance over every hour that she had lived!

I wrote, that on the night at Addison Lodge when Blake first kissed her hand, was shut the last white page of Susan Fielding's childhood. In this moment when their lips met, opened the first rose-colored one of her life as a woman. She looked at him, and a regenerate soul looked through the great, near-sighted eyes.

The clouds parted more and more. Not now in transient gleams, but in one broad wave of crimson, the sunset irradiated water, and wood, and hill-side, and the two faces radiant already with youth and love and the newness of their own delight: the last brightness before the storm. After a moment the red sun touched the horizon, the wind rose in a gust, a shiver like the first breath of autumnal dissolution ran through the beech-boughs, a prolonged moaning *huish* told that the tide was fast gathering strength as it rose in the river mouth beneath.

"We are better here, after all, than at the boating party," whispered Blake.

"We are better here," said Susan's heart, "than in any other place in the universe!"

As they walked back, half an hour later, toward the town, a few big drops of rain—the rain so long hoped and prayed for—were beginning to fall. The sky by this time was covered thick in cloud; far away upon the sands, dimly visible through the twilight, lay a white and ever-broadening belt of foam. When they had passed the barrier of the octroi and were in the long, unlighted, ill-paved lane that led down to the Petit Tambour, Susan's hand clung tighter to Blake's arm, a trembling despondency seized her spirit. In silence they passed the grass-grown entrance to the barracks; the gates were closed, the sentry at his post stood motionless: one of the gaunt St. Sauveur dogs was sniffing his famished way along the street: a minute later, and they had reached the Petit Tambour. The front door stood ajar; a light shone from Uncle Adam's bed-room window on the first floor.

"I shall see you early to-morrow," whispered Blake, as he clasped Susan's hand in his. "By ten in the morning I shall come—to tell Uncle Adam what good care I took of you."

And after this, a few more of the whispered words—so infinitely wise when they are spoken, so infinitely foolish when they are recorded—and Susan stood alone in the silent evening, listening to the steps of her lover until they died away in the distance. Then she turned into the house.

Something, she shuddered from asking herself what, was unusually amiss. Uncle Adam's favorite tortoise-shell cat, never allowed by Mrs. Byng to leave the kitchen, sat with solemn mien at the open door of the salon. A hand-lamp, evidently set down in haste on the passage table, was giving forth a fraction of a centime a minute of wasteful light. A strong pungent smell, like what Susan had smelt at the door of the cathedral during mass, went through the house. She advanced a step or two and saw that the stair window, usually so carefully shut at night, stood open. Her heart seemed to cease beating. She stopped, listening fearfully—afraid beforehand of what she should hear—a door upstairs creaked slowly on its hinges, a woman's figure glided, with cautious, noiseless step, down the stairs.

"Uncle—Uncle Adam?" broke from Susan's lips, almost with a sob.

"The will of the Lord be done, my daughter," answered the woman softly in French.

It was a Sister of Charity. The sight of the black robe, of the bowed, pale face, of the hands meekly clasped above the crucifix on the breast, told Susan all.

CHAPTER XXXVIII.

THE night was growing constantly wilder. Even here in the Petit Tambour, a mile and more from the sea, could be discerned the increasing roar of the breakers against the beach. Over in St. Maur, girt on three sides by the sea, men knew that the storm at every moment was gathering strength with the rising tide, and blessed God in their hearts! went down in groups to the shore—I speak of the citizens, not the fashionable visitors—and blessed God for the fresh salt wind, for the rain, scantily as yet though it fell, that was to bring back healing and life to the plague-stricken town.

But it must be a wholesomer wind than ever blew across our earth yet, that brings nobody any harm. The shifting of the wind from sultry east to cool south-west may save many a score of lives between this and this day week, yet wreck one life to-night. Portia Ffrench and her companion are abroad still; and the only hope Miss Jemima can gather from the conjectures of the people about her is that they may have landed at Sesame, an uninhabited island a league away from the mainland, before the storm reached its present height. They have with them brave men and true; in this may madame take comfort. Pierre Bresil and his son, two of the best seamen in St. Maur, are known to have left the pier this afternoon with an English gentleman and the young lady from the Benjamin. If they did but make Sesame before dark they are safe. Wine and meat they took with them in the boat; shelter could be got among some of the old ruins on the island. Even should the weather last over a couple of days, as was the case when the Parisian gentlemen were storm-bound, all would yet be well. Madame must not let her courage fail.

With a face white as stone, old Jemima Ffrench listened, as, with the ready garrulous warm-heartedness of French people, the host, and then the hostess, and then the serving-women of the Benjamin came by turns into her room to offer all they could of consolation. She had heard long ago as much as the lad who accompanied Portia to the boat could tell, or rather as much as Miss Jemima's scanty knowledge of his language enabled her to extract from him. Mademoiselle and the gentleman started from the Benjamin, yes, and he, Guillaume, carried the basket—'twas a weighty basket, too—to the pier. They spoke to other ladies and gentlemen on the road—could Guillaume remember how many? Well, two or three, it might have been more, he was thinking of the weight of his basket, not of these ladies; and then they got into the boat, and the gentleman tossed him a franc as they were pushing off. Pierre Bresil told them there would be a storm before long, and the lady said—Guillaume heard her say, in French—that, storm or no storm, she would go. Yes, he was quite sure no one but the gentleman and lady started. He set down to cool himself on the pier, and watched the boat till it was out in the great roads. The wind was rising then. She had her sails up before she reached the fortress of the city.

So much (possibly not so intelligibly told as I have told it) Miss Jemima, by slow questioning and cross-questioning, had succeeded in learning from the lad. What more should she seek to learn? Portia and John Dysart, alone, had started upon this expedition; were alone now. And, in the bitterness of her heart, Jemima Ffrench acknowledged to herself that such danger as these simple people spoke of, danger from wind and wave, was, in truth, the least she had to fear.

Her ideas on most points of feminine duty were, as you know, old-fashioned, her opinions as to truth and falsehood, honor and dishonor, transparently clear. For Portia, after all her promises, to have started under the protection of a man like John Dysart—the intention, not the accident that had followed upon the intention—was, to Jemima Ffrench's mind, disgrace. Not because of the world's condemnation—"the world may never know the truth," she thought as, with her measured "regulation" tread, she paced up and down the room, "but for *herself*, for Portia herself! better far that Harry's child should die, honestly, now in her youth, than live to become—what her mother, Portia Dysart, was before her." And then, even while she thought this, her eyes fell on some little trifle, some airy lace pelerine or neck ribbon of Portia's, carelessly tossed upon a chair as the girl had left it, and all the Spartan died, all the fond mother's heart began to beat in Miss Jemima's breast. Ah, let her once more fold her Harry's child in her arms, safe, and she would forgive her all, and tenfold all her folly! Folly—was this an hour in which to think of aught but heaven's mercy? Listen to the strong waves, as they beat against the ramparts, to the dash of spray—the first that has come so far—upon the window which was Portia's favorite place! Could an open boat, guided by the coolest nerves, manned by the stoutest arms, live on a night like this upon a rock-bound coast?

Toward ten o'clock a knock came at the door—an English rat-a-tat this time, not the discreet single "thud" of French knuckles. Miss Jemima opened it, and saw little Lord Dormer, a shade of color, almost an expression of excitement, on his weary white face. He had to enter upon the subject of his visit at once. Jemima Ffrench never asked him to sit down, nor did anything in her face or manner encourage the usual suave ambiguities which help men out in the commencement of a difficult conversation.

"Your—your niece is not at home, I fear, Miss Ffrench?"

"You fear aright, Lord Dormer. My niece Portia is out still."

Lord Dormer glanced uncomfortably round him. The tapestry swayed hither and thither with ghostly effect against the walls; the wind moaned and whistled in the windings of the huge old chimney; Miss Jemima stood erect, her arms folded, looking at him.

"Nothing more painful than this kind of explanation!" he stammered, at length.

Jemima Ffrench was silent.

"You see—I'm sure you will forgive me for saying it all out plain—Miss Portia Ffrench was to have seen me to-day about—about something of importance, something that *was* of importance, I should say. I hoped to meet her during the afternoon, and walked about—blazing hot it was—and fell in with the Ramsays. They were starting in a wagonette, with some other people, for a picnic up the river, and through them I heard of this boating party, and then—"

And then Lord Dormer stopped, his poor little soul thrown literally on its beam-ends as he found himself drifting into a narrative. Miss Jemima met his eyes steadily as ever, but said nothing.

"The whole thing is deucedly disappointing, Miss Ffrench. You've always been very kind to me, and I'm sure you must feel what—a-a-I'm sure you must understand my feelings!"

Jemima Ffrench looked stony.

"Of course I know that Madame de Miremont was to have gone, and no one could have foreseen that—"

"No," interrupted Jemima Ffrench, breaking silence at last, "no one could have foreseen that Madame de Miremont would have been otherwise occupied than in pleasure parties!"

"And so Portia—and so your niece, Miss Ffrench, chose to go alone with her cousin."

Jemima Ffrench's head drooped on her breast.

"I should never have believed it, I declare to you I should not, but I heard it from—another connection of your family, who, it seems, saw them start."

"Poor little Teddy," murmured Miss Jemima, half to herself.

"I don't know that he deserves pity. That is a matter of opinion," said Lord Dormer, gloomily, "and a matter, pardon me for saying so, that concerns me little now. I was to call on you to-day, Miss Ffrench, for an answer—an answer to a question I asked your niece a week ago, and I've kept to my part of the engagement. I want you to say so much for me. I've kept to my part of my engagement."

"An answer, an answer?" repeated Miss Jemima, putting her hand to her forehead. "Lord Dormer, I don't know what excuse to make to you for my stupidity. My anxiety about Portia has put everything else out of my head. There *is* a note for you somewhere, I remember seeing it not a quarter of an hour ago—a note directed in Portia's handwriting. The answer you speak of, no doubt." And, crossing the room, Miss Jemima, after some search, took a little three-cornered note from the mantel-piece, and put it into Lord Dormer's eagerly-extended hand.

Yes, it was the answer, the rejection: before he opened it, his heart told him that. And in a three-cornered note, too! An answer to "the greatest honor any man can pay any woman," an answer to a proposal which certainly not a dozen girls in England would have refused, conveyed in a three-cornered note! A fastened envelope might have taken something of the sting off rejection; but this!

"Dear Lord Dormer:" (He had to bend low by the candle to decipher Portia's enigmatical handwriting) "In case I should happen not to be back when you call, and there are storm clouds on the horizon already, I leave a line for you. St. Maur is getting horribly unhealthy. I don't know whether *you* know it, but there are quantities of cholera deaths every day. My advice to you is—to go away while you can. You may not care for yourself, but *is* it right to expose the crew of the Lily" (the crew of the Lily! thought Lord Dormer) "to unnecessary danger? I hope we shall see you at Halfont *some time before Christmas*, and please don't forget the set of waltzes you promised to get me from Coote's. I write all this under the firm impression that I shall get drowned to-night. If I do not I shall most likely see you on the beach to-morrow morning. At all events, till we meet, and wherever we may meet, believe me always sincerely yours.

"Portia Ffrench.

"P. S.—Whichever world I live in I shall never forget my *delightful* voyage in the Lily."

Lord Dormer succeeded in reading the note through, after some futile essays ; a choking feeling rose in his throat at the last words ; the candle seemed to him surrounded, like the head of a saint, by an aureola. He had come to the Hotel Benjamin in a mood of the very sternest virtue that can be engendered by jealousy. Portia Ffrench had chosen to make light of his suit, and he abandoned it without regret. If the woman he would have made his wife, chose to sail over any sea she liked, with or without disreputable cousins, let her sail ! The better for him that he was left safe in harbor ! These had been Lord Dormer's dispositions ten short minutes since ; and now, so true a fool is love, he knew that he did but desire more ardently than ever all which he had lost: that he would forgive Portia Ffrench, put himself and his possessions at her feet at this moment, would she only return to him !

" You will pardon my not asking you to prolong your visit," remarked Miss Jemima. " But I am really terribly anxious—about the weather. At such times we are all poor company'"

"And—and I suppose this is good-by, then ? " said Lord Dormer, taking up his hat and looking very dreary. " I suppose the best thing I can do will be to start by the first train to-morrow morning, and leave the Lily to follow when she can ?"

" It would be one way of getting over the Channel difficulty," answered Miss Jemima, too engrossed in her own thoughts to heed whether her words were cruel or kind.

"And if—I mean when your niece returns, you will tell her, from me, that I got her note and that—I thank her."

" I will try to remember to give her the message, Lord Dormer, but I promise nothing. My brain, what brain I have left me, is in a whirl."

And then, a sadder, if not a wiser man, Lord Dormer walked away out of the Hotel Benjamin, and Jemima Ffrench's lonely vigil went on.

She had kept many a score of lonely vigils in her life. Pacing up and down the room, and listening to the ever-heightening wind without, what midnight memories flock upon the brave old woman's heart ! Memories of the gaunt and bearded men, the wounded, fever-stricken, drink-stricken soldiers, beside whose pallets she had watched ; of little children (whose days of birth and death are unremembered by their own mothers now) ; of Harry Ffrench's face as she had seen it last—Portia innocent in her cradle then—in the Brussels lodgings. Aye, but this was the bitterest vigil of them all. Mingled now with impending dread, with threatened shame, was the sting of self-reproach—a feeling, be it said, new to the white conscience of Jemima Ffrench. If, instead of attending to the wants of aliens and Papists, she had guarded the life that it was her plainest duty to guard, Portia would be at her side at this moment—Portia had never been thrown among the evil influences of her old Dysart associates. Miss Jemima stopped abruptly in her walk, and leaned her face down against the window pane : something nearer a sob than any living ear had ever heard from that stout old heart escaped her.

" Save her ! oh my God, save the child ! " she prayed, but without words, as we pray when our prayers mean most. And suddenly from out a phalanx of black cloud strayed the palest ghost of moonlight, and Miss Jemima could see the tossing waters white with foam, and the ramparts, and the figures—could it be true ?—the figures of a man and a girl, darkly distinct at this instant against the back-ground of sea, not a dozen yards away from the window.

The girl was Portia: no doubt of that. Something in the poise of head, in the turn of shoulder, could never leave Portia Ffrench's identity long doubtful. Portia was on dry land, unharmed; and Miss Jemima's first impulse was to thank heaven rapturously for the child's safety, her second to begin lashing herself into a state of towering anger ready for battle. *Never* should Portia guess what anxiety she had gone through to-night! The pity, the pity of it—the moral suffering caused her by this midnight escapade—this was what should be borne in upon the girl's hardened conscience to feel.

Miss Jemima drew herself aside, letting down the muslin window curtains, the better to shade the light from those outside, and watched. We have the old adage to tell us that listeners seldom ever hear what they would care to learn: the same fate, as a rule, befalls watchers. Portia and her companion (bad, selfish man! Dysart that he was! scarcely from indignation would Miss Jemima look at him) walked together to the bottom of the flight of steps that I have mentioned as existing in the wall of the Hotel Benjamin. Then—and scarcely could old Jemima Ffrench believe her eyes—then did Portia, the cold, the reticent, throw her arms around his neck and of her own free will—I am almost as shocked as was Miss Jemima—kiss him. In went the friendly moon; there was a minute's pause; and then came a loud, perfectly assured knock at the window, and "Aunt Jem, Aunt Jem," cried out Portia's voice, not a quaver of conscious guilt in its tone, "let me in." It had been an agreement, made in jest between them on the first night of their arrival, that if ever Portia met with any romantic adventure she should glide " with soft step up the turret stair " and plead to be taken in: indeed, without romantic adventure at all, she had more than once returned from the ramparts by this fashion.

Miss Jemima stood motionless, long enough, she hoped, to set the culprit's heart beating with wholesome dread; then, stiffer, sterner than Portia had ever seen her in her life, she moved forth and turned the handle of the window. It opened with a burst. In came a storm of wind, rain and spray, and Portia, wet from head to foot, her black hair floating on her shoulders, her hat and veil a wisp, the water literally streaming from her yachting dress as she stood.

"Aunt Jem, dear old Aunt Jem, what a fright you have had! I'm too wet to kiss you, and—"

"And are you cold, too?" cried Miss Jemima, anxiety for Portia's bodily welfare holding virtue, for the moment, in abeyance.

"Cold? not a bit. If it hadn't been for thinking of you, I should never have enjoyed anything so much. You've called me a coward about this cholera business, but I'm not one. We have been in danger every minute of the last three hours, in danger from the moment when we failed to make Sesame—the boatmen said so—and I love it, I love it! I'd like to *live* in a small boat on the sea, always in a storm—"

"—And always in the society of your cousin, I conclude," said Miss Jemima. "Or at least, till the excitement of the novelty had worn off."

They had now reached the centre of the room, and the light showed the expression of old Jemima Ffrench's face.

" And you are going to scold me, after all ? " cried Portia. " And I came in expecting an ovation ! After being saved by a miracle from drowning to be reminded of propriety ! It is not like you, Aunt Jem."

"Go and take your clothes off, child. I will talk to you when you are in your bed. Go at once."

" Not until you look better-tempered, old lady. After being wet to the skin for four hours or more, an additional five minutes can't be a matter of life or death. Don't be hard, don't think bad things of me, Aunt Jem! I don't care a fraction what the rest of the world think, but don't you join issue against me!"

"You leave me no choice, Portia. I am not over-suspicious, as you know. I have trusted, since you were little, more to your honor than to my watchfulness. But what I am forced to see I see. You lower yourself, child, you lower yourself fatally. Men see you, like you, admire you—do all but love you—then they tremble and draw back. Lord Dormer has paid you his farewell visit, Portia."

"Thank heaven for one mercy, then!" said Portia, cheerfully. "Poor little wretch, how did he look? You gave him the note I left for him? Well, how did he take it? Was he cut up? Really and truly, did he seem cut up?"

"Not the very least in the world," said Miss Jemima, with decision. "He bade me say that he had got your note, and that—he thanked you! Even Lord Dormer, with his intelligence, with his fraction of a heart, does not, you see, seek to marry a woman carrying on the kind of flirtation that you are carrying on with John Dysart."

"With John Dysart? I like that—good, too, the idea of Lord Dormer giving me up! Well, if the whole remainder of my life is as innocent as my flirtation with poor old Jack, I shall not have very much to answer for when I die."

"Innocent!" Miss Jemima's face grew scarlet with blushes. I don't know what may be called 'innocence' now-a-days. When I was young, for a woman to part from any man but her own husband as you parted, five minutes ago, from John Dysart, would—"

"I parted five minutes ago from John Dysart? I parted from John Dysart six hours ago, at least; I left him, not at all in good temper, upon the St. Sauveur harbor between four and five."

"And your companion—the companion who left you at the foot of the stairs?"

"Was Ted. Who else should it be? I'm sorry you think so badly of me, Aunt Jem;" Portia's fine face suffused and fell; "and sorrier still that it is not in my power to set you right. Perhaps some day you'll do me tardy justice. You saw—I know what you saw. Well, then," suddenly and unashamed lifting up her head, "you ought to know I could never bring myself to marry any man but Ted Josselin."

"I know nothing about you. I seek to know nothing. That you could start upon a boating expedition alone—that you have been all these hours in the society of Edward Josselin, not John Dysart, is just so much better in this—that Edward Josselin is not a married man. I say no more. When you persuaded me to come here in Lord Dormer's yacht, you certainly did not speak as though your cousin Josselin were the only man you could bring yourself to marry."

"But accepting the use of a yacht—oh, and accepting a bracelet or two, and a certain quantity of foolish attention, is not marrying, Besides, where's the good of going over all this now? Lord Dormer has paid his farewell visit, you say; Jack Dysart has gone back to the society of the Ramsays, who, I believe, return to Paris to-morrow. Do you know, Aunt Jem, this horrible cholera is really gaining ground, Jack told me so when we were on our way down to the boat."

"Well, yes, this horrible cholera is gaining ground," said Miss Jemima, coolly; "has taken some decisive steps indeed, during the last few hours. Did you meet Susan Fielding? You must remember I know nothing at all of what you have been doing."

"I met Susan and George Blake on our way to the boat. The De Miremonts, at the last, sent word madame was too ill to come—an excuse, likelier than not—

Miss Jemima looked up at the ceiling.

"And John Dysart was here, waiting for me, and I thought as Susan Fielding was to go, too, and—and as Jack was a married man, it would be ridiculous
to put the party off. Well, we started, and I must say I never felt more ill-hu-
mored in my life ; first, about the De Miremonts ; next, that Teddy Josselin had
not appeared. I gave him a quarter of an hour's law, and then Jack reminded
me we should only lose the tide by waiting ; and over in the Place Dauphin at
St. Sauveur we met Susan and George Blake, and found they were not going
either. The old uncle was afraid of the sun, or of the sea, I don't know what he
was afraid of—at all events, they were not going.

"And then you decided to start alone with John Dysart ?"

"Decided ! Have I ever decided anything in my life ? I thought it a pity
the good food and wine should be lost, and the boatmen's fares paid, for nothing ;
and that Jack and I might just put out half a mile to sea, eat our dinner, and then
come back—I don't know what I thought, I'm sure. We went a little further
along the lane, looked down through a gap in the wall to see if the boat was
waiting, and—lo and behold ! Ted had turned up after all, and was sitting on a
barrel upon the shady side of the quay, smoking cigarettes. He had made one of
his usual foolish mistakes ; thought we were to meet at the water-side, not at the
Benjamin—however, there he was waiting for us—"

"And John Dysart ?" interrupted Miss Jemima, who was beginning to see
the cross purposes at which she and Lord Dormer had played.

"Oh, well, Jack—upon my word, I shall cause an inundation ; look at the
waves rushing from me across the floor—Jack got cross. Seemed to think three
rather a silly number, and insisted upon my reducing it by one. I reduced it by
one. Jack, I fancy, betook himself to some picnic of the Ramsays, and then
Ted and I went off to sea, and ate our dinners, and drank our champagne, and
got caught in the storm, and, as you see, reached shore safe. The story is told."

"And if Teddy Josselin had not 'turned up,' as you call it ?"

"Aunt Jem, it may be a defect in my powers of reasoning, but, as I have told
you before, I can't follow out sequences from awful things that might have happened, but did not. If Teddy Josselin had not turned up, I should not have gone
to sea with Teddy Josselin. So much is certain. Now let us speak of something else. Tell me, before we say good-night, how your day has passed."

"My day ? oh, in quite humdrum, uninteresting occupations, Portia. You
wouldn't believe how little novelty there is in scenes of sickness and death !
The same patience, the same suffering ; the rigid hand—the glazed eye. How
can you expect me to have any news fresh enough to be worth repeating ?"

"You look cadaverous, ashen, yellow, aunt. Let us go away from this place.
What good is there in stopping here any longer ?"

"What good ? Portia, in a mud-hovel to-day I saw something worth travelling to the end of the world to see. A girl was dying—nothing new in that,
certainly—a girl about your age dying of rapid cholera, a child a few months old
in her arms. The husband—a gaunt, starved skeleton, who had recovered not a
fortnight ago from fever—and two miserable children, stood helpless, tearless,
conscious only, I suppose, of their own hunger, by her side. She died, and I
could only pray that the babe on her breast would die with her. But as we stood
there—I and a Sister of Charity and the man—one of the neighbors came in, a
woman no better off than the other, also with a child in her arms. Portia, this
woman took the babe straight from the dead girl's breast to her own ! Then,
little though I understand their patois, I know she told the husband she would

nourish it for the future. Do you think more highly of human nature when you hear that?"

"I think the whole story horribly, unspeakably nasty," answered Portia, with a shudder. "All these things make me ill. I can't help it. Of death itself, a clean, brave death on the white waves out yonder, I was not afraid. Ask Ted some day if I was afraid! Dirt, mud-hovels, famished babies—everything to do with poor people and sickness, I *loathe*. Good-night."

But Miss Jemima lingered. "The sickness is not confined to mud-hovels and poor people now," she remarked, her eyes fixed full on Portia's face. "What hour was it, do you say, when you met Susan Fielding?"

"I suppose it was between four and five. Why do you ask? Why do you look so strange?"

"Adam Byng is dying. The doctor who attends him told me so this evening."

"And you have been there?" cried Portia, turning white. "Good God, aunt, don't tell me that you have been there!"

"Nothing very much to fear, if I had. No more contagion in the Petit Tambour than in all the other cholera houses I have visited lately. Well, no; I did not go. The good old man was calm and collected, they told me, and one of the Sisters of Charity was at his side. I was not wanted. Besides, I had a duty to perform nearer home—prepare yourself, Portia, you must know it to-morrow morning—I had a duty to my hand, here in the Hotel Benjamin."

"Don't tell me!" exclaimed Portia. "I can do no good by knowing. We will leave by the seven o'clock train to-morrow. The De Miremonts, I'm sure will go, too, and Teddy—I'll send round to him the first thing in the morning—and we can all travel in a party. I'll take off my wet things, and begin to pack at once—"

"As half the visitors in St. Maur are doing at this moment," said Miss Jemima, quietly. "Yes, we will go to-morrow, and you may bid Teddy Josselin, or any other of your lovers whom you choose, go with us. But we shall not travel quite in the party you speak of—Madame de Miremont died in my arms at six this evening."

CHAPTER XXXIX.

EVERY carriage the St. Maur railway station could muster was in requisition for the first train next morning; and still more places were wanted; still a crowd of disappointed, eager candidates for flight had to be left behind upon the platform to wait for the Brest express at ten o'clock.

The violence of the wind was now over; bounteous rain had fallen during the night, the air was fresh and cool, the place healthier, in reality, than it had been for weeks past. But the cholera had struck down a person of distinction. The little Countess de Miremont, who was dancing—the beauty of the ball-room—on Thursday evening, lay in her coffin on Friday. What more natural than that her sorrowing friends and acquaintances should wish to escape from the possible recurrence of such a catastrophe? Away flew everybody, French and English alike, in the general contagion of terror. The Ramsays and John Dysart, Portia and Miss Jemima, Teddy Josselin, Lord Dormer—all are gone! to England, Paris, Trouville, anywhere where they believe the cholera is not. The bathing-machines stand unoccupied, in a row; at the Hotel Benjamin a dozen people in-

stead of a hundred sit down to breakfast. In vain the doctors, the hotel keep-
ers, cry aloud that the epidemic is passing. In vain the Casino directors placard the town with announcements of a ball, a concert, a regatta, all forth-com-
ing in the next eight days. Balls, regattas! Had not Madame de Miremont
been at a ball the night before; was she not to have been at a boating party the
evening she died? Merely to advertise such frivolities seems like wilful tempting of Providence in a time like this! And the ten o'clock train clears out all the
people who were left behind perforce, this morning, and scores of others as well.
The St. Maur season is over. In the prime of summer, with fresh air blowing
and warm sun shining, the Casino and *tables-d'hôte* are empty. Grim death
this year, not a royal personage or other leader of fashion as was wont, setting
the signal of departure.

By ten o'clock was effected the second great clearance of fine ladies and gentlemen, with their accompanying band-boxes. At the same hour George Blake,
with the light step of five-and-twenty, the happiness of a lover whose suit is not
a day old in his heart turned into the narrow shade of the Rue de la Guerre.
The colza mill was clinking merrily; one of the mill-girls sang clear and sweet
over her work; the morning sky showed blue above the roof of the Petit Tambour; a freshness almost of spring was in the air. Blake rang discreetly at the
door; with a smile pictured to himself the little figure that would trip to meet
him along the passage, the face, suffused with conscious blushes, down-bent so
that his first kiss must be given to the forehead not the lips! Meanwhile his ring
remained unanswered, and he repeated it, somewhat louder: then he heard a
step descend the stairs. The door opened, and he saw Susan Fielding. Where
were the blushes, the dimples, the coyness of young love, of which he had
dreamed? Her face was heavy, her dress uncared-for; some of the wild-flowers
plucked during their walk last night were in her breast, dead.

"You!" she cried, starting back, horror-stricken, as her blind eyes caught
sight of Blake. "Don't touch me, don't come near me. What do you mean by
coming near the house?"

"What do I mean! Susan, my dear little girl, what is this foolish jest?
Don't you know very well what I come for?"

"Then you have not heard?—you don't know that my Uncle Adam has got
the sickness? Go, Mr. Blake, go. I may never ask another favor of you—do
this for my sake! There, then, I will give you my hand if you'll only promise!
The Southampton boat leaves St. Maur at midday."

She snatched her cold hand back after it had lain a moment in his, and made
an attempt to shut the door. Blake quietly slipped his arm within the lintel.
"You are saying you know not what, my poor little child. You think that in
your trouble I would leave you—now that every trouble, every pain is as much
mine as yours! What use can I be of? What help can I give? Has Mrs.
Byng returned?"

"She came back late last night; and one of the Sisters of Charity has been
with him from the hour he was seized. All that could be done for him has been
done."

"And is there no way in which I can be of use?" repeated Blake.

"Yes, there is one way," said Susan. Her voice was set, almost hard: all
the happy youth of yesterday had fled from it and from her face. "I told you so
just now. Go. Let those who have no duty here escape, while there is still
time."

"No duty! You can't really mean to be cruel, Susan, although your words

are cruel. No duty for me to stay near you, to feel with you—if I may do nothing else—in your sorrow?"

"No, it is not your duty, Mr. Blake. Your duty is—to help me to fulfil
mine."

"And yours?"

"Is to forget you. Oh, I am talking soberly now, this is not a time to talk of
love-matters, but I must say so much. I had lost my reason and my conscience
last night. You took me by surprise, and—"

"And you don't care for me? and all that you said during those two hours
was false? Tell me that and I will go away from you as quickly as you bid
me."

She hesitated—her lips quivering, her poor little clasped hands twitching nervously. "I *can't* say that I don't care for you, I think it would be a horrible sin
for me to say that, but I've been thinking, all through the night, and I know now
how wicked I was to let my heart go from—the person I've promised to marry.
It came on so easily, from one thing to another, and last night under the beeches
I forgot him—indeed that's the truth—I forgot him. If Uncle Adam had not
been taken ill, I don't know what I should have gone on to. I think I had forgotten right and wrong altogether. I think I've been getting further and further
from my duty ever since I knew you."

"Duty!" repeated Blake. "You, child as you are, talking of the duty of
marrying a man like Collinson, of whom you know nothing, for whom you care
nothing—"

"I promised to be true to him," cried Susan Fielding, a light coming into
her eyes. "My duty is to keep my word. I can't deceive myself with fine
words now. In the night, and the house so silent, and death coming so near,
I thought of the time when papa died, and felt just as if his voice had spoken
what he would have told me was right. Tom Collinson isn't a gentleman, I
know; and I can't care for him as—as I could care for some people! But whatever he is, I'm bound to him the same as if he had married me before he
left. I can never be free till he sets me free. I should bring no good to you,
sir, if I did a great wrong for the sake of my own happiness."

"And you mean to give me up? Let me hear the plain truth."

"If my heart breaks for it, I'll keep my word to Tom Collinson. God knows
I will!"

Blake was silent for a minute. "You think all this now," said he, gently,
"and I think better of you for thinking it. This is no time, as you say, for talking of love-matters. All I can do is to stay near you, my poor little girl. Let
Collinson have the lover's love when he returns; meanwhile, let me be your
brother." His head bowed, his lips all but touched her forehead.

"And what will be the end of it all?" cried Susan, almost with passion. Collinson will *not* have the lover's love, and you know it—do you think I'll deceive
myself anymore? Collinson will never have a lover's love, and you—you can
never be like a brother to me while I live! The way you can help me is by going. You know what must be the end of your staying near me! You know
that every hour I am with you will make it harder for me to marry Tom Collinson!"

Now no coquette, versed in the intricacies of men's hearts, could have
worded a lover's dismissal more flatteringly than did Susan, unversed in everything, speaking only honest truth, and looking up, with honest eyes, full into the
face of the man she loved, and whose love she was giving up. And still Blake

felt, while she confessed his supremacy over her affections, that over herself, over the steadfast, upright soul of Susan Fielding, his will was powerless. On this solitary point of " moral obligation "—conscience once arrested, the sense of duty once confirmed—this child of seventeen, so immeasurably weaker in all things else, would be his conqueror. With a woman of more complex nature— I think in that moment's disappointment, he would have said of larger intelli- gence—he had stood a better chance. Many-sided minds can look at indi- vidual responsibility, as they can look generally at life and men, from higher ground than that of written law. From Susan Fielding (out of whose ductile heart a lover could draw as wide a diapason of emotions, as a skilful violin- player can draw tones from his instrument) it were vain to expect a single fluc- tuation of "principle." She loved him, confessed her love, confessed his pow- er over her ; and would go and marry Tom Collinson, cook Tom Collinson's dinners, rear Tom Collinson's children, say her prayers and believe herself on the road to heaven by virtue of having kept to the letter of a senseless oath ! Which indeed were best : the woman with too little heart, or too little brain ? The former were incalculably easier to manage. Vanity, pride, a sense of the picturesque, a sense of the ridiculous, all might have been brought to plead for him, and against Tom Collinson, with a woman as slow to feel, but as quick to perceive as Portia Ffrench. With poor little honest, unimaginative Susan, all were powerless. She had promised.

"You are strong, you are generous enough to forgive me," she said. " You won't remember me in any way with unkindness. *I* am the loser, you know. You will meet with people better suited to you in every way than I am. You'll wonder some day that your choice could have rested, even for an hour, on a girl like me ; and I—"

" You will marry Tom Collinson."

She stood for a moment silent, then a great sob broke from her, and Blake took her in his arms.

" You'll never love him, you'll never love any man as you have loved me ! " he whispered, a selfish, exquisite pleasure even in the bitterness of his pain.

" No," said Susan, " that I never can. But I will do my duty by him."

" And you will write to me ? "

" Yes, I'll write when I'm left quite alone in the world. Never again."

" Let me look in your face ! Let me have one kiss before I leave you ! "

" Mr. Blake "—shivering in his clasp—" let me go. I never meant that you should touch my hand. There may be death about me at this moment—I came straight from Uncle Adam's side to open the door."

" If death were on your lips, child, do you think I would count the cost of a kiss ? "

These were their last words to each other. An hour later, and Susan, with a breaking heart, watched the Southampton boat steam slowly out of the St. Maur roads,

GRAY walls, draped by the sodden skeletons of last summer's roses : dank and untended flower-beds : a snow-charged sky :—such is the winter prospect from the back windows of the Petit Tambour. In front, the narrow street, along which the solitary figure of a priest or sister from the neighboring convent may be seen to pass at lengthened intervals during the day ; the silent colza-mill, the tall, gaunt block of barrack, shutting out for four months of the year, whatever southern light or warmth heaven, in this Breton climate, may vouchsafe to send, from the mouldy, death-still precincts of the Rue de la Guerre !

Silence, lifelessness, grayness, outside the house : silence, lifelessness, grayness within. No fire, no inmates, in any room but one, the dining-room ; and there a few smouldering logs, carefully kept below blazing-point, and two joyless women, stitching with heads downbent, without the interchange of a word or look, at their needle. Joyless, I say, both of them ; yet is the heart of the elder one the least heavy. In losing poor old Adam, Mrs. Byng had lost much ; a diligent servitor and companion, a patient sharer of her toils, a meek participator in her profits. But she has not lost the closest, sweetest interest of her life : her money is safe. She is thinking of money at this moment. A faint additional warmth circulates in her veins as she listens to the drifting sleet against the window, and reflects that her house-keeping is now reduced to a positively fractional item ; the straw a day, the visionary ideal of economy attained ; and yet her own body and soul kept together ! The charges she makes to Susan Fielding are strictly fair ones. Half a century's battle with her kind has taught this woman that probity in the long run pays a steady dividend, and she respects it, as she would respect any other safe investment. But the coffee, the cider, the pumpkin-soup, that will keep one will keep two : this is a mere natural elasticity of matter over which Mrs. Byng has no control. The menial work of the household is, at this season, nominal ; but, mindful of the world's respect, Mrs. Byng still goes through the form of a servant (without nourishment), and Susan's money not only defrays the market outgoings but pays the servant's wages, twopence-half-penny a day. The woman is joyless. What has a life l'ke hers to do

with joy? Can joy be hoarded and put out at interest, or rented, with chance
of profitable breakage, to summer visitors? But in her soul is the solid satisfaction of a passion gratified. She is existing, and costing herself nothing.
Never in the nighest point to starvation through which she and Adam had
passed together has she before drawn breath in December on terms so cheap as
these.

December: yes, the year is on his death-bed. Autumn has come and gone,
sweeping the leaves from the beech-trees, and hope and youth out of Susan
Fielding's heart, since that night when she and Blake walked together in paradise upon the hill-side, the night before Adam Byng's death. She knows very
well what sort of a paradise the hill-side is now. Every afternoon when the
day's task is over, she goes up there alone, rain or shine, stands with her arm
round the tree beneath which Blake rested when he made his sketch, looks at
the colorless, sunless landscape; listens to the beat of the wintry sea, and tells
herself that all is over: summer, love, happiness—all.

I have read that there is only room in the heart for one profound sorrow at a
time. Is this practically true? Susan's master-sorrow was, assuredly, the ship-
wreck of her love. Of the impossibility of being Blake's wife she thought when
she awoke, thought during the day, thought till dreams bore her back to the
canal-bank and to the time when she was a girl, catching minnows, chasing drag-
on flies, hiding torn frocks from Miss Collinson. But blent with this, heightening every tender memory, sharpening every present pain, was her grief for her
father; the grief held in abeyance only during the past months, and which now,
like a stream swollen by accidental obstruction, was having its course.

This little creature, so devoid of sentiment in speech and action, could, in
truth, live only in the life of the feelings. Love, and its attendant jealousy;
despair when what she loved was gone from her: these were the very fabric of
Susan Fielding's nature: the coquetries, the vanities you have seen in her, lights
and shadows on the surface only. To hear Blake say again that he loved her,
to know that he had loved no other woman since he left St. Sauveur, to feel his
arms round her once more, and then die and be carried home and laid under the
chancel yew beside her father—this was the nearest approach to a hope she
could have felt now. And from Blake she had long ago ceased to hear. He
wrote her one long letter in answer to the promised announcement, in which she
told him that she was "quite alone in the world," her Uncle Adam dead. And
she had had the strength of will not to write to him again. And there was no
chance at all of her dying! Her life was to be passed in sewing, and silence, and
grayness: in listening to the hopeless convent bell: in walking (her nearest approach to pleasure) for fresh draughts of poisonous, regretful memories to the
beech knoll. And by-and-by Tom Collinson would return, and she would marry
him, and—no, at this point Susan invariably thought no further! Her interest,
her desire, her life was over. Whether her remaining twenty or sixty years of
existence were to be spent in the Petit Tambour or with Tom Collinson she did
not speculate. There had been better prospect of her cure could she have roused
herself sufficiently from the apathy of present despair to picture trouble beyond.
On the day when we begin to look forward to the future we begin, little as we
may know it, to hope again.

The mixture of snow and rain which the Bretons call the *verglas*—the dis-
tinctive feature of their climate in winter—continues to beat against the window.
Though it is only three o'clock, twilight already is deepening the shadows in the
garden. The great bell of the convent sounds, and gives a last Dantesque

touch to the gloom of Susan's spirit by reminding her of the two hundred frozen hearts; women's hearts to whom human love and human joy are accursed things; waiting for death within its walls.

"Three o'clock," she remarks, not because the hour of the day interests her, but because change, even the change of hearing her own voice, seems all at once an imperative necessity.

"Three o'clock," repeats Mrs. Byng, without looking up from her work, "and nearly too dark to sew. In these short days it might be well if you got up an hour earlier. We had the oil burning yesterday by four in the afternoon, and oil is rising."

Get up earlier! make the days longer than they were already! With a sinking heart Susan folded her work, with weary, patient neatness, and laid it down on the table. "May I go out a bit, Aunt Adam? My eyes ache. I shall work faster this evening if I have an hour's walk now."

"My eyes never ache," said the widow, "and I am fifty-five and have been working all my life. Go out, of course, when you choose. I can get your seam done for you in your absence."

On this grudging permission Susan rose, went upstairs for her hat and cloak, and started. It was biting cold; the north-west wind drove the cutting *verglas* full on her face as she opened the front door; the road leading toward the beech knoll was ancle-deep in half-melted snow and mud; and suddenly a kind of inspiration bade her give up her pilgrimage for to-day and walk down to the post to inquire for letters. If the factor came as far out of his beat as the Petit Tambour during the bad season, he expected a handsome gift at the new year. By Mrs. Byng's orders all letters for the household were therefore, from November till February, left at the office until called for.

The usual tide of life was flowing along the cheerful high street of St. Sauveur; two old market-women on donkeys riding back toward the country; a crippled street-sweeper extending his palsied hand for alms at the principal crossing; detachments of the unhappy ragged regiment of English taking grim exercise by pacing up and down the only piece of pavement the town could boast, a space just opposite the second-floor room wherein our countrymen played whist for glasses of gin and water, and which they called "the club." Susan passed through these people, with none of whom had she acquaintance, and made her way into the post-office, where other English, poorly-clad, depressed looking like the rest, were waiting for letters. (It amazed you to think how people so obviously forgotten by heaven and man could look for communication from their fellows; and, of a truth, they rarely received any. But in a life as near petrifaction as theirs, even to pretend to one's self to have an expectation may be something.)

"Any letters for the Petit Tambour?" asked Susan, when her turn came, and hearing beforehand the "No letters for Mademoiselle" she knew so well.

The civil little clerk searched through his row of pigeon-holes, and handed her two; one from Eliza Collinson, the other—. How did she get over the up-hill length of street? Where was the cruel *verglas?* Where was the bitter wind? She reached the Petit Tambour in about a third of the time the distance had taken her in coming. The servant chanced to open the door at the moment when her hand was on the bell, and, without encountering Mrs. Byng, Susan put off her sabots, ran softly up to her own room, locked the door and gave herself up to the pleasure—pleasure! the very word sounds unnatural connected with her life now—of reading George Blake's letter.

Her window, the one from whence she watched the steamer that bore him away, faces the west. There is a strip of pale primrose light on the horizon; enough, if she loses no time, to enable her yet to read. Which letter shall she keep to the last. Through conscientiousness (or epicureanism) she puts Blake's aside—holds it passionately tight, I mean, between her numbed little red fingers —and opens that of her lover's sister first.

101 RED LION STREET, LONDON.

MY DEAR SUSAN,—The melancholy demise of your respected uncle—though who shall doubt that *your* loss is *his* gain?—has, I fear, by the tone and shortness of your letters, cast a lasting gloom over your spirits. It is therefore with lively satisfaction that I take pen in hand to be the harbinger to you of welcome tidings. My beloved brother is now on his way to England, having completed business in the Colony earlier than expected, and looking forward to our being ready for the wedding immediately on his arrival. You will, I doubt not, under these happily-altered circumstances, see the propriety of at once returning to England. My dear brother has inadvertently mislaid your address, and begs me to communicate. He also asks me to take an inexpensive temporary apartment in London, which, as you see, I have done, so that you may be quietly married at once. I will leave all important subjects till we meet; but if Tom's business calls him to live in the metropolis you had better see to furnishing without delay. I looked at some sweet chintzes to-day in the Edgware Road, slightly soiled, but would not show when made up, and two pence a yard cheaper than at Hounslow. However, more of this when we meet. I saw old Miss French and Miss Portia just before leaving home, and told them the news of Tom's return, and how your marriage would take place immediately. They were on their way to London, and they stopped the carriage most *civilly* to speak. Old Lady Erroll is feared to be on her deathbed, and strange stories are afloat as to Miss Portia. Expecting so soon to see you, and with seasonable compliments—though, I fear, *but* compliments—to your bereaved aunt, I remain, your affectionate friend,

ELIZA COLLINSON.

P. S.—Tom may be here before you. I mention this to avoid giving you a turn if you should find him on your arrival. In due course his letter ought to have reached its destination more than a month ago, but fortuitously, through the poor fellow's indistinctly writing the word "Hounslow," it went first to *Halifax*.

And this is what Blake wrote:

MY DEAR LITTLE FRIEND,—I have just seen Josselin, and he tells me some news very bitter for me to hear. Mr. Collinson is on his way home, and you are coming to England to be married directly. Will you let me see you once before your wedding-day? You are to be married in London, I hear. Well, write a line and give your address, and tell me when I may come and wish you good-by? Do you remember my telling you once that you and I would not see the last of each other for the next forty or fifty years? I'm afraid we shall have to see the last of each other now. Don't think I am asking you to do anything wrong or to deceive Mr. Collinson. Tell him everything about me, and ask his permission for me to come, as an old friend, and offer you my good wishes. Are you well? are you better in spirits, my poor little Susan? Write to me, and believe always in the affection of your friend,

GEORGE BLAKE.

Susan went down straight to the dining-room, her letters in her hand. The nearest approach to a fire that Mrs. Byng ever permitted herself was at this hour when the shutters were still unclosed and ghostly shadows glimmered in the dark garden outside. As Susan opened the door the draught caught up the carefully-piled embers; they flickered into a blaze, and showed the girl's face distinctly. It was white and tired-looking, as usual; but a lustre they had not worn for months past was in her eyes.

"I am to go to England at once; yes, by the next boat from St. Maur," she exclaimed. "I have got a letter that calls me back."

"You must pay your quarter's board just the same," said Mrs. Byng. "I stipulated at the time that you should pay in advance. What necessity can there be for you to travel at a time of year like this?"

"I have got to be married," said Susan, hanging her head. "You know what I have told you about Tom Collinson? Well, I have heard from his sister, and he is coming back sooner, a year sooner, than he expected. Don't talk about my quarter's board, Aunt Adam! I hope you will take all the money I have to give, for your kindness to me and for Uncle Adam's sake."

A sudden, softening gleam came over Mrs. Byng's face, then it hardened; her eyes sank, and shifted about uneasily under the blazing fire-light. Money, money—the very thought of touching money roused, for one minute, all the slumbering giant desires of her narrow soul. But avarice has almost as many delicate shades of superstition as her half-sister, gambling! Susan's offer was the first disinterested one Mrs. Byng had received during her fifty-five years' cold experience of life, and she shrank from it, that momentary instinctive impulse over, absolutely as one shrinks from a thing of evil omen. What profit could accrue, what luck come home to *her* with money gotten through such unwonted channels as another human being's generosity?

"You are liberal, Susan: in time you will grow wise. I shall receive the remainder of your quarter's board as a right; not a sou besides. I never take more, I never take less, if I can help it, than is due to me, and you will find other uses for your money than alms-giving! If you light the lamp and begin at once, you may finish your seam before dinner."

By the post that night Susan dispatched two letters. One was to Miss Collinson—neither expressing pleasure nor the reverse at the prospect of Tom's return; but simply stating that she would be in London, and would drive to the address given on such a date, a few days hence. The other letter bore no signature. It consisted of three lines in the centre of a page; an ominous blister in their midst.

The address is 101 Red Lion Street, Holborn. I shall be there on January the second. Yes, I *should* (three times understroked) like to see you once more.

And this was directed to "Mr. George Blake, the Treasury, London."

CHAPTER XLI.

ELIZA, but no Tom Collinson, stood waiting for Susan on the cold January night when she arrived at the door of One Hundred and One, Red Lion Street, Holborn.

"He's not here, my dear," were Eliza's first words. "Don't be disappointed—my foolish mistake. Tom can't be here before to-morrow afternoon at earliest. In one way I'm glad, for we can go together to see after the chintzes and things. Dear, dear," as the white-faced little traveller came into the light of the parlor, "you are looking much older; Susan, you have grown very thin. I'm sure I hope Tom won't be shocked when he sees you! Tom, who used to think so much of your good looks!"

Susan took off her travelling wraps, and began to warm her frozen hands; and Miss Collinson, as she bustled about preparing tea, descanted more and more upon her changed appearance. "You have grown two inches, your face has got quite pointed—you who used to have dimples ! I'm sure I hope you'll make a good tea. I'd have had something substantial, only I knew what a poor hand you are at meat. Yes, you had dimples, you looked a girl of fifteen when you left Halfont, and yet—I don't say Tom will think you uglier for the change."

Then Susan took sudden courage. If plainest truth-telling could yet save her, she did not mean to be Tom Collinson's wife. So much, during her long journey from St. Sauveur to London, she had resolved.

"It would be just as well Tom *should* think me uglier, Eliza. If he only asked me to marry him because I had dimples, I hope he'll see at a glance that my dimples are gone."

"Susan, what are you talking about ? You can never mean—"

"I mean that Tom and I had both lost our senses when we got engaged that night. What did we know of each other ? What was there in me, that Tom should want to have me at his side for his whole life ?"

"And your promise to him ? and the poor boy returning (overland, too) to marry you ? and the cake as good as ordered at Webb's—for the only thing I left open was the number of pounds. If your papa could hear you, Susan !"

Miss Collinson was at this moment on her knees toasting a muffin, and looked up with piteous supplication at Susan's face.

"Ah, if papa could hear me !" said the girl. "If papa could know all ! Well, he would'nt blame me, perhaps, for what I'm going to do now. Don't think I ever mean to break my word to Tom, to deceive him in any way. If he likes to marry me still, I will marry him—yes, the day after he returns. I only mean to tell him the truth, and—and—" she began to stammer a little, "the truth is, we both of us were in too great a hurry from the first."

"Oh, is that all !" cried Miss Collinson, looking relieved. "I declare you quite frightened me for a moment. Of course, you will tell Tom that he was in too great a hurry, and of course, Tom will only like you the better for saying so. Ah, Susan, my dear"—and now Eliza rose, the muffins toasted, and with a melancholy little air of sentiment, took her place at the table—"*I* was a young girl, *I* had a lover once. Well do I know what hopes, what fears, beset the female soul in such a position as yours."

"But perhaps you loved your lover ?" remarked Susan, crimsoning.

"A modest girl does not talk of loving a man till she is married to him," replied Miss Collinson. "It is quite enough that I have been in your position and can enter into your feelings."

So the first opportunity for confession was slurred over ; and Susan had not strength of mind, to-night at least, to seek another. After all, the confession she had to make belonged to Tom Collinson himself. Let Tom first hear the black story of her infidelity ; hear how, promised to him, wearing his ring upon her hand, she had listened guiltily to words of love from another man ; and let him pronounce the fate of both. She was silent: and Eliza, her momentary misgivings over, fell at once to babbling of wedding cakes, and wreaths, and dresses. She had seen a sweet worked muslin for forty-eight shillings, in Oxford street this morning ; and, talking of weddings, Susan would never believe it, but report said Portia Ffrench had refused a *lord*, and after travelling half over Europe in his yacht, too ! The Misses Ffrench, aunt and niece, were staying at the Langham Hotel, daily expecting Lady Erroll's death, but Lady Erroll—after putting them to the expense of coming to town—had not, as yet, consented to see her granddaughter. "All this I know from a gentleman who was here this afternoon," finished Miss Collinson. "A Mr. Lake or Drake—stay, his card is somewhere about—ah, here it is under the tea-tray. 'Mr. George Blake.' He must be a friend of the Ffrenches, I suppose, for he called here to see if you had come, and—bless my heart, child, what a wretched appetite! and after a journey, too! Done your tea already?"

Susan had started up at Blake's name, and was standing before the fire, leaning her tell-tale face down against the mantel-shelf. "Mr. Blake? Yes, he is a friend of the Ffrenches—and of mine—I'll come back in a minute when I'm warmer—don't you remember I met him at the Manor on my birthday? You told him I should not be here to-night. Was he—disappointed at not finding me?"

"Really, my dear, I did not remark the young man very closely. He just asked if you had come, and I said no; and then, after a little gossip about the Ffrenches and old Lady Erroll, he told me of this terrible accident in the park—fifteen people under the ice at once!"

Half through the night Susan lay awake in a fever of dread, lest Blake, having missed her once, should not take the trouble to call in Red Lion street again. Next morning she was too weak and languid to get up for breakfast; and, when at length she managed to creep into the parlor, looked such a poor little shadow of her former self, that all hope of seeing about wedding dresses to-day died in Miss Collinson's heart.

"You want good nourishing things, instead of wishy-washy soup, Susan. All your French water-souchy and stuff don't suit English constitutions. A pity you didn't stop quietly at home with me, while Tom was away."

"Yes, a great pity," said Susan, absently.

"It was my wish, as you know, but Tom talked such nonsense about the cavalry barracks! What harm have the cavalry barracks ever done *me*? And then your head was so full of change and seeing fresh places. Do you remember the evening before you left? I was cross with you; I couldn't help it, because you took everything so easily. Don't you remember you said you felt as if you were in a dream?"

"I remember," said Susan. "Ah well, Eliza, you needn't be cross with me any more. I've awakened from dreams of all kinds now."

When their two o'clock dinner was over, Eliza prepared herself to go out. After the Misses Ffrench's kindness in sending to inquire for Susan, it would be only civil for her to take a 'bus as far as the West End, and tell them she had arrived. "And do you try to sleep, and get up your good looks while I am gone," was her last injunction, as she wheeled round the one arm-chair the room possessed to the fire. "Your eyes seem bigger, and your face smaller, every time I look at you. Just suppose Tom was to walk in, and see you as you are now!"

Suppose Tom were to walk in, indeed, Susan thinks, when she is alone! and it is possible: the New Zealand mail is already due, Tom Collinson walk in, take her in his arms, kiss her, bid her prepare for their instant marriage! And all the time her heart passionately yearning to see the face of another man; her hands turning cold, the blood rushing to her cheeks, if she only hears the rattle of a cab down the street, at the thought that it must be *he*. Ah, how great is the gain of people who haven't got to live life out—how she wishes she had died when she was twelve years old, and had the fever! Little Polly Dawes of the shop died—they ran in the fields together and made a big cowslip ball, the evening before Polly was taken ill. She can smell the cowslips—she can see the green oaks waving above the path where they played. "Susan, Susan, I can toss higher than you!" says Polly's voice. She runs to snatch the ball from her companion—her companion is Blake—his arm is round her—he is whispering in her ear. The tired eyes close : the flushed face has drooped. For once more, at least, in her life, the poor little girl is in paradise.

Sweet is her sleep and deep: so deep that she never hears a cabman's thundering knock at the house door, nor the entrance into the parlor of a visitor, vaguely announced by the small maid-of-all-work as "a gentleman." The well-piled fire is blazing high, and there is a street lamp just outside the window ; so, although it is between four and five o'clock, the room is full of light, the picture of the small figure curled up in the arm-chair distinct. Susan's face looks younger than ever as she lies asleep ; her lips are parted ; her breath comes soft and noiseless like infant's ; two little white hands are clasped upon her breast. The visitor bends, gazes at her long and sorrowfully : and under the gaze she gives a start, and wakes.

"Mr. Blake—" she was dreaming of him : quite naturally, his is the first name she utters ; "it is time to go. Uncle Adam—ah, where am I?" pushing back her hair from her forehead. "Eliza—I am very sorry, sir, that you should have found Eliza out."

She doesn't know what she is saying. She has started up frightened, both her hands in Blake's. She was with him, they were lovers, a minute ago, in the happy sunset, on the Breton hill-side. She must have time before she can realize that he is here, in this London lodging, to bid her good-by, to offer his congratulations upon her marriage with Tom Collinson.

"You were resting—tired after your journey," says Blake, "and I have disturbed you. My poor little friend, how grown you are—and how thin ! "

He holds up her hand—very loosely Tom Collinson's ring fits her finger now—and looks at it with grave tenderness, never offering to raise it to his lips.

"Every one says I'm grown," answers Susan. "At least Miss Collinson says so ; that is my 'every one.' It used to be the dearest wish I had, to be two inches taller."

She tries to laugh, to be at her ease ; she moves away from him. They look at each other a moment in the fire-light ; a mist swims before Susan's eyes, her head droops. "Wishes don't bring much happiness, when they come true," she remarks.

After this a silence. Then, as people do when their hearts are full to overflowing, they try to begin a conversation on indifferent subjects. "Is there any news from Brittany, Susan?" Blake asks. "What have the St. Sauveur people been doing since I saw them last ? "

"They have been burying each other, sir. At least that was their chief employment till late in autumn. The sickness got better just after Uncle Adam died, and when the visitors went away, but in another month it was as bad as ever again. Nothing but the bell tolling, the priest's voice chanting down in the cemetery. I was glad they took my Uncle Adam away. They buried him in Guernsey, by his first wife. I like to think of him lying in the quiet graveyard, by the sea he used to talk of."

"Do you remember your Uncle Adam's last words to me, Susan? Do you remember his standing at the door of the house, and how he bid me—"

"Yes, yes, I remember," interrupted Susan swiftly. What need to recall that last vain injunction ! Who but Tom Collinson would she want to take care of her now, and till her life's end ! "I don't know why it is," she went on, "but everything to do with France, seems farther away to me than leaving Hal-

font. I only left St. Sauveur thirty-six hours ago, and already the place, and
everything belonging to it, seems like a dream."

"A good or a bad dream?"

"Oh a bad—bad one!" cried Susan; thinking of the lone gray house, with
the *verglas* beating on the pane, and the convent bell marking the dragging
length of the sad hours.

"What," said Blake, "was the summer bad? How warm the sun used to
shine—how full the little garden was of flowers! Do you remember the last
duet we sang, and how silent the house was—only you and me alone together?
Do you remember the hill-side? Susan, whatever comes of it, I won't let you
say that all your recollections of St. Sauveur are bad ones."

She clasped her hands with bitter eagerness. "I wish there was no such
thing as recollecting! If I could only begin afresh from this moment, and recollect nothing, I might be happy, perhaps!"

She meant (I believe she meant): "If I could only forget you, I might be
happy with Tom Collinson." But Blake's heart gave another interpretation to
her words.

"And what is there to hinder your beginning afresh?" he asked, his eyes
intently reading her down-bent face." Why should you and I go on talking
polite insincerities to each other? You have come back to marry Collinson, and
you are miserable at the prospect. Don't marry him. You have a day—an
hour of freedom left you yet. Use it well. To keep such a promise as you
have given, is perjury. What sort of life do you look forward to spending at
this man's side?"

The moment of fiercest temptation had come at length. The past dark
months of suffering, the tender pleading of her lover's voice, the casuistry that
passion only too promptly awakened in her heart, all conspired against Susan
Fielding's honor. "If I was dead!" broke from her lips with a sort of sob.
"If I was at rest with papa! There's nothing more in the world for me to live
for!"

"Nothing?" exclaimed Blake, and in a second his arm was round her waist.
"Susan, do you call the warmest love a man's heart can give you—nothing?"

She faltered, trembled, broke away from his touch. "Better to die miserable as I am, than live and win your love through—falsehood," she cried. "I'm
bound to Tom Collinson, so that nothing but his word can set me free. He
wanted me to swear—and I told him yes or no was the same to me as an oath—
and then I said yes, I *would* hold faithful to him."

"And have you done so? Have you kept true to the spirit of your promise?"

"No, I have broken it, shamefully, because my heart—my heart was stronger than myself! You are cruel to make me say such things."

"Susan, my dear, your principles are beyond all praise. If you had ever
loved—no, I won't use the word—if you had liked me even, as I once thought,
you would not have your feelings under such fine control."

"*If* I had liked you!" her great, dilating eyes looked up to his full. "*If!*"—
a sudden passion swept over Susan's Fielding's girlish face, she clasped her
hands with a gesture, almost of bodily pain. "And you doubt me after all,
then! Why, but for this promise, do you think there's anything would hold me
from you? Wouldn't I follow you to the end of the world? You have made
me say this—you shall hear the truth now—for this last time while we live, that
we shall talk together. I liked you from the first evening I met you at the
Manor, and when I knew you had never a look or thought, but for Portia

Ffrench. Oh, sir, but I will show you, in my own writing, that what I say is true!"

And quitting him abruptly, she walked into the adjoining bed-room, and came back a minute later with a book (her old Halfont journal) in her hand.

"I was a child in those days—who'd think it was so few months ago? I wrote very sillily, because I wrote what I thought, but you must take it for what it is worth. I knew no better."

And she opened the book at the part containing her account of the first evening spent at the Manor, and put it into Blake's hands. He stooped till the fire-light rested full upon the page, and read it through: the school-girl raptures on Teddy's embroidered linen and blue eyes, the discriminating remark that he, on the other hand, had "a dark, serious face, but no pretty ways like Mr. Josselin ;" the confession, evidently written with extra care in the cramped, childish hand, "*I like Mr. Blake.*" He read it though, and as his eyes still rested on the avowal contained in those four last words—avowal, more pathetic, it seemed to him, than any spoken one to which he could have listened—some small object rolled out from the pocket of the book, and fell to the ground. Blake picked it up—'twas only a three-inch end of pencil—and examined it with the sort of mechanical interest the eye sometimes bestows on external things when the thoughts are far away. It was one of his own: a little square cross, that he had an idle trick of carving on the top of his pencils, arrested his attention.

"Give it to me—it is nothing?" exclaimed Susan, betraying her secret by her vehemence. "I—I found it! Mr. Blake, give me that pencil. I found it on our river-bank. I never meant—it has nothing to do with what we spoke of. Pray give it me!" She held out her hand with humble entreaty to his.

"And you have kept this, Susan—through all these long months you have cared to keep this bit of worthless pencil?"

"Worthless!" She had got it safely back in her own possession now. "Ah, if you knew what it is to be alone, as I have been—without a companion, without a hope—you would not talk so. Why, during all these months what have I had, but—"

Rat-a-tat, went the knocker; an apologetic little feminine knock: they started guiltily asunder.

"It is Eliza," said Susan. "Go away when you have spoken to her. This must be your last visit."

"Susan, do you mean to do Collinson the gross injustice of marrying him?'

"I know nothing about injustice. I shall I tell him the truth, just as plainly as I have told it you. It will be for him to decide the rest."

The door opened and in came Eliza Collinson, looking more like a frightened little bird than ever, with the snow resting on her small, gray-clad figure. She gave a twittering start of astonishment at seeing the tall male figure on the hearth-rug ; Blake moved forward, and, with as good a grace as he could command, made his bow to Tom Collinson's sister.

"You must really excuse me? Mr. Blake—oh, of course—Mr. Blake, for not recognizing you at first, sir ; but coming in out of the dark—and such a night as it is!" And then Miss Collinson paused, looking a little curiously at George Blake's face, then at Susan.

"I called," said Blake, feeling an excuse was needful, "to inquire if—if Miss Fielding had recovered from her journey. Your brother has not arrived, I hear, Miss Collinson."

"No, sir, but for certain he will be in England in the course of to-morrow.

I called round at his agents—Susan, my dear, I called at Tom's agents—and they have had a telegram from Marseilles. By dinner-time to-morrow our dear boy may be with us."

Susan's heart turned sick. "How will your brother know where to find you?" she stammered.

"Oh, he will go straight to Messrs. Cox and Braddell, and they will give him our address. He settled that in his letter at the same time he bid us be in town to meet him. You can understand our anxiety, I'm sure, sir?" added Eliza, turning round, with a flutter of girlish diffidence, to Blake. "But *under* the circumstances—"

"Oh, certainly," said Blake, taking up his hat, and moving across the hearth-rug to say good-by to Susan.

"We shall be a very small party, and everything quite quiet, by my brother's desire, but if, as a well-wisher of Miss Fielding, you would join us at the church? Tom has few friends in London, we shall want a best—gentleman." Miss Collinson's delicacy would not allow her to use so common a word as "man."

"Eliza," broke out Susan, her face crimsoning, "what are you talking of? You know things are not settled. You know—"

"Oh, my dear, I said nothing about the day, did I? I was telling Miss Ffrench about it, an hour ago—old Miss Ffrench; Miss Portia has been sent for to her grandmamma's, whose last hour they fear has arrived. (Most painfully anxious their situation is, Mr. Blake! Lady Erroll, it appears, has been in the habit, all her life, of making at least two new codicils a year). Well, I was telling Miss Ffrench that everything but the day is settled, and how *that*, of course, must be left till after Tom's arrival. I hope you will do my brother the honor of making his acquaintance, sir?"

"You are extremely kind," observed Blake.

"We might try and get up a little party to the British Museum, or somewhere of the sort. Miss Fielding is rather low-spirited, Mr. Blake, and my dear brother is always so fond of pleasure. Susan, my dear, we should have much pleasure if Mr. Blake would join us in a cheerful party to some of the Metropolitan sights?"

"I think everything had better be left till Tom's arrival," repeated Susan, ready to sink with shame.

And upon this George Blake shook hands with her, and bade them both good night. When he had got to the parlor door, he turned. "If I might be allowed to call at about this hour to-morrow, Miss Collinson, to inquire if your brother has arrived?"

"Most delighted, sir. You will, I hope, at the same time, do Tom the honor of making his acquaintance," said Eliza, with her best company curtsy.

"A very elegant young man," she remarked, the moment the house-door had shut—Susan standing, with quivering lips, with downcast eyes, before the fire. "It was a good thought of mine to ask him to the wedding, particularly as a friend of the Manor family. I wish"—plaintively—"poor Tom had a little more of that style, Susan!"

"Yes?"

"So considerate of him to call again; but I fancied"— Eliza glanced at herself in the glass above the mantle-piece—"I fancied, from the little I saw of him yesterday, that Mr. Blake was anxious to become better acquainted with our family."

CHAPTER XLII

THE snow-fall that had just begun when Eliza Collinson entered, grew thicker and thicker, and long before midnight all the miry length of Red Lion street was pure and white, the distant roar of Holborn hushed.

Looking out through the dingy lodging window, something in this altered silent world struck tenderer chords in Susan Fielding's memory, and for the first time to-day, brought tears into her eyes. " I like the snow: it makes me think of Halfont churchyard," she said to Eliza, almost in her old voice. "At this minute I think I see the old peacock yews, each with its topknot of soft snow outside the chancel."

" Like the ice on a bride-cake," said Eliza, whose thoughts could never at the present time, stray far from nuptial subjects. " Ah, my dear Susan, such are the chances of our transitory life! You and I thinking of bride-cake, and our friend Miss Portia watching beside a deathbed—and such a fever of excitement, too, as she must be in about her grandmamma's intentions ! "

A fever of excitement! Aye, in all her tolerably chequered existence, never had Portia Ffrench really known the meaning of the word *excitement* till to-night. Here, at length, was the genuine, concentrated, overmastering emotion, at which, through cards and other mimic warfare of society, she had hitherto sought in vain to arrive ; life, or all that to her constituted life, the stake.

She had been summoned, late in the afternoon, to her grandmother's house ; but by the time she reached Eaton Square, Lady Erroll had grown rapidly weaker—or so Miss Condy sent word by the lady's-maid—and could not see her granddaughter. And now, midnight coming on, Portia Ffrench is still on the watch, still alone in the drawing-room.

About all the house is the faint, chill impress, indefinable by words, of coming death. The door stands open ; Portia, unobserved herself, can watch the figures of those who pass, can tell, without asking, all that is going on. She knows that the family apothecary, and the family physician, came down-stairs a couple of hours or more ago, grave, like men who feel that their patient's last earthly fees have been paid. She knows that a messenger has been dispatched in haste for Teddy Josselin, that Mr. Bloxam, the family lawyer, has been in the house for hours. She knows what visitor is with the dying woman now ; can guess what that visitor's errand, in such an hour, is likely to be !

Her hands are cold, though blazing fires are burning in both drawing-rooms. She has taken nothing but a glass of Lady Erroll's sherry for hours, yet is unconscious of hunger. Every fibre of her nature, moral and physical, is strained to one tensest point of agonized doubt. What—what will be the latest act of the woman who lies adying overhead? Will pitiful rancor, will sordid care, survive to life's last gasp? If Lady Erroll learn the truth (and some instinct of Portia tells her that it will be so) will no premonition from a world into which money and ambition may not follow, tempt her, in these her last hours of mortality, to be generous and to forgive ?

Her thoughts are interrupted by the stealthy rustle of a silk dress. The visitor who has been spending the last half-hour in the sick chamber is descending the stairs. The visitor's face changes color ; her eyes sink ; she tries to hide under her shawl a morocco box that is in her hand—in vain. Portia saw it at the first glance, and guesses only too well the meaning of its being in the other's possession. 'Tis an old-fashioned box, of somewhat singular shape, the case of one of Lady Erroll's finest diamond necklaces.

"You here, Laura? A wild night to be abroad." And now the visitor has no choice but to look up. The friends stand before each other, face to face.

"I was sent for—at such a time I could not refuse to come."

"And have broken faith with me? But that I need not ask."

"I—I could speak nothing but truth beside a deathbed," stammers Laura Wynne.

"I see, and have received your reward. From the time of Judas when has not betrayal fetched a good price!"

"Portia, you have no right to speak to me like this. I don't know what you mean by using such words as reward and betrayal. Poor dear Lady Erroll insisted upon my taking a little parting remembrance from her hands. There has not been too good a feeling between us lately. I was glad that things at the last should be made smooth?"

"Made smooth! Mrs. Wynne, have you been trying to make things smooth for me?"

"I have answered a direct question. What else could you expect me to do? Ask yourself if, in everything, you have been a true friend to me? Oh, Portia, I have always cared more for you than you for me? You—you will be too generous to betray any poor little folly of mine?"

"Can you ask me," returns Portia, with icy coldness; "knowing me even as you do, do you think I have so little self-respect, so little worldly wisdom, as to criminate a woman I once called an associate?"

And then—Mrs. Wynne gladly making her escape down the stairs—she walked back, with her grandest air, with a bursting heart, to the companionship of her own thoughts. She paced up and down the room: she chafed over her own powerlessness. Oh, fool that she had been, to *risk* an hour like this! fool, with so many possibilities yet open to her had she remained free, to cast the die of her own life beyond recall! If only she and Teddy could live the past again, from the hour in which Macbean found them together in the conservatory! If only—she turned, hearing her own name softly spoken, and saw Teddy himself.

He came up to her side, took her hands tenderly, and kissed her. "'Tia love, I've a notion things are going rather badly for you and me."

"Just as badly as they can," said Portia. "Laura Wynne has been upstairs for the last half-hour, and went out just now, with a jewel-case in her hands. What secret but one could Mrs. Wynne have had to sell, or Lady Erroll to buy? Bloxam is here; Miss Condy does not leave grandmamma's room. Nothing but hard swearing of yours can save us now."

"Hard swearing!" cried Teddy, drawing back; "and what have I got to swear but the truth. Money is not worth a solitary falsehood, Portia! Let grandmamma cut both of us off with a shilling. We shall have each other still."

"We shall," said Portia, with a hard smile: where was her youth gone? she looked thirty years old. "Each other, and starvation. Teddy," she went on, after a minute, "if you have ever loved me, if you would not see me the most miserable woman living, put away all these copy-book platitudes, do your best to be sensible. Grandmamma, I am positive, is altering her will—meaning mischief of some kind—or why should Laura Wynne have been sent for, why should that horrible old Bloxam have been all these hours in the house? If she should require you to take an impossible oath, and by so doing, you could make her death-bed easier—"

"—You would advise me to perjure myself!" interrupted Teddy Josselin. Thank you, my love! I have invented facts enough. The invention of facts at a time like this would be, my dear child, something unpleasantly like—dishonesty."

"Dishonesty! dishonesty means defeat," said Portia, turning from him coldly. "Act as you choose. When we are beggars, perhaps you will see how highly the world will rate your delicate sense of rectitude."

"I don't believe I'm thinking of the world at all," said Teddy, looking foolish, but in a singularly firm voice.

Portia answered him not a word; and in two or three minutes' time, Miss Condy, her eyes swollen with weeping, entered the room. She gave a chill little nod of recognition to Portia Ffrench; then came to Teddy's side, and, with real feeling in her voice, told him that Lady Erroll felt herself somewhat stronger and was asking for him.

"And for me too, Miss Condy?" said Portia, with admirable self-command. "Does not grandmamma wish to say a parting word to me?"

"Yes, Miss Ffrench," answered the old woman, still keeping close to Teddy Josselin. "It is her ladyship's desire to see you, also, and in Mr. Josselin's presence."

And so together, Miss Condy stealing on first to marshal the way, the two cousins went up to hear their fate decided. They caught a glimpse of Mr. Bloxam, the solicitor, on their way. He was sitting in a small room between the drawing-room and the second floor; some open parchments on the table before him; his head resting on his hand. Not altogether an exhilarating sight this, of a lawyer with parchments, in the eyes of heirs-expectant, when a rich relation, wont to make new codicils twice a year at least, lies in extremity!

A disease of many syllables had been assigned by the physicians, as a justification for the Countess of Erroll's having done with life at fourscore; and to alleviate its symptoms, Miss Condy was ordered to give a spoonful of some restorative ether draught every half-hour. Never while she lives, will Portia encounter the smell of ether without the overpowering atmosphere of that chamber of death, and the pinched face of the dying woman, and the misery of her own eager, despairing heart coming back upon her vividly!

A low snarl met her as she entered: it came from Arno, who, shivering in his scarlet coat, and with a wistful sapience on his bleared dark eyes, sat at the foot of his mistress's bed. The old dog showed his fangs with unabated animosity at Portia, as she passed; raised his ears and gave his tail a melancholy wag, as Teddy followed.

"Dear grandmamma," said Portia, approaching and stooping over Lady Erroll's pillow. "I am so glad to hear that you are feeling rather stronger now."

The dying woman raised her hand with just sufficient strength to make Portia know that she was waved back. "Teddy," she murmured, indistinctly, "where's Teddy?"

Teddy Josselin on this came forward, and a slight sidelong movement of the little white old face upon the pillow told him that Lady Erroll expected to be kissed. He kissed her; then knelt down, took her shrivelled, nerveless hand in his and held it. The tears stood in Ted's blue eyes.

"You've been a good boy," whispered Lady Erroll, "till of late—and that hasn't been your fault. You were ten years old when I took you—Miss Condy?"

Condy, in a second, was leaning over from the other side of the bed.

"—He was ten years old when I took him?"

"Ten in the August, that he came to your ladyship in the October," said Miss Condy. "His dear papa and mamma both no more, and—"

"Child," turning her sick eyes—the fatal, fixed look of death already in them—to Teddy's face, "you'll not disobey me, now that I've come to this? I've done what I could for you."

Teddy Josselin made no answer. Portia moved a step nearer the bed. "Teddy," said she, very low, "you will surely not refuse to follow out all dearest grandmamma's wishes now?"

Her tone, but not her words, arrested the dying woman's ear. "Miss Condy," she called again: Condy knelt upon the bed, and bowed her ear down to the pillow. "Tell my granddaughter Portia what I wish her to hear. All that I have strength to say, I will say to *him.*"

Then Portia knew that her doom was about to be spoken. She folded her arms across her breast; and, with uplifted head, stood and listened to it.

"It is a most painful office, I am sure," said Miss Condy, "most painful indeed—ahem! but duty is duty."

"Go on. Be brief," said Lady Erroll, almost in her old imperative voice.

"A good many months ago, Miss Ffrench, you promised—"

"—Swore," interrupted Lady Erroll, impatiently. "Let me speak! You swore never to renew your engagement with your cousin Josselin, save by my consent. How did you keep your oath?"

"To the letter," answered Portia, firmly. "I have renewed no old engagement, I have formed no new one, from that hour to this."

"And where," said Miss Condy, "her ladyship, if she had strength, would ask—where did you go on the evening when you and your cousin dined here, the following day to that on which this oath of yours had been taken?"

"Do you readily require me to answer, grandmamma? Laura Wynne has been here. Has she not exposed my folly sufficiently, without my being forced to expose it myself?"

"Mrs. Wynne has been here," exclaimed Miss Condy: a cubit seemed to be added to her shrunken stature in the intense, culminating triumph of this moment: "but we were convinced—her ladyship was convinced of the truth, without Mrs. Wynne's testimony. I saw you with my own eyes, Miss Ffrench, descend at a place of impious resort! I had my suspicions; and anxious to carry out her ladyship's wishes—"

"You set a watch upon my actions," said Portia, perfectly cold and unmoved of manner. "So I half suspected at the time. Grandmamma, in going where I went that night, in associating with Laura Wynne, in asking Teddy Josselin to meet me, I sinned against good taste—well, if you choose, against propriety. I did not break my word to you. And Teddy Josselin—yes, you must let me say it, was not to blame. You have always loved him. Don't let your feelings toward him be changed, now that you are so ill, by any folly, past or present, of mine!"

Portia Ffrench, as you know, was an actress by nature. At this moment she acted so well as entirely to carry away Teddy Josselin, very nearly herself, somewhat her implacable enemy Miss Condy, into believing that she was ready to sacrifice her own prospects from unselfish, generous motives. But dim though the senses of the dying woman might be, not for one moment was *she* so deceived.

"Forgive! Aye, you care so much whether I forgive!" she said, with the faintest little ghost of a laugh. "Portia Ffrench, come nearer."

Portia obeyed in an instant; a flutter, that could scarcely be called one of hope, at her heart.

"I am going to do something better than forgive you. I've altered my will, and I'm going to leave you what you would have had if you had married Macbean—Teddy will be well enough off to spare it—and I want to give you the best chance I can of settling reputably yet. I've thought a great deal of it all during the last few days—I don't want to be harsh to you, badly though you have behaved—I remember whose child you are."

She stopped, exhausted. Miss Condy held a spoonful of wine to her lips, and after swallowing it and resting quiet a minute, she went on.

"But you—you shall never marry Teddy Josselin! Never. You are both here to learn that."

"Grandmamma!" cried Teddy, raising his head.

"Oh, I know what you would say, child. Portia has compromised herself by her intimacy with you. Has she not done the same with other men? Condy—' she looked round faintly towards her attendant.

"Yes, my lady—I entreat your ladyship to spare yourself the fatigue of talking. I am in a most distressingly-delicate position, Mr. Josselin, but her ladyship would allude to the rumors that were afloat in the autumn about my Lord Dormer in France. Also—we could not avoid hearing them—about Mr. John Dysart. A married gentleman, too!"

The color flamed up over Teddy Josselin's cheek. "And all these rumors," he cried, looking full into the dying woman's face, "all these rumors I know have been scandal of the vilest kind. *I* was at St. Maur. *I* countenanced, *I* allowed whatever Portia did."

"Teddy, I implore you—" began Portia.

"No. Let him speak," said Lady Erroll. "This is conclusive. I have—I have no time to lose! Bloxam must have finished?" looking anxiously towards Miss Condy.

"Mr. Bloxam, I am sure, only awaits your ladyship's pleasure."

"Bloxam has drawn out a fresh codicil to my will. I am making you a poorer man, Ted—by this codicil I leave my granddaughter, Portia, the sum of ten thousand pounds, and also to my faithful attendant, Miss Condy, an annuity of one hundred a year—"

"Oh, my dear, dear lady!" sobbed Condy, bursting into tears.

"To you—to you, child, will belong this house and every remaining shilling that I have—upon one condition. You will take your oath, here in Miss Condy's presence and in Bloxam's, never to make Portia Ffrench your wife."

Portia moved a few steps towards the door: she hid down her face between her hands. Before the thought of all that she was losing, before the prospect of all the blank to-morrows which, as far as she could look on, must constitute her life, her fortitude at length gave way.

"It is an oath I can never take, grandmamma," said Teddy: his voice was low, but quite firm. "You have given me enough already. You took me home here, you showed me kindness when I was a small boy, and had no one to look to but you. Do with your money as you choose. I don't suppose I'm such a fool but that I could earn my own bread—yes, and hers, too."

"*Hers!*" cried Lady Erroll, with a sudden start of energy: an expression, horrible to see at such a moment, sweeping across her face.

"Yes, hers," repeated Teddy, with quiet deliberation. And he bent forward, and whispered a word or two in the dying woman's ear.

"Leave my presence, both of you. I will never look at your faces again. Let Bloxam be called. I—must set my house in order—this—this is the bitterness of death—"

She sank back upon her pillows.

CHAPTER XLIII.

THE New Zealand mail has arrived; an open letter from Tom Collinson is in Susan's hand as she waits at dusk next day for George Blake's promised visit.

I have read in some advertisement a description of the toys called Magical Flowers: flowers dead to the eye, and yet so chemically prepared that a breath will bring back life and odor to their withered petals. Surely some magic has been wrought on Susan Fielding now! There is color in her pallid cheeks, hope once more lights up her eyes, as she reads over again some passages in Tom Collinson's closely-scrawled letter; she smiles—the dimples have got back to her cheeks!

A knock she knows comes at the door: quickly she hides the letter in her pocket; lectures herself stoutly on the impropriety of allowing her happiness to be so legible on her face; when Blake enters, a minute later, runs joyfully across the room, both little hands outstretched, to meet him. "The New Zealand mail is in, sir!"

Blake glanced suspiciously round, expectant of Eliza Collinson, of Eliza Collinson's brother. "I congratulate you, Miss Fielding," he remarked, stiffly. "I congratulate you upon your anxiety being happily ended at last."

They moved together to the fire-side, and stood there, as they stood yesterday evening: Susan's eyes fixed diligently upon the pattern of the hearth-rug, and Blake's upon her face.

"I wonder at my own good luck in finding you alone," he went on, after a time.

"Eliza has gone down to Halfont, Mr. Blake. She had a letter from the next-door neighbor this morning, to say something had gone wrong with the roof. Eliza was very sorry to miss the chance of seeing Tom on his arrival, still she had to think of the roof—oh, how silly I am to laugh! it was very natural she shouldn't like the thought of melted snow on the stair-carpets."

And out aloud Susan laughed, the most light-hearted, merry little laugh conceivable.

"I can really only stay a minute longer," remarked Mr. Blake, growing stiffer and stiffer. "No doubt"—looking round him again, as though Tom Collinson must be hidden behind the window curtains—"no doubt your time is fully taken up. I came, as I promised, to offer my last words of congratulation, and now I must hasten off to visit the Misses Ffrench. They return home to-morrow, and I am anxious to be the first to see Portia under her altered circumstances."

Straight went the keen, cold knife of jealousy to Susan's heart. "Good evening to you, sir:" holding out her hand frigidly. "Don't let me detain you. I had not heard of any alteration in Miss Portia's circumstances."

"Lady Erroll died last night. Didn't you know it? It was in to-day's papers—and I have a notion has cut her granddaughter out of her inheritance. I had a note from Portia Ffrench this morning, asking me to visit them in the course of the afternoon, and from its tone I guess the truth. Poor Portia," he added, throwing the utmost expression of sentiment of which he was capable into his face, "now the true nobility of her character will show itself."

"Now," remarked Susan, emphatically, "she will marry Teddy Josselin."

" Well, no. I fancy the last act of Lady Erroll's life was to extract a promise from Josselin that such a marriage should never take place."

" And he was selfish, wicked enough to make it ? " Susan asked this question with a sort of gasp.

" You call all promises wicked that are made against the inclination of one's own heart ? "

The answer died on Susan's lips : with sudden, cruel clearness the whole future shaped itself before her sight. Portia (abandoned by faithless Teddy Josselin) in poverty : Blake offering the love that in reality had belonged to her all along; and *she* left desolate, to live an old maid's life at Miss Collinson's side ! This was the reward to which the narrow, uphill path of honor and duty had brought her. The tears rose heavily into Susan's eyes—brimmed over.

" Susan, my dear little child," said Blake, quite with his old tender manner, " what are you crying for ? Surely you and Mr. Collinson have not had a lover's quarrel already ? "

" Mr. Collinson is in New Zealand. I don't care where he is. If—if you had had any thought but of other people I would have shown you his letter. I shall never see Tom Collinson again while I live."

Upon this Blake threw his arm round the small, shrinking figure, and clasped it in a sort of bewilderment. " Collinson in New Zealand ! And you have been unkind enough to keep me in misery all these minutes ? "

" In misery ? Will you please to let me go, sir. You have your visit to pay to the Misses French."

" I have no visit to pay to pay to any one, and I will not let you go. I can't realize this news. Is Miss Collinson's invitation a sham ? Am I not to be best man at the wedding after all."

" You will be best man I dare say—' best' in the real sense—at another wedding before long ! For me, I will never marry. I'm glad to think I've done with engagements, and lovers, and all *that wretchedness* forever.

" Susan, will you show me Collinson's letter ? I want confirmation of this good news. I can't look round without expecting to see your lover ! coming forward to claim you."

Susan drew the letter from her pocket. " It is for Eliza, as you will see, but there are no secrets you may not read. It was settled that if a letter, instead of Tom himself, should arrive at the agents, it was to be sent here by a messenger ; and before leaving this morning Eliza gave me leave, in case such a letter came, to read it. He—he writes rather badly," added Susan, not even yet without a blush of shame for Tom's deficiencies, " but I think you may make it out."

And this was what Blake read : his arm round Susan still, her little curly head pressing round his shoulder as she read her lover's letter with him.

DEAR ELIZA,—When you see this shaky scrawl you will not be surprised to hear of my sickness. I suppose you have got my last letter and are expecting me, and when I wrote it meant, as true as a man ever meant anything, to come by the next mail, but ' *Lumb proposé*,' as you used to say. My dear sister, you must prepare your mind for a sad blow. I wish I could say I thought it would be the same to S. F. ; but in her heart, it's my belief, she never cared for me, and that's a comfort—not to me, but to my conscience. I was never much of a hand, as you know, at a letter, and so must say my say in few words. I've got a wife here and a little daughter ; you must make the best you can of that. From the first day I saw S. F., I was sweet upon her, but I could say it on my deathbed—and this has been pretty near me—I should never have got into the mess I did but for you. That night you spoke to me on the heath—and the day Susan dined with us—well, well, let bygones be bygones, but this I do say, it's often along of religious people, and their tantalizing ways, that fellows like me get drove to their worst actions. This is duty, and that is duty; till a man, who hasn't too much *steadiness* at starting, don't know which way to turn to get out of it at all. I never meant to injure the girl, and I love her —to this day I love her. I think that little face of hers will go with me to my grave. If I had married S. F., she would have been my lawful wife—I trust to you to make her believe so much good of me—the injury would have been to—well, I see I must write the story plain, if I ever want to have done with it.

You remember the time, long ago, when I first wrote to you that I was meaning to get married to that blackguard Scotchman's sister! My dear sister, I deceived you, for we were married then, in a fashion. You know what the Scotch are, about marriage. Well, Matty (that was my sweetheart) held the same notions as the rest, and one day a Methodist parson chap came along by our station, and we said we were man and wife in his presence ; and Matty thought it as true a marriage as if we had been to church and had a couple of bishops to pray over us. I looked upon it of course as a marriage, too— *but I knew it wasn't one*—and by-and-by came that villain Phil's smash, and everything in the colony going to the dogs—what was there for me to do, but try my chance in England again, and leave Matty to shift the best she could for herself and the child? It's all very fine for lucky men to talk about " principle." I've never been lucky, and consequently, nothing I've done has been " principled." I don't know that I ever deliberately harmed man or woman in my life, but I've got into more scrapes than most, and generally managed to drag some one else down with me. I was never one of your cold-blooded, long-headed fellows, who can see from the first what line of conduct will turn out profitablest to themselves, and stick to it. I did what looked like best for the moment, and let the future take care of itself. And it didn't—there's the truth—and there's no accounting for anything.

I came back, and you know all that followed. I did honestly mean at that time to turn over a new leaf. I felt sure poor Matty would get on better without me than with me, and I thought I'd take some place under government, and make you a home against your old age. And then one morning came a letter—Susan Fielding knows the day it came—and my fine intentions were upset. I suppose no man was ever on the horns of such a *dilemma* as me that day. If Susan had been a little kinder about my going, I believe at the last I would have stopped. But she wasn't kind, although she pretended all she could. I dare say you'll say she saved me from committing a great crime. I'm sure I don't know about that. I came back and found Matty pretty well off in the world— three thousand pounds or so left her by her uncle. And I told her the truth—that'll show you if I meant to act dishonorable, and said it might be better to leave her and the child where they were, for the present, and how I saw a good prospect of my getting on in England, *et cetera*, and all I asked was, she should pay me out of her fortune an equal sum to what her family had robbed me of. It was then I wrote you word to expect me by the next mail. Matty took things easy for one of her high temper, (it strikes me sometimes she had other plans than I knew of) and it just seemed to me, matters might be squared off comfortable to all parties, when—for my paper tells me I must cut it short—I was struck down by my old enemy, the nervous fever. Well, Matty, she nursed me through it, poor girl ; and in the *d. t.* I believe I let fall more than I ought. At all events when I got better, the first thing I saw by my pillow was a parson—a *real one*, you may be sworn, this time—and between them they made me see what my duty was ; and we were married, you may say, before I had strength to know what I was doing. Dear sister, I leave it to you to break this to Susan, I could not bring my hand to write to her ; and ask her at the same time to let me have back my ring—I shall want you to send us out a chest of things soon—and I know *she* won't care to keep anything belonging to me. My dear Eliza, I brought your diamond ring away by mistake, and will take care of it till we meet, as I hope we shall again in this life ; for I hope, if ever you want a home, you'll come and make it here, with me and Matty. The young one's a fine child, a great look of poor father about the eyes. I'm sure, dear sister, you'll always remember me and the baby as the nearest you have belonging to you in the world. Let me down as gently as you can with S. F., and in the neighborhood, and believe me, your affectionate brother,

TOM COLLINSON.

Does Susan (who, I conclude, is in England) keep company still with Portia Ffrench and her fine London friends?

"Poor Tom Collinson—jealous to the last!" said Susan.

"'Poor Tom Collinson,' indeed! And it was for your promise to a man like this—a scoundrel who only did *his* duty by accident, after a bout of delirium tremens—that you were going to sacrifice everything?"

"I am not sure that he is a scoundrel. He confesses, you must remember, that he didn't know what was right and what was wrong. I should have known quite well that it was wrong to break my word to him. My guilt would have been greater than his."

"That is right. Stand up hotly for Collinson now that you are sure he did his best to injure you! I wonder whether it would be possible for a woman really to love a man who had never shown a disposition to behave badly to her?"

"I never loved Tom Collinson at all," said Susan, appositely.

The whole of this time Blake's arms had held her close. "Susan, my love," he remarked presently, "what are we trying so hard to quarrel about?"

"I am not trying to quarrel, sir, and—and I don't wish to keep you from visiting the Misses Ffrench."

"Miss Collinson has set her heart upon having a wedding-feast. Don't let us disappoint her. What reason is there that you and I should not be married at once."

"The best of all reasons," said Susan, in a faltering tone. "Portia Ffrench is free, is in poverty, and in your heart you care about her still. If you married me, it would be from pity."

"It is not your place to analyze motives—Will you have me for your husband?"

"If I was quite sure you didn't care about Portia!"—

And in this wide city of London there were two happy hearts at least.

After an hour or so they began to think of other people. "Eliza will be back by tea-time," said Susan, "I shall never have the face to tell her all this."

"Well, I should think not," said Blake. "Even a hardened coquette like Susan Fielding would find it difficult to announce that she had got off with an old love and on with a new in the same day. Such things are not to be told by word of mouth. Write Miss Collinson a line confessing what you have done. Inclose it and Mr. Collinson's letter in an envelope, and come away with me to see the Misses Ffrench."

"I should certainly find it easier to meet Eliza if she was prepared first—if you would tell me how to word it?"

"I don't think there need be much difficulty about that," said Blake.

And upon this Susan got writing materials, sat down at the table and wrote: but without Blake's assistance. It was the easiest note she had ever composed in her life!

DEAR ELIZA,—Tom's letter explains everything. Don't be angry with him, for I am not. I am quite sure he never meant to injure me. I have gone to see the Misses French, so don't wait for tea for me. Yours affectionately,

SUSAN.

"Go on," said Blake, looking over her shoulder. "The subject of the letter comes, of course, in the postscript. ' I am going to marry that worthless fellow Blake !' "

" Indeed I won't say 'worthless.' Eliza might not know I was joking. Do you think really, I ought to tell her at once ? "

" It will show how little you concern yourself in the matter if you don't."

And down went the postscript, carefully understroked : " I am going to marry George Blake."

The note and Tom's letter were inclosed in an envelope and laid in a conspicuous position on the mantel-shelf; then Susan ran to put on her hat and cloak, and they started forth into the night.

It was dismally wet and cold, Holborn a river of black mud, the sleet falling fast ; but Susan insisted pertinaciously upon having a Hansom cab. As soon as they were on their road : " Every wish I had has came true at last," she cried. " That night at the Chelsea Gardens in summer, I thought the greatest happiness the world could give, would be to ride in a Hansom by moonlight, us two. And it all has come true."

—" Except the moonlight," Blake remarked.

" Oh how I wish, for *one* day, I could be sure you were not laughing at me ! " said Susan.

CHAPTER XLIV.

A DRAWING-ROOM—warm, curtained, wax-lit—on the first floor of the Langham : two figures, a young man's and a girl's, in two easy chairs drawn up luxuriously close to the fender, at either end of the hearth-rug. The man's eyes are closed, his hands clasped with lazy listlessness above his head. The face of the girl is keen with eager thought : animation, unrest, are in every line of her graceful figure as she sits upright, her cheek resting on her hand, and builds castle after castle while she gazes in the red depths of the fire !

Castles not in Spain, but London : guests of the kind that shall amuse herself ; little dinners ; little round games, such as those at which she and Jack Dysart used in old days to bank together ; the most perfect pony carriage the town can show ; the most artistic dresses ! Surely the cup of existence sparkles to the brim at last. She likes Teddy Josselin : his character suits her own better than that of all the men the world has shown her : she likes Teddy Josselin's fortune. And yet, and yet—" incomplete " nature, dissatisfied heart, that she possesses ! Portia sighs bitterly in this, the crowning, long-coveted moment, when every desire, every ambition of her life has come to fruition.

" Teddy, dear, do you think you could manage to keep awake for five minutes ? "

Teddy's eyes unclosed, he turned his head round slowly. " I wasn't asleep, my love. I was listening to the cinders falling from the fire."

" The house in Eaton Square is too big. It was very well for grandmamma, who could live on a cutlet a day, and had her jointure to depend upon. We could never keep it up. Besides, no nice people live in big houses. We'll let it and get a nutshell in Park Lane ; spend our money on ourselves, not on a great, useless house and servants."

" Money. Ah, that reminds me of poor Condy," said Teddy Josselin. " I'd write the poor old soul a line to-night, if I wasn't so done up. We must let Condy have the annuity just the same as though that last codicil had been signed, Portia."

"For doing her best to ruin us! Hadn't you better pension Laura Wynne, at the same time? I am going to cut her; but that is beside the question."

"I don't suppose Condy wanted to ruin anybody. Grandmamma made her follow people about—'twas one of her duties, likelier than not. At all events, some one will have to take care of Arno. We'll make them comfortable together, and old Sam, too. And I think Condy has got a sister."

"What an interesting menagerie! Fortunately we shall each be able to have a private allowance to spend on our hobbies. Ah, Teddy, a number of things will have to be altered. You are not going to have anything more to say to Nelly Rawdon, for instance."

"Nor you to Dormer?"

"Don't be absurd. Lord Dormer's position is a very different one to the Rawdons'."

"And Jack Dysart?"

"Oh, poor, dear old Jack!" but a blush forced itself into Portia's cheek. "The next time we meet, how I shall laugh at him! There's not a doubt in the world that he did really see us both in Paris. And yet, how thoroughly I succeeded in hoodwinking him!"

"And a good many other people with him," observed Teddy, a little drily. "Thank heaven," he added, "we shan't have to hoodwink any one again. You can't imagine what a relief it is to me, 'Tia, to think I told the truth to the last!"

"I can quite imagine it. If one was always sure of such a result to truth-telling, who would be at the trouble of another falsehood?"

Teddy's eyes closed again: the proposition required mental exertion: and after a minute or two of silence, a door communicating with another room opened and Miss Jemima came in. She walked up the room, the roar of Regent street without deadening her footstep, and looked long and earnestly at the two young figures beside the fire.

"Aunt Jem!" cried Portia, suddenly catching sight of her. "And with red eyes, too?" She rose and put her arm round Miss Jemima. "Confess now, slenderly though you loved each other, that you have been crying for grandmamma."

"No, Portia," answered Miss Jemima, "I have been crying for you."

"A little for me, too, I hope, Aunt Jem?" said Teddy, looking up.

"Yes, a little for you, too. I trust they are the last tears you will either of you make me shed."

"Trust?" repeated Portia, "I don't know, aunt, that you need put such a stinging emphasis on the word. I shall make a better wife to Teddy Josselin, depend upon it, than I should have made to a better man."

"And vice versa," said Teddy, sleepily. "Stay, is it vice versa? 'a better husband to so-and-so than I should have made to a better—never mind, Portia. You may laugh, but I know what I mean myself."

Portia, on this, laughed aloud; then, stooping down, she patted Ted Josselin's shoulder encouragingly. But Miss Jemima's face kept grave as ever. "I would give all the little I am worth," said she, "that you hadn't entered upon life together with a falsehood."

"And was not falsehood forced upon us?" cried Portia. "I knew that I liked this poor little foolish Teddy better than I could ever like any one else, and I had heard the story of the past too clearly from your lips, Aunt Jem, not to be very sure my one chance of life was to marry him. If I had told this openly, acted honestly with grandmamma, what would have been the result? Starvation to both of us. Will grandpapa, will anybody living, blame me now for having acted as I did? Does not the end," she glanced at Teddy, "more than justify the means?"

"We ought to have told Aunt Jem," said Teddy, rousing himself, "I always said that. We ought to have told Aunt Jem."

"Not a bit of it," said Portia. "Aunt's honest heart would have been sure to ruin us. No honest-hearted people can be trusted with a secret. Do you think, if Aunt Jem had known the truth, she would not have spoken at St. Sauveur?"

"Do you think if Aunt Jem had known the truth she would ever have been at St. Sauveur?" said old Miss Jemima. "Oh, Portia, be a good child now, if only to make amends to me for what I suffered—"

"The night when Ted and I were shipwrecked, and when you thought I had run away with Jack Dysart! Aunt, if we had been shipwrecked, and our bodies found, you would have guessed something of the truth, for my ring was tied, as it has been since last July, round my neck. My poor little ring—" she began to falter.

Teddy at once rose and closed her lips with a kiss!

"All these months have been a mistake," said he. "Let us forget them. Where is the ring, Portia?" He turned to her with a flush of genuine feeling on his face. "Let Aunt Jemima be the witness while I put it on for good."

And Portia was just drawing a hidden bit of ribbon from her throat, when a knock came at the door: a waiter appeared. "A lady and gentleman are below, waiting to see if they might be admitted?"

"Certainly not. We can see nobody," said Miss Jemima, in a voice of choked emotion, and without looking round. "Say there has been a bereavement in the family."

"The gentleman wished me to give his name. Mr. George Blake."

"Show him up at once," cried Portia, pushing the ring hastily out of sight again.

"Now Teddy," as the servant left the room, "you must be the one to tell mind."

"Perhaps there is to be a double surprise," remarked Teddy. "We hear of a lady. Is Blake also going to impose a wife—"

The door opened and Blake appeared, with Susan Fielding on his arm; her face, either from the wintry night air, or happiness, or both, blooming as a rose.

The usual salutations passed: the ladies kissing each other, the two young men shaking hands with more of the thorough heartiness of their old schoolboy days than they had felt for months past. And then the four young people stood and looked at each other a little awkwardly; Miss Jemima holding aloof.

"It snows very fast," observed Susan, at last; the only time on record when she attempted to begin conversation. "But we came in a Hansom cab," she went on, coloring up furiously as she made the confession.

"You have come to us, my dear, in a time of great family—." Honest Miss Jemima paused for a word. Could Lady Erroll's death be called an affliction?

"A time," exclaimed Portia, "when every one is speaking the truth. I will speak it, too. Mr. Blake," turning to him full, "grandmamma is dead. That you know from my note; and she has left me nothing; that, also, you know. My name was not mentioned in her will."

"Portia, my dear—"

"Oh, of course, Aunt Jem. The will has not been read, but Bloxam, Condy, everybody, knows perfectly well what is in it. Poor grandmamma, at the last, died somewhat suddenly, Mr. Blake. Had she lived a quarter of an hour longer, we have reason to fear her money would have been left away from us all ; but—she died, and everything she possessed in the world goes to my cousin. Congratulate him on his good fortune."

"Money, by itself, is a thing scarcely worth congratulating a man about," said Blake, looking doubtfully at Teddy Josselin's face.

"Money is the only thing, it seems to me, that a married man can be congratulated about," said Teddy. "Oh, I was forgetting ; we have not mentioned it sooner, but my cousin Portia and I were married last July. The ceremony took place here in London, but quietly, (Portia says we were married from her grandmamma's house), and we spent our honeymoon in Paris. So, you see, whoever congratulates one congratulates the other." He smiled, and looked contented.

Married ! Married months ago ! The slightest spasm of disappointment crossed Blake's heart at the news. The one supreme touch of felicity was given to Susan's. Not even in imagination could Portia be a rival any more.

"It would be a long story to tell all the *pros* and *cons*," said Portia : never had she looked fairer in Blake's eyes than at this moment, as she stood, with downcast, blushing face at her husband's side ; "but there were, unhappily, good reasons for our deceiving even our dearest friends. Ah, Mr. Blake," and for an instant she raised her dark eyes reproachfully to his, "you need not have been so terribly hard on me that evening in the summer. Teddy was with me all the time."

"Have I ever been hard on you in my life, Miss—Mrs. Josselin ?"

Blake stammered over Portia's new name, then got red, and every one laughed. If there had been just the slightest element of tragedy in the situation hitherto, it was dispelled now.

"It sounds so funny to hear people called 'Mrs.,'" remarked Susan.

"Ah, very funny," said Ted Josselin. "Wait awhile, Susan ! See if the fun strikes you in the same light by and by ! What news from Otago ?"

The poor little girl's face grew hot with confusion : Jemima Ffrench came to her assistance. "There is nothing for you to be ashamed of, my dear Susan ; we are all friends here. I know from Miss Collinson that her brother is expected daily, and—"

"He's not coming—he'll never come again !" exclaimed Susan, with all the courage she possessed.

"Mr. Collinson not coming back !" said Portia, and in a moment her eyes were reading Blake's face. "This seems destined to be an evening of congratulations."

"But I call such conduct infamous—infamous !" cried Jemima Ffrench. "I've known a man cut by his whole regiment for less cause. My poor little friend—"

"Oh, ma'am, don't pity me !" Susan hastened to interrupt. "Indeed, everything has turned out for the best. We were both very foolish—we didn't know our own minds. And Tom Collinson has married Matty, and I am so delighted."

Old Miss Jemima lifted her hands and eyes in bewilderment. "Tom Collinson has married Matty, and you are delighted ! The times are beyond me !" she said. "Fidelity, love, honor : nothing is as it once was !"

"But I was never really in—I mean, I never really cared for—" then Susan broke down, and stole an appealing look up at Blake.

"Susan gave her word but not her heart," said he, and moving to her side, he took her hand, before them all, and held it in his. "Considering her age, we must not judge her too harshly."

"Particularly when we reflect on her manner of keeping her word," suggested Teddy.

"Oh, but I did keep it," said Susan. "Mr. Blake knows if Tom Collinson had returned I would never have broken my promise to him."

"But Tom Collinson has not returned," said Blake; "and Susan is able to be true to herself, and to make me the happiest fellow in existence."

Congratulations from every one.

"And so the curtain descends on universal felicity," said Portia. Was there the slightest tinge of bitterness in her voice? "The money is left to the rightful heir; stern old parent (you, dear Aunt Jem) reconciled; the good and the wicked heroine both marry and live at peace forever after, as the people do in novels."

"'Marry and live at peace forever after!'" repeated Teddy, thoughtfully. "And the fellows who write novels would make us believe they take their pictures from life."

"Mrs. Josselin has omitted one important detail of the closing scene," said Blake—"the inequality in fortune between the two heroines. Susan has only a life of poverty before her, while—"

"Poverty!" cried Susan. "I don't think we shall be at all poor, and if we were, would it matter? Can we be more than happy?" looking up, with a smile of the most absolute contentment, into her lover's face.

Once again Portia sighed in the spirit. She had won much: ease, position, a London life, with its attendant ever-changing round of pleasures, were before her. She had not won all. The commonplace heart of Susan Fielding was satisfied: the life barren of riches, excitement, ambition, of all save love, would be complete.

THE END.

www.ingramcontent.com/pod-product-compliance
Lightning Source LLC
Chambersburg PA
CBHW030624030726

47497CB00006B/1621